Autumn Changes

B.G. Thomas

Published by
DREAMSPINNER PRESS

5032 Capital Circle SW, Suite 2, PMB# 279, Tallahassee, FL 32305-7886 USA
http://www.dreamspinnerpress.com/

Autumn Changes
© 2015 B.G. Thomas.

Cover Art
© 2015 Paul Richmond.
http://www.paulrichmondstudio.com
Cover content is for illustrative purposes only and any person depicted on the cover is a model.

ISBN: 978-1-63476-071-3
Digital ISBN: 978-1-63476-072-0
Library of Congress Control Number: 2015901361
First Edition April 2015
Passages from the play Drunks © Pete Bakely, 2008. All rights reserved.
Used with permission of Pete Bakely.

Printed in the United States of America
∞
This paper meets the requirements of
ANSI/NISO Z39.48-1992 (Permanence of Paper).

Readers love the Seasons of Love series by B.G. THOMAS

Spring Affair

"This book is full of pain and hurt, but also hope and elation. He really hit it out of the park for me with this one."

—My Fiction Nook

"*Spring Affair* by B.G. Thomas is more than a simple love story. It is an exploration of all we can be and all that we push away in fear that we will never be the person others expect of us."

—Joyfully Jay

"B.G. Thomas's special touch in dealing with… issues, his humor, and the way he lets the story play out make it a fascinating character study and a touching, gentle romance at the same time. Bravo!"

—Rainbow Book Reviews

Summer Lover

"This is yet another fabulous read from BG Thomas! I am totally smitten!"

—MM Good Book Reviews

"You better make sure you are ready for the ride because I will guarantee you, this book will take you on one for sure!"

—Love Bytes

"I loved how the author really brought the reader into this world. The descriptions were written so well I felt at times I could actually see, hear, and smell every word."

—The Novel Approach

By B.G. Thomas

All Alone in a Sea of Romance
All Snug
Anything Could Happen
Bianca's Plan
Bones (Multiple Author Anthology)
The Boy Who Came In From the Cold
Christmas Cole
Christmas Wish
Derek
Desert Crossing
Grumble Monkey and the Department Store Elf
Hound Dog and Bean
How Could Love Be Wrong?
It Had to Be You
Just Guys
Men of Steel (Dreamspinner Anthology)
Red
Riding Double (Dreamspinner Anthology)
A Secret Valentine
Soul of the Mummy
Editor: A Taste of Honey (Dreamspinner Anthology)
Two Tickets to Paradise (Dreamspinner Anthology)

SEASONS OF LOVE
Spring Affair
Summer Lover
Autumn Changes

Published by DREAMSPINNER PRESS
http://www.dreamspinnerpress.com

For Paul Richmond, who continually and constantly gives me the best covers a writer could ask for. And who has so brilliantly created the Alphonse Mucha inspired covers for this series....

I was a fan before I discovered Dreamspinner Press.

Now I am honored to call you my friend!

Acknowledgments

Special thanks to Rabbi Barry Albin and EM Lynley for all things Jewish. It is the Rabbi Barry who taught me about the scriptures you will find within these pages. It was incredibly eye-opening. If I have made some blunders herein, it is my fault and not theirs.

Thanks also to Phillip Maugaotega, Melanesia FofoaiVaoese Toese, Ammaron Taula, and Masau for all things Samoan. Again, any blunders are my fault and not theirs. *Fa'afetai tele!*

Thanks to Sandra Harden and Stacia Aurore Rose for betaing and helpful insights. And to Ian and Jenn, who did so much. And as always, to Andi Byassee for waving her editorial magic wand over my words and making them readable!

Special, *special* thanks to Pete Bakely for letting me use his play *Drunks* in this book, and a wonderful *Twilight Zone* thanks to my good friend and wonderful actor Curtis Smith. I called him up to ask him some questions about plays and such (I grilled him during the writing of *Anything Could Happen*, as well as my friend Paul Burns) and got a shock when I found out he had *just* been in a production of *Drunks*! Now what are the chances of *that* happening?

I've got a magic life, my friends! Thank *you,* readers, for helping the magic happen!

Autumn passes and one remembers one's reverence.

—Yoko Ono

No man can taste the fruits of autumn while he is delighting his scent with the flowers of the spring

—Samuel Johnson

To everything there is a season, and a time to every purpose under the heaven.

—Ecclesiastes 3:1, KJV

CHAPTER ONE

IT WAS Asher Eisenberg's turn to host "Porch Night," the must-not-miss night for the Fabulous Four. They might not be the most popular people in the world (well—Asher considered *himself* to be pretty popular), but they had lives (such as they were), they *did* things (some of them pretty darned silly), and sometimes life got busy enough that weeks would fly by without them seeing each other.

Thus the agreed-upon pact: thou shalt not miss Porch Night.

Porch Night was the night that—barring floods (there weren't many in the Kansas City area, although Brush Creek had risen once or twice), terrible sickness (the FF were as healthy as horses), or an impending end-of-the-world, catastrophic meteor collision with Earth—Asher and his three friends got together every month to simply *be* together. A time for catching up, laughter, and, now and again, crying on a shoulder.

It was also a time for cocktails. Sometimes *lots* of them, especially if it was Asher's turn at bat. Porch Night rotated each month, one of the four taking his turn to host the evening's entertainment.

And when Asher's turn to be in charge of the festivities came around, it was usually an evening he relished.

Usually....

First of all, Asher *liked* to host. He had a natural talent for entertaining. He went out of his way to provide the most surprising and unique food and drinks and make sure he created the most enjoyable atmosphere possible.

Asher had been a bartender on and off for years—what actor hadn't worked in a bar or waited tables at one time or another?—so he had the advantage of being able to find distinctive cocktails the boys might never find on their own. All he had to do was head over to The Male Box or The Watering Hole or The Corner Bistro, sit at the bar with one of the bartenders he'd worked with (and most probably also tricked) at one time or another, and ask what the new "in" drink happened to be. Out of the three bars, the Bistro was usually the gold mine because the fags who worked there all wished they lived in LA or New York instead of Kansas City (*any*where *but*, actually), so they had their ears to the wall for anything to make them look cool or more sophisticated. People working at or patronizing The Watering Hole or the "Box," on the other hand, were more likely to argue which beer was better, Bud Light (*shudder*) or Pabst Blue Ribbon (*double shudder*).

Asher almost always took the prize (not that there was an actual *prize* per se) when it came to his cocktail offerings.

The four of them really did move the heavens to make sure they didn't miss out on their monthly soirée, and the only way Asher missed it was if he had a play.

(And damn it all, there hadn't been one since last year's *Tearoom Tango*—and he wasn't even going to let himself *think* about the movie audition in LA….)

Next week, he told himself. *Next week. Wednesday afternoon at the Pegasus Theatre. Next week. Make it your mantra….*

(Too old! He'd actually been told he was too old! He was thirty-two, for God's sake! Too old? He'd always gotten by on his looks. Did "too old" bode well?)

Tonight Asher was going to blow the socks off his friends with his cocktail! Let anyone *try* to top this one.

Scott, bless his little heart, always served frozen margaritas made from one of those bucket kits, where all you had to do was add tequila (cheap in Scott's case) and stick it in the freezer. Wyatt—like Scott—had a standard. It was always the cosmopolitan (maybe with slight alterations). The chubby little bear, God love him too, couldn't help it. His favorite color was pink, and he delighted in the pink sugar on the rim of the glass (but damn him for serving something last month called an Aviation cocktail—*that* had been a major score). Sloan at least tried and had come up with one or two through the years that weren't bad at all.

So this month Asher was serving a Corpse Reviver #2, which was simple looking, but quite simply delicious. He was sure the drinkie would top Wyatt's. Asher found he actually *needed* to be King Cocktail once more.

He was serving blue-cheese-filled endives as well, along with a small pimiento-olive-stuffed pastry, which he was taking out of the oven when one of his friends asked…

"Can I help?"

Asher turned to see Sloan, sweet goddamned Sloan, standing there—beautiful as always with his bright red hair and dimples deep enough to fall into.

"In a minute you can help me take all this out to the balcony." Which was of course Asher's answer to a porch since he lived in a hundred-year-old apartment building instead of a house like Sloan and Wyatt.

"You okay?" Sloan gave him a considering look. "You seem a little… off tonight."

Damn, thought Asher. Sloan had gotten here all of ten minutes ago and seen that already? *My acting abilities are slipping.* Had the others noticed?

Others!

He tried not to growl.

Of course, Sloan knew him like no one else—in fact *anyone* else—in the world, even Asher's own family. That was saying something considering how little of himself he ever let Sloan see.

He flashed Sloan a smile he reserved for directors, or for photographers taking his headshots. "Nothing that some cocktails can't take care of." He hoped Sloan would buy it.

His friend—his *best* friend in the universe—looked at him for the longest moment and then nodded. Returned the smile. "Sure. Just asking. Speaking of cocktails, what's tonight's concoction?" He bent slightly and turned his attention to the martini-style drinks on the tiny kitchen counter.

"You'll see," Asher said, smile now totally genuine.

Cocktails. The *drinking* of which was the second reason Asher liked to host so much. Alcohol served at his own place meant he could drink himself under the table if he wanted. He wouldn't be driving any-fucking-where. The farthest he had to go was down the short hallway of his boxy little apartment to his bedroom.

He wondered which of his buddies was the designated driver tonight (and if it even *was* one of his friends). Since the other members of the FF all lived in Terra's Gate, about a thirty- to forty-five-minute drive, depending on how heavy the foot of the driver, they pretty much always drove in together. If they took turns driving, that meant there was only one night a year they had to watch how much they drank! He, on the other hand, had to be careful every time he wasn't hosting. Of course, if he did drink too much on other nights, one of his buddies always offered up their couch. It happened fairly often. Asher *liked* to drink.

In fact, he *loved* to drink. It was the one time he could definitely relax and just be happy (well, except when he got mean, and damn if sometimes he wasn't a mean drunk).

Asher turned back to the oven, shut the door, pulled off his oven mitt, and arranged the hot pastries and Blue Boy endives on a platter. When they were arranged to his satisfaction, he handed the food to Sloan, along with some paper plates, and grabbed his biggest serving tray with its six—

(six! not four!)

—cocktails, and with a nod, the two of them headed out to the balcony.

The *very* crowded balcony.

A balcony that had always been quite comfy for the four of them—the *Fab*-ulous Four as Wyatt liked to call them. But now? With the boyfriends? Well, now the little brick, screened-in balcony was like a can of sardines.

There's just not room for six, dammit! This is supposed to be the four *of us. No boyfriends.* It had *always* been the rule that Porch Night was for *just* the four of them.

And fuck! Look at the way Sloan's… boyfriend (Asher's gut clenched at the word) was looking at him. Like he wanted to jump up and kiss Sloan right then and there. Kiss? No… ravish him was more like it.

Sloan could have been mine.

After all, hadn't Sloan carried a torch for Asher for years? Three years and—

"I'm telling you," Wyatt was all but shouting (of course). "The *fuckin'* lyrics are better on the album! They should just play the damned song on the radio the way it was *meant* to be played. Who *doesn't* use the word 'fuck' these days?"

"My mother," said Scott with a grimace.

"What the 'fuck' are you talking about?" Asher asked their resident bear (who was looking especially chunky lately). *Putting on a little weight, dear heart?* He began serving his six (*should be four*) guests their cocktails.

"The P!nk song," cried Wyatt. Asher could practically hear Wyatt pronounce the "!" in the singer's name.

"So like you honestly think the country's ready to hear the word 'fuck' sung on the radio?" Scott—the FF's curmudgeon—asked.

Well, at least he *used* to be a curmudgeon, thought Asher. Ever since he'd met Cedar a couple of months ago, Scott had been a changed man. *Will it last when they break up?* Surely they would break up. They had to.

Asher eyed Scott's boyfriend appreciatively. Slim and well muscled, *maybe* thirty years old, sexy as shit, with an *almost* Mohawk and a high, round, perfect ass to die for. How in the steel-blue fuck had Scott scored a man that hot?

Not that Scott was ugly or anything, but damn! Cedar was *way* out of his league, no doubt about it. Asher had tried to flirt with the little stud, and Cedar had even flirted back. The hunk had given him long looks with a dangerous flash in his eyes. Had even bent over (on purpose—had to be!) and showed off that that damn-*tacular* ass that was *meant* to be fucked. And then the little bastard totally rebuffed Asher!

Not that Asher would fool around with a friend's lover. He *did* draw the line. It was a razor-thin line, but he did draw one.

"It's censorship," Wyatt exclaimed, continuing his rave. He shook his fist and then stopped the second he saw the cocktails and reached out and took his. "Party!"

"Censorship?" Max asked, Max being the total hunk Sloan had practically married late last spring. But only practically because the bearded beefcake was already married—to a woman. Of course, she was living in France now, and they were getting a divorce. And he was here, in Asher's apartment, sitting on the small wicker love seat with Sloan.

The place where Sloan and I used to sit.

"Believe me, I'm against censorship." Max was a teacher at Wagner University, so of course he was against it. "But at least they didn't bleep out any words to her song. Her feistier version *is* available. Her label let her include it on the album."

"And the 'feisty' one is so much more powerful," Wyatt exclaimed. "All you have to do is listen to both versions!"

Asher sighed. Who else besides Wyatt would be so worked up over a P!nk song?

"The 'fuckin'' version is so much more powerful," Wyatt cried. "She tells us in that song that we're *fuckin'* perfect, just the way we are!

In the other version, she just says we're perfect." Wyatt said the last word in a whiny tone. "It just doesn't have as much punch. *Fuckin'* perfect is so much better." He sighed dramatically.

"Wyatt, to quote Bob Dylan, 'the times, they are a-changin',"" Max continued. "Look at it the bright way. It used to be you couldn't say bitch or bastard or ass either. Have patience."

"The times really are changing too," Scott said enthusiastically. "For the better. All you have to do is look, and you see it. It's all around us. The world is waking up!"

Asher's eyes almost bugged out at the words. Surely the world was coming to an end. *Surely* it was one of the final signs of the Christians' apocalypse when Scott, of all people, said something positive!

Almost as if he'd read Asher's mind, Scott continued, "I didn't used to believe that—"

No shit!

"—but I'm learning." He smiled and placed his hand on Cedar's knee. His new lover smiled back, placed his hand on Scott's, and leaned in and nuzzled noses with him. Actually nuzzled noses!

You two are going to make me puke.

Sloan took a sip of his drink, then looked at Asher and nodded. "These are *lovely*, Asher! What are they?"

"They're called Corpse Reviver #2." Asher took a healthy swallow of his own, and since they were in martini glasses, it was a respectable portion indeed. "They were popular in the '30s— supposedly because they were a 'hair of the dog' hangover cure. I don't know about that, but they are *delish*!"

"What's in them?" Wyatt wanted to know, hopefully forgetting P!nk and whether perfection needed the word "fuck" attached to it.

"Equal parts gin, Cointreau, Lillet Blanc, and fresh-squeezed lemon juice, with a few dashes of orange bitters. I rinsed the glasses with absinthe first. Tried it without, but I didn't like it as much."

"Absinthe?" Wyatt looked at his glass in horror. "Isn't that supposed to be deadly? Highly addictive or something? Didn't Edgar Allan Poe, like, *die* from drinking absinthe?"

Asher smiled. "No, little bear. Absinthe's no more dangerous than any other booze. You think I would poison you?"

"But I was sure...."

"I think I read somewhere that the rumor started because it was so popular in Bohemian culture. Any psychoactive properties absinthe is supposed to have, have been greatly exaggerated. There are like two hundred brands made now."

Wyatt sighed in great relief. "Thank the gods! 'Cause this shit really *is* to *die* for."

"To *live* for," Scott corrected. "Remember, we can manifest our words."

Asher had to bite back a groan. *I am going to puke! I am. I am going to puke.*

Cedar leaned over again—

(*He doesn't have to lean very far....*)

—and kissed Scott on the cheek.

"How fuckin' *perfect*," Wyatt sang.

"And who *doesn't* like to fuck?" Cedar said with a growl, and they all laughed.

All! Geez. "All" was two people too many. No matter how hot Cedar or Max were.

Are we going to have Max's fourteen-year-old gay son and his boyfriend join us next month?

He decided to go back to the kitchen and grab the pitcher of Corpse Reviver #2. He, for one, needed seconds. There was no time like the present.

"ARE YOU sure you're okay?"

Asher jumped at the voice, turned to see that it was—of course—Sloan. His friend, his best friend, was looking at him with those unbelievably blue eyes. They hardly seemed real.

Asher sighed. *How did I not see how beautiful you are?*

"You're not okay." Sloan wasn't asking. He was telling.

Asher shrugged. "I've got an audition, and it's got me a little anxious," he lied. Well. He did have an audition. But it wasn't why he was upset.

Sloan's entire face lit up. It made him even more beautiful. "You do? Where? What?"

Asher shrugged again. "It's at the Pegasus."

"Oh my God! That's terrific!" Sloan jumped forward and gave Asher a big hug. "What great news!"

It's an audition, baby. I don't have the part.

Baby? Had he just called Sloan "baby"?

"It's an audition," Asher said aloud. "There could be a host of actors trying to get the same part. There's a lot of out-of-work actors in town since the American Heartland Theatre and others closed down."

"Yeah, but none of them are as talented as you."

Oh, Sloan. Always so fuckin' nice. You don't even want me anymore. You've got you a man now. And you still treat me like I'm fucking gold. How did I ever deserve you?

"Is it a specific play or just general auditions?"

Only Sloan would think to ask him that. Only Sloan would know that's how it worked sometimes. That Jennifer Leavitt, producing artistic director of the renowned Pegasus Theatre, sometimes specifically called in actors and offered them the parts she thought best for them. And word was there were some great plays in the Pegasus's pipeline.

"I don't know yet," Asher said. "I think—I'm hoping—that she might actually have something in mind for me."

"Asher!" Sloan hugged him again, and he couldn't help but remember a drunken night, not so long ago, when he had this man in his arms and made a terrible mistake. A mistake that through some miracle (not that he believed in miracles) had not driven his friend away forever. "This is incredible!"

"What is?" asked Scott, who was standing on the other side of the counter that separated the tiny kitchen from the barely bigger dining room.

Sloan spun around. "Asher got a call from the Pegasus Theatre. They want him to try out for a part."

Scott leaned against the counter. Asher quite suddenly noticed he wasn't wearing his pretentious Versace reading glasses tonight. Interesting. And his hair. It wasn't gelled within an inch of its life. "Really? *They* called *you*?"

Asher nodded reluctantly. He shouldn't have said anything. Now they would all know. And if didn't get a role, like he hadn't gotten the movie part, then everyone would be feeling sorry for him and consoling him, and he couldn't stand that.

But then again…

He did *have* friends after all.

Sometime he marveled that he had these three to begin with. Three friends he could always count on to be there for him. Friends he was too embarrassed to invite to parties where his peers congregated. The thought made Asher feel ashamed.

"So isn't that a good thing?" Scott grinned, and wasn't it remarkable? Scott had been frowning for so many years Asher was amazed his mouth hadn't become stuck that way. Scott—grinning! Not too long ago, seeing a genuinely happy smile on Scott's face would have been akin to seeing Bigfoot or the Loch Ness Monster. And almost as scary.

Will Scott be so smiley when Cedar figures out his mistake and dumps his ass?

And again, Asher had the good grace to be ashamed at the thought.

What's wrong with me? Why have I been like this lately?

So fucking bitchy?

What's crawled up my ass?

Not like Asher ever let *anyone* in his ass. That was something that was never going to happen.

"Look, I don't know that it's anything. I'm not going to hold my breath. There are a million actors and a handful of jobs. I'll go. I'll audition. We'll see. Now let's go join the others."

This time Asher tried not to be bitter about that last word.

The times, they are indeed a-changin'.

They got back to the balcony just in time.

"Okay, now," Wyatt said and popped a pastry-coated noshy bit into his mouth. "Stop me if you've heard this one but—gosh, these things are good. Can I get the recipe?"

Asher stifled a groan. The worst thing about Wyatt's jokes were not the jokes themselves—which we often not so bad, even funny at times. It was that he kept getting distracted while telling them so by the time he got to the punch line, the zing wasn't all that zingy.

"I will give you the recipe," Asher said, "under the condition that you tell the joke, along with the punch line, *now.*"

Wyatt's eyes widened in mock horror. "*Now?* How can I build any anticipation if you rush me?"

"I'm going to go get more snacks," Asher said.

"Okay, okay!" Wyatt shook his head. "Yeesh! So two men are hunting when one accidentally shoots the other. He freaks out and calls 911 on his cell phone. 'Hey,' he shouts into the phone. 'I just accidentally shot my friend while we were hunting! I think he's dead! What do I do? What do I do?'"

Wyatt nodded enthusiastically. "So the lady on the phone says, 'Ok, Sir. *Calm down*. Now *first* let's make sure your friend is really dead, okay?'

"'All right,' says the guy." Wyatt smiled and then lifted his hand, index finger pointed and thumb raised. "BANG! 'Okay!' he tells the lady. 'He's *really* dead. Now what?'"

There were groans, and there was laughter.

Then more laughter as people really got the joke.

"Isn't that *hil*-arious?" Wyatt cried.

And Asher was struck again by how many people there were on his small balcony. Good thing Wyatt's partner of ten years, Howard, had never shown any interest in joining them. But.... *What's happened? Everyone is paired up except me.*

Thank God I don't want *to be.*

The last thing Asher wanted was to be paired up with anyone. Even Sloan.

At least, that's what he kept telling himself.

CHAPTER TWO

THE TATTOOS. It was the tattoos that called to Peniamina Faamausili.

He didn't search the Internet for porn. Well, maybe a little, but not much.

No. He looked for the *tatau*. The *pe'a*. The tattoos. The kind that started at the waist and then swept over the hips and buttocks and down. Down over the thighs and to the knees in intricate tribal patterns, arches, and designs with meanings unknown to him.

I should have asked.

Peni's father had had them. Of course, the man had been a chief, whatever *that* meant today in America—thousands of miles from Samoa. It seemed there were a lot of men who called themselves chiefs, but what did that *mean*? Especially in Independence, Missouri—the place where Jesus Christ would supposedly, according to his mother, one day return to the world.

But whatever the meaning, Peni would look at his father's tattoos and the pictures on the Internet and lose himself in the patterns, the lines, the black on brown.

"Four days," his father, Iakopo, had said. He was—had been—a big man. In height, shoulders, and girth. So many Samoan men were (and no wonder with the way Samoans ate!) and Peni fought like mad to stay slim and muscular. What gay man wanted a man who looked like Peni's father for a lover?

Four days. "Four *twelve*-hour days," his father had gone on to say. "No breaks."

"No breaks?"

Quick shake of the head. "No breaks."

Peni would think about that, and his jaw would clench and his back teeth would hurt. He had a high threshold of pain, always had. Rarely cried even when he was a kid, even when he wiped out and scraped his thigh half-raw on the sidewalk riding his bike the day after the training wheels had been removed.

But four days being hammered with those spiked wooden tools?

Sometimes Peni would look down at his thighs and wonder what he might look like with pe'a of his own. In fact, when he was in fifth grade he'd taken a Sharpie marker and used one up entirely drawing on himself to see. His mother had almost killed him. His father had laughed.

"Think you can skip the pain, *si ou atalii pele*?" his father had said. *My dear son.*

Peni had seen that corny (but scary) movie *The Tattooist* (with the incredibly hot Jason Behr) about Samoan tattooing, and it looked like the pain could be bad. *Really* bad.

Could I do that? Could I?

"If you start, you have to finish." His dad. "Big shame if you stop. Not only for you but for the whole family."

Four days.

And they tattooed you "right up to your hole," his father had told him.

Not your penis, thank goodness. But "right up there to your pucker," and how the heck did they do that? Did someone spread your cheeks? Did you have to reach back and do it yourself? And then everyone was looking at your butthole? Wouldn't that be humiliating? Or was the pain so bad that you just didn't care? And what if you had to go to the bathroom? How did you make sure you didn't get an infection? All that raw skin.

Peni wanted to ask his father. But he couldn't very well do that now, could he? His father was gone. Dead for over a month, almost two now, and he kept forgetting, despite the funeral and all that had gone with it.

Dad. Gone. Forever.

"You'll see him on the other side," Tina, his mother, told him, her big black eyes wet with tears.

The only problem was Peni wasn't sure he would get to the other side.

Or even worse, if there *was* an "other side."

Peni winced at the thought. He'd been having doubts. They'd been building for some time now, but a lifetime of religion wasn't easily shed. There was the fear. The fear that…

What if it's true? What if they're right?

Did an angel *really* appear to Joseph Smith and did he *really* find golden plates that he translated with a "seer stone" so he could restore Christ's true church?

It was so hard to believe.

But it could be true. Couldn't it? An angel *could* have visited Joseph Smith.

Right?

After all, what Christian had a problem believing an angel had appeared before Abraham? Or Mary? Why not Joseph Smith— especially if the church had drifted from where God wanted it to be?

But then Peni would remember the musical episode of *South Park* poking fun of the whole story and calling it all *dum, dum, dum, dah, dumb....*

And oh, how he had laughed!

Because didn't the story really sound, well, *dumb, dumb, dumb, dah, dumb...?*

But was it dumb? If the Bible could have been written thousands of years ago, and it was true and real, then why *not* some two hundred years ago as well? Were God's miracles confined to millennia past? If somehow man had messed up God's true word, mightn't God have wanted to set things straight? Surely He loved mankind enough to do such a thing. God *could* have revealed his true word through an angel to Joseph Smith.

Peni had grown up believing it all. Totally. Without question.

But now?

Now, he wasn't so sure anymore.

But then, was the religion of his parents any "dumber" than the idea of Adam and Eve or Noah's ark or burning bushes and water turning into blood? How about the story of how the Buddha was born and was immediately able to talk and walk, and how lotus blossoms burst into bloom everywhere he'd taken a baby step? Or how about the angel Gabriel appearing before Muhammad and commanding him to recite the verses that would become the Quran?

Peni thought maybe he could have sailed through his whole life believing everything he'd been taught. That Joseph Smith had a vision when he was fourteen years old, that Jesus and God had come to him while he was praying in the woods and revealed to him that all the churches were wrong and given him a way to reveal the true wishes of God. When Peni was young and thought about the story, his heart would pound with awe and excitement. That such a thing could have happened. That God could love the world so much.

But then God setting mankind "straight" had become the problem, hadn't it?

Because Peni wasn't. Not at all. He wasn't even bisexual. He was gay. He'd learned that with one kiss.

One kiss from a man.

And what if being gay meant he was going to be cast into the outer darkness?

Don't think about it.

Miss you, Father.

So much left to talk about. So many things unsaid.

I never told you I was gay.

"*Oka!* Honey… we knew," his mother had told him—only two hours ago.

Peni's mouth had fallen open. He was still reeling from the surprise of it. The shock. At his mother's house for dinner and the words had simply fallen out of his mouth. No prep. No plan. No idea. Just out. *He'd* come out.

"Y-you knew?"

His mother had just rolled her eyes. "You are twenty-eight, son. You've never had one girlfriend. Not one *date*—"

"But Nicole—"

"Please!" She rolled her big dark eyes again. "You two shopped for clothes and hung out at the mall. She might have been a 'girlfriend'"—she made quote marks in the air with her fingers—"but she was never your *girl*friend." She shrugged. "But it was okay. Hey! I never had to worry you would get some girl pregnant. I *always* worried about your brothers. Girl maniacs, the both of them. Thank God they married nice Mormon girls. Not Samoan." She cringed. "Not your older brother, anyway. But at least they were Mormon. When you find a nice boy, please make him Mormon?"

Peni and his mother had been in the kitchen, rinsing and then loading dishes in the dishwasher, when he had quite suddenly told her he was gay. Of course, they weren't just rinsing. They might as well have been washing them. Heck! He would eat off of the plates she put *in* the dishwasher.

"I can't help it," she had told him more times than he could count. "I remember when you *had* to rinse them off—when dishwashers, they weren't so good. The first one your father bought me? More work than it was worth!"

"Mom"—he had fallen into a kitchen chair by that point—"w-when did you know?"

She shook her head, closed the washer, pressed a button, and then sat down to the sound of hissing water. "Son, a mother *always* knows. I knew! Your Uncle Iosefa is *fa'afafine*. You have never been as effeminate as he, but still, I knew. Had you grown up in Samoa, you would have been *fa'afafine*."

Fa'afafine. The third gender. Samoans claimed there was no such thing as being gay. There was male, there was female, and there was fa'afafine. Something different. Fa'afafine could be extravagantly feminine and had sexual relationships with men who were not fa'afafine. They were trained to do the daily work of women, and some even believed they were female.

But Peni had never felt that way. He had never felt female. He had never liked the "work of women." He didn't like to cook—he could burn water. Forget laundry! Once he'd turned an entire load of white clothes pink when he'd carelessly added a red shirt to the washing machine. He'd never enjoyed babysitting either, not even Lagi, his *tuafafine*, beloved younger sister.

Even in Samoa, he would be on the outside, once more not belonging. He liked being a man. He liked hanging out with his brothers and his uncles and loved his time with his father. He liked what they did—carpentry, yard work, puttering over cars—and he liked learning the ancient dances of men. How many times had he danced with his brothers and friends at social gatherings through the years? Dozens? A hundred?

He also liked being with men who wanted to *be* with men.

Well. One man. He'd only been with one man, really—discounting the games of boys.

Peni hadn't responded in any way to this mother's words when she told him she knew he was gay. His tongue had been shocked dumb in his mouth.

"And then there was your mission. Now that... *that* made me sad—that you didn't go on your mission. And now that you are twenty-eight, you can't."

Which was true. In Mormon tradition he was supposed to start his two-year mission by the age of twenty-five. It wasn't a hard and fast rule, but it wasn't recommended past that age either. A woman could go at any time. His Aunty Natia, one of his father's sisters, was on a mission—after a failed marriage—at the age of forty-two! Of course since she was divorced, she wasn't allowed to do it full time, but she was still part of the missionary effort of the church.

Peni had wanted to explain to his family. Explain *why* he couldn't go on the mission. Certainly couldn't share a little apartment with several other young men. Not in such close quarters. Not when he knew how he would look at them.

He couldn't lie. Couldn't go on a mission that demanded certain things he couldn't do. Couldn't *be*. So it had been better to avoid explaining at all.

But hadn't that been lying as well?

Because Peni had known he was gay for a long, long time. When he was young, he would spend the night with his cousin Tupe (who was now married with kids), and Tupe would want to touch Peni, want Peni to touch him. Touch each other *there*. And it had been fun.

But of course Peni had lied to himself, hadn't he? Told himself all that "touching" with Tupe was just games.

Until a kiss.

Until a man kissed him….

Then the games were over.

PENI HAD gone into the city to have dinner with some friends from work. Specifically, he had gone to have dinner with Sloan McKenna, who he had a silly crush on. He knew it was going nowhere. Sloan was dealing with the death of his mother, was mooning over some man of his own, and worse, Peni had stupidly told Sloan he wasn't gay. So what did he think *could* happen? He would have been too chickenshit to be sexual with Sloan anyway. Truth be told, Peni was as afraid of Sloan as much as he hero-worshipped him. Sloan was the first out and proud gay man Peni had ever met. Being around Sloan was dangerous. What if someone saw Peni and Sloan together in public? Mightn't they think he was gay as well? Or might it confirm suspicions that had to be there already?

The thing was he *liked* being around Sloan. Being with Sloan made his heart race. Made Peni unable to help but wonder what life would be like if *he* took such a plunge and finally admitted that he might be gay.

Might? *Might?*

Was there any question anymore?

Of course there was the fact that Sloan was undeniably attractive. Far more attractive than any *girl* Peni's family had ever tried to set him up with, or any girl with whom he'd ever gone to school. Maybe it was Sloan's creamy white skin and bright, copper-red hair—all so very *un*-Samoan. Not that Peni was ashamed of being Samoan.

(...in fact lately, something, some indefinable *something*, had begun to stir in his heart... his very blood... about his ancient heritage....)

It was just that he'd never thought Samoan men were sexy.

(Except for the pe'a!)

It was men who were the antithesis of Samoan who appealed to Peni the most. Blonds, most often. Blue eyes. Or green eyes! And slim. Hadn't Bobby Brubaker been anything *but* Samoan?

But first, there had been dinner. A birthday dinner with a coworker at the Blue Koi, a little Chinese-style restaurant in the 39th Street West district. What a bitch it had been when everyone had squeezed into the narrow area around the table and Peni found he hadn't even gotten to sit next to Sloan.

But why get upset? What was he going to do? Play footsie with his crush under the table?

The dinner had been fun and anticlimactic all at the same time. Anticlimactic because it was over and done with in what felt like a flash. But nice because he had enjoyed seeing a side of his coworkers that he couldn't see on their rush-rush-rush work schedule. At work they came in and sat down and put on their headphones and plugged into the system, and suddenly the calls were pouring in. Breaks were fifteen minutes, and you had to be back on time, even now that Sloan had been promoted and watched out for everyone. There were calls coming in, after all: calls about baby formula and gift certificates from various companies and kitty litter and blood glucose monitors for diabetics. You hung up with one caller, and the next came through. There was no real chatting with anyone in your neighboring cubicles. Lunches were half an hour, and most of that you were scrambling to get your food and get it microwaved and eaten. Not a lot of time for socializing. So how nice to see people with their hair down, listening to them laugh and talk about their lives—

(Hey! Jon Harington had a new baby. How had Peni not heard about that?)

—and even seeing them get a little tipsy. Really see them as *people*.

Peni had even been tempted to get a cocktail or a beer. Thing was, he wouldn't really know what to order and had no idea what his alcohol tolerance was. Crazy that he was gay and had so little experience with drinking, huh? (Hadn't Wyatt assured Peni that when you were gay, you weren't allowed to skip alcohol?) Peni knew Samoan boys who had been getting drunk in high school. He'd been too afraid. Plus there was the fact that he had to drive home after dinner. Not ever having been drunk before, he had to be especially careful.

So weird, then, wasn't it, that he wound up in a gay bar, heart pounding so hard he could hear it over the drag queens lip-syncing to Lady Gaga and Emeli Sandé? He wasn't even sure how it happened. He was in his car one minute, driving past The Male Box the next, and then there he was, standing inside the door of a bar. A *gay* bar.

Again, he'd had no idea what to order when he was finally brave enough to walk up to the bar, so he played it safe and got a Diet Coke.

Then a man named Bobby Brubaker bought him a drink. This one had rum in it. A *lot* of rum.

And Bobby was sexy—so *very* sexy! Chest hair grew thick over the collar of his shirt, and most Samoan men didn't have hairy chests. Most could hardly grow beards.

Bobby had a great beard.

They talked in a corner, or tried to over Miley Cyrus pounding from the beer-patio speakers, and then there was a second rum and Coke. A third.

And then the kiss.

EVERYTHING HAD come to a head just recently, when he met one of Sloan's friends, a guy named Scott Aberdeen. Sloan seemed to have a lot of friends. A lot of gay friends. Friends that not only knew what he was, but were gay themselves. Imagine.

Scott had been quite vocal in his belief that there was no God. The idea had startled Peni. It wasn't the fact that Scott was an atheist.

Peni knew there were people who didn't believe in God. But Scott was actually *angry* that there were people who did.

Except lately Scott had been acting differently, hadn't he? He'd changed. Something about that men's festival he'd gone to at the end of July. He'd stopped his anti-God talk.

Then there was Wyatt, a short, slightly dumpy, funny, very sweet man. A bear is what they called him, or maybe it was a cub? Was that right? Because he was hairy and not skinny and apparently had no interest in spending half his life in a gym trying to sculpt his body into something that resembled the statue of some Greek god.

Speaking of Greek gods…

Asher.

At least that's how people seemed to treat him. Sloan had been in love with him until he met Max. People deferred to the man, this Asher, and Peni couldn't figure out why. Yes, he was beautiful. He had to admit that. Like Matthew McConaughey or a very young Robert Redford. Everyone seemed to think he might one day be a big star himself.

The thing was, as far as Peni could see, Asher was an ass. It was one thing to know you were attractive, and it was stupid to pretend you weren't aware of the fact. But it was something else to act like your looks could get you anything or anyone you wanted. He'd met Asher at a Fourth of July celebration held at the home of the millionaire (billionaire?) Peter Wagner. Asher's date had looked like he was *maybe* eighteen—and Asher had ignored the boy so he could flirt with Peni.

A complete and total jerk! How could Sloan have been in love with that man? Even if he was gorgeous. Incredibly gorgeous. It made Peni angry he found the man so attractive.

So those were Sloan McKenna's best friends.

Scott the pessimist, Wyatt the flamboyant, and Asher the jerk.

Yet there was no denying that these three men were Sloan's *true* friends. It almost made Peni jealous. He could do with such friends.

But it was Scott, least fun of the three, who had splashed the cold water on his face. Made Peni think about what he had tried *not* to think about. That maybe, just *maybe*, there was no God—Mormon or any other kind. That was pretty scary. The only thing more frightening than a God who would cast him into the outer darkness was the idea that God didn't exist at all. That life was just some big cosmic joke, some celestial accident, and that there was no purpose to life. No purpose for the drive to continue the species or for life's suffering or the search for love.

Which was why Peni had gotten excited when he'd heard about Wyatt's "Witchy-Woo-Woo Camp"—Scott's words, not Peni's (and certainly not Wyatt's). Wyatt offered a whole different view of God and spirituality and an opportunity to explore those ideas. Going camping with Wyatt would have been ten days in the woods with over a hundred gay men who believed that there was a sacredness to being gay! That there was some purpose—perhaps even a divine reason—for there to be men who loved other men.

If a gay man's purpose wasn't creating children, continuing the family name, then what was it? It certainly wasn't anything his father would have understood.

But Peni's father was gone, wasn't he?

He had died in a stupid car accident. A Samoan chief! Dead when some drunk had gone through a red light and plowed into his father's side of the car. The drunk with barely a scratch. Peni's father—blood of chiefs for who knew how many generations—dead.

That had ended Peni's camping trip before it even began.

So now what?

So now Peni very suddenly realized he needed a drink—not one from the local liquor store, either.

He was going to go to a gay bar.

Peni was walking out of his apartment door when the thought hit him: What if Bobby was there?

Peni had thought he was in love with Bobby. Was sure of it. But the man took his virginity and then basically cast him aside like used Kleenex.

Seeing Bobby was one thing he couldn't deal with.

Could. Not.

So what, then?

What indeed?

CHAPTER THREE

ASHER WAS in fourth grade. Or was it fifth?

No. Fourth.

He was in his bedroom with his best friend, Ronnie, and they were playing "I'll show you mine, if you show me yours." They had pilfered an issue of Asher's father's men's magazines (had it been *Penthouse*? *Playboy*?) to see what all the excitement was about. Neither of them had been all that excited.

"She doesn't have anything down there," Ronnie said.

"Just hair," Asher agreed.

Of course they had known this intellectually, but neither had ever seen a female "down there" for themselves. They'd heard all the boys talking excitedly about what girls had, and so they'd been curious.

"That's what all the fuss is about?" Ronnie asked.

They turned the pages past an article or two ("Best Motorcycles for Your Money," "Saving Libraries Will Save Our Children," "Base Jumping—A Near Death Experience") and came to a spread that stopped them in their tracks. It was a fantasy piece of a woman *and* a man.

"Wow," said Ronnie. "*Look* how big his dick is."

Asher nodded. "I think it's bigger than my dad's."

"Do you have any hair on yours?" Ronnie asked.

Asher shook his head. "No. Not yet."

That's when the "show me" game began. They stripped down to their underwear and then pulled the fronts down and snagged the elastic bands under their balls.

"I wonder if we'll get that big," Asher said and pointed to the picture.

"I sure hope so," Ronnie replied.

Then the game turned to "I'll touch yours, if you'll touch mine."

"Want to kiss each other down there like they're doing?" Asher asked with a husky tone in his voice. He was getting *very* excited. Nothing like this had ever happened to him, but lately he'd been peeking at the men when he went into public restrooms and the locker room at the community pool. He liked what they had much better than what he'd seen in his father's magazine.

They were just climbing onto Asher's bed, getting into a position he would learn in later years was called "69" when the bedroom door opened.

They both looked up in surprise.

Standing in the doorway was Asher's grandfather, Yeshiyahu.

Their surprise was nothing compared to the expression that morphed over the old man's face. One moment he had that beautiful, calm look on his that always gave Asher the most wonderful feeling of peace, and the next his eyes had gone wide and his mouth had fallen open and drawn back into an ugly rictus.

"Abomination," his grandfather shouted. He pointed at the two of them with a long bony finger. "*Abomination!*"

Asher and Ronnie could only look up at the old man—frozen in place and too stunned, too terrified, to move.

Asher's grandfather stepped into the room. He let out a long moan and began to shake. "Anathema!"

Ronnie was the first to come out of his paralysis. He scrambled off the bed and went for his jeans, grabbing Asher's first by mistake and then tossing them aside to snatch up his own. The old man shouted (screamed) again as Ronnie, unable to get his left foot in his jeans because one of the pants legs was pulled inside out, began to cry.

"Grandfather" Asher was finally able to say. He jumped out of bed and was dressed in his pants and shirt before Ronnie was able to get his jeans on (an ability that would serve Asher well when he was older).

Yeshiyahu, his grandfather, was still moaning, head thrown back, eyes now closed, and shaking so hard Asher was afraid the old man was having some kind of fit. He reached down, plunged his hand through the leg hole of Ronnie's pants, and pulled it right side out. Ronnie fell, jammed his foot into the leg, and scrambled to his feet, pulled on his shirt and stuffed his feet into his shoes. He ran past Yeshiyahu without bothering with his socks.

"A man shall not lay with a man as he would with a woman," Asher's grandfather said, his voice hoarse and rasping. "It is an abomination."

Asher stood there a moment, confused, trying to figure out just what his grandfather was saying, when the man slapped him. He was so startled he staggered back, nearly knocked to the floor. He let out a cry and reached up to touch his stinging face.

"Grandfather!" he cried.

"And a man who lies with a male as one would with a woman, both of them have committed an abomination," Yeshiyahu reiterated. "They shall surely be put to death; their blood is upon themselves."

"But…. But…." But what? What was he going to say? That he wasn't lying down with Ronnie? He was. But what was that stuff about a woman? Abomination? Asher wasn't even sure he knew what that word meant except that it was the name of a really cool bad guy who got into fights with the incredible Hulk. Abomination?

And… his grandfather had hit him! *Hit* him! Yeshiyahu had *never* hit him.

"You!" Yeshiyahu screamed suddenly. "*Naked*. In that bed. With another boy! Do you know what you have done? Surely God cannot even *look* at you now! You have made yourself an atrocity in his sight! God vomits at the very sight of you!" He stepped forward, towering over Asher despite his frail frame. He hand flashed out, grabbed Asher's wrist in a painfully tight hold. He dropped to his knees with a grimace, pulling Asher with him. "Pray! *Pray* for forgiveness. You must make yourself clean in his sight. Do you want to be put to death? Do you want your blood to be upon you? Pray, Asher. *Pray*!"

Finally coming out of his shock, Asher burst into tears and yanked his arm away from his beloved grandfather. He jumped to his feet and pushed past the old man, fled the room, the house, ran barefoot down the street. He ran and ran until he could run no more, winding up at school. The building was locked, of course. Where had he thought he was going to go anyway? He was going to have to go home eventually. And his grandfather would be there.

Hating him.

Asher sat against the building, under the entrance awning, and buried his face against his knees and cried again. Yeshiyahu hated him. He said that *God* hated him.

All because he had been curious about another boy's body. It had been so exciting. It had felt… *right*.

So why would God hate him? Why would Yeshiyahu hate him?

When Asher finally got home, both his parents' cars were in the driveway. He'd been sick with fear and worry at the sight.

But Yeshiyahu was not there. They had taken him home, apparently.

Asher didn't see the old man over the next few weeks. Didn't hear from him either.

A month later he was dead.

And even though his parents never mentioned the incident—had Yeshiyahu even told them?—the echo of his last words never, ever, went away....

ASHER WAS nervous. He was beyond nervous.

Jennifer Leavitt, *the* producing artistic director of the Pegasus Theatre, had asked him to come in and see her. Was she offering him a play? She'd implied it. Told him to be ready to read. He didn't think that meant she was going to see if he wanted to work the box office or concessions.

What kind of part was it? Minor? Starring?

Asher had tried to pass it off as if it were all no big deal, but it *was* a big deal. It was a big fucking deal.

The Pegasus did about eight shows a year and was highly respected, not only in Kansas City, but as far as New York City. Jennifer managed to get shows for the Pegasus that had been nowhere except the Big Apple. Actors onstage at her theater went on to Broadway. One, Spencer Morrison, was a big movie star now.

Last year Asher had been thrilled to get a part in the Pegasus production of *Tearoom Tango*, directed by the incredible Guy Campbell. It had been a remarkable experience, although it had made Asher a little nervous. What if his family had taken it in their heads to come from Chicago to see the show—a play about anonymous gay sex in public restrooms? Thankfully, that hadn't happened. His mother hadn't been in the best of health, and it was a miracle if his father drove more than five or ten miles from their house, let alone as far as Kansas City.

Asher had played a cop, and he'd gotten rave reviews, which had given him high hopes for more shows. Yet here it was a year later and he hadn't done a thing except audition for a movie for which he'd been told he was too old. He tried to tell himself it was okay. The role had been for some kind of pirate, á la Han Solo, in a medium-budget sci-fi movie. Not the kind of role that would bring him to the attention of Martin Scorsese, Woody Allen, up and comer Derek Cianfrance, or even Seth Nichols.

Except now? Now something *might* be happening.

So it was with his heart in his throat that he parked in the north lot of the old red building that housed the Pegasus. He got out of his battered pickup and walked around to the front of the building. The first set of doors were locked, so he walked on to the office entrance and pressed the doorbell. A buzzing noise let him know he'd been seen, and he quickly pulled on the heavy glass door before the noise stopped. A few steps took him through a second door, and he was standing in the small office lobby, the walls dark red and gray, bedecked with pictures and posters from previous shows.

"Hi, Asher," said the lovely Iyanha. She was standing behind a counter, a headphone somehow managing to stay perched on and over her high-piled convolution of braids.

"Iyanha! How are you?"

She rolled her dark eyes comically. "Oh, you know. The girls are trying my patience, and the man is on the verge of getting kicked to the curb. He got home last night at three and couldn't go to work today. I have *had* it!"

Asher nodded. Drama, drama, drama. No wonder she worked box office for a theater.

"And you, tall and handsome? What about you?"

"Great as always," he replied. "A little curious as to what Jennifer wants."

"I'll let Jen tell you. She had a meeting downtown, but she'll be here soon. Guy should be here any minute, though."

"Guy?" Guy Campbell? The director of *Tearoom Tango*? Asher's heart skipped a beat. He couldn't help it. This could be a good thing. A *really* good thing.

Iyanha nodded. "Who else? Didn't you know?"

He shook his head.

"Sit down, Ash, relax—

(Ash? Why did Iyanha always insist on shortening people's names? Ash? No one called him Ash. And he suspected no one else called Jennifer Leavitt "Jen.")

—all is well, my brother."

He didn't have to sit long.

Guy, a very handsome man, came through the door a moment after Asher sat down. "Asher!" he said. "Good to see you. Hope you haven't been waiting long."

Asher was back on his feet in a flash and walking up to meet the director. "Not long at all. A minute. Less than."

They shook hands. Guy was shorter than Asher (but then most men were), with close-cropped dark hair and a thick shadow across his face that looked like it was trying to be a beard. Asher knew better. This was Guy's style. It seemed to be the rage recently, but as Asher had gotten to know Guy, he'd seen that copying someone else's style was far from Guy's. The director and playwright did what he did because *he* wanted to. What surprised Asher was the man was wearing a shirt that actually *fit* him and showed off his muscular chest. Guy had always worn almost ridiculously baggy clothes. Asher had been hot for him for a while now, and the new look made Asher want the man even more. Too bad he was taken. Asher had never quite managed to get him in the sack, and now word was he was in a relationship and as exclusive as a gay penguin. Damn.

"I'm glad you're here, Asher." He looked up at Asher with brown eyes that seemed to sparkle with electricity.

"I'm glad to be here," Asher said. "I'm a little nervous, though." *God! Did I say that?* Never let them know that!

"Nothing to be nervous about, Asher. You've faced far worse."

Just then the front door opened, and in came Jennifer. She gave a little nod. "Ah, Asher. You're here." She was a short woman with tight curly black hair and large dark eyes framed by wide red-and-black glasses, and as usual she was accompanied by her two constant companions, an old border collie and a small, shaggy, undefinable mutt.

He squatted and the smaller dog ran up to him, nudging for some petting. He couldn't remember if this was Robbie or Kane, but he dutifully scratched the happy dog behind his ears and then stroked his wavy fur. "You're so sweet, aren't you?" Asher looked up to see the expression on Jennifer's face.

"Kane!" she snapped. "Come here and leave Asher alone."

Kane didn't budge, of course.

"Kane! Come here, boy."

With an almost sigh and a longing look in his big brown eyes, the dog stepped back and then trotted to his master, who turned and picked him up. He couldn't have weighed more than ten pounds, so it was no problem for the little woman.

"Why don't we head down to the conference room," Guy said. There was a tension in the room that Asher couldn't identify. Had these two had a fight this morning?

Jennifer gave a nod, a weak smile, and headed down to the end of the lobby. They followed her into a room with a long conference table. It was piled high with papers spread out in piles. An obvious mailing project in the works. For one awful instant Asher was afraid that was all the two of them wanted him for. To stuff envelopes!

"I think this part is perfect for you," Guy said, going through the piles on the table.

A part I'd be perfect for! Asher thought with relief. *Yes!* He bit back the urge to do the Snoopy Dance. *Maintain. Maintain.*

"We did this as an onstage reading last year, and it's funny and it's crazy and you'd be great as the actor."

"The actor?" Asher said. He could do that. He fought back the foolish grin that wanted to take over his face. "I can do that."

"It's a pretty wild play," Guy continued. "The reading was controversial. People will certainly be talking about it."

Asher found his voice. "*Tearoom Tango* was controversial." He gave a shrug. "Since when is the Pegasus *not* talked about?"

"True, true," Jennifer said quietly.

Guy nodded. "Well, the story is all about this producer who puts two actors and a screenwriter in a remote motel room to get a contractual approval on a film script. The three start drinking. *Insane* amounts of drinking. They talk, panic, fight, vomit, and have sex. Lots of vomiting. *Lots* of sex."

Asher blinked. Vomiting? Fighting? He wasn't supposed to actually vomit, was he?

"Now, as your scene opens, you'll walk into the hotel room like you own the place. You are full of yourself, and you are full of shit. You are probably bipolar, and you recently tried to commit suicide when your wife left you."

Asher nodded. He got it. This was already more direction than he'd been given in the past for an audition. He thought this could be a piece of cake in fact.

"It's right here," Jennifer told Guy, who was still looking around the big table at the piles of paper. Jennifer leaned across and handed Asher and Guy several pieces of paper stapled at one corner. Asher glanced down and immediately saw the highlighting. Matt, in each case, stood out in bold piss-yellow.

"Thanks," said Guy. "Asher, I'll read for Don, the screenwriter. Jennifer will read Kensie, the young film producer, as well as Cindy, a very young actress who is known for doing a lot of those sitcoms."

Jennifer nodded. For some reason she was making Asher uncomfortable, and his heart was suddenly trip-hammering. She wasn't the warm woman he remembered. And today she was totally no bullshit. They were jumping right into this. That was Guy's way. Jennifer's too. But this time there hadn't even been an offer of coffee and a doughnut.

"Ready?" Guy asked.

"Ready when you are, CB."

Guy laughed. Then with a blink said, "And you are walking into the hotel room—*now!*"

Asher nodded, eyes widening for a fraction of an instant before…

…he *became*.

He surged forward, as if just coming to a stop, and flopped down onto a small love seat that was just inside the room to the right. Letting out a long sigh, he read, "Wow. Did they actually have to hide this place in the middle of nowhere? What the *fuck?*" He glared at Guy, i.e. Don, and Jennifer, aka Kensie/Cindy.

"Hi," Jennifer read from her script.

"Yeah," Asher continued.

Jennifer: "OK. First thing. The studio has spared no expense to put you up in this charming motel far away from the temptations and distractions of Los Angeles. They have rented out the entire place. There are no other guests here. Everyone, give me your car keys."

Guy pretended to hand Jennifer his keys.

Asher sat up, felt a moment of inspiration, started to reach into his pants pockets, then leaned forward, resting elbows on knees. "You know this is bullshit."

Then Jennifer began what turned out to be half a page of monologue. It started with, "I do not need to remind you that our earlier attempts to set up this session failed. You partied instead of working. We are now down to the wire." It went on for a bit and ended with,

"So, if you do *not* give me your *fucking* keys, I will have to move back in with my parents, and if *that* happens, I swear to God, I will *find* you, I will get past your entourage—and I will *end you.*"

It was weird to hear Jennifer use the F-word.

Asher held up his hand. "Wait." He pretended to press a button on an imaginary key fob. "Had to lock it." He handed Jennifer the "keys," then turned to Guy. "I absolutely *fucking* love her," he said without a trace of irony. Just like the script instructed.

This set up another monologue and left Asher with very little to say except some "Yeahs," "Wow," and an "Oh no. Please stay." Weird scene for him to read. He wasn't getting much to say. How could they know if he could do this or not with so little? Was the whole play like this? Despite himself, he was getting even more nervous and was surprised to feel a trickle of sweat roll down his ribs. He never sweated. Not outside a gym or a bedroom.

Guy ended the scene just as Asher left the room and came back with a make-believe bottle of alcohol, which apparently the character wasn't supposed to have. So the drinking was to begin right away?

Asher gulped and bit the insides of his cheeks. Fuck. Disaster. This was a disaster! Why hadn't they given him a scene where he actually talked? Acted?

But it was then Asher saw Guy smiling.

"See?" Guy said, nodding to Jennifer.

"It's almost creepy," she replied.

"What is?" Asher asked.

"It's like we waved a wand over the script, and he—" Jennifer pointed at Asher and sighed. "—popped out of thin air."

"Yup," Guy agreed. Was he stifling a grin?

What the hell was happening?

They turned as one. "Why don't you take the script home and read over it," Jennifer said, this time handing Asher a whole lot more paper.

Asher looked down and the script. Take it home? Read it over?

"I think we just may have our Matt."

Wait. What? "Are you offering me the part?" Asher asked, astonished. She was so matter-of-fact that she could have been talking about her grocery list, while Guy was grinning. It was confusing. What was happening?

"Read the script," she said, her own voice unreadable. "Tell us what you think."

Asher gulped and managed an "okay."

"Can you get back to us…." She looked over at Guy. "How long can we wait?"

"I want to do it," Asher offered quickly.

She smiled. *Was* that a smile? Had her expression finally cracked? "All right. But I tell you what. You read the script. Call and let us know for sure. Meanwhile, Guy and I will talk."

They would talk? Were they offering the goddamned part or not?

Guy came around the table and held out his hand.

Asher took it, sure to wipe his hand up along his jeans as he did so. He was sweating. He couldn't believe how much. "T-thank you, Guy. For this opportunity."

"Thank me after reading the script. *Lots* of throwing up. *Lots* of drinking."

"I trust I won't *really* be drinking?"

"Hell no. Not booze. We want you to make it to the last scene without passing out!"

Asher nodded. Gulped again. "Okay."

A few minutes later he was sitting in his car.

Sometimes life moves really fast.

CHAPTER FOUR

"Tangaloa lived on high, and he was alone. There was no sky and no land or any peoples. He went to and fro, high above, for there was no sea either, and no earth, and when he grew tired there was no place to rest...."

Peni was in fourth grade. Or more properly, the summer between fourth and fifth.

They were sitting on his grandfather Afona's back deck. That is what Peni called him—Afona—because in Samoa, children called their parents and grandparents by their names. And while Afona's house was not Samoa, it was Samoa as far as Peni's grandfather was concerned. There were tiki torches burning, and they were both wearing lava-lavas, Samoan sarongs. Grandfather insisted. He always insisted. It was a hot evening, and they had come out here because Afona was not Mormon and he was telling Peni of the old ways. Afona had the pe'a and sometimes he would talk about how painful it had been to get and how Afona's half brother had died getting his. But he was a chief, a high chief, and he was Samoan, and there was no question. No "had to." He simply did it. He had gone through the ritual, gotten his pe'a, just as Iakopo, Peni's father, had.

"If we were in Samoa, *you* would get the pe'a too," he would often say. "When it was time for you to become a man."

But tonight Afona talked of other things.

Tonight was the story of the creation of the world by the great god Tangaloa.

The story was complicated. Not nearly as easy to understand or picture as, "In the beginning God created the heaven and the earth." No simple "And God said, 'Let there be light.'" No scooping up a handful of dust and breathing into it to, presto chango, make a man. Sometimes Afona's story seemed to change, and Peni couldn't keep it all straight. But Peni *loved* to listen to the old man, who was big and heavy like so many of the men in his family.

"And finally Tangaloa stopped from his moving back and forth," Afona said, his big black eyes wide and dramatic. He nodded. "And where he stood there grew up a Rock—a place to rest at last. His name was Tangaloa-fa'a-tutupu-nu'u, and he was ready to make all things!"

The old man took a drink of his ava, which was made of the root of the kava plant and could get you high. Grandmother wouldn't let Afona have alcohol. She was Mormon and wouldn't let a drop in the house. But this was tradition, and she didn't dare step on tradition.

"Tangaloa faced the west," Afona continued, "and he spoke to the Rock and struck it with his right hand, and it split open and the earth was brought forth—the parent of all the peoples of our world. And the Sea was brought forth and covered the Papa-sosolo, and all the rocks called him blessed."

That was another part of the story that confused Peni. He wasn't sure who Papa-sosolo was and how there could *be* any other rocks. Hadn't Tangaloa just created the only rock? It was like when God marked Cain and exiled him and told him that wherever he went, people would hate him. How could there *be* anyone to hate him when the first people were Adam and Eve, and Cain and Abel were their only sons? But Peni didn't ask. Somehow it seemed wrong to do so. Irreverent. Instead, he just listened. Listened and remembered because one day it might be *his* job to tell the stories.

"Then Tangaloa turned to the right side and all the Fresh Water sprang up. And he spoke to the Rock, and out of it the Sky leapt upward. Then he spoke to the Rock again and Ilu—Immensity—came forth. And then Mamao—Space—and Tui-te'e-langi and Niuao...."

It was around here that Peni would get totally lost in the Samoan names and words, and he would get so frustrated because he wanted so much to understand. Afona told him not to worry because one day he *would* understand.

But Afona was gone now. He was on the other side, or maybe somewhere else? A Samoan paradise? Peni didn't know, and his mother wouldn't talk about that. She insisted that the Heavenly Father made the world, not Tangaloa.

But Peni loved those stories! He loved to hear about how Tangaloa spoke to the Rock and how from it Man and Spirit and Heart and Will and even Thought were created. He would try to imagine it. Try to picture these things coming out of the Rock. And wasn't the

Rock Samoa? He thought it was. He thought that was what the story meant. That the whole of existence came right out of Samoa.

Peni tried to picture what Tangaloa looked like. Did he look like a man? Was he perhaps a giant since he had rested on a rock and that Rock was Samoa? Did he have the pe'a? Peni liked to think so. He liked to picture a giant with brown skin and flashing black eyes and his body—from waist and lower back to his knees—covered in the intricate black lines and jagged triangles and squares and dots and *x*'s. Peni would imagine until he could *see* this giant, this god, towering over all of Samoa, above the palm trees, the blue sky and the white clouds resting on his shoulders.

And Peni liked to hear the story of the two beautiful ladies, Tilafaiga and Taema, who swam away to visit Fiji and, when they came back, brought a basket full of tattooing tools with them, singing a song that said the tattoo is for women and not for men. But when they reached Samoa, they saw a beautiful oyster beneath the water and dove down to take it for their own, and when they came back to the surface, their song was mixed up. After that it was the men who got tattooed.

There were so many tales, and Peni listened to them all. He loved to hear about Sina and the eel. Sina was a lovely young girl, and she had a pet eel that fell in love with her. It made her afraid, and she tried to run away, but the eel followed her. Sina hid in a village, but when she went to the village pool to get water, she saw the eel staring up at her! *"E pupula mai, ou mata o le alelo!"* she cried, which meant "You stare at me, with eyes like a demon!" The village chiefs came and killed the eel and as it lay there dying, it made one last request. It begged Sina to plant its head in the ground and, feeling sorry for the eel, Sina did as it asked and—*Oka!*—a coconut tree grew from the ground.

Afona would pick up a coconut at this point in the story and point at the three spots on one end that looked like a face, and say: "See? Now whenever Sina poked a hole here and drank from the coconut, she was kissing the eel!"

Sometimes Afona would scare him with stories about Pulotu, the spirit world, or of Telesā the ghost, or the powerful devil called Nifoloa, who had a long tooth that continued to grow long after it had died and could still bite people. Peni would shiver in delicious fear at these stories, and when he had nightmares, he couldn't tell his parents because he knew they wouldn't let him sit with Afona alone anymore if he did.

Peni cherished all these stories, and he would dream of going to Samoa himself. He had gone once, when he was very little, but all he could remember was the sun and beautiful beaches that seemed to go on forever.

One day, he would think. *One day I will go back.*

His grandmother came out then, bringing him a big mug of kokosamoa, and his eyes lit up. So much better than the hot chocolate his friends' mothers served. Kokosamoa was rich and thick and so sweet he would get dizzy!

"Thank you, Ioana," Peni said, and then she stood and listened for a moment and rolled her big dark eyes like all the women in his family seemed wont to do.

"*Oka*," she muttered and shook her head and left them there to spin their tales.

Peni laughed and drank his cocoa and listened and listened until his eyelids grew heavy, despite all the sugar and caffeine. At some point his grandfather gathered him up in his big arms and took him to the couch and laid him there and covered him with a light blanket, and Peni slept all night with dreams of coconut trees holding up the sky and black tattooed lines across brown skin.

PENI WAS happy when Wyatt called and asked him if he wanted to hang out with him and Sloan for the afternoon. He liked Wyatt a lot, even though at first his flamboyant behavior had made Peni self-conscious. It was back to those feelings of *if someone sees me with him, will they think I'm gay?*

But now as he thought about it, he saw it all came down to one thing. He *was* gay, wasn't he? His mother knew. His brothers and sisters must know by now, right? Of course Lagi, his younger sister, knew. He had told her, and to his surprise, his revelation had been no news to her either. She just rolled her eyes comically—looking so much like their mother when she did it—and said one word. Two, actually…

"Like, *duh*!"

So what if someone *did* see him with Wyatt? What difference did it make?

Peni tried to tell himself that. It *sort* of worked.

But then the echoes of the people from his church threatened from the corners of his mind. Words that said it was all right that he was homosexual—as long as he didn't *act* on it. And why? Well because it was a serious sin to have sex outside the bonds of marriage. And since God himself had created the definition of marriage to between a man and a woman, and he couldn't marry another man, then he couldn't "act on it." As a Mormon, he had no right to question or change what God himself had designed.

That meant his only choice was either to live a celibate life or to marry a woman. And how was that going to work? Because what a shock it had been to find out he didn't even like kissing a woman. How could he marry one? Have *sex* with a woman? No. Not happening.

Sometimes it made him angry. Angry at fate. Angry at the universe. Angry at *God*! Because damn it, men were *supposed* to want women. All his life, that was all his guy friends had ever done—talk about girls, and then later, women. They talked of the mysteries of women. The beauty of women. There was a movie called *Scent of a Woman* for goodness sake!

And when Peni would think that way, he would hear Scott's words in his head...

("It's religion! It gets its fucking hooks in you and you can never escape! Abusive is what it is! How can you believe in God?")

But then Scott had changed his tune, hadn't he?

Something had happened to him when he went to that men's festival back in July—a festival Peni had been packing for when word had come that his father had been killed in that stupid car accident. All because someone had chosen to drive drunk. *That* man was alive today, while Peni's beloved father was gone.

Peni still forgot. He'd reach for the phone to call his father... only to remember that he was dead.

His family took comfort in the fact that they would see him again one day in the Celestial Kingdom. But Peni? He just didn't know....

He also didn't know how his people could throw away a thousand years of their own ways and religion for this new one. They were a proud race, quite possibly the *very* first of the island peoples—and they had just given it up?

Which was a big part of the reason Peni was enjoying getting to know Wyatt. Wyatt was what Scott liked to call—or at least *used* to call—"witchy-woo-woo." Wyatt believed in ancient ways. He spoke in words that excited Peni and made him want to know more about what the Samoan people had once believed. The problem with that was his mom. Now that his father and grandfather were gone, there was no one who would talk about the old ways. He had to resort to Wikipedia to find anything!

But in the meantime, thankfully, there was Wyatt. He wasn't Samoan and knew nothing of their ways, but he *did* believe in gods and he *did* believe in all kinds of magical stories.

Peni pulled his little Dodge Intrepid in front of Wyatt's house and got out. It was a lovely day, still quite warm—the first day of autumn still a week away. The place was a cute little American Craftsman-style home with a front porch (of course) and sets of windows on the second floor with their own little peaked roofs. Peni didn't see Sloan's aged silver Oldsmobile Ninety-Eight, so that meant that he'd beat him here. Of course, sometimes that old car wouldn't start, and that might mean he'd have to go get him—that being no big deal considering nothing in Terra's Gate was much farther than fifteen minutes from anything else in Terra's Gate.

Peni got out of his car and was greeted by the music of P!nk blasting all the way to where he was standing. He grinned. Ah, Wyatt. He had passed under the two huge old evergreens in the front yard and up to the front porch and was just about to place his foot on the first step when he heard the screaming inside.

Crap. Were Wyatt and Howard fighting again?

He stopped where he was, hesitant to embarrass his friend. Maybe he should just go back to his car and drive around the block a few times. But then, just as P!nk was singing out that she was still a rock star, Peni's decision was taken from him. Wyatt came slamming out of the house and onto the front porch, hand and middle finger raised in the universally recognized salute. An instant later P!nk came to a sudden stop, mid-*Na-Na-Na*.

Wyatt's eyes flew wide when he quite suddenly noticed Peni standing there. "Oh, shit! I didn't mean you!" He was wearing a lavender shirt that said, "Gay By Birth, Fabulous By Choice," and a large matching lavender wristwatch with little rhinestones around the edge.

Peni's hand flew to his mouth. He didn't want to laugh, but it wasn't easy. "Where did you get that watch?" he asked.

Wyatt shrugged. "Avon. I'm thinking of becoming an Avon lady."

"Over my fucking dead body!" Howard came charging out of the house after his lover. "No—*fucking*—way!"

Wyatt spun back around. "You don't own me!" he shouted angrily, and then throwing his hands over his head, he launched into the classic Leslie Gore song of the same name.

"Goddamn it, Wy! Could you *be* a bigger faggot?"

Peni took a step back. Howard was a big man. He towered over Wyatt, and sure, Wyatt was short, but Howard was a *big* man. Taller than Asher even, a good six five at least, with broad shoulders and a big (a very big) gut and hands (clenched in fists) the size of small hams.

How was it that Wyatt could be brave enough to continue his song? How could he continue to sing (swiveling his hips and cocking his crotch) about how he was free to live his life the way he wanted? Peni would be terrified. He *was* terrified. He could easily imagine—the way he could see Tangaloa towering above him, sky resting on his shoulders, pe'a stretching for miles—Howard bolting down those steps and pounding the shit out of chubby little Wyatt.

Howard stood there on the porch, face red, breathing in great heaving gulps, eyes opening wide and then squinting in deadly threat, those hands (those huge hands) clenching—opening—clenching—opening....

Then Howard's big bald head turned, and he noticed Peni standing there. They locked eyes, and it was all Peni could do not to turn and flee. Howard shuddered, abruptly broke eye contact with Peni, and swiveled back to Wyatt.

"Fuck you, you flaming little *faggot!*" he shouted and turned his hulking form around and slammed back into the house.

"Takes one to know one!" Wyatt called after him.

Peni raced forward and laid a hand on Wyatt's shoulder. "Are you okay?"

To his surprise Wyatt jumped as if he'd been goosed and pivoted around, his face white, sweat beading up on his forehead. He looked terrified. So much for his brave front. For a seemingly endless moment, they stared into each other's eyes, a strange repeat of what had happened seconds ago with Howard, though the message crackling back and forth between them was a completely different one.

Then Wyatt smiled, and the color came back to his face in a blink. He grinned, his dark eyes flashing, and launched back into his song, letting Peni and the whole block know that he could say and do whatever he pleased.

And dammit if Peni didn't, despite himself, burst into laughter. "Wyatt! I can't believe you did that. He could have *killed* you!"

Wyatt laughed (not quite convincingly) and waved Peni's concern away as if the idea were as crazy as Howard announcing he was a closet heterosexual. "Howard? *Please!* He's all bluster. *Fuck* him."

For a moment there was a look in Wyatt's eyes—just what, exactly, Peni wasn't sure. Fear? Yes. Panic? Could be. And sadness. But all those emotions were there and gone in a flash, and Peni thought he very well could have imagined it, because just that fast Wyatt was smiling and swiveling his hips and giving Bette Midler and Diane Keaton and Goldie Hawn a run for their money.

Then somehow, Sloan was joining in—

(and when had *he* gotten there?)

—and he was singing too—

(with only one quick glance at the front door of the house).

—and why not, what the hell?

Peni didn't know all the words, but he knew the parts about you not owning me, and because he'd danced the traditional Samoan dances at weddings and dozens of other events for years, he moved with the best of them. Maybe better.

How cool was that?

("I'm impressed!" Wyatt squeaked.)

Who cared if they looked like some queenie gay version of the trio of stars from *The First Wives Club*?

And look! There was Sloan's boyfriend, Max (although he certainly didn't join their dance number), and after that they all climbed into Max's Scion and headed into the city, plans of watching *Shelter* on Wyatt's big flat-screen television abandoned in favor of cocktails at The Male Box. After all, it was Saturday, right? Peni didn't have to work the next day, and he wasn't driving, and maybe once, for *once*, he should see what it was like to get shit-faced.

After all, what could it hurt?

What could it really hurt?

CHAPTER FIVE

SATURDAY NIGHT and still no word from Jennifer or Guy, and goddammit, why not? He'd called and let them know he wanted the part of Matt, vomiting or not. They'd made him feel like it was all over except the ticker tape parade. What could be taking so goddamned long?

Asher didn't like this feeling. Not one bit. Not one *goddamned* bit. He was pacing! He never paced for anyone or anything. It was enough to make him tell Sloan that he wouldn't be joining the FF for movie night. Hell, it was just *Shelter* again anyway. So it wasn't like he would be able to pay any attention. His nerves were eating him up. He'd even had nightmares two nights running.

In one he was sitting in an audience and the lights went down, and when they came back up to a lighted stage, he realized he was seeing a production of *Drunks*. Two actors he didn't know, playing Kensie the film producer and Don the screenwriter, were performing the argumentative opening, and when it got time for Asher—as Matt—to get ready to go onstage, he discovered he couldn't move. He was tied to his seat.

He began to panic. He only had a few more seconds until the second actress, who had just come on (someone else he didn't know and goddammit, there weren't many actors or actresses in Kansas City that he *didn't* know!) would deliver the line cuing him to step onstage!

Oh, God and—"Wow. She's your mentor."—there it was!

Asher tried to yell out his line, to somehow save the scene, and that was when he realized there was a gag over his mouth. A new panic set in as the actors onstage waited for him—for *him*!

"Wow. She's your mentor," the young actress said, repeating her line as Asher struggled madly with his bonds.

The audience began to get restless around him. They were beginning to suspect something was up, and how could they help it? The three actors onstage were looking at each other and mouthing unheard words to each other, actually shrugging for God's sake (how fucking unprofessional!) and then (no, no, no!) the actress repeated her line yet a third time (could you be so frigging obvious?).

"Wow. She's your mentor."

Then, just as Asher began to think that maybe, just maybe, he was getting one of the ropes loose, an old man stepped out onto the stage.

Asher's eyes went wide in alarm.

It was his grandfather Yeshiyahu!

Even from where he sat, he could see his grandfather was angry. *Furious.* The old man was trembling and quite suddenly pointed a long bony finger out into the audience—at Asher.

"You!" Yeshiyahu shouted. "You think I can't see you out there in the dark? *Naked?*"

Naked? But he wasn't naked....

But of course, he was, wasn't he? This was a dream, and wasn't that just par for the fucking course in a dream?

A woman in the row ahead of Asher turned around and looked at him. Her eyes went wild. "Oh, my, *Gawd,*" she cried in a thick Yiddish accent. "He *is* naked."

A man next to her looked then, and his eyes bugged out as well. "Look at that *cock.*" He grinned lewdly.

"Oh, no. Oh, Asher" came a familiar voice next to him, and when he turned to see who it was, of course it was his mother—wearing one of her hideous babushkas. "Oh, Asher." She shook her head.

"Do you see him, Hanneleh?" Yeshiyahu shouted. "Do you know what he's done? With men? God cannot even *look* at him now. He is an abomination!"

Asher had woken at that point with a scream, words echoing in his head. *"Pray, Asher! Pray!"*

What the hell was wrong with him? What was all this anxiety? He'd waited weeks to hear back on parts in the past. Why all the anxiety over this one?

And why had his grandfather shown up in his dream? Asher hadn't thought of that old bastard in years!

Liar, said a voice deep in his head.

What if he had another nightmare tonight? What if the old man showed up again? The prospect made Asher break out in a sweat. It was an idea he didn't relish one bit.

A drink was what he needed. Several, in fact.

So he had gone down to his old truck and headed over to The Male Box. He thought briefly about going to The Corner Bistro instead, because what if Sloan or Scott or Wyatt had decided to go out? The Male Box was the only bar they'd go to. But no. They were watching *Shelter* yet again, and he'd told Sloan he couldn't make it. Told him he wasn't feeling well (and of course Sloan had offered to come stay with him, bring him goddamned chicken soup!) when in fact what he didn't want was to be grilled about the part in *Drunks*, and did he have it or did he think he had it, or "Come on, Asher. You must have *some* idea how it went!" He couldn't stand that, and even thinking about it now made his stomach clench into knots.

No. His buds wouldn't be out tonight, and while he liked The Corner Bistro best for atmosphere and new cocktail recipes, tonight he wanted a *crowd*. A bigassed crowd, which he wouldn't get at the small Bistro. It wasn't a tenth the size of The Male Box, and the crowd was so different there. Mostly dates or little groups of friends chattering away the hours and sipping at overpriced drinks—the music simply for background. "The Girl from Ipanema" and "The First Time Ever I Saw Your Face" and "I'm Not In Love."

No. He wanted to be bombarded by music—have his senses slammed by Iggy Azalea and Demi Lovato and Ellie Goulding. He wanted to *dance*!

And he wanted to get laid.

He wanted to get a man to take him home, and then he wanted to fuck the goddamned hell out of him. Maybe some guy who claimed he never bottomed. Oh, and how many times had Asher heard *that* one? Well, if he could get a straight dude in bed with his legs up in the air, what gay man stood a chance of resisting him? Especially after they got a look at the size of his cock or after he ate their ass?

Asher loved to fuck—had ever since Jane Berenbaum let him have her in the back of her car when they were both sophomores in high school, and then (damn!), Buck Summers, the school's star quarterback (and later practically collecting the cherries of his alma mater's sports heroes like notches on his belt).

Sex was the only thing (perhaps) that Asher liked as much as booze. Both made the bullshit go away for a while. He was *happy* when he was drunk or when he was fucking some hot stud. The only reason he didn't like sex better was that it didn't blot out as much time. Not that he didn't have the stamina to make a bedroom (or bathroom, or alley) romp last as long as a good binge. He did. *Hell* yes. But somehow the fucking didn't drown out the voices as well—

(*"Abomination!"*)

—because he lost interest in his conquest as soon as he shot his load. Which was why he always made sure his trick came first. Let it be said that he was conceited or even a slut. But never bad in bed. *Never* that.

So once again he wound up at The Male Box, making a beeline to the back patio with its tacky little tiki bar (and where the hell else did you find a tiki bar anymore besides the Box?) and, oh good, Ziggy was serving up the cocktails.

"Asher!" cried the *almost* hot bartender (hot enough that Asher had had him).

"Ziggy," he said with a collected cool. "What's new?"

"What's new," Ziggy said with a gigantic smile, "is that I've got a new shot for you!"

"Oh?" Asher asked, showing interest (but not *too* much interest).

Ziggy raised his thick brows in a way that Asher guessed was supposed to be sexy or something. He wasn't sure.

Ziggy got out two shot glasses. Then he reached for the white bottle that no one had heard of a year or so ago and now seemed to be *the* party alcohol—RumChata. Not a good start. Asher wanted original. Then came… was that whiskey? RumChata—which tasted like kheer, the Indian dessert—and whiskey?

Asher raised an eyebrow.

As Ziggy poured, he gave Asher an enthusiastic nod. "Go on. Try it. Have I ever steered you wrong?"

Yes, thought Asher. *More than once.*

But it was free alcohol, and when did he turn down free booze? That would be alcohol abuse.

So they nodded and clinked glasses and back and down they went, the shot hitting first with its cloying sweetness and then… *whoa!* Hot! And not "hot, damn hot," but a burn that was somehow *not* since it came with that silky sweetness.

"Yeah?" Ziggy asked excitedly.

"What's it called?" Asher asked, careful not to show *too* much approval.

"Demon Semen." Ziggy laughed. "RumChata and Fireball Cinnamon Whisky. Starts sweet and ends with a *burn*."

"Thus—Demon Semen."

Ziggy smiled the smile that had gotten Asher to go home with him once upon a time.

"Not bad, buddy," Asher told him. "Not bad at all."

Ziggy could have been a puppy in the way he all but wagged his tail at Asher's approval. "Another?"

"Later," Asher said. "I want something I can nurse…." *And how….*

Ziggy nodded again. He was starting to remind Asher not of a puppy, but one of those little toy dogs with the bobbing heads, like the one that used to sit in the back window of his mother's car.

"G and T?" Ziggy asked.

Asher let him know that would be *just* fine.

"Bombay Sapphire?"

Asher let him know that would be fine as well.

Then he took his drink and paid the man—along with a generous tip—and settled in a corner and waited. He would dance later. After a few cocktails when a nice little buzz had begun to take hold. Right now he was beginning the hunt.

ASHER SPOTTED his evening's target just a sip into his second gin and tonic. He knew it. This was no keep-this-guy-in-mind-until-I'm-sure-there's-no-one-better. This was *him*.

The man was tall, although not as tall as Asher, and that's the way he liked it. His height automatically gave him a sense of power over the men he singled out of the herd. He was beautiful, too, dusky skinned enough to make Asher think he was either mixed or… what? Filipino? No…. Maybe he was…. Well, who gave a shit? He was hot. That was what mattered. He was slim and well-muscled, with a lovely round butt that was just begging to be held—and more. And his eyes! As glittering black as his hair, which was cut short but not too short.

He was looking for someone, that was obvious from the way those dark eyes kept darting to the patio door.

Me, thought Asher, standing up and making his way to the sexy man. *You're looking for me*. He was already imagining the guy on his back, legs wrapped around Asher's waist, eyes rolled up in his head from the pleasure Asher was sure to give him. Pleasure he was always sure to provide.

"May I get you something to drink?" Asher asked as soon as he reached the exotic man's side.

Beautiful jumped. "What?"

"Drink." He gave his most dazzling head-shot smile. "May I get you a cocktail?" He sidled up a little closer.

"I… well… gosh. I guess so." He gave Asher a look he couldn't identify. Surprise, maybe?

"What'll you have?"

"I…." Beautiful blinked. "I don't know."

"Can't make up your mind?"

The man shrugged. It was cute. Adorable, even. "I've only drunk a few times before. I had some wine once…."

Only drunk a few times before? Was the guy bullshitting him?

Something began to tickle around the corners of Asher's memory. Wait…. Wine…. Something…. What?

"You know, Asher. Fourth of July, remember? Wyatt gave it to me."

What? Fourth of July? This guy knows Wyatt?

Wait….

Tickle…. Tickle, tickle…. Something familiar….

Quite abruptly, Beautiful's expression changed. The sweet little lost look vanished from his face to be replaced by…

"You don't remember me, do you?"

Remember…. *Shit!* Yes… it was coming now…. Dancing?

"Yes, dancing!"

Asher's eyes widened. Had he said that out loud?

"You tried to grab my ass even though you had a date."

Then it hit him. Asher remembered, saw it like a figure emerging from the fog—misty, obscured, and then *there*! Clear and real.

"Peter Wagner's party," Asher said, then opened his mouth to say the young man's name and realized that he couldn't remember it. "I'm sorry," he managed. "I was pretty wasted. The alcohol was flowing pretty free."

The dark eyes studied him, and Asher couldn't help but feel it was as if he were a bug under a magnifying glass.

"*Oca*, Asher! You were at my father's *funeral*. Or were you drunk then too?"

A breath caught in Asher's throat. Funeral. *Fuck me!* He had been drunk. *Really* drunk. Why, he'd been tipsy on the drive there, although he'd kept it to tipsy since Independence wasn't a short drive from

Kansas City. He'd waited to *drink* in the car before he went into the chapel. Stumbled was more like it.

Peni.

The name came to him like that figure in the fog—not there, and then *there* in a snap. "Peni," he mumbled, pronouncing it "Pea-knee."

"*Penny*" came the corrected pronunciation. Like the coin.

Was that a note of contempt in Peni's voice? Well, what flew up his ass?

"Asher!"

He turned to find Sloan standing in his personal space. Fuck. And he had his fucking "boyfriend" with him, and great, Wyatt too.

"I thought you weren't feeling well," Sloan said.

"Well, I thought you guys were watching *Shelter* for the eleventy-first time."

Hurt? Was that hurt in Sloan's big brown eyes? *Christ.*

"I thought you were feeling bad," Sloan said again.

"I had to get out," Asher snapped before he could say it a third time.

"Your friend was just offering to buy me a drink," Peni said and shit, that was condescension in his voice all right.

"Oh, *really*?" asked Wyatt, eyes flashing and filled with knowledge. "Were you offering for all of us?"

"I think he was trying to pick me up," Peni said.

Wyatt smirked and Sloan's heart-on-his-sleeve expression said it all. "We were just showing Peni that you could go to a gay bar and have a good time without it being about sex," he said.

Wyatt nodded, and Max simply crossed his arms.

"I don't think your friend knows that," Peni said.

"I know that!" Asher clenched his jaw. He wanted to lash out. How dare his friends judge him? Jealousy. That's what it was. They just wished they could get laid as easily as he could. As if any of them *could*. Except for maybe Sloan. Wyatt, but only if he was at a bear convention. And.... Wait. "Where's the fourth musketeer?" he asked, trying to dispel his anger.

"Asher. Scott and Cedar went on a road trip. They got him a motorcycle to match Cedar's. He's hasn't talked about anything else for the last two weeks!"

Really?

He turned just in time to see Peni give him a look of disgust. "Can we go somewhere else, guys?"

Rage flashed to the surface, and Asher practically snarled. Who did they think they fucking were? "No need," he barked. "I was just leaving. This place sucks tonight."

Asher pushed past them and headed into the bar proper and the slamming music of drag queens lip-synching to Katy Perry's "This is How We Do."

He was stopped by a hand on his arm, and he spun, ready to lash out until he saw it was Sloan. The look of disappointment was gone from his face, his only expression now one of concern.

Of course.

"Are you okay?"

Asher wanted to say, "Fuck you!" In fact, had his mouth open to do just that, and instead (to his surprise) said, "I still haven't heard back about the play."

"But wasn't your audition only a few days ago?"

Yes. Yes, it was, dammit. So the hell what?

"They made it sound like it was mine. Like I was the one they were thinking of for the part. So what the fuck? What are they waiting for? I told them I wanted it. I've left two frigging messages!"

"Asher. You'll get it." He smiled. "I know it."

Asher shook his head. "You *don't* know—" and then somehow bit off that last word—*Shit*. As in, you don't know shit. "Look," he said instead. "I gotta go." And he did go, ignoring the offered hug.

That would have been just a little too much.

So Asher went to The Watering Hole instead. He had to listen to country and western, but he also didn't even have to finish his first beer—

(Bud Light—*shudder*)

—before a hot, *very* hot, guy was hitting on him. His name was Frank (at least that's what Asher thought he heard over Steve Grand belting through the bar's speakers), and he was shirtless, with just the right amount of chest hair, and wearing very tight black jeans that showed off his cock and balls. Not as big as Asher's, but impressive, and who knew how big it got when it was hard? Asher sure aimed to find out.

"Look," Asher all but shouted less than five minutes after they started talking. "You want to get the hell out of here?"

"I thought you'd never ask," said Frank (Frank?), and they were off. How nice to meet a guy who was apparently just as big a slut as he was.

Even better, they went to Frank's place, which was only a couple of blocks away. That meant Asher wouldn't have to endure small talk after the sex, and he could leave as soon as he wanted.

That's just what he did.

CHAPTER SIX

"How can you like that loser?" Peni asked Sloan. It was Monday, and they were on break.

"Liam Neeson?" said Sloan. "I wouldn't call him a loser."

"What?" Liam Neeson? He looked at his friend in confusion, saw the confusion on Sloan's face, and realized—well—they had been talking about *A Walk Among the Tombstones* and whether Liam Neeson had sold out, hadn't they? How he used to be such a good actor and now....

And somewhere along the line, Peni had started thinking about Asher. He didn't like it one bit. The man was a pompous jerk. He sighed. "No. Not Liam Neeson. Your buddy Asher."

"Asher?" The look on Sloan's face was complete surprise. Then understanding. "Gosh, Peni. Are you still thinking about Saturday?"

Like it was a year ago or something! Yes, he was still thinking about Saturday. The "famous" Asher—at least in his own mind—had tried to pick him up. He had been—what was the phrase?—cruising him. And that? Well, that was kind of okay. Flattering even. Peni had been immediately attracted to him. He'd thought he was hot the second he'd laid eyes on him months ago.

But then Asher had gone and proved he was a *valea*—an idiot.

The day they'd met had been a beautiful one, a Fourth of July celebration at the home of the wealthy and renowned Peter Wagner. The man might as well have owned the college town of Terra's Gate—or at least that was the way it seemed to Peni. The billionaire's palatial mansion atop the hill overlooked the town, and Peni couldn't help but think of some story from myth—as if Peter Wagner were Zeus gazing down at Greece from his throne on Mount Olympus or Tangaloa standing over Samoa. At the height of the evening, there was a tremendous fireworks display that outshone Kansas City's, some forty-five minutes away. But what was wonderful to Peni was that the man was gay—openly gay. The whole world knew.

Mr. Wagner owned Horrell & Howes, the company where Sloan and Peni worked. Sloan had so impressed the man with his performance and bold ideas (or at least his boldness) that he'd been promoted, leapfrogging over several intermediary positions. He'd also been invited to the huge private party the man threw every year, and to Peni's shock and happiness, Sloan had scored Peni an invitation as well.

Peni had been very nervous. He almost hadn't gone to the party. Why, the drive alone, especially that last bit—stopping at the foot of the hill and showing his invitation to the security guards and then taking the private road that wound up and around and up again to Peter Wagner's house—had almost been enough to send Peni racing back home.

Once at the top, he was guided to a parking space on a great expanse of lawn, and he called Sloan so he could find him. It was easy enough. He was directed to look for Wyatt's huge rainbow umbrella—and when he made his way to it through the crowd, there they were: Sloan and his friends.

Peni had already met Wyatt. It was the first time for the rest, including Max, Sloan's lover, Scott (who had bombarded him with all the antireligion stuff), and of course, Asher.

One look at the man took Peni's breath away. Sloan had told him he was good-looking, but the words just hadn't prepared him for *how* good-looking. Asher was stunning.

Sadly, Asher also proved himself to be a jerk.

He was lying back on a picnic blanket making out with a young man the first time Peni laid eyes on him. That didn't stop him from sitting up and giving Peni a look that made him feel naked. Asher's expression was absolutely lascivious. "Well hello, Peni," he said, drawing out the "hello" in an almost pornographic way.

Despite himself, Asher's words sent a bolt of electricity straight to Peni's crotch. Then Asher jumped to his feet and held out a hand, either oblivious to or totally unselfconscious of the hard bulge in his jeans. It was a considerable bulge. From what he could see, Sloan hadn't been exaggerating the man's endowment.

Peni held his hands out, but not to shake. It was to ward the man off. "I've heard all about you," he told Asher.

Asher, consummate actor that he apparently was, got a wounded, innocent look on his face at Peni's words. "What about me?" he asked. Two seconds later he was folding himself back down on his blanket and patting a spot next to him. "You can sit here." He said it with his date cuddling up next to him. Had he no shame? This was the man Sloan, Peni's hero, had fallen in love with?

Lust. Yes, he could see lusting after Asher. Peni instantly found himself lusting after the man. He was one of those men that straight men would admit they'd fuck if they were drunk enough.

But love?

No. No way.

Peni sat down with Scott instead.

That's when they offered him the wine.

He'd liked it quite a bit. Something called… mush-cot-oh?

Later, when they were all dancing on the coruscating dance floor that had been set up for the night, Asher tried again. He moved in and snagged Peni by the belt loops of his jeans and pulled him up against his hard and muscular body. He looked at Peni with those incredible eyes, and it was all Peni could do to keep himself from falling under the man's spell. Asher leaned in several times trying to kiss him, and through the grace of… God? …Tangaloa? Peni managed to turn his head to the side so he avoided that sexy mouth.

And then Asher actually suggested they go find a dark corner and get to know each other better. With his date not five feet away! Worse, the offer actually tempted Peni. It was only the alcohol rolling off Asher's breath that shocked Peni back to reality. He laughed and squirmed free and left the dance floor as fast as decorum would allow.

Later, Peni asked Scott to go for a walk. He wasn't sure what made him do it. Especially with all of Scott's anti-God talk. But Wyatt and Sloan had their boyfriends there, and Peni wanted to talk.

And what should he find himself talking about?

Why, Asher of course!

"…he's the guy Sloan was in love with forever?" Peni asked.

Scott sighed and assured Peni that Asher wasn't only a jerk but a slut as well. The word surprised him. He didn't know you used that word to describe a man.

He went on to tell Scott how awesome he thought Sloan was—he was still pretty deep in the throes of his crush on the man—but then found himself trying to excuse Asher's behavior. "He must see a quality in Asher that I didn't see tonight, right? I mean, Asher's your friend too."

Peni had found it a relief when Scott was able to say something nice about Asher.

"Yeah. Asher's all right. He's got some good qualities."

He held on to that thought as well. As the weeks passed, on lonely nights when he was masturbating, he found that Asher's face came to his mind over and over again.

So it was pretty frustrating to find out what a *muli elo* he really was.

When Peni found himself finally returning—mentally—to the break room of Horrell & Howes and saw Sloan was doing a crossword puzzle and eating the last of his lunch—whatever it was, probably something vegetarian, knowing Sloan's boyfriend—he realized there were only about five minutes left of their break. He had been sitting there for nearly half an hour thinking about that *komo* Asher.

What was wrong with him?

And God, was it bad enough to make him use a word like asshole? Even to himself? Peni prided himself on keeping his thoughts clean, even while he wondered what Asher looked like naked. If the big bulge in his jeans, and Sloan's description, were really true.

Sloan looked up at him over his crossword puzzle. Peni had thought he was working the thing. Why, looking down he saw Sloan hadn't done a quarter of it. "What?" he asked.

Sloan shook his head. "He's done it again, hasn't he?"

"Who?" But of course Peni knew just who Sloan meant.

"Asher. He's done it again. And he hasn't even kissed *you*...."

"What are you talking about?" Peni snapped, feeling—for some reason—naked and exposed.

"You know exactly what I'm talking about. Or who. He's gotten to you. He's wedged himself under your skin, and you don't even *like* him...."

"No!" Peni all but growled. He was repelled by the idea. And still, somehow, he felt as if Sloan had managed to peek into the secret stash of naked tattooed men on his computer. Peni shook his head. "No. Asher is a *komo*." And there he had done it again. But this time he'd said the word out loud! He shut his mouth with a click, ashamed at using such a crude word.

"It's okay," Sloan assured him, leaning forward and laying a hand on Peni's. "That's what Asher does. It's why he's going to be a huge star. He doesn't even have to be a good actor, and he is, Peni! He really is. No. It's the magic of Asher. Everything about him. His looks. His way. Those eyes. His lips! When he is finally on that big screen, he's going to make women melt in their seats, gay men cum in their pants, and straight men wonder what it would be like to suck cock. Don't feel bad about it. Just be glad he hasn't kissed you, and God, that you haven't had sex with him. Otherwise you'd be one of his worshipful minions. Trust me. He had me under his spell for years. You're lucky."

But the thought that kept coming back to Peni's mind—during the incoming phone calls when he got back to his desk, and worse, between calls—was this: Was he lucky?

Or might it all be worth it for one kiss?

Because Peni had the idea that he would never be the same again.

And he all but hated himself for the thought.

THEY DANCED.

And had cocktails.

Too many cocktails.

The music was loud, and it was powerful, and as Peni's friends led him onto the upstairs dance floor, the beat took over and he was moving like he had only moved when his bedroom door was closed (and locked) and headphones were on. Oh yes, he had danced at Peter Wagner's Fourth of July extravaganza, but somehow he had never let go. Perhaps it was because he was embarrassed. He'd never danced anything but the traditional Samoan dances in front of anyone else. Maybe it was trying to keep Wyatt's lover's hands (as well as Asher's) off his butt. Maybe it was because all he'd had was two tiny little bottles of "mush-cot-oh." Whatever the reason, it was only child's play compared to the dance floor and the pounding music of The Male Box.

Wyatt had shoved a rum and Coke in his hands—

("Don't worry, it's a light one.")

—and nervously Peni had drank it down fast—

(It wasn't a light one—Peni had almost choked on the first swallow.)

—and then they were pulling him out into the music and the flashing lights and the thrashing bodies. Lots of bodies. Mostly men's bodies. Nearly-naked men's bodies! *Gay* men's bodies.

It was scary as hell at first, but the (strong!) rum and Coke was hitting Peni already—

("Hey! I'm not used to drinking!")

—and Lady Gaga was compelling him to "just dance," so he did.

It was glorious.

It helped that he had Wyatt and Sloan to dance with, which was fun and a little less daunting. He even took a turn with Max—who assured Peni that he was one of the only men he'd ever danced with as well—and that somehow made it okay. Even more than okay.

After he'd had two more drinks, he accepted a dance from a really cute guy—after all, that song from *Frozen* was telling him he should let it go, so he did.

It felt magnificent.

Or was it the booze?

Or the beat—as deep in his blood as his Samoan dances?

Or was it that he was dancing with a man (a man!)?

He was hard. So hard his cock actually ached. He senses were full to overflowing. There was the smell of a dozen colognes and sweat. There were the shadows and flashing lights and the sight of those near-naked men dancing on raised platforms. The taste of the rum on his tongue. The pounding of music filling his ears—Beyoncé and Meghan Trainor and of course, Wyatt's P!nk—and soon the cute guy—

(was it the *same* cute guy?)

—started grinding up against him—

(God! Grinding his hard *cock* against Peni's!)

—while Nicki Minaj sang about her anaconda—

(*Godgodgod!*)

—and then the stud was leaning in and asking Peni if he wanted to go home with him.

Peni did. He *did* want to go home with the guy. The *cute* guy who had taken off his shirt while they danced to the pulsing beat, muscles shimmering with sweat, and who had helped Peni pull off his.

That's when Sloan suddenly showed up—right out of *nowhere*!

"*Heeeey*, buddy!" Sloan said, a big happy smile on his face.

"Hey, Sloan!" said Peni, feeling just as happy as Sloan's smile.

"You ready?" Sloan asked.

"For what?" Peni was confused.

"To go home" came Sloan's reply.

Peni giggled. "Hey!" he exclaimed. "I'm ready to go home with *him*!" He pointed to his right and then looked but—*hey, wait!*—where'd the cute guy go? He felt someone tapping on his left shoulder, and when he turned—*oh! There he was!*—his grin spread so wide it made the muscles in his cheeks twinge. "*Him*, Sloan! I'm going to go home with *him*!"

The cute guy nodded.

"Whoa there, Peni," said Max (where had *he* come from?). "Who is this?"

Peni turned to the cute guy. "This is…." He paused. He squinted at his dance partner. Peni opened his mouth. Closed it. Name? Did he know the cute guy's name? Things were fuzzy. The music was *so* loud—Taylor Swift singing that he should shake it off.

"Peni?"

"Yes?" he said, turning his head through air that seemed to have the consistency of Jell-O.

"Do you know this guy?"

Peni glanced back. This guy? Know him. He grinned. "Yeah!" he announced. "This is Cute Guy."

"Okay," said Max. "It's time to go home. Sorry, Cute Guy." He nodded politely to the man who had asked Peni to go home with him. "My friend here is a little drunk. He's not used to it."

"I'm not drunk!" Peni objected, and then staggered. Through a fraction of the grace he had managed to retain and a heaping helping of Max's strong arm, Peni didn't hit the floor. "*Kae*," he swore under his breath. *I think I am drunk. So this is what it feels like. Niiiiiiice…. Weird….*

"Let's go, Peni!" Max said and put an arm around his waist.

The fresh air helped a lot, the slight chill bracing to his senses, pulling him somewhat from the fog of alcohol. Peni found he didn't need his friends' support quite as much. But he liked it. Liked the feeling of these men's arms around him, supporting him. What must it be like to be able to feel this whenever you wanted?

He especially liked being so close to Sloan, and a rush of memories filled him—the months of riding the feelings the crush on his friend had given him, and the horny nights where he'd pictured Sloan in his mind when he brought himself to orgasm.

They crossed the street and found Max's white, boxy car in the parking lot. Both Max and Sloan helped Peni into the backseat, asked him if he was okay, if he thought he was going to be sick, and he didn't remember anything after that until he woke and it was time to get out of the car. He saw that he was at his friends' adjoining homes, saw his car in Sloan's driveway, and started to stumble in that direction.

"Oh, no," Sloan told him. "No driving for you tonight. You're sleeping here."

"I am?" Peni asked and found he was still swimming through intoxication. Were you supposed to get this drunk on three cocktails?

"Maybe you're just a lightweight," Sloan said, and Peni realized he must have asked his question out loud.

"Or it's just the fact you aren't used to it," Max added. As Peni was assisted up the porch steps the world began to swim again. Peni was beginning to realize he didn't like being drunk after all. Everything was so swimmy. So weird. He'd lost all control, and he didn't like it. Strange feeling. *Strange* feeling....

They were inside now, and Peni saw the couch and pointed—or tried to. "I think.... Mmm*aaaaay-beeeee* there," he managed.

That was the last thing he remembered until he woke up the next morning.

"I CAN'T believe you don't have a hangover," said Sloan from across the kitchen table.

"I...." Peni closed his mouth. His head felt like it was stuffed with cotton, and he was finding it a bit difficult to put his thoughts together. His head wasn't hurting, and he didn't feel like throwing up, but maybe he still had one after all? He told them about it.

Max set a mug of steaming coffee in front of Peni, who took it gratefully. "Yes, that sounds like a hangover. You're just lucky you aren't paying the price in pain." He went back to the counter, poured two more coffees, and sat down, pushing one over to Sloan.

Peni tried to remember what had happened when they got back to his friend's house. For the life of him he couldn't. "I guess I must have passed out? How did you guys get me upstairs?"

Sloan and Max looked at each other, a funny look on Sloan's face and an inscrutable expression on Max's. They didn't say a word, simply stared into each other's eyes as if they were speaking telepathically.

"Max?" Sloan said. "Ah.... Do we...?"

Max raised an eyebrow. "You're going to make me do this?"

Sloan gave his lover a big puppy-dog look.

"You little shit," Max replied, raising the other brow.

Peni's stomach clenched. What? What were they talking about?
I've got a bad feeling about this.

"What?" he asked aloud.

Sloan nodded. Max sighed and turned back to Peni. "You didn't pass out, Peni."

What? "I didn't?"

"It appears you blacked out."

"Doesn't that mean the same thing?" Peni asked, confused.

Max shook his head. "Nope. Blacking out is where you are still conscious, but you don't remember anything."

Peni sat up straight and did it too quickly. He *did* get a little stab of pain after all. Right between his eyes. "Huh?"

Max looked back at Sloan. Sloan didn't respond. "You really are going to make me do this?"

"Max," Sloan all but whined. "I have to work with the guy."

The bad feeling intensified. "Oh no," Peni whispered. "What happened? Did I throw up or something?"

Sloan shook his head. "No. You didn't do that, at least."

"At least?" Peni squeaked.

"I have to go to the bathroom," Sloan said and slipped out of the kitchen, but not fast enough to avoid hearing Max call him chicken.

Peni's stomach clenched again. *Baaaad* feeling about this. "Max?"

Max sighed and took a drink of his coffee. "Well, Peni…. Sloan got you onto the couch and you got, well, amorous."

"Amorous?" Peni was still confused. It was all that damned cotton batting.

"And touchy." He drank more of his coffee.

"T-touchy?" Peni's stomach clenched once more.

"You kept trying to touch Sloan's face and told him how you used to have a crush on him."

A burning crept across Peni's cheeks. "Oh, no…," he whispered.

Max gave him a little smile. "It's okay, Peni. Sloan had pretty much figured that out already."

The heat of embarrassment spread out over Peni's face.

Max nodded. "It's pretty normal. To get a little crush on the first gay man you ever really get to know," Max continued. "God knows I got one on Sloan."

Yeah, but you got him, Peni thought, staring down at his mug.

"And then…. Ah…. Are you sure you want to hear this?"

Peni looked up, and Max's face was once more completely unreadable. Peni bit his lip. *God....* He nodded.

Max's cheeks pinkened. "You told him you used to masturbate thinking about him."

Peni's eyes widened in horror. *Oh, please no. Please no.* But yes, there was a flicker in Max's eyes, and why would the man lie about that? It was clear Max was uncomfortable. Peni closed his eyes and slumped into his chair, wishing he could disappear. "Please tell me I passed out *then*."

"Well... no." Max cleared his throat. "You told him you've been wondering since the day you met him if his... pubic hair was as red as the hair on his head."

The horror deepened. *Please stop*, he thought, covering his mouth and eyes in his palms. He couldn't cover his ears as well.

"You wanted to see...."

Peni dropped his head and buried his face in his arms. "Oca...."

"You got pretty insistent too."

No, no, no.... "Please tell me that's the end of it...."

"Well, we made you go to bed then, and that was when you begged us to have a three-way with you."

"Oh God," Peni moaned.

That was when he felt the hand touch his. He flinched and then looked up—peeked up, really.

Max's smile was back, and a sweet sympathy. "Oh, Peni. It's okay. It really is. I'm flattered. We both were. No offense. Really. Just be glad it happened with good friends, and not a couple of strangers. Who would have taken you up on it."

Peni felt tears prick at the corners of his eyes.

"I mean it," Max said in a quiet and gentle voice. He squeezed Peni's hand. "We all mess up. You messed up with us. And it really wasn't so bad. It could have been worse."

"I'm never, ever going to drink again," Peni mumbled.

"Never say never," Sloan said, coming back into the room. "Eggs? Bacon? Max, do you mind having greasy meat this morning? I'm not fixing that vegan stuff."

Max laughed. "Sure."

Peni looked up to see Sloan getting a frying pan from a lower cabinet.

"I am so sorry, Sloan," he said.

Sloan put the frying pan down on the stove and then covered his ears with his hands. "La la la la la!" he cried. "I can't hear apologies! Especially one that aren't needed." He dropped his hands. "Will your stomach take breakfast?" He went to the refrigerator.

To Peni's surprise his stomach rumbled. "I—I think so."

"Good. But I'm not making omelets. I suck at omelets. I tear them up every time."

"You want me to make them?" Max asked.

"Sure!" Sloan exclaimed and sat back down at the table.

Max rose, chuckling. "Omelet, Peni?"

"S-sure," he answered.

Max began to putter around with eggs and bowls and vegetables and a cutting board, and Peni dared a look at Sloan. He opened his mouth to say he was sorry, feeling the heat slip over his cheeks again—

(and quite suddenly had a clear memory of tugging at Sloan's belt and giggling out a, "Oh, come on! Show me! I wanna see!")

—and then he was blazing with embarrassment.

Sloan pointed sternly, shook his head, and covered his ears again.

Peni sighed. "I'm not going to drink. That was it."

"How about saying you're going to skip getting slam drunk and consider this a lesson well learned instead?" Sloan offered.

Peni shook his head. "I never had a drink until the last year, and look what it's done for me. I think alcohol is the thing I want to skip. I don't need it." A determination began to build inside of him.

"I say don't make up your mind this morning" came Sloan's response.

Peni shook his head more determinedly, bringing up a wave of ugly dizziness (which only built his resolve). "Sloan. It was drinking that killed my father. He would still be with me if it wasn't for booze."

Sloan bit his lip, said nothing for a moment. "It was a drunk that took your father from you," he said. "But I understand."

"Onions, okay?" Max asked. "And lots of cheese?"

"Sure," Peni replied, and Sloan agreed.

A few minutes later there were huge omelets for all and big thick-cut slices of toast. Peni fell on his like a starving man. He'd had no idea he was so hungry.

CHAPTER SEVEN

IT WAS the ringing phone that saved Asher from the worst of the dream. He came out of it with a cry that startled the blond man sleeping next to him—

(*Who the fuck are you?* he wondered)

—and sat up, looking around the room and trying to figure out where he was.

He remembered.

Oh shit damn fuck....

He was in a hotel room at the Meridian.

The man next to him was Jim Musgrave, the hotel's bartender.

Asher groaned. *Stupid, stupid, stupid! How could you? Never, ever shit where you eat!*

The phone continued to ring, and it was Asher's cell, he knew it, unless Jim had the same ringtone—Beethoven's Fifth. Somehow he doubted it.

Da, da, da, daaa.... His phone continued.

Where the hell is my fucking phone? He got down on his hands and knees on the floor—

Da, da, da, daaa....

—and just in time saw his cell's screen flashing under the bed, snatched it up, and answered it before he had the time to check the ID. No one called on that ringtone unless Asher actually wanted to talk to them. "Hello?" he barked into the phone.

"Asher?" came a man's voice from the other end of the line.

"Who is this?" Asher asked way too harshly—but it was too late. He could hardly take it back.

"This is Guy—"

"Guy?" This was a guy?—*Oh!* "Guy," he cried. *Shit!* "Hello, Guy. Sorry." *Is this it? Is this the play?*

"Is everything all right, Asher?"

Shit! "I couldn't find the fuh—ah—the phone."

"Nice view" came another male voice, and when Asher looked up, he saw Jim peering down at his butt while rubbing his eyes. "Too bad you're a total top, Asher. That is one *fine* ass."

"What?" asked Guy.

"Nothing," Asher said, jumping up and dashing for the bathroom. "Just the TV."

"Okay. Well, I have something to tell you, Asher."

His stomach twisted into one huge knot, despite Guy's cheerful demeanor.

"Y-yes?" he stammered and hated himself for it.

"Well, we'd like to offer you the part."

The world froze, and Asher had to sit down on the toilet before he fell down. It jolted him awake in a way he didn't expect. The water level was very high. His balls hung low. The water was chilly. "Whoa!" He leapt to his feet.

"Excuse me?" came Guy's voice.

Asher leaned on the sink, smiling despite himself.

Then it hit. It *really* hit.

They want me to do the part!

"Oh, Guy. You don't know how happy I am to hear this. I wanted this. I'm just now realizing how much."

Got to call Sloan! Oh. My. God! Got to call Sloan!

A thrill raced through him.

I got the part!

"Hey, man. Mind if I come in there? I gotta pee."

It was Jim, of course, and that brought back what he'd done the night before. *God!* He groaned again. Stupid?

"You sure you're okay, Asher?" Guy asked.

He laughed. "Oh my God, yes. I am wonderful. And I can't wait." He opened the bathroom door and was greeted by his trick, with full morning wood. Holy shit, it was nice. Enough to make his own cock twitch. Why didn't he remember it being so big? How drunk had he been? He hated when he couldn't remember things. Well, at least he remembered doing the guy!

"Can you come in next week?"

"For what?" he asked. He caught a glimpse of Jim trying to aim a cock that was determined to point upward into a downward position instead. *He's going to piss everywhere*, thought Asher. "Pee in the tub," he whispered, holding his hand over the phone.

Jim laughed. "Might as well. I want to shower anyway."

"Well, we would like to do the first read-through on Monday" Asher just barely caught Guy saying. "Then start rehearsals right away. Tuesday even."

He stepped back out of the bathroom. "Tuesday?" Asher asked, surprised.

"We'd start this week if we could, but I figured I had to give you at least a few days to make arrangements. Your file with us does say that you have a flexible job."

"I—yes. It was just, well, you gave me a little bit more notice when the Pegasus did *Tearoom Tango*. I mean, this is like Fringe Festival timing."

"Well, yes, then, I understand. But I'm still asking. Do you think you can do it?"

"I'll do it, Guy." And he meant it. That was for sure. The Meridian Hotel would just have to understand.

"There's more, and we'll explain it Monday, all right?"

And didn't *that* sound mysterious? "Whatever you say," Asher told him.

"Six o'clock?"

"A.m. or p.m.?" he asked.

"P.m.," Guy said with a laugh. "I haven't been up that early in years."

Thank God! He'd begun to suspect Guy didn't laugh anymore. Had something happened? Death in the family? "I'll see you there," he replied.

They signed off just as he heard Jim calling to him from the bathroom. "You want to wash my back?"

Asher glanced at the clock. He didn't have to be downstairs for an hour. He had his Meridian uniform, he realized, seeing it tossed here and there all over the floor. Then he turned to the bathroom door.

Oh, what the hell?

ASHER'S UNIFORM wasn't too badly rumpled, and he figured his body heat would take care of smoothing out the worst of it. His slacks and white shirt had the majority of the wrinkles, and the vest covered the most notable part of the shirt, and he'd be standing behind a counter most of the day, so that took care of that. He also knew where to swipe a toothbrush and tiny tube of toothpaste—always a courtesy of the Meridian Hotel for travelers who had forgotten to pack something. That and the restrictions on the airlines kept a lot of people from packing things like toiletries when they didn't have time to find the itsy-bitsy proportioned items the airlines demanded.

Nellie gave him raised eyebrows when he showed up at the front desk. "Don't you look like the cat that ate the canary," she said. "What did *you* do last night? Or should I say who?"

Asher gave her his best "I don't have a frigging clue what you're talking about" look and cursed himself. Was everyone reading him lately? He was an actor for God's sake. He should have been able to arrive on the scene totally deadpan.

Of course, he had just had sex not fifteen minutes ago, a right wonderful fuck, and Jim had given him an incredible kiss in the elevator on the way down—along with a good ass-groping.

"Are you sure you won't let me have some of this?" he'd asked while squeezing Asher's bun quite thoroughly. "I mean, it's a crime to let that masterpiece go to waste."

"I'm sure," said Asher, who had never, nor would ever, let a man have him that way.

Abomination!

He might "lay" with a man as he would a woman, but he *wasn't* going to *be* the woman. No way.

"You're late," Nellie said, pushing a little lock of dark hair out of her face. She looked like an elf with her bob-style cut and huge blue eyes. He'd thought she was a lesbian when they met, but she was sticking to her story that she liked men.

"Ten fucking minutes," he said. "Did Rodger notice?" Rodger was the hotel's day-shift manager. He was also an asswipe. Doubly so toward Asher because he'd turned down the man's advances. "I don't sleep with coworkers," he'd told Rodger.

Then why had he slept with Jim Musgrave?

He gave an inward shrug. The free cocktails had helped.

"No. You're in luck. He had a meeting with housekeeping first thing."

"Good," he replied. "I'm in a fucking awesome mood, and the last thing I need is him ruining it."

Nellie began going through a printout of the guests who would be leaving today, knowing that soon the onslaught of check-outs would begin. "You know, I didn't see you come in. Usually when you're late, you slip in from there." She nodded toward the doorway that led to the shopping center that was attached to the hotel. Staff weren't supposed to use the center's parking garage, even though it was a lot more convenient. Those spots were, of course, for actual shoppers. Employees were supposed to park in the allocated lot across the wide and traffic-heavy street. But what Asher would do was park where he wasn't supposed to and then move his truck on his first break. He hadn't gotten a ticket yet. Security rarely cruised the garage before ten o'clock, which was after his break.

Asher shrugged. "Maybe you were too busy."

"Nope." She shook her head and raised a high-arching brow— which furthered her elfin appearance. "I haven't had a single guest. And I've been watching for you."

This time Asher made sure his face was impassive. Unfortunately, it didn't work.

"Give," she said firmly.

The corner of his mouth twitched. *Dammit!* He couldn't help it. Despite the fact he regretted what he'd done. Not because Jim hadn't been fun. Far from it. It was the whole shitting where you ate thing. What if Jim wanted a rematch? What if he wanted to go on an actual date? It was far harder to avoid someone when you worked at the same place.

"Oh my God. What did you do?"

He leaned in close to her. "I spent the night here in the hotel."

"With a guest?" she asked, wide-eyed. "You tricked with a guest?"

"No," he said quietly. "But I used a room."

"Asher! You *didn't*. You could get fired for that! You don't think they'll try and figure out who messed up one of the rooms?"

"We didn't 'mess it up,'" he explained. "That second-honeymoon couple stormed out last night around eleven, and I kept it quiet. Used it after they left. So it was already messy. We just messed it up more. They'll never have a clue, especially since there's no hallway cameras these days." There had been lawsuits about a respect for guest's privacy. In other words, they didn't want recorded proof that they'd been cheating on mates, hiring prostitutes on their company expense accounts, or other general shenanigans.

She looked at him in amazement. "You are something else, you know that?"

He grinned sheepishly.

Then…. "Who?" she asked suddenly, clearly excited. "If it wasn't a guest, who? I can't imagine you calling some trick and telling him to come over." Her eyes went wide. "My God! Someone who *works* here?"

But with that she crossed a line. "Nope," he said resolutely. "I do not kiss and tell. *Ever*." Well, except for the Fabulous Four. He'd been known to brag to them, hadn't he?

"Of course it might not make any difference," Asher told her. "I might not have a job when Rodger hears what I have to say."

"*What?*" Her eyes looked even wider. "Asher, what are you telling him?"

This time there was an entirely different kind of smile on Asher's face—one of genuine happiness. "I got the part, Nellie."

"In the vomit play?" she asked.

"It's not a *vomit* play," he defended.

"Well, *you're* the one who said it. You said there's a lot of vomiting and sex and blood and—"

"It's about a lot of things," said Asher. "It's funny and it's over the top, and it's…." He paused as the realization hit him. "Nellie. It's *brilliant*. It's going to be the talk of the town. They're going to love it and they're going to hate it and they're going to be *talking* about it. This could be *it*! This could be the play I've been waiting for!"

"So why would Rodger fire you? He knew when you started here that you need your schedule adjusted for your plays."

Asher bit the insides of his cheeks. "Rehearsals start Monday."

"*Monday?* Next *week* Monday?" Her brows came together.

"Yeah. I'll need out of here by four for I'd guess at least six weeks."

"Asher!" Nellie put her hands on her hips, and her eyes flashed dangerously. "I'm going on vacation at the end of next week. If you fuck that up…."

Asher threw his hands up in the air. "It can't be helped, darlin'."

"Don't give me that *darlin'* crap," she snapped. "I've been planning this vacation for weeks."

"What was I supposed to do, Nellie? Turn it down? I'm an actor. I'm not a front desk clerk!"

"Oh, but *I* am? You're better than me? Too good to work at a hotel?"

"I didn't say that!"

But it was true, Asher thought. He was too good to work at a hotel, even one as five star as the Meridian. He did feel he was meant for far better things. He was going to be a star. A *big* star. He *knew* it. He just couldn't figure out why it was taking so long.

Too old! Those big deal Hollywood directors had told him he was too old to be in their movie! Like he was seventy-five and auditioning for the part of Tom Sawyer or some damned thing!

"You're an asshole, you know that, Asher?"

He blinked at her and had opened his mouth to give her a snappy comeback when he saw she meant it. Asher was surprised at how much the words stung. Or at least one of them.

He didn't dwell on it long, though. It was right then that an elderly couple approached the desk, ready to check out, and after that the rush hit. Even Rodger had to help. Karol and Francis at the other end of the counter weren't enough.

Asher had to wait until break to call Sloan with his good news.

THEY MET at The Corner Bistro for celebratory cocktails. Asher arrived, and of course Sloan was already there—and *he* had a forty-five minute drive. Oh well. And hey, Sloan was alone. Well, what do you know? Mr. Right actually stayed at home? Let Sloan off his leash?

Sloan leapt off the stool at the table he'd claimed along the mirrored wall and embraced Asher in a hug that took his breath away and then gave him a friendly kiss. Asher was reminded of some very different kisses between the two of them. He hadn't thought about that in a long time.

"Oh, Asher! I am so damned excited for you!"

Asher grinned happily. Of course *Sloan* was. And didn't that make him feel wonderful? Almost giddy. Why couldn't Nellie have been happy for him? She didn't need to be bone-crushingly happy, but damn. Would a "congrats" have hurt her much?

"Thanks, buddy," he said.

"Didn't I tell you?" Sloan was practically bouncing. "Didn't I *tell* you not to worry? They would have been stupid to miss the chance to have you on their stage!"

Sloan hugged him a second time, this time not so tightly, their bodies simply resting against each other. There was a hardness to his best friend's chest that surprised him. He didn't remember, or think of, Sloan being quite so muscular. Maybe it was Max. Maybe he, a man in near perfect physical health, was coaching Sloan in their workouts. Toning him.

You could have been mine.

Hadn't Sloan wanted him? Been *in* love with him? Fallen in love with him the very night Asher had picked him up in the bar and taken him home with him?

They stepped back from each other, and Sloan's big warm brown eyes were full of emotion, and for one brief instant, Asher thought he saw…. No. It was his imagination. Sloan didn't have feelings for him anymore. Not like that. He was in love with Max now, and that was a good thing. Right?

But you could have been mine.

It's a good thing they never tried that, though, wasn't it? Because it wouldn't have lasted. Not a month. Not a week. Asher didn't do the lovers thing. And that would have meant they wouldn't be friends today.

That would have been bad. Asher looked at his friend and found he couldn't imagine a life without him.

"What?" Sloan asked him.

Asher smiled. "Just thinking about how lucky I am to have you in my life."

Sloan looked at him, mouth agape. Then he laughed.

"I CAN'T believe how nervous I am," Asher said. "I mean, we start Monday! Am I going to be ready?"

Sloan rolled his eyes. "Of course you are. You always are. Hey, want me to read lines with you?"

Asher grinned. Leave it to Sloan. "You'd do that for me?"

"Of course," Sloan said with a half shrug. "I don't have anything else to do."

"What about Maxie?"

"Max and Logan are camping this weekend, I told you that. Some kind of father and son bonding thing. They wanted to talk. I think there's something wrong with Logan and Devon. All those months he was away in France. And Scott and Cedar are still on their road trip—I don't expect them until Sunday. Wyatt and Howard are heading I forget where to some big bear festival. I think it's some place called Cactus Canyon? Sure, I'll help you. We'll have fun. I'll get to see this vomit play of yours raw."

Asher groaned. "Why is everybody calling it a vomit play?"

"Just going by what you said."

Maybe so. Maybe so.

"Want to start this evening?" Sloan asked him.

"Nah. I want to get drunk this evening."

"And drive? Maybe we should pick up something from Gomer's? Go to your place?"

"If you want."

So that's what they did. And Asher decided not to worry about the odd little looks Sloan had been giving him. There was simply no sense in worrying about it. Life was too good right now.

CHAPTER EIGHT

ASHER MADE it to the Pegasus with time to spare. It was a long redbrick building with a glass front and had—once upon a time, around a hundred years ago—been a garage. It had been transformed into a modern, intimate theater. As the Pegasus grew in popularity, it was able to buy the two spaces to the south and fully come into its own. It now had offices and ticket sales and had expanded from one to two stages. Even more importantly, the Pegasus Theatre had gained national attention in its fine selection of plays, and that meant an eye on the actors as well as the productions.

Asher knew it was a big deal for him to be here today to begin his second show at the theater. He hadn't slept for shit the night before. He'd been afraid to drink more than a glass of wine for fear he'd be exhausted after working a shift at the hotel and then coming in for the read-through. The trouble was, alcohol helped him sleep.

Guy was waiting for him right inside the glass office doors. The director was all smiles, and handshakes, but stiff and missing the bounce in his step.

"Glad you're here, Asher."

"Where else would I be?" he asked with what he hoped was a cheerful grin.

Guy gave a single nod.

Yeah. He was acting funny. What was up? God, they hadn't changed their minds, had they?

"Asher, mind if we talk real quick in my office before you meet the others?"

Asher's stomach clenched. *Here it comes.* "Not at all," he somehow managed in a clear and pleasant tone—as if there were nothing wrong.

He followed Guy to a set of offices that faced the street, both fairly small, one with Jennifer Leavitt's name painted on the glass door, the other name-free. It was this second one they entered. Of course.

Guy Campbell wasn't their only director, awesome as he was. He wouldn't have his own office.

"May I get you a coffee?" Guy asked, while motioning to the seat in front of the office desk. "A doughnut?"

Now he offered the coffee and doughnut?

Asher managed a short nod. Sat down. Nervous. But a leap in his stomach told him no doughnut. "Just coffee...."

Guy smiled. "It's good coffee. Got it down the street at The Shepherd's Bean."

Yeah, yeah, yeah. Get fucking on with it!

Guy was gone for only a moment, and Asher looked around the small room—desk piled high, a dying ivy hanging in the window, more piles on the floor. God. Was it hot in here?

"Here you go," Guy said in a voice so cheerful it reminded Asher of a parent in a kid's TV show.

Guy set the mug down before Asher, and he grabbed it and took a quick swallow. Not booze, and it was quite hot, almost burning his mouth, but it jolted him out of the strange sudden fear that had swept through him. *Relax! What's the fucking worse that could happen? They changed their minds?*

Well that would be pretty fucking bad!

Guy sat down, coffeeless, leaned back, squared his shoulders.

Oh, fuck me, thought Asher.

"Asher, there's something you should know. I thought about telling you when you read for the part, but Jennifer insisted I not do that."

"What!" Asher barked, and then cringed. *Get in control of yourself! You're a goddamned actor! Choose a role.* Any *role. But get a hold of yourself!* "Sorry." He smiled. He was Jay Gatsby—and he was *coooool*.

Guy took a breath. "Asher—we've been in rehearsals for over a week. Almost two."

Asher did not show his surprise. He was Jay Gatsby. "Oh?" he asked calmly.

That was a forced smile on Guy's face, wasn't it?

"Yes. We cast your role with someone else. But it soon became clear he wasn't Matt. We tried and tried, but it wasn't working. He just didn't have it."

"I see," said Asher. He understood that. Sometimes a part just didn't work with a certain actor. They could be an awesome performer, but still just not be able to be what was needed in a certain role. "So I wasn't your first choice."

Guy glanced out the window. Composing himself? What? He looked back. "Actually you were. I think you were born to play the part."

Asher nodded. "Ah…. Okay…. Then, what?"

"Jennifer didn't want you."

Asher froze for half of a half of an instant. He was Jay Gatsby. "Oh." Compose. Compose. "Well, she's the boss."

"Yes, she is. But I convinced her to give it to you."

Which was what had taken so fucking long.

"I see," he said, not sure that he did see at all.

"But all you had to do was those few lines last week, and she knew I was right."

"Well, thank you," Asher said. Jay Gatsby. He was *coooool*. "Your confidence means a lot to me."

Guy let out a long sigh and grinned. "Good! And you do have my full confidence, Asher."

Asher smiled. It wasn't *his* smile. It was Gatsby's. But it was a smile.

"I just didn't want you to be surprised is all," Guy said. "When we go in there and some of the actors are already close to off book."

Which meant they would have a big advantage on him. Luckily he memorized fast, and he and Sloan had worked on the lines most of the weekend. It was a mostly cocktail-less weekend. Asher hadn't really missed it while they practiced. Once he was into a part, everything else went away. Acting was his drug of choice. It was only when they relaxed later in the evening that he wanted to jump into a big bottle and make up for the drink-free hours.

"Thanks for the warning," Asher said.

Guy stood up, his bounce back, rocking on his heels. "Ready, then?"

"Sure." Asher stood up and with Guy's gesture, left the office first. Guy overtook him and led the way to the back, where the main and bigger stage was located. The smaller one, the Wagner Stage, was up front. It was used mostly for productions from outside companies, charity shows, and very sudden projects that were produced with little advance warning. Jennifer was known to cast roles months and months in advance. Because this had all happened so fast, Asher had assumed he would be working on the smaller stage. Halfway there, the question burst out of Asher before he knew he'd even thought it. "Guy, why didn't Jennifer want me?"

Guy stopped. Took a step. Stopped again. Turned around. "Does it matter?"

Asher found it did. "It does," he said.

"Really, Asher? Isn't it enough that you've got the part? That this could be big? That this could be the role you've been waiting for?"

It should. Guy was right. But Asher found that his ego couldn't let it go. Acting was all he really had. Besides the Fabulous Four.

The last thought surprised him.

"Tell me," Asher said. "Please."

Guy just stood there, looking at him for a moment. Then he gave a half nod and pointed back over Asher's shoulder. Asher turned and Guy led him back a few steps to the entrance to the Wagner Stage. They stepped though a black curtain and into an empty theater. "Sit," he said.

"I'm okay," Asher said, butterflies abruptly whirling in his stomach. He suddenly wasn't sure if he could sit.

Guy shrugged. "Okay, Asher. The reason she didn't want you is because you're difficult."

The comment couldn't have surprised Asher more. "Difficult? How?"

"Your attitude, Asher."

"Attitude?" Asher brought his brows together in a knot. Attitude?

"You really want me to go on?" Guy asked.

"Y-yes," Asher stuttered, Jay Gatsby forgotten.

"You're rude, Asher. You act like you're better than everybody else. Barking at people. You *yelled* at your fellow actors during rehearsals for *Tearoom Tango*."

"I was only trying to make it great," Asher said, defending himself. He had been better than the other actors. They kept frustrating him. Pissing him off. They'd fuck up a line over and over, and when he yelled at them, they'd finally get it right.

"That wasn't your call," Guy said. "*You* weren't the director. *I* was. And frankly, I guess this is the time for me to tell you that I'm the director this time too. *Not* you. If you have an idea or a remark, you tell me later. No barking at your fellow actors. I almost had somebody quit when they found out you had taken the role."

Asher's mouth fell open. He couldn't help it. "*What?*"

"You want me to be brutal, or do you get it?" Guy said.

Asher clenched his teeth. Then: "Spit it out." *Go on. Be brutal! Stop beating around the damned bush!*

"All right, then, Asher. You're a good actor. No. You're *great*. One of the best I've ever seen. The best I've ever worked with by far. One of these days, you could be a legend."

That was being brutal? Asher grinned foolishly. "Thanks."

"But frankly, Asher, you're an asshole. You're a Russell Crowe. Brilliant, but notice hardly anyone wants to work with him twice? You're a Terrence Howard. So much better than Don Cheadle will *ever* be, but Marvel Studios didn't care. One time with Howard was enough. They were done with him. They did the same to Edward Norton. There aren't many actors who can hope to be better, but they cast Ruffalo nonetheless. That's your problem, Asher."

Asher was frozen. He didn't know what to say. His mind could hardly process what he was hearing.

"You're an asshole, you know that, Asher?" Nellie's voice echoed in his head.

"Let me ask you something, Asher," Guy said. "That part you tried out for in Hollywood...."

Asher jolted, Gatsby totally gone. Had he told Guy about that horrible audition? How unprofessional it had been? And the girl who had read him lines? How terrible she had been? How he'd wondered who she'd fucked to get her job?

"When you were there...." Guy continued. "Did you boss anyone around? Bitch at them?"

Bitch at them? Boss them around? Well, no!

But for God's sake. They didn't know what the hell they were doing. He had no choice but to take over! And... "...the girl that was reading me lines. She sucked! All she had to do was *read*!" The words were out before Asher even thought about them.

Guy's mouth turned into a tight, thin line, and he nodded. "Was she an actress?"

Asher shrugged. Probably not. Certainly not! Hopefully not.... He shook his head. "I don't think so."

"She wasn't even a professional actress and you bitched at her, Asher? She wasn't *supposed* to be able to act. She was just reading you your lines...."

"So what?" Asher said, defending himself once more. Sloan wasn't an actor either, but he was far better than the skinny, big-boobed girl. "She should at least be able to *read*. If she couldn't even get her lines right, how was I supposed to read back?"

"What do *you* do when you're onstage and someone fucks up a line during a performance?"

"That's different!" Asher trembled, fighting an anger welling up inside. How could Guy even ask that? It was totally different!

"*Why* is it different?" Guy asked him, crossing his arms across his wide chest.

"Because you never break the illusion in front of your audience. You keep going. Make it look like it was *meant* to be that way."

"And when an audience isn't there?"

"Then there's no illusion to *break*," snapped Asher. "That's when you learn to get it right. When you *make* it right! And if people can't get it right, you keep doing whatever you have to do to get it right. And if it hurts someone's feelings, then so—the—fuck—what!"

Guy nodded. "And you're doing it now," Guy said.

"Doing what?"

"Being an asshole."

Asher was startled at the sting of the words.

"What? Did that hurt your feelings?" Guy asked.

Asher didn't answer. He did sit down.

"Listen," said Guy. "Listen good. Now that I think of it, I'm glad you asked. This is the way it's going to be. No yelling. No attitude. If you have an idea, you take it to me later, on the side. I don't want a Russell Crowe, Asher. I want a Tom Hanks. I want you to be Jake Gyllenhaal. Hugh Jackman. Nice. Considerate. Polite. No entitlement. No bullshit. I want you to be so nice that it makes me sick to my stomach. Can you do that?"

Asher still didn't answer. He was numb. He couldn't believe what he was hearing.

"You're an asshole, you know that, Asher?" came Nellie's voice once again.

An asshole? He wasn't an asshole, was he? He knew assholes. His boss Rodger at the Meridian was an asshole, getting mad when Asher told him he had a part and not wanting to change his hours. Nellie for not understanding, for thinking her vacation was more important than his career.

"You think you're more important than other people, don't you?" Guy asked him. "That your life is more important than other people's lives because of your talent?"

Once more Asher was surprised into speechlessness. It was like Guy had been reading his mind.

"You are not entitled here, Asher. You are an actor. Frankly, you need this part as much as we need you in it. So I am going to ask again. Can you be a Tom Hanks for me?"

Asher trembled. Was shocked at how he felt. He wanted to run. He wanted to fucking run! He saw Guy watching him. Waiting for an answer. He swallowed hard. Seized composure. "I can play any part," he said, voice like steel.

"If that's how you have to think about it, then fine," Guy said. "Make it your finest role yet." He stood. "Ready?"

This time Asher didn't tremble. Not so that Guy could see. Ready? To face his fellow actors? One of whom almost quit because he was coming on board?

He nodded. Yes. He could play any part. He was *coooool.*

He'd win a goddamned Tony.

He stood. "Ready when you are, C.B."

Guy grinned. "Excellent."

And then they went into the lion's den.

ASHER BARELY made it through the next day. Nellie was being cold, even more so than yesterday. She hadn't asked one question about the read-through, which had gone better than expected but was still tough as hell. His fellow actors had known their parts. Luckily that had turned out to be a good thing. In fact, it had brought out his best—an unexpected level of best—from somewhere deep inside him. But he also couldn't help but wonder which of them had wanted to quit. As he watched them, and tried not to be *seen* watching, he couldn't help but see hostility in all their eyes. Was it real? Was it his imagination? He didn't know. And it drove him crazy. He'd gone home and drunk half a bottle of his Black Label, and was paying for it today with a killer hangover. Thank God he didn't have to work that night, either at the hotel or the Pegasus. Rehearsals were starting on Wednesday.

The frustration and headache had also made it hard not to be rude to the hotel guests. Every time he opened his mouth to answer a stupid question with an equally stupid answer, he would hear both Guy and Nellie in his head, calling him an asshole. An asshole! *Really?* Sure he could be low on patience, but did that make him an asshole?

He called Sloan, but he wasn't answering. He left messages, but when Sloan called back, Asher hadn't been able to answer his cell. Then when he called Sloan back, his friend hadn't answered. It was just that damned voice mail over and over.

Then Sloan didn't answer after work, either.

Fuck it. He would drive to Terra's Gate. Show up at the door, and screw it if there was some kind of damned Family Night with the Homosexuals going on.

Asher was pulling off at the Terra's Gate exit when Sloan called back, and dammit, by the time he managed to pull over and get his cell out, it had gone to voice mail again. Asher tried calling back first, tried twice, and when Sloan didn't answer, he checked to see if his friend had left a message.

"Hey, Asher." (laugh) "We have been playing phone tag all day, huh? Sorry to—yes, Logan. Hold on! Give me a minute!—sorry about that. Logan was asking me a question. Anyway, sorry that your day hasn't gone well. I'd like to talk, but we are going into a conference with the teacher. Can you believe it? Me? I'm included in a parent-teacher conference?"

Asher couldn't believe it. He wanted to puke.

"Anyway, I will try and call you when we get out, but we're rushing out to see a movie right after. We're actually taking Devon too. I'm thinking, hoping I guess, that the kids have worked out whatever was wrong. I so want to see them work. It would be so cool if—"

That's where Sloan's voice cut off. End of time for his message apparently.

Dammit!

Now what was he supposed to do?

Then, without really thinking about it, he headed to Wyatt's instead. He wasn't Sloan, but he'd do in a pinch. As long as Asher didn't have to listen to one of the bear's stupid jokes.

Wyatt's place was only minutes away, and he pulled up in front of the house and look there—Wyatt was sitting on the porch. Perfect.

Asher parked in front of the house, even though he knew it would annoy Howard (which gave Asher a certain pleasure), and waved at his friend, his truck coming to a sputtering stop.

No response. Didn't Wyatt see him? It wasn't like Asher's crappy truck was quiet.

"Hey, Wyatt," he called out. Still no response.

Dammit! Ignored again? What the hell was going on in the world?

He strode up the small walk to the porch. "Hey," he said, and still Wyatt didn't seem to see him. He just sat there on the old couch under the big window not saying a word. "Wyatt!"

The little bear jumped and looked up at him, eyes swollen and puffy. "H-hey, Asher." He cleared his throat. "W-what are y-you d-doing here?"

God. Had he been crying? Now what? Had someone scratched "faggot" on his mini-coop again? Asher decided to ignore it. He sure wouldn't want anyone noticing that *he* had been crying.

"Hey, Wyatt." He sat down on the chair across from his friend. "Have you talked to Sloan today?"

Wyatt shook his head. "I... I tried to call him, but he's in some kind of parent-teacher thing with Max and Logan."

Asher sighed. "Can you believe that shit? Sloan playing Daddy? And not even the fun way! As in a *father*. Stepfather, I guess." He shook his head. "One of us. A father!"

Wyatt didn't say anything.

"Any idea what movie they're going to?"

Wyatt shook his head. "No. But they're taking Logan's boyfriend."

"And can you believe that? A boyfriend! It's like some *Twilight* version of *Seventh Heaven*, staring Sloan and Max as the mom and dad, and Logan and Devon as the kids."

Wyatt gave a little nod but still didn't say much. What was wrong with him today? Did P!nk get another one of her songs censored?

"Did you hear I got the part in the play?" Asher asked.

Wyatt's head turned slowly in Asher's direction, face blank, like some kind of creepy special effect in a movie where the antique doll came to life. "Play?" Wyatt blinked. "Oh. Yeah. Con-congratulations." He blinked again.

Asher really was getting uncomfortable. He hated it when people acted this way. All these emotions—it made it all the creepier when they didn't show them, like Wyatt was doing now. He was used to Wyatt's roller coaster ups and downs, not this zombie look.

Ignore it.

"The director told me last night that I was second choice for the role. That Jennifer didn't want me. Can you believe it?"

Wyatt looked at him again. Seemed almost to be focusing, finally. Was he high? Wyatt didn't usually get high except when he went away to that camp of his every summer. Drunk? It was a little early for his friend to drink—although not for Asher. Maybe Wyatt had something prepared?

"Who's Jennifer?"

"The artistic director of the Pegasus!" Wyatt knew that.

"Oh, yeah. That's right. Howard broke up with me."

"She said I was an asshole," Asher cried, flinging his hands up in front of him. "Can you believe it?"

"He told me he wants me to move out."

"Guy said that one of the actors almost quit when they heard I was joining the cast!" Asher ground his teeth together.

"Move out. How can I move out? Where would I go?"

"I could hardly concentrate last night." Asher shook his head. "I kept wondering who didn't want to fucking work with me!"

"This is my house, Asher! My God! What am I going to do?"

Wait. Asher closed his mouth. What did Wyatt just say?

Wyatt burst into tears.

Wait. Broke up? Did Wyatt say Howard had broken up with him?

Asher rolled his eyes. Yeah, sure.

The crying grew stronger.

Wait. Wait a fucking minute.... "Wyatt?"

Wyatt covered his face. "And—you d-don't even f-fucking *care*, do you?" Wyatt looked up for a second, eyes red and crazed. "You a-*are* an asshole, A-Asher. You *are*!" He leaned over and began to rock. "Oh my God. What am I going to do?"

Asher blinked.

Holy shit.

He jumped up and ran over to his friend, got down on his knees in front of Wyatt and placed his hands on his heaving shoulders. "Wyatt.

Hey, baby bear. Come on now. What's going on? You know Howard isn't kicking you out."

Wyatt cried all the harder.

Fuck. This was messed up. He didn't know how to handle stuff like this! Where the hell was Sloan?

Shit!

Asher got up and sat down next to Wyatt and put an arm around his shoulders. He tugged Wyatt toward him, but the bear resisted. He pulled harder. Wyatt fought another second and then came.

Asher patted Wyatt's back, resisting the urge to say, "There, there." He would hate if someone said that to him. On the other hand, would Wyatt? Probably not…. "There, there," he muttered. "It'll be all right."

Wyatt shook his head. "N-no it won't," he cried.

Asher was starting to get worried. This didn't feel like one of Wyatt's big drama productions. But he refused to believe Howard had kicked him out. The two of them fought like dogs sometimes. They'd been together for years. And besides, if anyone was going to break up with anyone, it should be Wyatt kicking Howard to the curb.

"M-my dad w-will be h-happy," Wyatt managed through his tears. "He said m-me and Howard wouldn't l-last. That two men can't make a home." He chocked. "That's not the word he used of course. It was a lot more c-colorful."

The words surprised Asher. He didn't think he'd ever heard Wyatt talk about his family, not even once.

"*Goddess*, I thought I was going to prove that old son of a bitch wrong!"

"Wyatt, honey," Asher said, hardly believing he had used the endearment. "You two fight all the time. You'll be fine. You're both just blowing off a little steam."

Wyatt sat up, eyes wide and slightly scary. He shook his head. "N-no! Not this time. My gods, Asher. It's over!" Tears began to run down his face.

It was crazy, but Asher felt the urge to laugh. Because this was crazy. Way too crazy.

"Wyatt, why do you say that? What makes this time worse than any other?"

Wyatt trembled.

"Wyatt?" Asher felt a wave of panic, all thoughts of Jennifer Leavitt goner than gone. What the hell was going on here?

"I-I came home early today." He trembled again. Asher could actually *see* Wyatt fighting for control. Wyatt never worried about controlling himself. "The b-boss told me to go home early and have a nice evening." Wyatt's face went blank again. "I picked up Indian. H-Howard loves c-curry."

"Okay…." Asher said cautiously.

"And when I walked in he was having sex…"

Asher nodded. Nothing new for Howard.

"…with like four or five other guys…"

Asher shook his head. Howard could *find* four or five guys that wanted to have sex with him?

"…and they weren't—using—condoms!" Wyatt's eyes went wide and he dropped his face into his hands.

"Fuck," said Asher. That wasn't good. And hadn't there been some big deal about Howard maybe or maybe not fucking some kid bareback at that gay men's festival they went to last July?

Wyatt jumped up and began pacing. "I started shouting of course! Who wouldn't?"

"Yeah, sure," Asher agreed. The no-condom thing was not good. Even he followed that rule most of the time. He'd slipped once or twice, when he was pretty sure the guy was neg. But that had been a long time ago.

At least he hoped so. Sometimes when he got to drinking a little too much, he forgot stuff…. Luckily, he was an exclusive top, and they now considering topping, even if you were topping a poz guy, pretty low risk and—

"The guys freaked out and got dressed and ran out of there and I was screaming like a girl and then Howard slapped me!"

Asher sat up. "He hit you?"

"And then he said he was done! He said he was done with my shit and he wanted me to get out!" Wyatt burst into tears again, staggered, and almost fell. Asher helped him back to the beat-up old couch and let Wyatt fall into his arms again.

This wasn't good.

Was this real? Had Howard really broken up with Wyatt? Shit.

Not good at all.

He needed Sloan. He wasn't any good at this stuff.

"Look, Wyatt. You two have worked through worse than this. I'm sure you'll work this out too."

Wyatt sat up so fast his head almost bonked Asher on the chin. "No, I don't think so. He told me I had to be out by the end of the month! He told me to pack up my shit and leave. He said he'd throw it out on the sidewalk if I didn't. He's never said anything like that!"

Sloan. He had to call Sloan. And he told Wyatt that.

"They're going to a movie," Wyatt said. "With the boys. Asher, we can't interrupt that."

Wyatt? Not wanting to interrupt? Not wanting to be the center of attention. And then Asher saw Wyatt meant it. He really did want Sloan left out of this.

"What time does their movie start?" he asked.

"I'm not sure," Wyatt mumbled.

"I'll call him in an hour, that way he'll know the first thing he gets out."

Wyatt began to tremble again and tears began to flow anew. "What am I going to do? I don't have anywhere to go."

Shit. "Wyatt, we'll cross that bridge when we come to it. But I'm still betting this will all blow over." That it was just more of Wyatt and Howard's drama. They lived for big, loud, over-the-top drama. Exactly that kind of thing Asher avoided like the twelve plagues. Or was it ten? Give him swarms of locusts and darkness and water turning into blood, but please, please no public spectacles. Except onstage. That was different.

Asher pulled out his cell phone. "Give me Howard's number." Because there was no way he'd ever been interested in having it in his phone.

Wyatt shook again. "I don't know...."

"Come on!" Asher snapped, making Wyatt cringe. Shit! "Just give me the number, Wyatt...."

Wyatt did and Asher punched it in and decided to get away from the little bear for a moment. He went into the house. Maybe if he had a sensible talk with—

It was not a sensible talk.

Howard answered the phone.

Howard answered the phone shouting. Calling Asher a kike and what the fuck did *he* want?

Kike? He called me a kike? Who does *that anymore?*

Asher was so pissed trying to think of a response to "kike" (tub-oh? fat ass? lard-o?) he almost missed what he hadn't expected to hear.

Howard was serious.

He *was* done with Wyatt.

He wanted the little guy out as fast as possible.

Not good.

Not good at all.

So Asher made the call to Sloan early, but there was no answer. It went straight to voice mail. Then he went back to Wyatt.

Jay Gatsby. I'm Jay Gatsby.

It didn't work. Wyatt took one look at his face and burst once more into tears.

Oh, this sucked. This sucked a blue whale's cock.

CHAPTER NINE

AND SO it was that the Fabulous Four gathered early that Saturday at Wyatt's house.

Wyatt's *once* house.

The leaves were just beginning to change along Wyatt's street (once street?) with a splash of red and a dash of orange, as if giant kids had snuck out during the night and sprayed here and there with huge cans of spray paint. The temperature was perfect, not hot, not cold— very conducive for all the work ahead of them that day. Autumn had snuck in so quietly that Asher had missed it, hadn't noticed Wyatt carry on about the equinox or solstice or whatever the hell it was like as he usually did—*it* being one of the little bear's "high holidays."

Of course, Asher had been a little busy. He might have missed such carryings on. And the last week had gone particularly fast, with jumping right into rehearsals for *Drunks*, and wouldn't Peni have a field day with that?

It was the first Saturday of the month, October the fourth, and while that meant it was Porch Night, and Scott's turn to host, plans had obviously been changed. And while there were cocktails on the schedule, there was much to do before they all relaxed.

Another difference for this first Saturday, of course, was that there were more people there that day than just the Fab Four. There needed to be. Moving was not an easy thing to do even for four. And while it would have been a lot more work had Wyatt had a more reasonable ex than Howard—he wasn't letting Wyatt have even close to his half of the many things they'd bought over a decade of being together—there was still quite a bit to move.

And people call me *an asshole*, thought Asher. He knew the reason—as did the rest of the Fabulous Four—why Wyatt couldn't, or at least wouldn't, fight harder with Howard for his share, but it was frustrating as hell to watch.

Luckily, the problem of where Wyatt should go was solved almost instantly. He'd move into Sloan's place.

"Really?" Wyatt had asked that afternoon, eyes red and swollen, when they had all gathered together for their friend on that fateful afternoon.

"Of course," Sloan had told him. "Hey. It solves a problem."

Wyatt had thrown himself into Sloan's arms and burst once more into tears. And for once, Asher hadn't felt as if Wyatt was being a drama queen. In fact, he'd had to fight back tears of his own. Not because of the breakup—Asher knew that was a good thing—but because Wyatt was brokenhearted. It was a terrible thing to see the perpetually cheerful man so deeply crushed. Asher could only hope that Wyatt would see that he was finally free of the fucker he'd been with for so many years. And yes, now he had a place to stay.

How perfect that Sloan and his lover Max, who had met because they were next-door neighbors, had been going through a strange living arrangement ever since it had become abundantly clear that they really *were* a couple and not just two men caught up in a rush of hormones. Asher had been in doubt. He was *sure* that Max would panic when he began to see that he had abandoned a lifetime of safe and quiet straight-a-tude living and would have long since flown to Paris to set things "right" with his wife by now. Many a straight man was interested in gay sex until the moment after he shot his wad, and then he was running for the hills as if a mob of torch-carrying villagers were after him. Or there were the "straight" men who lived on the down low, married but with a male "mistress" on the side (which would never be enough for Sloan). And then there were those who happily took on a boyfriend until someone noticed—usually a straight friend. Then it was all over but the crying—the gay boy crying, that is.

In this case none of those things happened. Apparently even Max's hardass father had been unable to stop the couple from merrily falling more and more deeply in love.

So the problem of which house they should live in had been solved. The biggest reason Sloan hadn't been able to put his house up for sale was the memories of his much-loved mother. That and the garden she cared for so deeply. Sloan had been terrified that if he moved in with Max and sold the house, someone would buy it, plow the beloved garden under, and roll out new sod instead. Now he didn't have to worry about that, and he could go live in a love nest with Max.

Love! What was love? It was enough to drive Asher crazy, but apparently Sloan and Max were happy. And Max did care for Sloan. So

Asher guessed he should be happy for his friend. It wasn't even that Asher didn't believe in love. Hell, if push came to shove, it was love he felt for Sloan, as well as for Wyatt and even Scott.

Scott.

Who had also found love.

Wow. Who would have ever believed it?

Scott was only the biggest curmudgeon who had ever lived. A man who put the word "Doubting" in "Doubting Thomas." Asher had been sure Scott's relationship with Cedar would end faster than it took the average twink to decide what to wear to the dance club on a Friday night. A while, but not long. Scott had been known to fall in love faster than that. Yet here he was, three months or so later, with the decidedly hot Cedar, and the two of them were fawning all over each other like lovesick teenagers. It was enough to make Asher want to puke.

Because while Asher did believe in love, he found the whole lovers thing hard to believe. You loved your friends. You tried to love your family. But being *in* love? That was something different.

But then again, Scott was happy. Had he ever known Scott to be happy? Ever? Unless it was when he was *un*happy? Not only that, but his lover Cedar Carrington, son of the famous rock stars Cyan Carrington and Laird Addington, was happy too. Happy as could be. Happy as a frolicking puppy. With Scott!

Yes. As crazy as it all was, Asher supposed he needed be happy for them. Scott was his friend, and it was good to see the changes that had come over his life since he met Cedar. And while Scott was now a card-carrying, crystal-holding, tree-hugging, you-can-manifest-anything-your-heart-desires New Ager, Asher supposed that it was better than the negative, pessimistic malcontent he used to be.

Here was hoping both couples would last.

Because Wyatt and Howard sure hadn't, had they?

They were as dead as the brontosaurus.

They had sat on Sloan's porch the night it happened, *Sloan's* and not Max's, and Wyatt sat in the center of the four friends, shell-shocked. One minute he would be sobbing and the next sitting there completely overwhelmed, as if suffering from some kind of post-traumatic stress syndrome. Who knew? Maybe he was.

Then there would be the moments he could talk (those were just as bad): "It was so fast. I mean, one minute I was holding a bag of Nilgiri chicken korma and samosas, strolling in the front door excited as could be, and the next I was staring at Howard fucking this kid over the coffee table while this big dude was fucking Howard! Howard had a prick up his *own* ass. Howard hasn't let *me* fuck him in eight years. *Eight years!* He says I'm too big." Wyatt let out an awful little bark of laughter. "*Me!* Too big. But there he was, taking one right up the old poop-chute. A *big* dick too. *Huge*. Without a condom!"

Wyatt began to shake again. Took a deep breath. Went on. "I'm standing there and suddenly I'm screaming and all of a sudden…. All of a sudden, I'm homeless…. *Homeless!* I mean, I don't understand. How could this happen?"

Then Wyatt had looked up, pale and with a look of horror on his face.

"Oh my gods…. *Bareback*, guys! They were *all* fucking with*out* condoms." He was just then finally realizing that his day was far worse than he'd imagined. Just then finally realizing the full consequences of what he'd walked in on—what he'd seen—and what it meant. "What…? What if I've got it? What if Howard has given me HIV?"

Asher had found himself with his arm around Wyatt's shoulder, pulling him tight, shushing him softly, rocking him, whispering that he was getting ahead of himself and they would take him into town to the KC Free Health Clinic first thing and get him tested, and he was sure everything would be all right and….

And then Asher had looked up to see Sloan and Scott looking at him slack-jawed.

"What?" he growled. Did people really think he was an asshole? Surely they knew he cared for Wyatt. Cared for all of the members of the so-called *Fab-ulous* Four?

And here they *all* were on this sad day. Not only the Fabulous Four, but more besides. A mob helping move poor Wyatt out of the house he loved so much. Asher wondered if there would be half this many if Howard had been the one who had to move out.

There was Peni, who had volunteered the second he'd heard what was going on. Hot as he was, Asher hoped he wouldn't have to worry about the sanctimonious little prick's attitude.

Although that attitude did seem to be aimed at Asher. He'd actually showed up with flowers—pink—for Wyatt. Asher had no idea what the hell he was going to do with flowers on a day like this, but Wyatt seemed pleased.

It surprised Asher to see Katherine Grimsley—Wyatt's boss and the owner of Treasures of Terra, the New Age store that Wyatt managed—there as well. She was an older woman, with snow white hair—from what Asher had put together, at least sixty if not more. And yet there was a power about her that defied description. Look out! She was moving boxes and directing traffic like a four-star general.

Then besides Sloan and Scott, there were their partners as well, both Max and Cedar, as well as Max's fourteen-year-old gay son Logan, and lo and behold, *his* boyfriend as well.

Asher had his mouth open to say that he was the only single gay man here besides Peni when he realized he was about to put his foot in his mouth in the most colossal way. What was today about, after all?

A breakup.

Of course Wyatt was still a mess. He wasn't good for much of anything, especially with Howard, the hulking giant with his big belly and his glistening bald head and the sweat stains under his arms. Howard wasn't doing shit! Just making sure that Wyatt didn't take anything he didn't think Wyatt should take. Which was quite a bit.

Howard had even made the two of them go through the CDs one by one, choosing them like grade schoolers picking members for their baseball team. Luckily, Wyatt had every bit of the music downloaded to his computer, but he *loved* his CDs. Especially since he had a number of them with autographs, including some by Celia, an artist who did pagan music. Wyatt loved her and had been to every one of her local concerts. She wasn't to Asher's taste, although he had to admit she was talented. Sadly, Howard didn't care about that. It was like he was doing all this to purposely hurt Wyatt. And why? Hadn't they been together for ten fucking years? Why be such a douche? Howard had actually picked out one of the P!nk CDs, which had just shown how mean he was. As far as Asher knew, Howard hated P!nk.

"I'll get you a new one," Asher had told Wyatt when the little bear looked like he might start crying again. "At least he didn't get the autographed one. It's irreplaceable."

Which was probably why, at his next turn, Howard had snatched up one of the signed Celia CDs. "It says 'to Wyatt *and* Howard'," the big creep argued.

So it went, item by item, throughout the whole house. It was an ugly, ugly day, and it was all Asher could do not to down the entire six-pack he had waiting in a cooler in his truck. It soon became clear that the only way Wyatt was going to have any semblance of a household was that Max and Sloan didn't need two households' worth of furniture. It was a good thing too. Asher didn't really have anything to offer Wyatt. His apartment was small, his possessions few. He didn't really even have much in his storeroom in the basement of his building, and certainly nothing Wyatt could use. Asher had never been one to "own" things. Things could be taken away. Witness this horrendous day.

Fortunately, there was no way Howard could wear any of Wyatt's clothes. He didn't try for any of those. And there was a painting that Wyatt's grandmother had done. Apparently, she had been someone famous. It was the one time Wyatt stood up to the man, puffing himself up like a cat. Asher was happy to see it.

Over and over Howard made the whole ordeal far uglier than it needed to be, choosing to keep things he surely didn't really want or need and that Wyatt loved. The fucker almost hadn't let Wyatt take the guest bed.

"It's *mine*," said Wyatt. "I had it before we met."

"But you sold it to *me*." Howard stated that loud and clear. "When you had a big bill due. *Over*due!"

"You made him *sell* you something to pay one of his bills?" Sloan asked suddenly, incredulity clear on his face. "You didn't just pay the damned bill? Are you…. Howard. Were you two a couple or not? Jesus!"

Howard snarled, and for one brief minute, Asher had been afraid he might take a swing at Sloan. He was just moving to get in between them when Howard said, "A couple doesn't mean one of us has to pay for everything!"

"You don't pay for everything!" Wyatt cried.

"I pay more! I pay more every—*single*—time," Howard said. "That's always been the problem with you." He thrust a big blunt pointed finger at Wyatt, looming over the little man. "You have that *shit* job, which pays for *shit*, with no goddamned benefits—I have to have you on mine, and I pay that *too*. You haven't offered to make an insurance payment *once*. You can't afford *any*thing, let alone half our expenses. Never have."

"Excuse me," said Katherine Grimsley.

She had come up on them and their argument as silent as a rolling mist. She was tall for a woman, even though nowhere near Howard's stature. And yet….

"That for-*shit* job you are talking about is the manager of *my* store."

...and yet somehow Howard stepped back when she advanced on him. They all saw it. They all froze and watched. Asher actually felt goose bumps rush down his arms at the sight. She kept going and Howard retreated. He seemed to shrink, get smaller with every step she took.

"And *you*... whom I have never had anything for except contempt, you are going to *gift* that bed to Wyatt, aren't you?"

"Why—why *should* I?" Howard asked in a voice several decibels higher than the one he'd been using.

"*You* come up with a reason. And maybe one of them should include the fact that you call yourself pagan.... Have you forgotten the Rule of Three? That whatever you put out into the world comes back to you three times? I shudder to think what awaits you when that Law is enacted. And something else, Howard. You know that *I* am a witch. Care to see who is what they say they are?"

Howard had backed up against the front door by this time, all but cringing.

Asher let out a laugh.

Which broke the "spell." Howard actually snarled, lunged at her, and then vanished into the house with the slam of the screen door.

"Wow," Wyatt said and then collapsed on the old sofa—which Howard said he couldn't have either—and buried his face in his hands once more.

It was Peni who got to him first that time, sat by his side, and hugged him. Wyatt had cried a lot today. Through the carrying out of things he was allowed to take, through Howard's curses and insults, and even more when Howard had smashed a large photograph of the two of them right there on the front steps.

At one point, with a loud laugh and eyes flashing, Howard had cried triumphantly, "Imagine next year at Festival when I'm camping in the Rolling Brothel—"

(the name he and Wyatt had given their new, for them, pop-up camper)

"—and you're sleeping on the ground in our old tent."

(Which Howard had graciously let Wyatt take.)

Curiously enough, that had been Wyatt's biggest breakdown. Asher hadn't gotten it. But apparently Scott and Cedar had, and they'd walked poor Wyatt down the street to a convenience store for coffee while the rest of them continued to pack the various cars and Asher's truck and Katherine's big work van (on the side of which were painted the words "Treasures of Terra—As Above, So Below.").

It was all terribly hideous, and it was only the fact that they had to move everything no more than a mile away and into a house that Wyatt had visited hundreds of times that kept them all from losing their minds.

Through it all, what had really impressed Asher the most was Peni. For a man who had been so judgmental of him, today Asher had witnessed only sweetness and comfort from Peni.

Interesting.

It added a different level to the man, and once more Asher felt himself drawn to him.

Maybe he should try to be nice to Peni?

THE ONE man who surprised the heck out of Peni during all the awful unpleasantness of moving Wyatt out of his home was Sloan's friend Asher. Until today all Peni had ever seen was Asher the drunk. Asher, the sanctimonious, thinks-he's-better-than-everybody-else drunk. For some inexplicable reason, Asher was a hero to Sloan, and for the life of Peni, he couldn't figure out why. Sure Asher was gorgeous. Quite possibly the most handsome man Peni had ever seen in real life, up close and off the silver screen. But so what? You could be good-looking and still be a total jerk. So what if, according to Sloan, and even Wyatt, the man was an extremely talented actor? Charlie Sheen was a talented actor—but from everything Peni had ever heard, he was a horrible and narcissistic person.

Yet Asher was a full and firm member of Sloan's so-called Fabulous Four. Sloan insisted he had lots of good qualities.

Peni had to admit he'd been impressed that Asher had stood there the *entire* time Wyatt's *muli elo* ex-boyfriend—

(and there Peni was, using horrible words—what would his mother think?)

—made Wyatt chose those CDs, one by painful one. While the rest of them carried and lugged and loaded. What's more, Peni realized that Asher wasn't doing it to get out of work. He was being there *for*

Wyatt. He was making sure Wyatt wasn't ripped off. To Peni, the CDs weren't all that important. In fact, at first, it had been all he could do to keep from saying, "Wyatt, it's just CDs! They're the least of your worries. You can get new ones."

But then he remembered that day not long ago when P!nk had been blasting from Wyatt's house. Or how they had all danced and sung to "You Don't Own Me." Then it was suddenly very clear that music meant more to Wyatt than even a bed to sleep on.

Asher had taken care of Wyatt. Even told him he'd buy him a copy of the P!nk album that Howard had taken. To Peni's shock, he saw there just might be more to Asher than he realized. Was there perhaps a human being beneath that gorgeous exterior?

And Asher *was* gorgeous! Not only his face, but from what Peni had seen, an incredible body. If he ever became the movie star everyone said he would be, he wouldn't have to worry about nude scenes.

From what Wyatt had once told Peni, he wouldn't need to fear the full-frontal scenes either. Wyatt had said that Asher had a dick so big he would use it to prop himself up when he was drunk!

But—*oca!*—so what? Peni didn't care about dick size. In fact, the idea of a huge one intimidated him. What did you do with something that big anyway? And the whole prop-himself-up-when-he-was-drunk-idea only led to one thing; the word "drunk."

"How did you even see it?" Peni asked before he could stop himself.

"Locker room," Wyatt said with a mischievous smile. "We all work out at the college gym a couple times a week." Wyatt raised and lowered his eyebrows suggestively once or twice. "Wanna join us some afternoon and see for yourself?"

"N-no," Peni said. "I don't think so...."

"Are you sure?" Wyatt asked. "It's the eighth wonder of the world. Seeing *is* believing."

But there was no way. Because of course that would mean Asher would see *him* naked as well. That was all he needed, Asher's lascivious eyes on his naked body. Plus he wouldn't be able to measure up. He wasn't all that big. And what if he got hard?

But worst of all was the fact that Peni *had* wanted to see Asher naked and that made him mad. Why would he want to see such a jerk naked? Who cared what Asher looked like without his clothes? But the thought was there. It also upset Peni because it meant he was objectifying the man. He didn't even like Asher, but he wanted to see his penis? What was that about? Yet with all the talk, how could Peni help but be curious?

Sloan had talked about it too. Told him one night as they sat on Sloan's porch. It was back before he fell in love with Max. Or maybe it was right after? It blurred....

"I couldn't believe it when I saw it, Peni. It was huge. I thought, there's no way I can take that. It would kill me. But God, Peni. Asher is the most amazing lover I've ever had. He made sure I was ready. Touched me in ways I'd never been touched before. Kissed me in ways I couldn't believe. Used his mouth in ways that made me...." Sloan had trembled at that, and Peni had felt a stirring of his own. "I couldn't believe how easy I took him when it was time. How easy he took *me*. Not that it didn't hurt. But good. I don't know if you understand...."

Peni understood. Bobby Brubaker hadn't been small.

"But surely Max...." Peni had started to say. Surely he's better?

"Oh! Oh, Max is wonderful. What he lacks in experience and technique, he more than makes up for in loving. Sure Asher knows technically how to touch and kiss and... well, you know. But when Max touches me"—he smiled then—"he's adoring me. And there is nothing better than that. He's also a lot more... ah... human down there, if you know what I mean." Sloan blushed furiously at that. "I shouldn't be telling you this. Max is perfect, okay? Please don't think...."

Peni had understood. Or thought he had, and they'd changed the subject.

Yet remembering those words now, and Wyatt's, made Peni think about Asher's... well... dick, once more. It wasn't the first time. He could hardly help it. Asher was wearing sweats today, perfectly understandable clothes to be wearing while helping a friend move. But could he possibly be wearing underwear underneath them? With what Peni hadn't been able to help but see swaying inside the loose gray fabric? It was enough to make Peni check his own crotch, since he was wearing sweats as well, to see if he were making a spectacle of himself as well (not that he could compete!). But no, his tighty whities were keeping everything in check—even with the fact that his penis was beginning to shift inside those same underwear.

It was thoughts like those that made it all the more embarrassing when Asher quite suddenly showed up at his side and asked if he might share the couch where Peni had decided to take a short break.

"No. I-I don't mind." Peni scooted over.

Meanwhile out on the street, Katherine Grimsley was directing the way the bed should be put in the back of her van so that there was the maximum use of room. What must it be like to work for that woman?

Peni took a sip of his bottled water and noticed Asher had a beer. He couldn't help but sigh.

"Oh for God's sake, Peni. It's *one* beer. I'm lugging breakables and driving. I'm not going to get drunk. Certainly not on one beer."

"I'm sorry," Peni said. Besides, it wasn't any of his business, was it?

Asher twisted the cap off his bottle and took a quick swallow.

They sat for a while in uncomfortable silence—at least it was for Peni. Then, just to break that quiet, he blurted, "Happy Yom Kippur!"

"Huh?" Asher said.

Peni looked at him. "Yom Kippur. Wasn't it yesterday? Isn't that a big Jewish holiday?"

Asher looked at him blankly for a moment and then, slowly, understanding came to those eyes. "Oh. Wow. I guess it was." Then his eyes clouded over, and he looked away. "I'm not a practicing Jew." He went silent. In fact, it felt like stone-cold silence. Like he couldn't go more silent for any reason at all.

Did I say something wrong? Peni wondered. As the silence continued, he found the need once more to say something. Anything. The quiet was unnerving. "Tell me the part I don't understand."

"What part is that?" Asher asked without looking back, still staring out into the busy front yard.

"Why Wyatt? Why does *he* have to move out?"

"Do you want the real reason?"

Peni nodded. "Yes, I do. This is just awful. It's killing poor Wyatt. I thought this was *their* house. Why does Howard get to say who moves out?"

"It's because he's a motherfucking prick," Asher spat.

Peni let out a sudden, surprised bark of a laugh, then covered his mouth quickly. This was no day to be laughing, and he certainly didn't want Wyatt to hear it.

"Wyatt messed up. *Big* time."

"Messed up how?" *Or is this any of my business?*

"You mean besides getting mixed up with that bastard in the first place?"

"Yes!" cried Peni.

Whether it was or wasn't Peni's business, Asher explained—after a long sigh and another swig of his beer. "A few years ago, Wyatt got himself into a little financial trouble. Not for me to go into, so I'll leave it at the fact that Wyatt declared bankruptcy. I think I know why he had to do it, but I'm keeping it to myself. Anyway, last year Wyatt and Fuckstick decided to refinance their house. They wanted to redo the kitchen, bathroom, that kind of stuff. Bank said they'd do it, but only if they left Wyatt's name off the mortgage because of his bankruptcy."

"Oh no," Peni said.

Asher nodded. "We all tried to talk Wyatt out of it, but he wasn't having any truck with our advice. He was determined. He said the bank said if he waited a year or two they could put his name back on the mortgage. And then we got weekly and daily reports, not to mention Facebook, as they transformed the place. They even got that damned camper Wyatt loves so much. And now he's out in the cold. He's lost it *fucking* all, and there's not a damned thing he can do about it."

"Gosh." What else was there to say? Besides going on about the injustice of it all? And what a horrible man Howard was? But they knew that. Today was all about that.

"I'm smart enough not to tell him, but you know what? This is the best thing that could happen to our little bear."

Peni looked at Asher in shock. "What?"

"He doesn't see it that way now, of course. But eventually, with our help, I hope he does. His whole identity and ego are wrapped up in Wyward."

"What's Wyward?"

"You know all that cutesy shit where couples combine their names? Wyatt and Howard. Wyward. 'Course Fuckhead would say Howaratt or some such shit. Anyway, Wyatt doesn't believe in himself. All he has ever seen is Wyatt and Howard. He doesn't see just Wyatt anymore. He's been nothing but a half of something for way too long. And Peni?" He shifted on the small couch and looked Peni in the eyes, his blue-green eyes swimming with unexpected emotion. "Wyatt is *so* much more. He's so much better than Howard. He deserves so much more. Howard has treated him like shit for years, and this barebacking stuff is just the end of it." Asher's beautiful face twisted into something ugly. "I swear to God if Wyatt becomes poz because of that fucker, I *will* kill him!"

Peni froze. Because he thought it was just possible that Asher meant it. That it was no figure of speech. No venting.

Goodness….

"A coward, Peni. Wyatt has been nothing but a coward."

A coward? A sting of anger hit Peni. How could Asher sit there and call his friend a coward in the same breath that said he'd kill Howard?

"That seems a little harsh," Peni said, remembering again dancing and singing "You Don't Own Me" in front of Howard. It had amazed Peni. He'd been terrified that Howard would come bounding toward Wyatt and punch him. "I don't think Wyatt's a coward."

"He's a coward because he didn't leave that scumbag years ago." Asher's expression softened, and he became again the work of art that kept—despite himself—taking Peni's breath away. "He believes that no one will ever love him. That Howard was his one shot. And that's not true. Plenty of men would want Wyatt. He's not my type, but look at the guy." He nodded toward the sidewalk where Scott and Cedar were just coming back with Wyatt. "Even all sad and down and torn apart… he's adorable."

Peni had to keep himself from going all wide-eyed. *Or* tearing up.

Asher really did care about Wyatt. Who would have known? Not from the way Peni had heard him talk to Wyatt, needling him, poking fun at his passions, even his wardrobe.

Asher only got more and more interesting.

Was *this* what Sloan was always talking about? Was *this* why Asher was one of the Fabulous Four?

Asher leaned his head back and with several huge gulps and downed the rest of his beer. Damn. Even his bobbing Adam's apple on that strong neck was sexy!

"We should probably get back to work."

Peni nodded. "All right."

And so they did.

AMONG THEM all, they managed to get almost everything out of Wyatt's long-time home and to his new one in one trip. It was a lot of cars, really, and of course Howard had not really let his partner of a decade have very much.

At least Sloan's two-story shirtwaist wasn't going to look half-empty because of Wyatt's lack of furniture. Sloan would take some of his stuff next door, but that would only mean that he and Max would have to bring some of Max's stuff back. Wyatt was basically moving into a furnished house.

"You know," Katherine was saying, standing in the dining room, hands on hips, "I think we need to open up all these boxes before we go home. No sense in leaving it all to you."

Asher watched Wyatt's mouth fall open in surprise and then his eyes well up in tears yet again. At least this time it was for a good reason, if the word "good" could be applied to anything about this day. Anything that *Wyatt* could see as good, that is. Asher maintained that Howard ending their relationship *was* the best thing that could happen to Wyatt. Now Wyatt had a chance at a life. He could have wasted decades on that creep.

Wyatt collapsed, crying, into Katherine's arms.

Could one human being have enough liquid *in* them to cry as much as Wyatt had in the last few days?

But the thought dissolved as Katherine stroked Wyatt's hair. "Ah, my sweet friend. It gets better. It does. When Anthony and I went our separate ways, I thought the world had come to an end. It didn't. You'll be all right. You will…."

Wyatt looked up. "H-how?"

"Trust me, Little Bear."

Little Bear?

(Asher could hear the capital letters.)

Katherine called Wyatt "Little Bear"?

For an instant Asher almost felt jealous. "Little Bear" was how *he* thought of Wyatt. Then he remembered that Little Bear was Wyatt's "faerie name." The name he used at that camp retreat he went to every summer—all gay men, most of them tree huggers and nature worshippers. Literally. Wouldn't it make sense that Katherine, a woman who ran a New Age shop, would know Wyatt's witchy name?

"You do trust me, don't you?" Katherine asked Wyatt.

Wyatt nodded.

"Then trust me when I say it *will* get better. You don't see it now, but this is the beginning of the rest of your life."

Wyatt dropped his head back into her shoulder, and quite suddenly Katherine, looking over Wyatt's head, locked eyes with Asher. It jolted him for some reason. It was as if they were somehow telepathically connected in that moment. As if he could hear…

Yes. I agree. Getting away from that beast is the best thing that could have ever happened to Wyatt. And you and I and the rest, we're going to help him get there, right, Asher? Right?

And Asher felt himself nod, gooseflesh running in a rush down his arm, the hair there standing on end.

She smiled gently and gave him the slightest nod, and he couldn't help but wonder if it hadn't been his imagination at all.

They ordered pizza, all throwing in money despite Wyatt's protests—

"But I'm supposed to pay! It's what you do when friends help you… help you… m-move."

—and when the tears came again, they all assured him that *next* time he could pay.

They got just enough set up so when the pizzas arrived they could sit around and eat. Asher only had one more of his beers—he saw Peni watching and battled the urge to get mad at the judgment he thought he saw—because really, the beers could wait until they were all sitting around the porch in their traditional first-Saturday-of-the-month way.

Soon P!nk was pouring out of the speakers, and bless Wyatt, he tried to join his idol, singing halfheartedly to the lyrics that Howard was a tool and that he, Wyatt, was still a rock star.

It was a step, and Asher found himself joining the others as they backed Wyatt up.

After the pizza, Katherine gave everyone a duty, convincing them that together they could get the job done fast. They lost Max's son, Logan, and his boyfriend—

"Now you two know I'm trusting you over there, right?"

"*Dad!*"

—but at least the boys had helped take one of Sloan's bedroom suites down to the basement so Wyatt's could be set up in its stead. Katherine took charge of the kitchen, telling Wyatt he needed to do the bedroom, and if he didn't like where she put things, he could always rearrange it later.

Somehow Asher found himself, along with Peni, included in that chore. They put the bed together (and Asher couldn't resist winking when he looked at Peni over the expanse of the mattress as they made it) and then helped Wyatt unload his clothes and put them in the closet and the drawers of the battered dresser that went with the bed.

At one point Wyatt started to cry again, and at first Asher thought it was because Wyatt was thinking about how he would be sleeping alone that night... until he saw the T-shirt Wyatt was folding.

It featured a football helmet (which is what made Asher look twice—Wyatt had no interest in sports) with a bear on it and... *fuck*... arched above and below, were the words "Bear Backers."

Shit damn fuck.

Asher reached out, took the shirt, insisted with a gentle—and then stronger—tug that Wyatt relinquish it. "Trash, Wyatt. All right?"

"B-but," Wyatt burbled.

Asher held up a finger. Gave it a single shake.

"You don't want this. You don't. You don't ever want to see this again."

Wyatt's shoulders slumped, and yet another tear rolled down his face.

"Wyatt. *Look* at me." Asher wasn't sure where the words came from, but came they did. "You have survived a hard day. It's not over. But do something for yourself. For Wyatt. Throw this away. Because, my friend—you *are* a rock star. You don't want something to remind you every time you look at it what a tool *he* is." And of course there was no reason to clarify who "he" was.

Wyatt looked at him, eyes glassy.

"Rock star, Wyatt."

"Rock star," echoed Peni, surprising Asher. For a moment he'd forgotten the man was there.

Wyatt managed a weak smile, and then, reaching out, took the T-shirt back. Asher opened his mouth to object but then saw what Wyatt was doing. Or trying to do.

He was trying to rip it. That didn't work. And then without even communicating the idea, both Asher and Peni reached out and, between them, tore the shirt asunder.

Later, they all sat around the living room, some on folding chairs borrowed from next door, and listened to music. Quieter music this time. Celia, Wyatt's favorite pagan singer. It was something they could talk over. Katherine had a glass of wine and then, stretching and popping her back, told them she had to go. She worked Sundays, after all, and needed a good night's sleep after the long day's journey. Wyatt flew into her arms, and Asher was sure that there would be an encore of tears, but the little bear surprised him again.

Yes, when he stood back, his eyes were wet. But he fought the tears back, and Asher was proud of him for it.

A real worry began to creep over Asher nonetheless, and it had really begun when he was trying to flirt with Peni while making that bed upstairs.

Tonight Wyatt would be sleeping alone. Sleeping alone for the first time in years—not counting the few times he and Howard were separated by business trips or a drunken night on someone's couch. Why, Wyatt had even (and this boggled Asher's mind) slept in bed with Howard the night the man had broken up with him! Sloan had put Wyatt to bed in Max's (now Max and Sloan's?) guest bedroom, and when he got up the next morning, he'd found the bed empty. Wyatt had gone home.

"I couldn't help it," Wyatt had (yes, with tears) explained. "I guess I thought if I cuddled up to him, he'd say it was all a mistake."

That didn't happen.

What was worse was that Howard didn't tell Wyatt that until *after* Wyatt gave him a blowjob.

You're better off without him, little bear! You are better off without him.

It was all enough to make Asher break out his beers. It was more than time. Then, even though he wished he had more than the four that were left, seeing that Peni was without alcohol, he offered him one.

Peni declined, giving Asher the most peculiar look. *What?* Asher wondered.

He'd seen Peni drink some wine. It was at the big Fourth of July celebration up at Peter Wagner's house. And Asher couldn't help the moment of shame he felt for having forgotten in the first place.

So what was the big deal? It was a beer. One beer. Asher wasn't planning on parting with more than one.

Asher decided to ignore it, and further thought slugging the quartet of beers was a good idea. When you didn't have a lot to drink, drinking fast could give you the buzz you needed—and Asher needed it.

He surprised even himself when he asked Wyatt if he had any new jokes—he rarely, if *ever*, liked Wyatt's jokes. But this sadness was like a heavy blanket over them all. Heavy and smelling bad, like one that had been put away wet and gotten mildewed. It wasn't a comforting blanket, but a confining and dispiriting one.

Wyatt declined, which really wasn't all that surprising. Asher had just hoped Wyatt could find something to laugh about, even if it were only for a minute.

So Asher told them about what had happened the other day during rehearsals for *Drunks*, hoping that would help.

"I have this line," he said. "I'm supposed to say, 'Cindy, fucking you again would give me the will to live.' And I wasn't doing it the way Guy—he's the director—wanted me to. He tells me, 'I want you to say that line like you *mean* it, Asher. Say it like you're saying that you want to lick her pussy.'

"And I keep doing the line and he keeps saying, 'I don't believe you want to lick her pussy, Asher!'

"So finally I tell him, '*Guy!* That's because I *don't* want to eat her pussy! I don't eat pussy. I gave it up!' And everyone *bursts* into laughter! And then Guy? He blushes bright red and then points to Louis and says without blinking, 'Okay, say it like you want to suck his *cock*.' And then Louis was blushing, and I should have just left it there, but you know me...."

"We sure do," Scott said, rolling his eyes.

"So I said, '*Now* I get you. But can I say it like I want to eat his sweet little ass instead?' And without beating an eye Guy tells me to imagine whatever I have to, but just please get the line right. Well trust me, after that, I said the line *just* how he wanted it!"

Asher laughed, or tried to, and so did they. They tried. But it didn't really work.

Oh well. It had been funny when it happened. Because he really did want to bed Louis. Sadly, he was way too busy with Melanie, the actress playing Cindy. Louis was a straight man who seemed to still be straight even after a six-pack. Asher had tried after the Friday rehearsal. Hadn't worked there either.

More's the pity.

At least Asher's beers were working for him tonight. He had a buzz going at the end of the second, and a third would surely do the trick. Why not offer Peni the last one?

"No," Peni all but snapped. "I told you, Asher. I don't want one."

"For God's sake," Asher said. "It's *one* beer! What? Will you die and go to hell over one fucking beer?"

The room went silent. Asher turned and looked around him. Everyone was staring.

Fuck! What was with them?

"What?" he asked.

Peni jumped to his feet, and Asher looked up to see his eyes flashing. "*Palagi puki'o!*" Peni spat, then covered his mouth—eyes wide—and dashed to the front door.

What the fuck?

Peni stopped, trembling, and looked back into the room. "I'm sorry, Wyatt. I'm tired." He shook his head. "I'm so sorry."

No one said a word as Peni left, but as one they all looked at Asher as soon as he was out the door.

"What the fuck?" Asher cried. "I offered him a beer. I was being nice. So what was he acting so fucking self-righteous about?"

"Jesus, Asher," Sloan said. "What do you think?"

Asher rolled his eyes. "Yeah. I know. He's *Mormon*. He's not *supposed* to drink. But I've seen him drink. He's not supposed to smoke the bone either, but he does that. So what's the deal?"

Sloan all but goggled at him. "Asher. *Think!* You know how his father died, don't you? You *were* at the funeral."

Yes. Yes, he was. But that was one day he didn't remember at all well. He'd had a lot to drink.

He shrugged.

"Asher...." As if for some kind of universal dramatic effect, there was a brief silence as one of Celia's songs finished. "Peni's father was *killed* by a drunk driver."

Asher's mouth fell open in surprise.

It was more like shock. He tingled with it. It thrust him right out of his high.

"W-what?"

Sloan shook his head. "Oh, Asher...."

Shit.

Shit damn fuck.

Asher closed his eyes from the shame of it all.

"Oh God," he whispered, and Celia began to sing once more.

Then he was up and on his feet and bolting for the door. He had to say he was sorry. Had to.

He ran out onto the front porch, but he was too late. All he could see of the beautiful Samoan man was the flash of his car's taillights as it disappeared down the street.

Asher slumped.

Shit.

He didn't stay long after that.

He didn't even drink the last beer.

He was tired, and it had been a long, long day. And after the fuck up with Peni, he found he didn't even want it. So he offered it to the room, and when no one took it, he placed it in the refrigerator instead.

Then, feeling like the world's biggest shit, he left.

It was while Asher was passing Wyatt's old house on the way to the highway that he saw something that made him slam on his brakes.

There on the curb was the couch. The couch that Howard wouldn't let Wyatt have. He'd thrown it away.

"Motherfucker," he said aloud.

He sat there a full minute before deciding what to do.

At least I'm not the world's biggest shit, he thought.

That title was reserved for someone else indeed.

CHAPTER TEN

FOR SOME goddamned reason, Asher couldn't get Peni out of his mind. That face, those huge, beautiful black eyes, those full lips, and that wide nose (and the way it crinkled when he smiled). And his skin.... God. So smooth and the color of hazelnuts. The deep tan of a man who had lain out in the sun all summer. Men would kill for Peni's complexion. Flawless except for one tiny acne scar in the crease at the corner of his left eye.

And since when did Asher remember such details about anyone?

But most of all, Asher couldn't forget, couldn't get out of his mind, the ridiculous faux pas he'd made offering Peni that beer. No. Not in the offering. In the insisting that he take one. In getting bitchy about it.

"Will you die and go to hell over one fucking beer?"

Asher wanted to pull his hair out. How could he have said such a thing? *Asshole, it's because of his father.*

Peni's father had been killed by a drunk driver.

What must Peni think of him?

So fucking what? He's an uptight little bitch!

No. No, he's not.

What do you care what he thinks?

I do care!

But why?

For that, Asher had no answer. He only knew he did care what Peni thought.

In fact, he was quite suddenly caring what a lot of people thought about him.

"You're an asshole, you know that, Asher?"

Nellie had said it. Nellie! Who didn't use words like that. And Guy had said it. Said there was an actor who wanted to quit *Drunks* before acting with Asher.

Was he an asshole?

Asher shook his head.

No.

Jealous. People are just jealous.

But what could Peni possibly be jealous of?

All I did was offer him a beer.

No, I did more than that.

The offer of a beer had really been nothing but a courtesy. Asher couldn't readily think of anyone in his circle of friends, acquaintances, or peers who *didn't* drink—at least occasionally. But of course, Peni was Mormon and not the usual type of person Asher associated with. Asking someone if they wanted a drink was second nature to Asher. It was a polite, social thing to do!

But that hadn't been what was so stupid.

"Will you die and go to hell over one fucking beer?"

God!

I didn't mean anything by it. I wasn't being mean. It was just a figure of speech. I wasn't thinking.

That's the fucking problem, Asher. You don't think!

I.

Don't.

Think.

Goddamn it all. It was enough to make Asher feel the strange and foreign sting of threatening tears.

No!

Not cry.

Never cry again!

And so now Peni hated him. And Asher wasn't used to anyone hating him. Or at least disliking him. Not that he thought everyone loved him. He knew they didn't.

"I almost had somebody quit when they found out you had taken the role."

Isn't that what Guy had told him?

Well, so what?

He didn't give a shit if people liked him or not!

Not... not mostly.

In truth it mystified him when he met someone and couldn't win them over. Couldn't seduce them, figuratively or literally. People *liked* it when he paid attention to them.

He first became truly aware of it in junior high. Girls would get all giggly. Boys wanted to be his best friend. He'd even had a teacher—

Mrs. "Four Eyes" Garenthall—who would blush and get all tongue-tied, and one day he quite startlingly realized she *liked* him. In fact, hadn't the music teacher, Mr. Ryerson, "liked" him too? Given him A's even though he'd fucked off in the man's class? And *damn*, could it have been because he'd been assigned to the front row and tended to slouch down (he'd been getting tall already, and that height had made him self-conscious in those days) with his legs spread wide and…. Yes! Of course! Given the man quite a view, hadn't he? Because he was already bigger than all the other boys and filled out a pair of soft jeans quite well.

Then, of course, he'd gotten to high school and found out how easy it was to get laid—first with Jane Berenbaum and then Buck Summers.

(Oh God! Buck Summers. Sometimes he wondered what had ever happened to Buck Summers. Probably fat with five kids and working at a Walmart or something.)

Discovering how much he was wanted meant from then on there had been no stopping Asher. It was through finding the right approach, just the right line, to get into someone's pants that he'd learned he had a natural talent for acting.

Asher decided, as a lark and through the suggestion of a teacher, to try out for a play. He got his first role in *To Kill A Mockingbird* as Arthur "Boo" Radley—the crazy kid who lived next door, never spoke, and peered in people's windows at night. He so impressed the director of the theater department that he was soon getting parts practically without auditioning.

When he was a junior, he got the lead role in *Death of a Salesman*, a classic high-school production and the type of part that, until then, only seniors had gotten.

"No one can touch you," the director told him. "We'd be idiots to let anyone else have the part of Willy Loman."

Gary, the senior who wanted the part and was so pissed when Asher got it, begrudgingly admitted that Asher was good. But far better was what happened after Asher played George Milton in *Of Mice and Men*. Gary came backstage, eyes wet and swollen and red, and told him that Asher had blown him away. And then, later that night, had blown Asher. And then the next day let Asher fuck him.

Fuck him *hard*!

Had pulled him into the dark backstage (how he had gotten the keys for the theater Asher never found out) and bent over a set of sawhorses and all but begged for it.

Asher had never felt such power before.

Unbelievable power.

And when Asher fucked that boy, and every time he fucked anyone after that, the echoes of his grandfather Yeshiyahu's voice—

"*Abomination!*"

—went away.

Asher wowed the school as Tom in *The Glass Menagerie*. But it was when he got the part of John Proctor in *The Crucible* that his life truly changed. There was something about the character that called out to him from the script. Most particularly in the scene where John Proctor was asked to sign a document confessing to witchcraft. When he delivered those lines—"How may I live without my name? I have given you my soul; leave me my name!"—his heart leapt into his throat. When he felt he needed to lie about how much he loved boys, wasn't that what *he* was doing? Denying who he was?

It was with John Proctor that Asher discovered digging deep into himself to find the part of him that *was* the character he was playing. That was when he fell in love with acting. Before then it had been all about getting attention (and yes, sex). With *The Crucible*, he found his destiny.

How fortunate, then, that some college recruiter or other saw him in that role. Asher graduated and then went to Northwestern University and paid nearly nothing after his scholarships.

To Asher's great happiness, he found that while tearing up a stage, people wanted him not only for his looks and his big cock, but because of *him*, his talent. They wanted to be like... like minions or some damn thing. They held doors open for him. They actually asked for autographs. Autographs!

And yes, there was sex. Lots and lots of sex. He didn't even have to try.

So he was surprised when he realized Peni didn't like him. And then he'd made a mistake—yes, a stupid one—and now Peni seemed to actually hate him.

It had been a long time since anyone had *hated* him. And that person had taken his hate to his grave. Asher couldn't deal with being hated.

So early that day, when he saw that Preston dude wandering around the hotel lobby, doing that thing he did, making the lobby look bright and pleasant for the guests, Asher got a crazy idea.

Even crazier, he called Sloan, who knew Peni far better than Asher did, and asked if he knew what Peni liked. Highly unlikely, of course, but….

But Sloan *had* known. Had coincidentally talked about it with Peni the day before. Peni had blushed and admitted to the cliché of it all, and so Sloan knew just what Peni liked.

Asher had gone to pretentious little Preston What's-His-Name and asked if he could set Asher up—

"Really? *That's* what you want?"

"Yes, that's what I want."

"*Actually*, you have the name wrong. It's from the *Malvaceae* family and…."

—and by promising to have a few drinks with the man (which Asher had no intention of doing), Preston had set Asher up quite spectacularly.

Now if only it would work.

Preston's handiwork sat in the seat next to Asher as he headed straight from work to Terra's Gate. Asher was largely absent from the second act of *Drunks* and luckily had the night off. So it was with a stomach cramping with nerves—

(and what the fuck was *that* about?)

—that he drove, nearly turning around at every exit, and finally pulled off into the college town where Asher's only real friends lived.

Along with a beautiful Samoan man Asher could not get off his mind.

THE DAY had been a bitch, although Peni didn't like to use such words.

Wednesdays were usually good. It marked the halfway point of the workweek, meaning halfway to go, but thank goodness, halfway done. Not that Peni was one to wish his life away. In fact, it wasn't uncommon for him to quote his mother whenever he heard someone wishing it were Friday.

"Hey! Be careful there. You never know what's going to happen between now and then. Don't wish them away. Who knows how much time we have left?"

Sometimes he got smiles of understanding, sometimes frowns. Some people took it wrong. Only went to show that you saw what you wanted in life.

But this whole week had sucked.

With most of Saturday swallowed up helping Wyatt move out of his beloved house, a sad and gray mood had set in. Then the day had ended so nastily when Peni had fought—if you could call it that—with Asher. Sunday had been deeply shadowed by a dark and ugly cloud of emotions. He'd hardly heard the lessons at church. Of course, these days he hardly did anyway. The teacher would say "God," and Peni couldn't help but think of a giant whose torso disappeared in the sky and whose mountainous thighs were covered in roads and highways of black ink.

Over and over again, Peni had chastised himself about exploding at Asher. What had made him treat Asher so rudely? Things had been going well. Peni had been seeing a side of the handsome man he'd never expected, which in itself was enough to make him feel guilty. After all, hadn't Sloan, and even Scott, told him there was a reason they loved Asher?

But somehow there had been a part of their assurances that smacked too much of a line of Shakespeare. Something about "the lady doth protest too much." Or worse, reminded Peni too clearly of the way his Aunty Natia used to talk about her husband when it had started to become obvious that the man was treating her badly. She always made the excuse that he was a good man, and he would change if she just stuck with him.

He'd never changed.

And then there was a black eye.

Luckily, she hadn't stayed with him after that.

That was how it had felt to Peni when his friends talked about Asher. That was how it sounded. But Saturday had made Peni wonder if they were right and there really was a good man buried beneath all of Asher's conceited bluster—that Sloan and Scott and Wyatt really *did* see something good.

Then Asher had insisted on offering Peni that beer. How could Asher not have understood why he didn't want one? Asher had gone to his father's funeral, after all.

Except of course Asher hardly remembered being there, did he? He'd been drunk.

And how insensitive had *that* been? As attractive as Asher was, even with that flash of something good inside, Peni couldn't possibly consider getting involved with a drunk.

He *couldn't*.

It was a drunk who had taken Peni's father from him. What kind of honor would it show his father's memory for him to get mixed up with a drunk?

Mixed up with a drunk? Why did that thought keep swirling and cycling through his mind, especially when Peni tried to sleep at night? Taking a beer wasn't getting involved with the man, was it? Why was he even *thinking* that way?

After that night the week had only seemed to go downhill.

Sloan was insanely busy at work, so they hadn't been able to take any breaks or lunches together. Peni certainly wasn't going to ask his mother what to do. Accepting his being gay she might be, but that didn't mean he was ready for a heart-to-heart about men with her. He was pretty sure she wasn't either.

He certainly couldn't talk to Wyatt about it. Peni had been staying with Wyatt in the evenings, giving *him* someone to talk to—to cry to. That had been rough. Wyatt was emotionally destitute. How could Peni ask him for advice about his love life?

Love life? *Love life!* Why did he keep thinking that way?

The only good thing that had happened during the week was that somehow the couch Wyatt had wanted and been forced to leave behind had appeared on Wyatt's front porch. But even that had soured. Wyatt assumed Howard had changed his mind and brought it over while Peni and Wyatt were at work. He'd called his ex-lover, very excited.

"Maybe he's changed his mind!" Wyatt had squealed.

Only to be told Howard had thrown the "effing" thing away.

Of course, Howard had used a different word.

Then today, fate had somehow put every single troubled or evil customer in Peni's call-waiting queue at Horrell & Howes, the call center where Peni worked. And each one of them was yelling, angry at how long they'd been on hold, none of them accepting the answers he was required to give them. Sloan, who just happened to be Peni's supervisor (which was how they had gotten to know each and become friends in the first place), had done a lot to make the center's scripts better. More human. But Horrell & Howes *did* have to follow the guidelines the companies they represented. Peni couldn't offer recompense the companies refused to give.

The calls were swirling around and around in Peni's mind, blocking out everything else, and so he was shocked at what he saw when he pulled up in front of Wyatt's new home and parked his car.

Asher was sitting on the front steps.

And he had flowers!

Peni's heart skipped a beat. He couldn't help that. Hearts would do what they would. *Traitor*, he told it, and found himself wanting to smile.

Were the flowers for him? Or Wyatt?

But there was Wyatt's mini-coop in the driveway, so they very well couldn't be for Wyatt, could they? And when Peni got out of his car and Asher stood, shifting from foot to foot, Peni saw quite clearly that the flowers *were* for him.

Peni's heart skipped another beat.

Stop it!

Peni grabbed his backpack, slung it over his shoulder, and started up the short walkway to the porch.

"Hi, Peni," Asher said.

"Asher." Peni managed to get the man's name past his lips without his voice shaking. *Oca! Why am I acting like this?*

"I hope you don't mind me stopping here. Sloan mentioned you were staying with Wyatt a few days and…." The words stopped although Asher's mouth was still open. It stayed that way for what felt like an hour and then slowly shut. Asher squared his shoulders. "I brought you these." He held the bouquet out to Peni. "Sloan says you love hibiscus."

It was true. "I do." Peni felt the heat of a blush touch his cheeks as he reached out to accept the white and rose and pink flowers. His heart skipped another beat—and a shock shot up his arm—when their fingers touched as he took the bouquet. "It-it's such a c-cliché," he stuttered, unable to help himself.

Damn you, Asher, he cursed inwardly. *How are you doing this to me?* He was immediately ashamed. *Damn you? Really? You're damning him?*

"I...." Asher stopped. Cleared his throat. "Shit." His eyes went wide. "God, I'm sorry. I mean... darn? Shit! I don't know what I mean!" He blushed.

Asher Eisenberg blushed.

Peni could hardly believe it.

He fought back a laugh. Asher was being so... well... cute!

"It's okay, Asher." He looked down at the flowers, felt a wonderful rush. They were so lovely. He didn't care if it was trite that he loved them so. *'Aute Samoa*—what the Americans called hibiscus—was one of his two favorite flowers. *'Aute Samoa* and *puti fiti*—plumeria—the flowers his mother and sisters loved to wear in their long black hair.

And what was he thinking about hair for?

He looked up, and up, into Asher's handsome—no, beautiful—face, and instead of his heart skipping, it began to race instead. It began to pound in his chest so that he could hear it in his ears. *Traitor*, he told it once again and looked for words to say. But no words would come.

"Peni," Asher said, and his voice cracked. "I am so sorry. I feel like such a fuh.... Such a shi*iiiii*.... Crap!" He looked away, then looked back. "I'm sorry, Peni. I hope you can forgive me. I didn't mean what I said about dying and going to hell and...."

And Asher was so obviously uncomfortable that Peni couldn't stand it any longer. "It's okay, Asher. Besides... I need to apologize myself. I said something too. It was wrong."

Asher looked surprised. "You said something? What?"

Peni sighed. "I... I called you a *palagi puki'o*." He closed his eyes. Felt his cheeks burn. "I'm so sorry."

When he looked up, Asher was openmouthed. "You called me... what? Pa-langy puke what?"

"*Palagi puki'o*...." The burn got hotter. "It's like.... *Palagi* means 'white man,' but a lot of the time when we say it, it's a lot like using the N-word."

Asher's brows shot up.

"And *puki'o*...." The shame spread. "It means like—" He paused. Lowered his voice to a whisper. "—asshole."

Asher had started to close his mouth, but now it fell open again, as if the hinges that controlled his jaws had quite suddenly broken.

"So I have to apologize too."

Asher visibly got in control of his emotions. "I deserved it."

"No—" Peni started to explain, but Asher cut him off.

"Peni, please. I can't stop thinking about what I did the other night. It's all I *can* think about!"

Asher's features were awash with emotion. It made Peni's heart hurt. He reached out, touched Asher's arm (another shock raced up his fingers), and smiled. "I forgive you."

A look of total surprise spread across Asher's face. "You do?"

How can I help it, Peni thought, his heart now expanding so much with—with *something* (he knew not what) that he thought it would burst. He almost felt faint. His senses were buzzing.

Oca! Tangaloa! I've fallen under his spell!

It was all Peni could do not to kiss the man.

No. No, no, no! Not this *man.*

Peni took a deep breath. "Yes, Asher. Just forget about it." And another breath. "And thanks for the flowers. They *are* my favorite."

Asher smiled, and it was like the sun shining out from his face. "I'm glad. I have to admit, Sloan told me what to get you."

Sloan? Asher had asked Sloan about his favorite flowers? And Sloan hadn't said anything?

He's been busy.

He talked to Asher about me?

Asher talked to Sloan about me!

Peni managed to nod. "Th-that was nice of him." *Nice?*

"I hope you know I didn't mean anything by it. I... I was.... There was Wyatt and...."

"*Please.*" Peni couldn't stand to talk about it another minute. "It's done."

Asher shook his head. A desperate look flashed in his blue-green eyes. "Let me do something to make it up to you."

Peni held up the flowers. "You got me these."

"Dinner? Let me take you out for dinner."

Peni started. Dinner? "As in a date?" he asked before he could help it.

Asher gaped at him. "Date? I.... Ah... I.... You...."

Asher at a loss for words. Would wonders never cease? From what the guys had told Peni, Asher was never at a loss for words. Wait until he told Sloan.

"I just want to do something nice for you. There's this place I love. Monique's...."

"I can't," Peni said, not even knowing he was going to.

"You're busy? How about this weekend?"

Peni took a deep breath. *I can't, Asher. If I go out to dinner with you, I'm doomed.* "I can't go out with you, Asher." He shook his head. "I can't."

"W-why?"

Was that hurt in Asher's eyes now? *Oca! Don't do this to me....*

Peni looked away. Tried to think of what to say. Finally decided the truth was best.

"I can't go out with a drunk, Asher."

They both flinched at Peni's words. There was definite hurt in those eyes now, and—*Did I need to say "drunk?"*

"I... I'm not a drunk, Peni."

Peni couldn't help but look at Asher with skepticism.

"I'm not, Peni. I...." Asher stopped. His shoulders slumped. "Look, I know why you would think that. But I'm sober most of the time. You've seen me at parties. Well...yeah. And at your church. But Peni... I.... Funerals." He looked away and was silent for a long moment. He looked back. "I wasn't drunk Saturday."

Peni nodded. True. "But you were drinking again. Asher, I can't go out with someone—"

"Who said anything about us 'going out'? I'm talking about dinner. You go to lunch with Sloan and Wyatt all the time."

"—with someone who drinks," Peni finished, ignoring Asher's protests. "At least as much as you do. A drunk driver *killed* my—"

"I *know*, Peni. I know that. What if I promise not to drink more than one cocktail—"

No! No drinking at all. Peni shook his head quickly, decisively. "Why do you have to have a drink?"

"I don't *have* to have a drink. I just *like* drinking. There's a big difference."

Once more Peni couldn't fight his doubt. "What's the difference? *I* don't 'have' to have a cocktail. Why do you?"

"Well, for one thing it helps with my damned nerves!" Asher's eyes went wide.

Then, again before Peni knew where the words were coming from: "Have you considered the idea that you might be an alcoholic?"

Asher looked shocked. "Alco.... No! I'm not an alcoholic! I just like the taste of cocktails. I like the different flavors. Finding some new delicious recipe. Trying a new beer or discovering a new wine. It's a hobby. I don't *need* to drink, Peni. I like to drink. Some people like coffee. Some an expensive cigar. I like alcohol. That's all."

Peni sighed. Asher didn't even know. And here Peni was, having little to no experience with the stuff, and he could see. He moved his head from side to side, slowly. It took everything in him to do it. But he couldn't be like his Aunty Natia. Saying that Asher was a good man and could change. Peni had to nip this in the bud. Stop it before it could possibly get started.

"Peni! I'm telling you!" Asher reached out and took Peni's upper arm in one of his big, strong hands. "I'm *not* an alcoholic. *Really.*"

Fight it, Peni told himself. Told himself not to let Asher get to him with those big, gorgeous eyes. "Asher. I just can't go out with you." *You're the last man on earth I should be going out with.*

And whoa! Was that anger Peni saw?

If so, it was gone too fast to know for sure.

"I'm *not* an alcoholic," Asher insisted firmly.

Then, once more, words were coming out of his mouth that Peni didn't even know were on his mind. "I'll tell you what," he said. "You go thirty days without a drink—without so much as a glass of wine with dinner—and I will go out with you. I'll go wherever you want. A movie. Dinner. The zoo. You name it."

And yes! That was anger Peni saw. Asher was turning red, and it looked like he might explode, and… and then the look was gone.

"You'll go out with me if I don't have a drink for a month?" Asher asked.

Peni nodded. *What am I doing?*

"Why should I?"

Peni shrugged. "You don't have to do anything. I'm just saying. I'll go out with you if you can go thirty days without a drink. If you're not an alcoholic, it should be easy."

"I'm *not* an alcoholic!"

Peni gulped. "Then you'll do it?"

Asher opened his mouth, eyes flashing once more with what could only be anger—and then yes, it was gone. "How will you know? If I cheat or not?"

"I guess I'll have to trust you."

Again Asher opened his mouth to say something and then slowly closed it, comment unmade.

"Of course, I do know your best friends. We talk. Do you think it won't come up in conversation if they have cocktails with you?" *There. Say something about that.*

Another flash. "They won't know what I'm doing when they're not around."

"Like I said. I'll just have to trust you."

Say no, Asher. Go ahead. Get mad. Tell me to "F-off!" Go on. I need you *to!*

Because of course he did want to go out with Asher. Almost desperately. Maybe desperation was just what it was. *So say no. Because—*

"All right. You've got yourself a bet!" Electricity was shooting from those eyes now. Like Peni imagined the lightning in Tangaloa's.

"It's not a bet, Asher." Didn't he see that?

"Whatever. I don't have a drink for thirty days and you will go out with me. That's what you said, right?"

Peni gulped again. Gave a nod.

"All right, then. Thirty days from now. It's… what? The eighth? So if I don't have a drink between now and November eighth, we go out. Wherever I want. That's what you said."

Oca! What had he done?

"Well?" Asher's expression was pure defiant determination. Why, he could almost convince Peni.

"Yes," he snapped. "You go thirty days without getting plastered, and I will 'go out' with you."

"Then it's a bet!" Asher cried triumphantly and held out his hand.

I'm not the reward in some bet! Peni wanted to say but instead found himself shaking that hand.

And—*Oca!*—was jolted again by just the feel of that hand in his. No. No, *his* hand in Asher's. Asher's hand was so big.

So *man.*

Asher nodded. "Thirty days, Peni. Prepare yourself. Be ready to dress up too. Because this is going to be the night of your life." He grinned. Then wagged his eyebrows. "It will be something you never forget."

"O-o-kay," Peni managed.

Then with one last nod, Asher turned and went to his truck.

But he had to set one thing straight. "Asher!" he cried.

Asher turned.

"A *date*. I'm not having sex with you. Got it?"

Asher grinned. "See you in thirty," he called and got in and zoomed away.

What have I done? Peni wondered.

CHAPTER ELEVEN

IT WASN'T thirty days.

CHAPTER TWELVE

HOW COULD the two of them *help* but do things together when he was staying almost every evening with Wyatt to help him keep his mind off his troubles, and Sloan lived next door, and Sloan was one of Peni's only friends, and Sloan and Wyatt were two of Asher's three best friends?

So if Peni was going to be around them or do anything with *any* of them, it was likely Asher might be there too.

Goshdarnit!

The only thing keeping him and Asher from bumping into each other all the time was the fact that Asher was in rehearsals for his new play (and what more appropriate title could there be for such a show than *Drunks*?).

"I want to see *Dracula Untold*," Wyatt said that Friday.

"Umm." Peni looked over at Wyatt, KFC chicken thigh halfway to his mouth. He lowered his hand. "I don't really do movies," he said.

Certainly not scary ones. Those Mormon hooks were in deep, just like Scott had said once upon a time, and Mormons didn't go to movies. *The Tattooist* didn't count because it was about Samoans.

(And it starred the incredibly hot Jason Behr, who even showed off his bare butt—in the very first few seconds of the movie!)

Wyatt pouted. "Come on. *Please?* If we go tomorrow afternoon, it won't be busy."

"How about *Meet the Mormons*?" Peni suggested, not having any idea why. He wasn't even sure what it was about. His mother had been talking about it on Monday during family night, but his mind had been elsewhere, like it had been a lot lately. He couldn't remember if she was excited about the film or warning Peni away.

Wyatt gave him an are-you-crazy look, and all Peni could think was perhaps he was. He didn't *want* to see *Meet the Mormons*.

"What about the Fabulous Four, Wyatt? Wouldn't you rather see that with one of them? Surely Sloan or Scott or…."

"I don't want to depend on them," Wyatt said, eyes as big and round as those paintings of cats and dogs from the sixties. Peni's Aunty Natia had one in her bedroom. "Everybody is married now. Except *me*, of course."

Oh, please don't start crying, thought Peni. "Asher's not married," he said aloud. *I'm not either!* "Ask him."

Wyatt rolled his eyes. "Are you kidding? There is no way Asher would think of going. He'll call it crap. And maybe it is. You should hear what Scott's saying about it. He almost sounded like the *old* Scott with all his, 'Have you *seen* the previews? You can tell they didn't research the historical Vlad Tepes at *all*! That would have made a *great* movie! Blah, blah, blah….'" All in all, it was a great imitation of Scott. "I just know Luke Evans is in it, and he's frippin' *hot!* You know, he's the hunka-cola who plays Bard in the *Hobbit* movies."

But Peni didn't know. He hadn't seen any of *The Hobbit* movies. He hadn't seen the first ones either. He didn't tell Wyatt that, though. Instead, he just decided it couldn't hurt to see a movie and agreed to go.

It certainly perked Wyatt up.

But then guess what? Sloan was there. Sloan and Max and his son and his son's boyfriend and—*Oca! Yes! Of course.*—Asher. And when they filed down the aisle to take their seats in the theater, who should Peni find himself sitting next to?

Why, Asher of course.

He looked gorgeous too.

He seemed pensive, though. Not his usual suave self.

"You okay?" Peni asked. After all, it was only polite.

Asher nodded. "Yeah. It's only…. This play I'm in." He shook his head. "Never mind."

Sometime during the movie—it was pretty wretched, although the special effects were pretty good—Peni realized that Asher's knee was leaning against his own. Had Asher done it on purpose? Was he hitting on Peni?

Peni went to move his knee and found he couldn't.

The weight of Asher's knee against his own felt… pretty nice.

Besides, it was only a knee.

Right?

THE WEEK had been a crazy one. Days at the Meridian were rough due to lots of business. The hotel was hosting three different conventions.

And then there were the evenings.

Rehearsals.

For *Drunks*.

A lot of the scenes were bothering Asher. It was like, since the afternoon talking to Peni, the play had transformed into something... else. It hadn't, of course. It was the same play, same lines, same words. The same *damned* words.

But now....

What had been funny and crazy and over the top (and yes, brilliant) now seemed....

What?

Asher couldn't put his thoughts into any logical order he could make sense of, let alone think of communicating with anyone else.

He only knew the play wasn't turning out to be very enjoyable. It was making him... well... think too much.

Like the opening scene of act two. A scene he wasn't even in!

Lights up. Cataclysmic mayhem. The floor of the room is strewn with empty beer cans, towels, paper products, wine bottles, liquor bottles, clothing, and debris of all sorts....

Focus on beer cans, wine bottles, liquor bottles....

Focus.

On beer cans, wine bottles, liquor bottles!

Why, only the last thing he wanted to focus on right now.

But it was more than that....

And then there was Guy.

"Remember, everybody! Save your booze bottles. No recycling until after the show. Tell your friends. We need beer cans and empty bottles. That means *you*, Asher! I know I can count on you!"

What the fuck was that supposed to mean?

Why could Guy count on *him* for empty booze bottles?

Then there was one of his lines. "Oh, it's disgusting and moist back here."

Referring to the scene when he looks over the back of the set's big couch and finds a bunch of vomit. He quite suddenly couldn't get the image of a morning a few months back when he'd woken up to find his own vomit (at least he supposed it was his) on the floor next to the bed. The thing was he couldn't remember puking. And then there was more in the bathroom. He'd seen that more than once, of course, but on the bedroom floor?

Then he couldn't help but wonder why he'd thought *of course* about how he'd seen puke in the bathroom.

Had he gotten used to that?

When had he gotten used to a puked-up bathroom?

How had he gotten used to it?

He hated puke. He could remember nearly losing his cooking when he saw the movie *Stand By Me* the first time and it got to the scene where countless characters were barfing during the big pie-eating contest. The very thought of vomit was enough to make him gag.

Or at least it *had* been.

When had he gotten used to vomit?

Thoughts like these were affecting his acting. His role depended on him being nonchalant about such stuff—but he was suddenly having trouble finding that place, playing *that* character.

And on top of that, he kept thinking about the fact that Peni had called him an asshole. He couldn't stop. It would just sneak up on him at the oddest moments. Right during a transaction with a guest at the Meridian. While sitting down to eat lunch. Buying a lottery ticket at the local QT.

Peni had apologized, but it didn't matter. Asher would wake up thinking it. When he wasn't having trouble going to sleep without the word "asshole" banging around in his skull, that was. Peni! Who actually used the word "darn." *Peni* had called him an *asshole*! Even *if* he had said it in Samoan.

And Peni had called him that on the very heels of Guy and Nellie using the same word! And Wyatt too. It was like they'd all gotten together and decided on the word. Yes, that was paranoid and couldn't be true, but fuck! It would hit Asher right in the middle of a scene, and he would go completely blank and forget his lines. A prompt might not even help.

"What's going on?" Guy asked him during a break.

Asher had only shaken his head. He didn't want to think about it.

"You going to be able to do this? You've been off the last couple days...."

"I'll pull it together," Asher had snarled—and then heard his tone. *Heard* the *you're an asshole* echoing in his head, as well, and dropped his voice a few octaves. "Sorry."

Nellie: "You're an asshole, you know that Asher?"

Guy: "But frankly, Asher. You're an asshole."

Wyatt: "You a-are an asshole, A-Asher. You *are*!"

Then Peni on top of all that? Peni? Who used the word "darn"?

"...puki'o.... It means like... asshole."

If Asher hadn't known any better, he would have thought all of Wyatt's (and now Scott's?) witchy-woo-woo "Universe" stuff was real and that "someone" or "some*thing*" was trying to send him a message.

But no!

That was just silly. Ridiculous. A dumber idea than the one about them all getting together and choosing to call him an asshole.

He wasn't an asshole!

Jealousy.

It was jealousy.

Yeah. Peni was jealous. *Riiiiiggght!* He had *so* much to be jealous of! Why jealousy was just falling right out of his... asshole....

And now he was sitting in a movie theater watching a total crap movie, and why?

Because of Peni. He had come to a movie that he normally wouldn't be caught dead going to and all because he heard Peni was going.

Holy shit. I've turned into a teenage girl. One of those girls who used to giggle every time he walked—

(strutted)

—past them down the hall in high school.

He gave Peni a surreptitious look out of the corner of his eye, turning his head as little as possible. There was a sudden bright moment in the drab and dark movie and.... And he was struck by Peni's beauty.

Perfect.

Peni was perfect.

Please, he thought. *This can't happen to me. I will not act like this! I will not start fawning all over some pretty boy. I don't do that. I* won't *do that!*

That was power. That was giving *away* power.

I don't need anyone.

Never again.

So why did he let his knee ever so slightly lean up against Peni's? And why did his heart speed up? His cock begin to stir?

Because Peni is hot! I've never thought anything else. He is *hot!*

Then with a gasp, Asher suddenly and with full clarity remembered Peni dancing on the coruscating dance floor set up at Peter Wagner's huge Fourth of July celebration. The way Peni had moved. The way the light had played with his body.

Asher's cock grew to its full length and it was *not* a nice feeling. His hard-on was bending in the folded confines of his jeans, making him very uncomfortable. Asher didn't know what to do. If he adjusted himself, Peni would have to see. How embarrassing would that be?

So Asher endured. Finally, thankfully, the wretched film had a distracting effect on his libido, and his erection softened enough that he could shift and get it to move into a more comfortable position without his having to touch himself.

But he was sure to let his knee touch Peni's again. Juvenile it might be.

He liked it.

A lot.

CHAPTER THIRTEEN

OUT OF the blue, or it least it felt that way to Asher, Wyatt decided he wanted to get a tattoo.

Wyatt.

Big baby when it came to pain. *Big* baby.

Who'd once caused a scene worthy of a Tony when he got a splinter in the bottom of his foot. It had taken Sloan half an hour to get it out because Wyatt couldn't stop jerking his foot away. "*It hurts!*" he'd whined. It was all Asher had been able to do to keep from conking their bear over the head so Sloan could finish while Wyatt was unconscious.

As far as Asher was concerned, it was what Wyatt deserved, walking around barefoot on the rough floorboards in his (once) house. Getting them refinished was one of the things he kept saying he and Howard were going to get done, but never had. Now they never would, would they? Howard might. But not Howard *and* Wyatt.

Wyatt was also the guy who fainted last year at this time when he cut his finger carving a jack o' lantern.

Wyatt.

So the Fabulous Four gathered together to be his support and hold his hand. They did it on a Saturday when Asher wouldn't be working at the hotel or rehearsing.

Oh joy.

On the other hand, who else should be joining them? Why, Peni, of course.

"I asked him, guys," Wyatt explained. "He's been coming over most evenings, you know."

Asher knew. It wasn't like he could forget. It was a hot topic on Wyatt's Facebook page.

"Peni and I having pizza!"

"Peni and I watching *Shelter*! He loved it! I knew he would."

"Peni and I went bowling tonight! Damn is he good! He got four hole-in-ones, or whatever they're called!"

"Peni tripped and skinned the hell out of his knee, and—

Now that had snatched Asher's attention. Had Peni hurt himself badly?

"—it was bleeding like a bitch!—

Shit! Bleeding! Did he need to call and see if Peni was okay?

"—and I nearly passed out—

Of course he did! Absolutely no good in a crisis.

"—but Peni was right as rain! He just cleaned himself up and doused it with alchol and hydrogen peroside—

(Wyatt wasn't a great speller!)

"—and OW! God that must have hurt and he didn't even flinch! Boy, does he have a HIGH threshold of pain!"

If Asher didn't know better, he'd swear Wyatt was getting a crush on Peni. Asher didn't like it. It was silly, but he didn't.

Wyatt didn't tell them that Peni was joining them for the great inking ritual until they were standing outside the tattoo parlor. Peni had driven because Wyatt had been too afraid he might want to faint on the way home. "And after all, he's over all the time." Wyatt hugged Peni. Even kissed him lightly.

Asher stiffened at the sight.

Why should Wyatt *get to kiss him and I can't?*

"He's been making the place seem less empty."

It wasn't like the rest of the Fabulous Four weren't offering to be there for Wyatt.

Of course, Scott was practically in Cedar's back pocket and…. Well, look there! He was. Scott (Mr. Public-Displays-of-Affection-are-Disgusting) had his arm around Cedar—right there on Main St., Kansas City—and his hand in Cedar's back pocket!

Plus Sloan *was* at Wyatt's new place (Sloan's old place!) a lot, or having Wyatt over at his (his and Max's!) place.

And Asher couldn't be there for Wyatt except on the weekends. He was working at the Meridian during the days and rehearsing at night.

And dammit, why didn't Wyatt want some time alone? He'd been living day and night with his hulking, disgusting fuckwad husband for ten years. Wouldn't a normal person want some time to themselves?

But then could Wyatt ever be described as normal?

"I hope you don't mind that I'm here," Peni said to the group and then looked up at Asher with his big black eyes.

Asher almost gasped.

He had forgotten how beautiful Peni's eyes were, and why it was striking him this particular day, he wasn't sure. He also realized he didn't mind that Peni was joining them. Not one bit. He told Peni so.

"I'm just surprised he's doing it," Asher said.

"I know, right?" Peni agreed. "I had to hold his hand the other night so he could get a flu shot down at Walgreens. He almost fainted before they even got the syringe out."

"It didn't drive you crazy?" Asher asked.

Peni smiled. "I thought it was kind of charming. Wyatt is so sweet."

Sweet? You're calling him sweet?

"While the rest of the world is caught up in shootings and Ebola outbreaks, Wyatt's world is the fear of getting a vaccination. He lives in the moment. I admire that."

Asher had no idea how to respond. He came up with the first thing he could. "Do you think he'll faint today?"

"He might," Peni said as they were going into the tattoo parlor. "I hope they have a bed or a chair he can lie back on. Then all we have to do is distract him and make sure he doesn't watch what's going on."

"What's he getting?" asked Asher. He'd only heard about this whole tattoo thing the night before, although apparently it had been brewing all week long.

"A teddy bear," Wyatt answered and showed Asher a picture he must have printed out on his computer. Or Sloan's. Howard hadn't let Wyatt have the printer, but luckily, Sloan didn't need his. Max's was better anyway. Of course.

The picture was from a T-shirt site, showing the shirt and logo on an anonymous man's chest, the face off-camera. It was indeed a classic cartoon rendering of a teddy bear, with the words HUSBEAR MATERIAL in an arch over and under the picture.

"You're not getting the 'husbear material' are you?" Asher wanted to know.

"I don't see why not!" Wyatt exclaimed with what Asher detected as false bravado. He kept peeking over his shoulder, where a big butch woman with about a billion tattoos of her own was busily tattooing a man who looked like he should be on an episode of *Duck Dynasty* or a ZZ Top video. Wyatt seemed paler every time he looked.

"Because, silly bear," Sloan said, "you aren't going to be single for long! How do you think your future man is going to feel with you walking around with 'husbear material' on your arm?"

"*Hmmmm….*" Wyatt said, looking thoughtful and biting a thumb. "I could go with 'Hug me, squeeze me, tug at my fur.'"

"I think that's a little bit too much wordage," Asher said. "You're going to be going through enough with just the bear."

Wyatt gulped and paled further, if that was even possible. "B-but I want it to say *some*thing!"

They all looked at him blankly.

Wyatt looked a bit blank himself. "I could always go with a simple 'bears rule' or 'likes bears.'"

Asher shook his head, and the rest joined in.

"Should I remind you of a certain splinter?" Sloan asked.

Wyatt grimaced. "I guess 'save a horse, ride a bear' would be right out, then?"

"Let's save the words," Asher said, biting back exasperation. Shit. Would Wyatt be able to get more than an eyeball done? In fact, it was what he was going to suggest to the artist. If that was all Wyatt could get through, he could tell people it was a mole.

"So not even a 'woof!'?" Wyatt offered.

Once more all of them shook their heads. It might as well have been choreographed.

"So what are we getting done today?"

They all turned to see a big, bearish man who was so tall he stood over all of them except Asher. He didn't have as many tattoos as the butch woman, still buzzing away at her victim's arm, but he had quite a few—even one on his neck. Asher could never understand marking up parts of bodies that were always visible—

At least it's a faint one, Asher thought.

—and the big plugs in his earlobes, which Asher understood even less.

"H-hey," said Wyatt, already swaying.

Oh no, thought Asher. *And he hasn't even sat down yet.*

Peni put a hand on Wyatt's shoulder and gave it a squeeze, and Wyatt wordlessly handed the big man his picture.

Big Man looked down at it and gave a nod. "For you?"

Wyatt nodded.

The big guy looked down at him, a look of doubt on his face, then at the Fabulous Four plus One. "And you guys?" he asked.

"Moral support," Peni said before any of the rest of them could.

The big tattoo artist gave a "Fffff" sound, not quite a raspberry or snort of derision.

"Look," Asher said, surprising himself. "This is a big deal for him. Yes, he's scared. And he's probably going to faint. But we're proud of him for doing this. His fuckwad cheating husband just dumped him." He nodded at Wyatt. "Our friend here needs a badge."

Big Guy gave Asher a look of surprise and then nodded. "Yeah. Okay. I can grok that." He bobbed his head to the side. "This way. Come on."

He led them down a long hallway painted black and covered with drawings and photographs of tattoos. Asher clearly saw that Wyatt didn't spare any of them even a glance.

This could be a nightmare....

"I'm Nikko by the way," said the big bear as they went into a room with something that looked a lot like a dentist or barber's chair and a massage table.

"I'm W-Wyatt," said their little bear.

Without any of the derision Asher thought he had seen earlier, Nikko asked, "Where we doing this? Make me happy and tell me it's on your round sweet ass of yours."

Wyatt blushed furiously and then smiled. Without talking, Wyatt removed his jacket and pointed at his right upper arm, revealed because he was wearing a sleeveless T-shirt with the words, "I can do that tongue-thing with a cherry stem... just saying!" (complete with a big knotted red stem).

"We'll see about *that*," said Nikko with a bawdy smile.

"About what?" Wyatt asked.

The artist cocked his head at Wyatt's shirt.

Wyatt turned even redder. "Oh," he whispered. "*That*."

"Is it true?" Nikko said and pointed to the chair.

Wyatt sat down. He nodded.

Nikko waggled his eyebrows and went to a table and began to pull out his equipment. "What colors do we want this? Browns?"

Wyatt nodded again, but of course Nikko couldn't see that.

"Yes," Peni spoke up.

Nikko flashed Peni a look. "You the new boyfriend?"

Peni's eyes went wide. "Oh no!"

Wyatt laughed. "He's way too lean and smooth for me," Wyatt said. "Peni's a sister, not husbear material."

Nikko scanned the rest of them. Seemed to find something pleasing. "Good," he said.

He worked some more, then pulled up a chair. "You want me to photocopy this or can I just do my thing?"

"D-do y-your thing," Wyatt stuttered.

"Good. I'll do you proud, I promise."

Wyatt gave a halfhearted smile.

"Now I'm not gonna lie, little cub. This will hurt. But I'll let you rest now and then, okay? I don't want to do some girlie, tiny little thing. I'm going to make it a good six or seven inches."

A little whine escaped Wyatt's throat.

"But you do good, and I'll give you a reward that'll make you forget that shithead husband of yours in nothing flat, got it?" He winked at Wyatt, who promptly melted.

Asher smiled. He didn't know if Wyatt was going to get laid tonight or not (he suspected they would have to take Wyatt home and ply him with ice cream and other treats) but this Nikko was a good guy.

The artist looked up at the ensemble in the room. "We're a little tight in here for all of you to hold his hand. Why don't we do this in shifts?"

They all nodded, and Sloan stepped up. "Me first, all right, Wyatt?"

Asher sighed in relief, and as they filed out of the room, the buzzing of the tattoo gun started, and the last thing Asher heard was a "Now don't jump now, little cub, or I'll fuck this up, okay?"

He only hoped Wyatt had it in him.

CHAPTER FOURTEEN

"WE'RE GOING down the street to the bike shop," Cedar said, cocking his thumb at Scott. "You guys want to join us?"

Asher shook his head. "No, thanks. Not my thing."

Cedar looked at Peni, who shook his head as well. "Nah." The truth was, he wanted to stay here with Asher. You're *ulu kae*, he told himself.

Totally cracked in the head!

"The Radiant Cup isn't far from here," Asher said. "Want to get some coffee?"

"Should we go far?" Peni asked.

"We can get it to go," Asher offered.

"Okay," Peni answered quickly. Too quickly?

Asher started down the street, and Peni joined him.

"This one we're going to is the first shop," Asher said. "The one in Terra's Gate came second. It's not The Shepherd's Bean, but they're pretty damned good. And we can walk."

"Yeah. I guess Terra's Gate might take us a while?"

Asher laughed. "Enough time for Wyatt to get half his body tattooed!"

Yeah, Peni thought, and wondered what Asher would think of the Samoan pe'a.

The Radiant Cup was only about five blocks away and looked little like its sister location in Terra's Gate. This place wasn't as young or hip, but instead more middle class, more "metrosexual." As if reading his thoughts, Asher said, "The other place caters to the college crowd."

Peni nodded. Made sense. Terra's Gate owed its lifeblood to the students who attended Wagner University.

"What do you want?" Asher asked as they entered the shop, its inside all glass and brushed steel. "I'm buying."

"Nope. This isn't a date, Asher," Peni stated firmly. "I can buy my own."

Asher gave Peni an are-you-kidding-me look. "Really? You don't think me and the guys buy for each other all the time?"

"Well, I'm not really one of the guys, am I? It's the Fabulous Four, right? Not the Fabulous… well, I don't know how many counting boyfriends."

Asher winced. "Tell me about it."

That was in interesting reaction, Peni thought.

"I'll tell you what," Peni said. "I'll buy. You buy next time."

Asher shrugged. Was that a flicker of a smile Peni thought he saw? It made him want to smile as well.

Interesting.

"Okay," Asher said. "I'll take today's special. Black."

"Okay," Peni said and ordered two.

"The Shepherd's Bean is more true to the whole coffee movement," Asher said. "You can't get sugar or sweeteners or anything there. No tea. No chai tea. No cocoa. Sad to say that's why this place probably makes more money."

"I can't even drink cocoa when I go out," Peni said. "I'm too spoiled on Samoan cocoa."

"What's the difference?" Asher asked as the barista handed them their to-go cups.

Peni laughed. "There's a *big* difference!"

Asher put a tip in the jar set there for that purpose.

Peni looked at him funny. "I gave a tip," he said.

"Sorry," Asher replied. "I can't help it. I've waited too many tables. It's automatic." He pointed to a table. "We can sit for a few minutes, right?"

"Sure," Peni answered and took a small table in the corner.

"Now tell me about this cocoa of yours."

Peni smiled. Ah, the memories. "We call it kokosamoa. It makes your cocoa taste like water. It is very sweet and very dark. Thick, even. It's hard to explain. Maybe I can make you some sometime. Mine can't touch my grandmother Ioana's, though."

Asher gave Peni a smile that made his breath catch. "I'd like that," Asher said.

Breathe, Peni, he told himself.

"What do you think of that Nikko guy?" Asher asked, taking a cautious sip of his coffee.

"Well, I think it was sweet he was flirting with Wyatt. It's going to help him. Do you think the guy meant it? The flirting, I mean?"

"He meant it," Asher said. "I can tell when a man means it." He winked at Peni.

Now what did that mean?

"I just don't understand the tats on his neck and the big holes in his ears," Asher said, shaking his head. "What do these guys do when they're not working at head shops or tattoo parlors? Don't they think for one minute how fucking stupid they're going to look when they're fifty or sixty?"

Peni stiffened. "I guess they don't think that far ahead." What would Asher think of his family?

"I mean, I get the tattoo thing, I guess. Some guys look fucking hot with them actually."

Peni breathed a sigh of relief.

"I wouldn't get one, though."

"Why not?" Peni asked.

"Because I want to be a *star*, Peni. I dream of being on that huge screen being watched my countless people. Having fans, even." He held his hands up, flat in front of him, as if visualizing the screen he was talking about. "Actors with tattoos?" He lowered his hands. "It can be a bitch. Either the director just goes with it or he has them covered up. But what about shower scenes? Hot tubs? Swimming?"

"You want to do shower scenes?" Peni asked.

Asher raised an eyebrow. "Why not? I work out all the time, just in case I have a nude scene."

Peni felt the heat of a blush. "I could never do that," he said. Of course if he ever… ever dared… to get the pe'a…. Why…. Wouldn't there be a bunch of men looking at his most private of places?

"I think it might be hot," Asher said. "I sure like seeing my faves naked. Thought I'd pop my eyes out when Michael Fassbender did that full-frontal scene in *Shame*! Damn, is that guy hung!"

Peni blushed even more. "So you like guys with big… you know?"

Asher grinned. "Dicks? Ah, come on, Peni. You can say dick, can't you?"

And now the hot glow of his embarrassment was burning. "Dick!" he said defiantly and then laughed.

"How do you say it in Samoan?" Asher asked.

"*Poki*," Peni said, thinking he would die he was becoming so embarrassed.

"And how would you say…." Asher stopped. His expression changed. "I'm sorry."

Peni looked at Asher in surprise. Was *Asher* blushing?

"I really am. I'm being a… what did you say? Paw-law-ge pu-ko?"

Peni looked away, felt a wash of shame. "Pa-lawn-gi pu-key oh. And it's not nice, Asher. Not the first word. I told you. It's almost like the N-word. Or it can be. And the next word…. We don't really have *nice* words for some things. Samoans just do it. We're a very sensual people. Or at least we're supposed to be. We just make love instead of talking about it."

But when he looked back, Asher was looking away. "I'm sorry, again, Peni. I don't know why I even asked. Guess I thought I was being clever or something. It's the way most men want me to talk to them."

Peni looked at him in surprise. "Really?" Then thinking about it, *Well, of course they do, you idiot!* Embarrassed as he'd been, wasn't there a part of him that was liking it too?

"Wyatt's always saying I'm a slut. That I take men to bed and then throw them out. But you know what? The truth is, most of those men don't want anything else. They just want to be able to say they got Asher Eisenberg into bed. And to see if I really do have as big a—" He stopped, and this time he did blush.

Which got Peni off track. Because now he was wondering again….

"I suppose Sloan has told you all about how we met? And how I broke his heart?"

Peni gave a single nod. What was he supposed to do? Lie?

"Well, I'll tell you something I've never told anyone."

Peni held his breath. What could this be about?

"If I had ever maybe fallen in love, it would have been with Sloan."

It took everything out of Peni not to react. God. And Sloan didn't have a clue.

"Right from the start. He was so sweet. So innocent. Naïve, you know?"

Peni thought perhaps he *did* know.

"But the thing is? I *liked* him right from the start. I found myself telling him things. Things that I don't talk about. And it scared the shit out of me."

Peni's mouth opened. It would have fallen open, but somehow he stopped it and quickly took a sip of coffee.

"And I knew I would mess it up. I'd fuck up. So I tried to get rid of him. But within a few days, I couldn't stand it. So I called him. Told him we could only be friends.... Is that the way he told it?"

Peni gave another slight nod. "Well, pretty much."

It was Asher's turn to nod. "Well, what he might not know is that I made up my mind right then that I would keep myself from feeling too much. Because I was afraid to do more. Afraid I would mess it up. And I knew if we were friends, I could have the best of both worlds." Asher's eyes were strange and wild for a moment, and Peni, surprised at his words, reached out and touched Asher's hand. Asher looked down at Peni's hand, almost as if he didn't know what it was. "Don't tell him, okay, Peni? Besides, there's no need now, is there? Sloan has found someone."

Was that bitterness Peni heard? There at the end?

Was Asher in love with Sloan?

Asher looked up. "You want to know what is really stupid?"

Peni didn't know what to say. So instead he just gave him a nod of encouragement.

"I don't think I knew just how much Sloan meant to me until I saw him with Max. When I couldn't have him the way I know Sloan wanted me for so long, I was shocked. I don't know what I've been doing all this time, but maybe it was some dumbass thing like I was holding him in reserve or something! Like when I was finally ready, he would just be waiting for me.... Pretty fucked up, huh?"

Peni sighed. He almost nodded again. Because it was pretty messed up. But maybe.... "I guess it's human," he said aloud. "As humans we do some messed up things." Like going home with Bobby Brubaker. Almost going home with some nameless guy at a bar a few weeks ago. Getting so drunk he tried to take Sloan's pants off! And then asked if he and Max wanted—

"But it's better this way, don't you think? Because Sloan deserves love. He shouldn't have to wait until I get my shit together."

"But what about you?" Peni blurted.

Asher stopped.

"Don't you deserve love?" he asked.

Asher took a deep breath. "I don't know," he said very quietly. "I also don't know if I trust it. Because sometimes people you love, and who you think love you back, stop loving you."

Peni bit his lower lip. Gosh. That sounded….

"We should be getting back, don't you think?" Asher asked abruptly and stood up.

"Ah, sure," Peni said.

They headed out the door and then south, back toward the tattoo parlor. Then Asher was talking about the tattoo artist again. It was such an abrupt change of subject, it took Peni a minute to get what he was saying.

"I mean, what's the guy ever going to do if he wants a serious job? Or to run for office? What's a teacher or principle going to think when he shows up for his kid's parent-teacher conference? And you know he gets shit from cops all the time."

"I… I don't think he cares."

Asher shook his head.

"So I guess I'm not following. You think tattoos are hot, or you don't?"

"I think they can be *way* hot. I just don't think people should have them where they show. Like on their hands or even their lower arms. You can't hide them if you need to—and sometimes you would need to. That guy, Nikko. He has one of the left side of his neck. And those big ugly ear holes. If a cop stops him, that's the first thing he is going to see—and he's quite likely to give the guy shit about it. Now the ones you can cover with a shirt, that's different. You can show those off when you want to."

"And the legs?" Peni asked, afraid of the answer.

"That can be hot too."

Peni let out a breath he didn't know he'd been holding. "My people…. They believe that the *tatau*—the tattoo—is… like… spiritual. As a matter of fact, it is pretty much believed that the word tattoo *comes* from the Samoan word *tatau*."

Asher looked at him. "Really? I didn't know that. That's pretty cool."

"My father and my father's father—they had the pe'a."

"Pay-ah?"

"The tatau—the tattoos—that start at the waist…" Peni put his hands at his waist. "…and go down the back and front all the way down to the knees." He moved his hands down as if to show Asher lines that were there, but weren't.

Peni's stomach went cold. And in that moment, he saw something quite clearly....

Asher stopped. "Are you okay?"

Peni had to make himself talk. Pull himself out of the shock of his realization. And how stupid he felt for not realizing it already.

He wasn't attracted to men who *had* the pe'a.

"Peni?"

Peni swallowed hard. Walked on.

"It's a very big deal to us. It's tradition. Important. Not everyone is supposed to get them, but these days anyone can. But chiefs. And sons of chiefs. They are *supposed* to get them. It takes *days*, and it is horribly painful."

"Because it's so big?"

"Because they don't use guns. At least they're not supposed to. They use these sharp tools that they dip in ink. They looks like teeny-tiny little rakes. And then they take a little mallet and hammer the little spikes—like grooves—into the skin. And it goes deep. Into the muscle. And you bleed a lot. People have died."

"*Died?*" Asher asked, visibly paling.

Peni nodded. "My grandfather Afona's brother died getting his."

Asher stopped, reached out, and leaned on a lamppost. "How?"

"Afona told me it was blood loss, for one thing. They do it straight through. It takes several days. It took my father four days to get his."

"Four days?" exclaimed Asher.

Peni nodded, started walking. He needed to walk. "He used to tell me the story. He always told it that same. '*Four days*,'" Peni said, lowering his voice, trying the accent—*trying* to sound like Afona. "*Four* twelve-*hour days*." Peni could hear Afona in his head. "*No breaks*."

"No breaks?" Asher said, unknowingly echoing Peni's childhood words.

Peni gave Asher Afona's quick shake of the head. "*No breaks*."

"Then why would anyone do it?"

"It is a symbol of manhood, Asher."

"Oh. And that is still important these days?"

"It is to *me*!" Peni looked away. "My people have forgotten our ways. They've embraced the Mormon god and forgotten about *our* gods. It makes me sad."

Asher nodded. "I think—I think maybe I can understand. It made my grandfather very sad that my mother rejected Judaism."

Peni looked back up at Asher, not sure he *did* understand.

But it looked like maybe he was trying.

"It sounds like *you're* thinking of—" Asher began.

"Hey guys!" came a cry, breaking into their conversation.

They turned as one and saw Max standing there. "Hey," Peni said.

"Wyatt was just asking about you. I said I'd look to see if you were back."

"Is it our shift?" Asher asked.

"Well, I think you're going to be surprised. Nikko's already got the line work done. Now he's just giving poor old Wyatt a rest before he starts filling in. I think that's the part that's really going to hurt."

"Somehow I doubt that," Asher said, looking at Peni knowingly. "At least not as much as it could."

"What?" Max asked.

"Never mind," said Asher.

Then together he and Peni went inside to help Wyatt get through his own ordeal.

"It's fitting," Peni said to Asher quietly as they went down the hall. "Samoans help their friends get through theirs. They sit with them and talk to them. Sing to them. Urge them on. Make sure they eat."

"Eat?"

"Yes," Peni said. "Because you don't want to eat. And when you don't eat, you don't replenish the blood. My grandfather says that's why his brother died."

"Wow," Asher said as they entered the little room where Wyatt was getting *his* tattoo. "So do you think we should get Wyatt something to eat?" He grinned.

"I would just throw it up!" groaned Wyatt.

"Ah, you're doing fine, champ," said Nikko.

So then Asher and Peni stood next to their friend, and Sloan left, giving Wyatt a little kiss on the cheek.

And they helped Wyatt through the pain.

CHAPTER FIFTEEN

THIS TIME they all went to see *Gone Girl*. It beat *Dracula Untold* hands down. Thankfully, even Wyatt agreed.

"It's a toss-up," Wyatt said, "who is hotter, though. Ben Affleck or Luke Evans."

They went out for ice cream at Glacé after the movie. Asher didn't indulge in many fattening foods. He had his body to think of, and his body might very well one day be all but naked on huge movie screens. But Glacé was something else again. Only the best he'd ever had.

Who ever heard of French Lavender ice cream? Yet it was beyond marvelous. It was perfection.

Today, of course, the flavor of the week was Spiced Pumpkin. No surprise. And no surprise that when he asked for a taste, he practically got goose bumps.

"You have to try this, Peni," he said and asked for a second tiny spoonful. Then without even realizing what he'd done, he turned and held it out for Peni. Not so he could take the spoon in his hand, but so that he practically had to take the offered ice cream into his mouth.

Asher froze.

What had he done?

His cheeks warmed, and he knew he must be blushing. Were Wyatt and Sloan and the rest looking?

Please have them be too busy picking out their own.

"Well, isn't *that* cute?" Wyatt said, and Asher knew that at least one of his friends hadn't been too busy to notice what he'd just done. How karmic was it that *Wyatt* was the one to see? Wyatt, who usually by this time should have been trying to climb over the counter and *into* the buckets of ice cream in the cooler.

Asher found himself, eyes locked with Peni, unable to move and felt his cheeks heat up all the more. Then, just as he was about to lower his hand, Peni leaned in, opened his mouth—

Look at those lips!

—and closed it over the end of the spoon, his lips—

What would those lips feel like against his own?

—less than an inch from Asher's fingertips.

Peni closed his eyes and smiled in what could only be pleasure.

What would he look like if he and I were engaging in a totally different kind of pleasure?

Peni's pink tongue tip—contrasting deliciously with the brown of his skin—slipped out and flicked away the minute bit of dark orange that clung to his upper lip.

Asher found he wished he could have been the one to do it for him.

Peni chose a combination of Coconut Lime and Grapefruit Hibiscus sorbets.

"Cliché, right?" Peni said with what might have been a blush, but his lovely complexion was just a *tad* too dark for Asher to be sure.

"Who gives a shiiii…," Asher said, then edited himself to finish with, "shoot." He also caught the incredulous look on Wyatt's face.

Asher couldn't help it; he had to get the French Lavender and Goat Cheese & Wildflower Honey. He was all for trying new things, but how could he walk out without having the lavender?

He had been so close to getting the Butterscotch Bourbon but suddenly wondered if Peni would consider it a break from their bet. Decided not to have it, just in case.

I can do this. It'll be a breeze.

But it hadn't been, had it?

The last few days had been a bitch. Who knew that *not* having something to drink would be so hard? And it wasn't that he *needed* alcohol—

I don't. I don't need booze. I like booze. There's a difference. For Mom, it's coffee. Sloan likes a Diet Coke. Me? I like a cocktail!

—it was just habit. He reached for the liquor cabinet automatically, like some people reached into the refrigerator for milk.

Habit is all….

Why, he'd mixed a gin and tonic the first night, and the rim of the glass had touched his lips when he quite suddenly realized what he was doing.

He almost drank it anyway.

After all, how would Peni ever know?

"I guess I'll have to trust you."

Shit, damn, fuck!

Asher had found he couldn't do it. He'd brought that glass to his mouth two more times, but in the end, he didn't drink it.

But what a crime to pour it down the sink! What was one cocktail?

Alcohol abuse is what Wyatt would call it.

Would it be cheating to get high? he wondered the next night. He was pretty sure he had a little pot around the apartment somewhere. Asher wasn't big on pot. He'd never really liked it, which surprised him considering that so many people he knew claimed it made sex so much better.

"Orgasms are frippin' mind-blowing," Wyatt had said on more than one occasion.

But for Asher, altering sex with marijuana was akin to covering a steak with A1 sauce. It didn't make the steak better, it only covered up the flavor. When it was a good steak, why would you want to fucking cover up the flavor? Sure, marijuana might make some bummer sex better, but why take a chance? Besides, how often had *he* had bad sex?

Asher liked to think that he inspired men in the sack. That even a man who might have been a lousy lay for others rose to the challenge of being the best they could when they got Asher in their bed.

Foolish dreams of getting a second chance with Asher? Probably. Almost certainly. How many men got that?

Sloan was the only one he could really think of.

Jim, the bartender at the Meridian, didn't really count. That morning-after sex in the shower was just a bit of leftovers from the main course the night before.

Somehow, though, Asher thought it might, just might, be different with Peni.

Somehow, it was becoming clear that getting Peni in his bed would be the biggest challenge of his sexual career.

But after that look from Peni with those huge black eyes across the seemingly endless expanse of a tiny plastic taster spoon at Glacé, Asher thought it might just be worth the effort.

CHAPTER SIXTEEN

PENI AND Wyatt were at the Halloween Shop downtown. Wyatt was excited. Peni? He was nervous, and he wasn't even sure why.

"So Mormons can celebrate Halloween?" Wyatt asked while studying a wall of masks. The store had everything imaginable.

Peni nodded. "Just as long as we're not celebrating the pagan holiday. You know that the whole 'trick or treat' started to appease evil spirits that supposedly congregated on the evening prior to All Saints' Day? If they knocked on your door, you had to give them a treat so they wouldn't 'trick' you by putting a curse on you."

Wyatt smirked at him. "The evil spirits or the trick or treaters?"

Peni opened his mouth, then realized he wasn't sure of the answer.

"You do know Halloween is like, my most important holiday, right?" Wyatt asked.

Peni nodded. "I do."

"I hope you don't think I'm evil or someth—"

"No!" Peni said. In fact…. "Just the opposite. I think it is pretty cool. I like that you're honoring a different way."

Wyatt smiled happily. It was nice to see Wyatt smile. The past weeks had been tough on the little bear.

"We call it Samhain, though. It's like our new year. It's considered the time when the veil between life and death grows thinnest."

"Um…." He wasn't sure what to say to that.

"We have a big feast and dance around these huge bonfires. It's all to honor our ancestors."

That caught Peni's attention. Ancestors? "Really? That sounds pretty cool. Are you going to one of those bonfires?"

Wyatt sighed. Looked away. "I don't think so. Going to do it the modern American way. I just don't know who I'll bump into if I go to the places I usually go…."

Which meant Wyatt was afraid to bump into Howard or someone who would ask him where Howard was. That Peni could understand. He'd been asked about Bobby for weeks, and they'd only gone out for a week. Not even that—if "going out" is what you call what they did. He decided to change the subject.

"You know, I'm surprised you don't have a costume already," Peni said. "Sloan says you usually work for weeks and weeks on what you're going to wear."

Wyatt froze. He sighed. "I do. But it's a couple's costume." He bit his lower lip. "Howard and I always did a couple's costume."

Oh no, thought Peni. *I've gone right in and stuck my foot into it.*

"Howard was actually going to let me be Little Red Riding Hood, and he was going to be the Big Bad Wolf. Of course, I was going to boy it up. I wasn't doing drag. Howard wouldn't let me do that."

He sighed and Peni saw the tears welling up again. *I've ruined everything*, thought Peni.

"It was going to be pretty hot. Me in the big red velvet cloak, and underneath, a black leather jockstrap and harness and boots and everything. And Howard.... The same but no cloak, you know? And a big huge wolf mask. We even got a *werewolf* one instead...." A single tear started down his cheek.

"Gosh, Wyatt. I'm sorry." He felt like crap.

Then Wyatt took a deep sigh, looked at Peni, wiped his face, and shrugged. "Nope! I am not going to cry. We are going to have a blast Friday night, okay?"

Peni smiled. "You bet."

So they looked. They looked and looked. Wyatt thought about and then rejected many ideas. Harry Potter. "It would be appropriate, but there'll be a million of them, even with the movies all over with." An orange prison costume. "Orange *is* the new black." Wyatt laughed. "Of course there will be a million of these too."

They found themselves in an aisle of women's costumes. "You know, I could do one of these," Wyatt postulated. "Howard isn't around to tell me I can't do drag. What do you say? I could be Maleficent." He pointed to an elaborately dressed manikin. "I've always loved Maleficent." He checked the price tag and then visibly paled. "Oh. No. Not this year. Not on my new budget." A sad look came to his face.

Tough. This was going to be tough.

"Hey!" Wyatt grinned again. "*Frozen*! I can be Elsa the Snow Queen." Again he checked the price tag, and again he shook his head. "Gods. These prices are crazy!" He sighed. Looked at Peni. "What are you going to be? You're not even looking."

Peni blushed. "Well, I have an idea. It's a little crazy."

"What?" Wyatt asked excitedly.

Peni shrugged, looked both ways (as if anyone were listening, as if anyone cared), and then told Wyatt.

The bear's eyes went wide and a huge grin spread over his face. "Oh my gods! I love it!"

"You do?"

Wyatt nodded. "Oh yes!"

"It's not going to be easy. I mean, there are places a little hard to reach."

Wyatt waggled his eyebrows. "I could help."

Peni blushed even more.

"Oh, come on!" Wyatt exclaimed. "You know you're not my type. I won't be ogling you… much."

Now Peni was really blushing.

"I say you do it! Now let's find me something, and then let's get the hell out of here!"

That sounded like a good idea.

ASHER STOOD in front of the mirror and examined himself.

He looked hot.

He looked really hot.

But what would Peni think? Would it turn him on? Or off? Would Peni think he was sexy? Or some kind of slut?

Asher turned to the side, letting the black cape flow around him. God. He could almost turn himself on. He was Batman.

Of course, a very naughty Batman.

Because there wasn't much to the costume. There was the classic mask and cape, of course. But then it was a black leather harness onto which he'd affixed a yellow leather oval and then painted the bat symbol. Teeny-tiny black leather shorts and big black boots. And gloves, of course.

They'll be drooling the minute I walk in the door, he thought. *I'll be able to have any man I want.*

Except the only man he wanted was Peni.

How crazy was that?

He, Asher Eisenberg, wanting only one man. Crazy.

But he couldn't deny it.

Asher did a sudden turn and let the cape swirl around him again. *I'd fuck you*, Asher thought. *If I got fucked, that is.*

And if it wasn't Peni he really wanted to fuck.

I wonder what Peni will be wearing.

Probably something that covered every inch of his body. Too bad. Asher really wanted to see some of that body, even if he never got to see all of it.

I guess I'll just have to wait and see....

CHAPTER SEVENTEEN

"I NEED booze," Asher said. "You want a beer?"

"Don" shrugged. "How are we going to get beer? No one delivers out here. There might be a Heineken in the minifridge for fifty bucks." He pointed to the tiny hotel refrigerator next to the bar.

Asher lifted a brow, smirked at his fellow actor, and then walked out the door on the stage set. He picked up the cases of beer waiting for him on a table just off set as he overheard Louis—playing the character of playwright Don—say, "He brought beer?"

Of course I did, thought Asher. Would anyone be able to tell his character, Matt, that he *couldn't* drink? He waited an appropriate minute and then lugged the cases—or pretended to, most of the beer cans were empty—through the door and back onstage. It was an amazing set. Jennifer Leavitt never allowed anything less on one of her stages. It not only made it better for the audience to believe in what they were seeing, even if it was only for a couple of hours, but it allowed the actors to totally immerse themselves in their parts. Stage magic!

Asher put the pile of beer cases on the coffee table in front of the couch, pretending that they were heavier than they were. He even threw in a grunt. Various cast members had brought them in and they'd filled them with Styrofoam to hold the shape since the top case did have beer and really was heavier. Empty cases would have been crushed. He looked at "Don" and "Cindy." Smiled.

"What the fuck?" recited Don.

"Wait," Asher returned. "There's more."

He walked off set again as….

Don: "Um…. Want a beer?"

Cindy: "No thanks."

Asher returned to the stage with a box of liquor bottles. "Here," he said and placed them next to the beer. Held up a finger. "Ice!" The script hadn't called for extra emphasis on the word, but he liked the sound of it, and Guy hadn't told him otherwise. Once more he walked off set. He loitered for a moment, waiting for his fellow cast members to reveal that they too had brought alcohol—Melanie's character Cindy, eight bottles of wine, and Louis's Don providing Jack Daniels, Red Stag, Tanqueray, *and* absinthe.

It was so ridiculous, it was funny. Asher knew the audience would be laughing.

Why, it was a Porch Night for the Fabulous Four!

Asher smiled. Caught it.

Of course we *don't drink* that *much*—

"You already have an erection" came Cindy's line, Asher's cue to return to set.

—*do we*? he wondered and then hustled onstage with a big cooler. There was no ice in it tonight. There would be during the performance.

He began to empty beer from the top cardboard case—"Pabst Blue Ribbon Beer—This One Has The Touch!" was printed along its sides—and put them into the cooler. *It has the touch all right*, thought Asher. *The touch of death.* He shuddered at the idea of drinking any of it, and then.... To his surprise he found himself *wanting* a taste.

I've completely flipped. No one wants *to drink Pabst! You only wind* up *drinking Pabst because you can't afford anything else!*

At least with Miller you got the supposed "champagne of beers."

Asher finished what he was doing and looked back up. "Come on," he said with a side-toss of his head. "There's more outside."

So then they all left the stage and then all returned with more coolers. These characters loved to drink.

They make me look like a lightweight!

He took one of the empties that he had purposely left at the top of the cooler, pretended to open it, and sat down on the couch. He pretended to drain it—

...and God, he could smell the beer! He was sure they'd rinsed them all out, but he could smell it and felt the sudden inexplicable urge to grab one of the real beers from the cooler....

—then crushed the can and tossed it over the back of the couch.

"Yeah... nice one" came the voice of Guy from the darkened theater.

Asher reached into the cooler and grabbed a second beer, pretended to open it. Thought of all the beers he'd downed just that fast. Funny, you didn't think about it when you were actually doing it.

Unless you were showing off or something. Hadn't his father done that enough times in Asher's boyhood?

(*"Asher, go get your dad another one...."*)

He handed a beer to Louis/Don and then offered one to Melanie/Cindy. When she didn't take it right away (and he didn't give her much time), he said, "Come on!"

Melanie snatched it out of his hand, acted out popping it open, and then as she went to slug it back, Guy suddenly stepped into the light from the stage.

"Hold it a minute, everybody."

They stopped and looked down at their director.

"You know we haven't really talked about this, but the night that we perform this.... Well, you know we're going to have to have some real beers up there, right?"

"Huh?" Asher looked down at Guy in surprise.

Melanie nodded. "Yeah. Makes sense."

"You want us to actually drink?" Asher asked. "You *do* know how much booze we're supposed to be drinking up here, right? You want us *really* throwing up?"

Guy shook his head. "No. But that first one? Yes, I want you to have *one* real beer. What's *one* beer going to do? Hell, it's Pabst! What is it? Four? Five percent alcohol?"

Asher froze.

Wait a minute....

Four or five percent *alcohol*....

"This is 4.74 percent," Louis said, looking at his can. "But that's not the point, Guy! It's *Pabst!*"

"Which is certainly better than Milwaukee's Best," Guy countered.

"Wait," Asher said, speaking up before he was sure what he was going to say. "You really want us to drink? *Really?*"

Guy nodded. "Just the first one or so. I want that *pop!* sound. That hiss. I want the audience thinking, 'Holy shit! They're really drinking up there!' The booze will all be tea or lemonade or whatever, depending. But I want to start things off with that sound. It'll grab them. Make it real. Come on guys, you won't get drunk on one beer."

"Oh for God's sake, Peni," Asher heard himself saying. *"It's one beer."*

And while that still echoed in his head, *"You go thirty days without a drink"* came Peni's voice. *"Without so much as a glass of wine with dinner...."*

"Yeah.... Okay," Melanie said.

Louis nodded. "All right. But this is only under protest. I mean... *Pabst?*"

Then Asher heard himself agreeing, as if he were somewhere else, listening to an actor instead of *being* the actor. It was only one beer. It was onstage. Surely that didn't break the terms of his deal—his bet, whatever it was—with Peni, did it?

(*"...and I will go out with you...."*)

So they went on, and Asher pretended to drink beers—Guy hadn't suggested they drink real ones while rehearsing, after all—and Asher continued to *smell* the beer rising from the supposedly washed cans, and it smelled wonderful and... and then he had a thought so *huge* he froze and lost another line.

My God.... I can't be.... I can't be an alcoholic. I can't *be!*

Yet here he sat, and every time he raised a can to his mouth, he smelled that beer and could almost taste it. Wanted it more every time.

No. No.... Please no.... I can't be one of those pathetic....

"Asher!" cried Guy, and he snapped to, realizing he'd been lost in thought.

"G-Guy?" he sputtered.

"Are you okay?"

"S-sure...," he said. And then, acting, "Sure. Of course I am." He nodded. "Sorry, everyone. I just got an insight to my character."

"Oh," sneered Melanie. "Care to enlighten *us*?"

Asher started to shake his head, and then the words came out instead. "Matt.... My character.... He's an alcoholic."

Melanie rolled her eyes. "Oh, really? You're just now putting that together? Jesus Christ! And here we've all been told you're brilliant!"

"Mel," said Guy. "Let's be nice, huh?"

Like that was possible.

"Some of us would like to get out of here," Melanie said. "It is Halloween after all!"

"Sorry, guys...." Guy looked around the stage. "I know you want to have fun tonight. But come on. The bars aren't going to fill up until at least ten anyway. You'll have plenty of time."

Everyone nodded. Gave him their okays. He was right. They had plenty of time.

But in that second, Asher had forgotten about Halloween. Forgotten about the party. He was realizing two things.

That *he* just might be an alcoholic. And—

"I almost had somebody quit when they found out you had taken the role," Guy's voice said in his head.

—that he knew who had almost quit.

How had he missed it? In that moment, that second, he could see the utter contempt on her face.

God. She hates me!

But that look was only on her face for seconds and then gone, fast enough that in his confusion, Asher could have read it wrong.

Hoped he'd read it wrong.

He took a deep breath and banished echoes and thoughts from his head and allowed Matt to possess him.

Then when they were done for the night and Guy congratulated them on a great rehearsal—

Did Melanie glare at him? Asher wondered.

—and declared that they all needed some *real* beer and hauled out some Boulevard Bob's '47 Oktoberfest—

(*real* beer!)

—and when Asher's mouth was quite abruptly watering, it hit him and he knew….

Fuck me.

I….

I might be a fucking alcoholic!

Please, no.

"I know, I know," Guy said. "You want to get out of here. But you all can have one beer with me, right?"

Asher took the beer nonetheless, pretended to drink it—once, twice—then put it down. Guy was leaving the room, and Asher followed him.

"Guy?"

They were in a darkened hallway, and the director turned. "Mind if I take a quick pee?"

"No," Asher said and didn't mind at all. He didn't even know for sure what he was going to say. The pee gave him a moment to gather his thoughts. Although he still didn't know just what he was going to say until it started tumbling out of his mouth....

"Guy," he said when the director came out of the little bathroom.

Guy leaned against the brick wall and folded his arms over his chest. "Yes?"

"Ummm.... About that beer. I—I don't know if I can do it."

Guy tilted his head, gave Asher a curious look. "Why?"

Asher swallowed hard.

Just say you have a bet with Peni....

Oh, yeah. Like Guy is going to care about a bet!

So what do I say? That I think I might be a....

Asher stepped close so that he was only inches from Guy. "I... I think I might...." To his shock Asher felt like he might cry.

Fuck! Fuck fuck fuck!

"G-Guy...."

Guy reached out and touched Asher's arm. "It's okay, Asher. Say it."

Say it?

Say *that*?

"Guy...." And once more he was in the audience, *listening* to himself. It was the only way he could say it. "I can't drink."

One of Guy's brows rose slowly.

"I've realized something tonight...."

The brow lowered back into place, and Guy nodded slowly. Sighed. "You've realized you're an alcoholic."

No! Asher wanted to scream. *No!*

And the tears did well up. Filled his eyes, and if he didn't do fucking *something*, he was going to cry!

He shook his head. Then stopped. That look on Guy's face! Why.... Was that... sympathy?

It was almost enough to make Asher lash out at the man. But then....

Why am I angry? Why should he be angry with Guy?

That look! Contempt?

No.... It wasn't contempt. Sympathy *was* exactly what it was.

But could he stand to have someone look at him that way? Sympathy meant weakness!

"That's why Jennifer didn't want you for this part, Asher. She's suspected it for some time."

What?

"But you said it was because I'm an…." *Asshole.*

Guy shrugged. "That too. But the real thing was she was afraid you'd get fucked up and not be able to do the show."

Asher almost fell. He leaned up against the wall for support so he *didn't* fall. He was still weak in the knees, though.

Weak! I'm weak!

"We'll print up some kind of labels," Guy said. "Laminate them so we can put them in the cooler. We don't want the ink to run…." He was nodding.

"But won't they see? The audience?"

"We'll make it just yours. It's one or two cans. We'll move you right to the bottles…."

Why? Why are you doing this?

"Won't Melanie bitch?"

Guy shrugged again. "She might. Who cares? Melanie *is* a bitch."

Asher almost laughed despite himself.

Then: "Why… why are you doing this, Guy?"

One corner of Guy's mouth flicked upward. He sighed, squeezed Asher with a hand that Asher became conscious had never left.

"Because I'm proud of you, Asher. And I want you in this show. You are a great actor. You are going to blow this city away when they see you do this role."

God, thought Asher as tears threatened again. As he used that name once more.

"And fuck. We go into production in a week and a half. I can hardly replace you at this point." He grinned.

Asher gave a half laugh.

Then concern took over Guy's face. "Unless…."

"Un—unless?" Asher asked.

"Can you do it, Asher? Pretending to drink night after night. Acting drunk? Can you get through three weeks of that? And *not* drink?"

"I can for at least a week," Asher said and didn't explain about how a certain thirty days was almost over.

Guy raised both brows. "I need you for three."

Asher nodded. "I can do it," he said.

Because he *had* to.

That's all there was to it.

CHAPTER EIGHTEEN

PENI STOOD in front of the mirror and surveyed what he and Wyatt had done.

He could hardly believe what he was seeing.

I look hot. He'd never thought of himself that way. Not once. But tonight?

They'll be drooling the minute I walk in the door showing this much skin, he thought. *I'll be able to have any man I want.*

Except the only man he wanted was Asher.

How crazy was that?

He wanted Asher Eisenberg. Only the worst possible choice of a man ever. If he got involved with Asher, it was only going to be Bobby Brubaker all over again. Asher would tire of him and cast him aside. Asher didn't do lovers. Everyone knew that.

But he couldn't deny it.

Asher was who he wanted.

"Goddammit, but you are fucking hot!" Wyatt exclaimed.

Peni blushed. But wow…. He did look good, didn't he? He looked over his shoulder and saw Wyatt grinning. "Stop looking at my butt!"

"Then cover it up, darlin'! Cover it up."

Peni held out his hand. "Come on. Give me that sarong."

"Can I look just one more minute?" Wyatt asked.

"Wyatt!"

His friend laughed. "Okay, okay."

He handed Peni the colorful piece of fabric, and Peni quickly tied it around his waist. Then he looked back into the mirror once more. Gosh. It was amazing. He looked so real.

He turned so the cloth swirled around him.

Yes. Just enough was revealed without showing too much. He'd let Wyatt go a little crazy, but then who knew what would show on the dance floor? It had to be perfect.

"It's perfect," Wyatt said.

"You really think so?" Peni asked, even more pleased.

"Honey, if I liked smooth skinny boys, I'd be trying to bend you over right now."

Peni laughed. "Whatever!" He turned back to his friend. "Now you! Get dressed! We have a party to go to!"

LUCKILY, THE Halloween party the gang had chosen was the big charity event at the midtown VFW hall. That meant when Asher got out of the Pegasus and back to his apartment, he only had to shower and scramble into his costume, and the party was almost close enough to walk to. But not in his outfit! Unseasonably warm as it was, it was just not an October outfit! While the VFW hall wasn't a bar, if it was anything like the last two years' Valentine's Day events, the place would be packed. And since it was Halloween, Asher was betting the choice of clothing wouldn't be tuxedos!

It didn't take Asher long to get ready. He had only one brief moment of worry.

What would Peni think and…

…what about the booze?

What the hell would it be like going to a Halloween party and *not* drinking?

Crazy.

Would he have to live a life without alcohol?

Hell. Worry when the time comes!

But what would Peni think?

As it was, Asher had to park two blocks from the event. He was happy to see that there was security around, though. This was just begging for some straight kids to decide to cause trouble.

Asher got to the door, showed his ticket, and got appreciative looks from the doormen. Good sign. He was suddenly feeling good, despite how the evening had gone at the Pegasus. He would have a good time.

And he would prove to himself he could do it sober.

Sober.

Halloween sober….

You can do it!

Asher squared his shoulders, thrust out his chest, and entered the chaos.

He was right. The place was packed. And packed with hot men.

He was glad to see that Cueball was handling the music. He was only one of Kansas City's hottest DJs—both because of his talent and his looks. He was shaved bald, but had muscles that put Asher to shame, and he was showing a lot of them.

The music was good too. Right now Meghan Trainor was explaining that it was all about that bass, and the dancers seemed to agree. They were tearing up the dance floor.

Asher looked around him. Damn. Had there been any worries that the bars would be the place to go? Where had all these men come from? He hardly recognized any of them, and with his scorecard, that was saying something!

Now where was the Fabulous Four?

Where was Peni?

He found Scott and Cedar first, and damn! He could hardly believe it. Jockstraps. They were wearing jockstraps and little else except matching T-shirts (come to think of it, the jocks were matching too) and tennies. How had Cedar talked Scott, of all people, into showing his butt in public? Scott had always, always hated his body. And hmmmm.... His butt wasn't half-bad. What was it with Scott and Sloan getting better bodies now that they had lovers? And these outfits sure exposed Scott and Cedar's bodies! Were their outfits even street legal? Didn't the crack have to be covered? Not that Asher minded. He knew Cedar had an ass to kill for—he'd wanted to see it for months now, and there it was, shaking and waving and.... Strangely, he realized he wasn't really all that interested, now that he'd gotten a peek.

He decided he'd say hi in a bit and started to move through the crowd. He wanted to find the others.

He was startled to feel a grope now and again. Not that it was anything new, especially on Halloween, when he tended to go out practically naked. But tonight he was finding the wandering hands... well... unwanted. It was a most unfamiliar feeling.

He needed to find Sloan and Max. Sloan would make sense of things.

Asher finally found them—dressed as Bert and Ernie (could they be any cuter?)—and what were they doing? Serving. And should he be surprised at that? Of course that is what they would be doing. Helping the community.

"May I help you?" Sloan asked, pointing at two punch bowls, one marked "Alcohol" and the other "Alcohol Free." Then his mouth fell open. "Asher?"

Leave it to Sloan to recognize him. "You know it's me?"

Sloan rolled his eyes. "Of course. You think I don't know your—"

Max cleared his throat and Sloan looked at him and blushed.

"—chin? Your eyes?"

Max laughed and Sloan joined him. Asher could only shake his head.

"You look great," Sloan said. "Awesome!"

"Thanks," Asher said and then lied, "You guys too." But then, was it a lie? They did look cute. They had even painted their faces. Max yellow, as Bert, and Sloan orange, as Ernie. Thankfully, they had the black wigs as well. The orange would have clashed terribly with Sloan's red hair.

He glanced down at the alcohol-free punch and sighed. Shit. Halloween without a buzz. What the hell was that going to be like. "I'll take some of this," he said, pointing to the bowl.

Sloan gave him a dazzling smile. "Coming right up," he said and served up a cup.

Asher tried it. Nodded. At least it was pretty good.

"Based *very* loosely on one of your best cocktails," Sloan explained.

"Is Peni here?" Asher said and then froze. Now why the fuck had he asked that?

Sloan raised an eyebrow. "Peni?" His mouth turned into a thin straight line. Amused? Was Sloan amused?

Dammit!

"You know, I do think I *might* have seen him."

"Oh for fuck's sake, Sloan. Just tell me where he is!" He closed his eyes. Took a deep breath. Opened them. "Sorry."

The smile on Sloan's face had changed. Not so big now. Not amused, though. Shit. Was Sloan reading him again?

His friend raised a hand and pointed.

Asher turned in that direction—

His mouth fell open.

—and there was Peni.

He was practically naked.

A shock raced through Asher. He all but staggered.

He had never seen anything more beautiful in his life.

All his friend was wearing was a sarong, flip-flops, and a lei of hibiscus (no, *'Aute Samoa*) around his neck.

And paint.

From just above the waist and down to his knees were black lines, curves, arches, dots, dashes…. Why, it was the pe'a. Asher knew that not only from what Sloan had told him the day Wyatt got his tattoo, but from looking it up on the Internet as well. It had taken him a bit. He had no clue how to spell pe'a. But he had found what he was looking for. The pictures had been riveting.

And now? Now he was looking at a Peni that had been transformed into something otherworldly. Asher couldn't breathe. He wanted to cry at the beauty. Peni had bewitched him.

He was dancing, and his sarong swirled around him, giving Asher glimpse after glimpse of his body. His exquisite body. Just the quickest flash of his hip sped Asher's heart up far more than seeing Cedar's entire ass.

I want him. I want him so much.

But there was more. It wasn't just the speeding of his heart. It was as if something were happening *inside* his heart. In the depth of him.

What was going on?

Right then Peni saw him and, for just a second, froze. Then he nodded and continued to dance, and it was all Asher could do not to run to his side and shove away the guy who was taking "his" place with Peni.

My place? Had he really thought that? Peni wasn't his. Peni would never be his. There was no way Peni would want him, could want him, the way he wanted Peni right now.

I want him in my bed.

But it was more than that. Far more.

And Asher didn't know how to make sense of it all.

The song came to an end, and Peni nodded at his partner and then pointed at Asher. The shorter, chunkier man looked over as well and— *oh*! It was Wyatt! He was dressed in a long pink negligee, wore a blond wig, and had two… were those antennae on his head?

The pair approached. God. The two of them weren't *together*, were they?

"Hello, Asher," Peni said.

Asher tried to answer but had to try more than once. He couldn't speak. "H-hello," he managed.

"You look incredible." Peni looked at him from top to bottom, and was he blushing? It was hard to tell with his coloring and the low lighting.

"You recognized me," Asher said.

Peni nodded once.

"I…. I…. Peni. You…. You look amazing. I…. I….". Damn. He couldn't even speak. He always knew what to say. *What's wrong with me? What the fuck is wrong with me?*

"Do you think so?" Peni asked.

Asher opened his mouth, and once more, words failed him. Finally: "How did you recognize me?"

Peni shook his head. "Oh, Asher. You think I don't know your—" He coughed. "—your chin? Your eyes?"

Asher felt himself blush. Thank goodness the mask covered his face.

"Hello!" cried Wyatt. "Person here!"

Somehow, Asher turned from Peni to his friend. "What are you supposed to be?" he asked. Caught himself. That sounded rude, didn't it? "I mean…. Sorry. I didn't mean it to sound like that. But. I don't know." Yes. Antennae. Two pipe cleaners attached to one of those plastic hairbands. They were corkscrewed at the top.

Wyatt put his hands on his hips and raised both eyebrows dramatically. "Why, I am little Cindy Lou Who, who is no more than two!"

Asher gaped at his friend and then suddenly burst into laughter. It was all he could do not to cry, he was laughing so hard. He rocked with it.

And then he threw his arms around Wyatt and said, "Fuck I love you! You know that, right? Only *you*, Wyatt! *Only* you!" Then he surprised himself and kissed Wyatt. Right on the lips.

He stepped back and shook his head. Wyatt was looking at him slack-jawed. "Are you okay?" he asked, incredulity clear in his voice.

"I am," Asher said. At least his cock had stopped stirring. Then, taking a deep breath, he dared look at Peni. A slow song started to play, and somehow Asher found the words to speak. "Will you dance with me?"

Peni nodded. "But I don't know if I'm any good. I've never slow danced with anyone, let alone…."

Asher nodded and took Peni's hand. "Just lean against me and sway. I'll take care of you."

Peni nodded, and Asher led him out onto the floor.

It was like a dream. He couldn't believe it wasn't a dream. It *felt* like a dream.

Asher opened his arms. Peni stepped into them, and Asher pulled him close. But not too close. He did not want to scare Peni.

They began to move slowly to the music. "Oh, Peni," he said before he could stop himself. "You look like a god."

"I-I do?"

Then, as Katy Perry sang of how she would love unconditionally, Asher felt Peni's weight lean into him. Had anything ever felt so good? His heart was racing again. He didn't know when he'd felt like this before. Had he ever felt like this?

What is happening to me?

I can't be.... I can't be falling....

He felt his cock getting hard again.

Thank God, his jock was made of leather. It would be the only thing keeping Peni from feeling....

And he did not want to scare Peni away!

It was the last thing he wanted.

CHAPTER NINETEEN

PENI COULD hardly believe what he was hearing.

"Really?" he said. They were standing in the hallway outside the party.

"R-really" came Asher's reply.

"Y-you know, I would have been all right with you drinking," Peni found himself saying. "For the play…. You're an actor. Sometimes you have to do things. I mean… didn't Meryl Streep climb into a bunch of ice so she could look dead in some movie?"

And how did I even know that? He hadn't seen very many movies since he'd been dating Asher—

Dating? Wait…. I'm not *dating Asher Eisenberg!*

But hadn't he been?

Isn't that just what he'd been doing?

Waiting breathless for the next excuse to see him?

Insinuating himself on Fabulous Four nights?

I haven't asked to be included in Porch Night!

Of course, a Porch Night hadn't come up yet since his and Asher's crazy bet.

It's not *a bet!*

A bet! Like he—Peni—was some kind of prize!

Asher….

He would be a prize.

"…you know?"

What? He'd missed something.

"I'm sorry," Peni said, embarrassed. "What did you say?"

"Shit!"

Asher pushed his mask back and looked away. There was a pause.

Oca, what had he missed? Clearly something that bothered Asher. Something he didn't want to say again. *Kae!*

"I'm sorry, Asher. I…."

"It's okay."

Had Asher's voice just cracked?

"Guess it's just Wyatt and Scott's so-called 'Universe' fucking with me."

Peni could actually hear the capital *U* in "Universe."

"Fuck. I mean. Sorry that I'm swearing...." His voice? Peni had never heard Asher sound like this. Of course, he hardly knew the man.

Except....

It didn't feel that way, did it? He couldn't believe how much he felt he *did* know Asher. How much he wanted to know Asher more. How much he....

Peni shook his head.

Get control of yourself and stop acting like a teenager!

Except.... He hadn't ever really been able to *be* a teenager, had he? Between the restraint he'd been under during his teen years being raised Mormon—

"No dating girls until you're in college!" his parents had insisted.

—and the fact that he couldn't date who he really would have wanted to date anyway—

Oh, Roland, the out and proud gay boy, had been so sexy and had so obviously liked Peni. Had flirted with him. Shown off in the shower, and how many times had Peni masturbated thinking of him and then fallen deep into shame?

—he'd never experienced what normal teenagers went through.

Whatever normal meant.

"Peni?"

"Y-yes!" he said, just a little too loudly. He coughed. Tried again. "Yes." His voice more controlled this time.

"I can't say this more than once—more than one more time, okay?"

"Okay," Peni said—wondering, *wondering*, what could this *be*?

"I—I think there might be something to what you said. I... I might be.... Well, if I'm not, then I'm only like one step away..."

What? One step away from what?

"...from being an alcoholic," Asher finished in a tone barely above a whisper.

Peni froze, unable to even take a breath.

Breathe.... Breathe!

"Peni? Please tell me you heard that because I can't say...."

"I—I heard you, Asher."

Peni's heart swelled. God. How hard must it have been for Asher to say those words?

"I heard you," he repeated. To make sure Asher *had* heard—and to give him another few seconds to figure out what to say next. He looked up into those beautiful blue-green eyes. "I... I don't know if you're an alcoholic either, Asher. But if you're not...."

"I—I'm only a step away...."

And then Asher's voice did crack.

Oca! Was he crying?

"Asher...." Peni's heart swelled even more, swelled until it *hurt*. Then.... *Oh no. I've fallen in love with him. Ulu kae, Peniamina Faamausili! I'm cracked in the head!* "Asher... do you want to get out of here? We could—"

"N-no." And Asher's voice did crack. Peni was sure of it. "Not now. How about S-Saturday?"

Porch Night? "Isn't that Porch Night? Only the Fabulous Four?"

"Well, it *was*." He gave a half laugh. "Now everyone's boyfriend is there. So why not you too?" His eyes went wide. "Not that I'm saying that you are my boyfriend!"

"It's okay," Peni said, assuring the man. Assuring the man he quite suddenly realized he might—Oca! There was no "might" about it!—have fallen in love with. *I want to be his boyfriend!*

When had *that* happened?

And was Asher implying...? No.... Asher didn't "do" boyfriends.

There was that strange laugh/cry noise again. "Sorry. I know you don't want to be my boyfriend...."

"It was the thought that counts," Peni said, heart pounding in his chest. *Yes! I do want to be your boyfriend.* He wanted a lot more than that. Did Asher mean what it sounded like he was saying?

"But that's the goddamned problem. I don't think! I don't ever think of anybody but my fucking self. *Fuck.* There I go swearing again. I'm sorry, I'm—"

"Dammit, Asher!" Peni cried while some conditioned part of him gasped in surprise. "I don't give a damn if you swear!" And another part of him felt the most wondrous sense of relief. Relief and freedom from a lifetime of restraint. "Swear all you want. I don't give a shit."

Asher gasped, then laughed. Then, was that a sob? "L-look what I've done.... Corrupted you."

"You didn't corrupt me!" A steel resolve that was even more freeing than the use of a few curse words rose up in Peni. It almost took his breath away. "Asher, all I asked is that you try and not drink for thirty days. I didn't ask that you change who you are. Swear from now until the end of the world!"

"Peni…."

"And you're wrong. You think of others all the time. I was there when you helped Wyatt move out of his beloved house. I've seen other things lately too." He meant it. He had seen it. He had seen exactly why Sloan and their little group loved Asher. Asher tried to hide it, but he *was* beautiful on the inside as well as the out.

You just had to look.

"Are you sure you don't want to get out of here?" *Say yes. Say yes, say yes, say yes….*

And an image of them naked in bed came unbidden to Peni's mind.

"No, Peni…."

No! You're supposed to say—

"Not tonight. Saturday. We can even meet early if you want and—"

"Yes! Early."

"We can have dinner."

"Yes!" Peni cried.

"You like that vegan place, right? Café—"

"Namasté," Peni finished. "I like it a lot."

"Okay. Do you want to meet there? Or I can pick you up."

"Yes. Pick me up." Another image filled Peni's mind. A Madonna video. An old one. Before he was born, maybe. "Material Girl." Keith Carradine picking Madonna up in a battered old truck. Peni's heart tripped. He smiled.

Oh…. Oh, I'm in love with him!

"That way…."

That way what?

What had he been about to say?

He wouldn't have to leave his car at the restaurant?

Why wouldn't they?

Because if Asher picked Peni up, then they would have to go to Porch Night together, and Peni couldn't leave until they were both ready to leave and….

Who was hosting this Saturday? Was it Scott? Because he was supposed to host last time, but they'd been moving Wyatt, so he and Sloan had switched and—

"Okay," Asher said. "And I'll take you home the minute you want to leave."

"Okay," Peni said before he could change his mind.

"Five o'clock? Six? Enough time to eat and talk before we have to be at Scott's?"

So it was Scott's. And Asher could pick him up at *noon* if he wanted!

Noon? Why, Asher could pick him up at six o'clock in the morning.

They could go sit under that gazebo in Wagner Park.

He could sit there in the shade, and Asher could lay his head in Peni's lap. Of course, the floor of the thing wouldn't be comfortable for that, would it? Blanket? In the grass?

Cold. Too cold for that, probably. Summer was pretty much gone. The days had finally fallen on the cold side. Why, the other morning Peni had actually seen flurries before the temperature rose up into the lower sixties....

"Six is okay, then?"

What? Had Asher been talking?

"Six is okay," Peni repeated, almost disappointed.

"All right, then. It's a date. No! I'm sorry! Not... not a date. It hasn't been thirty days yet."

"Saturday," Peni said, heart slamming in his chest. "Six o'clock."

There was a long pause.

Neither wanting the moment to end?

Peni didn't.

"Maybe we should go back inside," Asher said, his voice once more barely above a whisper.

"Maybe we should," Peni said, just as quietly.

And then they both walked back into the chaos of the party.

CHAPTER TWENTY

IT WAS November first, and that made it the first Saturday of the month, and first Saturday meant it was Porch Night. Despite everything that had happened in the last few days and the dinner with Peni earlier that evening, it was still weird not to have a margarita at Scott and Cedar's apartment.

Scott *and* Cedar's apartment. Weirdness number one....

Weirdness number two: for once Asher *wanted* one of Scott's crappy, cheap-ass margaritas, and the *reason* he wasn't having one was because he couldn't. Not and honor his bet with Peni. For one tiny moment, Asher had even experienced a bolt of anger about it.

Porch Night without a drink!

He almost felt tricked.

He and Peni had made their agreement a few days after the *last* Porch Night.

That meant *this* Porch Night fell before the end of the thirty days.

It was still a full week before he could have a drink!

Then something else washed over Asher.

He wasn't even sure what it was. It seemed to be a mixture of lots of emotions.

Regret.

But for what? That he "couldn't" have a drink? Or that if he *was* an alcoholic, he might not *ever* be able to have a drink again? Had it gone that far? Had his drinking gone *that* far? That he couldn't even have a glass of wine with a nice meal? No bottle of champagne on New Year's Eve? No romantic glass of cognac by a roaring fire with someone special?

Someone special?

He couldn't help but look over at Peni.

And shame.

Shame? Shame that he'd let his drinking go so far? He'd always had nothing but contempt for drunks and addicts. He'd once known a good man, a man who did bar outreach, teaching in fun yet serious ways all about the importance of safe sex (and that sex could be fun even with condoms) and the dangers of drugs like meth. Then Asher had watched as that man became an addict and had his life destroyed by the drug. Seen and heard him lie over and over again that he had kicked his addiction and was sober only to see him juiced up or strung out a half-dozen times. By the time the man was finally clean, Asher didn't give a shit anymore.

And now that might be me?

Not methamphetamine, no, but booze.

Was he a drunk?

When Asher saw men stumbling out the door of a bar at the end of a night, slurring their words and falling down in the street, he'd been disgusted with them as well. How had they let it get so far?

Was that him, now?

Disgusting in all ways except stumbling into gutters?

And guilt?

Guilt that he *was* angry that he "couldn't" have a drink!

How did it get this far?

And confusion. More than all the rest, confusion.

But what he'd really been confused about was…

…well, hadn't the last month been nice?

Once he'd gotten past the first few days, the first week (which had seemed to last forever)? He'd waited for the DTs. The "delirium tremens" (he'd had to Google it to find what the abbreviation meant). But while he had gone through some days where he'd felt sick, one night where he'd been shocked to find himself trembling, sweating, and *craving* a drink, even some mornings where he felt pretty awful—he was relieved he didn't go through the more severe symptoms that were a sure sign of withdrawal. He hadn't experienced the delirium or hallucinations or convulsions he'd read he might go through and feared might occur. After a week, the cravings had stopped, although he still wished he could have a drink.

But then something occurred to him. He could have a damned drink any damned time he wanted. There was nothing stopping him. He could do what he damned well pleased!

But then he knew something else. He had something he wanted to prove. And it wasn't just to Peni. He wanted to see he could do it for himself.

He wanted to prove to himself that he could do it. That he could go thirty days without a drink. It hadn't been easy. There were days he had a bottle in his hands.

But then...

(when he thought about it)

...hadn't it been interesting to see things and experience things in complete control of his faculties—unaffected by a cloud of intoxication? To see things clearly?

It made him think what it must be like for someone who had never known they needed glasses to try on a pair and see things they hadn't known were there to see. That's what his sister had told him once: how she couldn't believe what she was seeing. Details she hadn't realized she was missing.

Sister.... When was the last time he'd even thought of her?

Wasn't there something wrong with that?

Yes, he missed drinking.

But then he had dinner with Peni. And it had been... well... surprising to say the least.

How different would that dinner have been if he'd had alcohol?

How different would everything have been these last weeks leading up to that dinner if he'd been drinking?

Not that there *would* have even been a dinner!

How many realizations would he *not* have had in these last weeks? Or more importantly, tonight?

It was almost too much to think about....

But oh, hadn't dinner been nice?

ASHER KNOCKED on his apartment door at 6:01.

It made Peni smile.

This is a date, isn't it?

He could deny it all he wanted, but that was *just* what this was!

Why, just the way he'd cleaned up had been ridiculous. The shaving was normal, but the thoroughness of his shower? It was only when he caught himself methodically cleaning the cleft of his butt that it hit him. Was he *really* expecting Asher to be anywhere *near* his butt?

Crazy!

This *was* a date....

He'd tried on nearly everything in his closet.

One outfit would be too dressy, one too dressed down. He'd look like he was going to the Oscars or like he was trying to be a thug. It was exasperating. He should have just asked Asher what he should wear.

But that would have made it seem even more like a date.

This is a date.

Hasn't been thirty days yet!

But who gave a *kae*?

Goodness, he really was swearing these days. What would his mother think?

She wouldn't be happy.

But oh, *he* was so happy. He couldn't remember being so happy. Just being around his gay friends made him happy. Made him feel like… well, like something he'd heard Wyatt talk about many times. As if he were a part of something much greater, much bigger than himself. Something spiritual. Something truly wonderful. Something unlike anything he had ever felt before.

The last month had made him feel far closer to some kind of "God" than he'd ever felt in his life.

The morning after he'd gotten drunk at that bar, Max had loaned him some books. They were part of a series called *Tales of the City*, written by a gay man named Armistead Maupin. Max had told Peni that the books had been helping him immensely in his coming-out process. Peni couldn't imagine what that might mean— until he started reading them.

Peni was flying through the books now. In fact, he'd ordered them all from Amazon and could hardly wait to get through them—but dreaded it as well. He didn't want them to be over as much as he couldn't wait to find out what happened. He was also living in worry that one of his favorite characters, the wonderful and eccentric transsexual Anna Madrigal, would die in the final book.

But what had literally and spiritually changed his life was the chapter early on in the series where the character Michael Tolliver came out to his family through a letter.

Imagine *having* to write letters instead of having the *option* to e-mail one! When writing it out had been your only choice….

Wouldn't that have destroyed spontaneity?

Of course it would also mean that it would be a lot harder to just rush your thoughts out in an e-mail and hit the send button before you thought through what you were doing.

In the book *More Tales of the City*, Michael Tolliver ("Mouse" to his friends) told his mother that her fears that he had somehow been recruited into homosexuality were unwarranted—but in a way, he wished he had been. He wished someone had taken him aside when he was younger and told him he wasn't evil or sick. That he could be whatever he wanted to be. And he could find lots of wonderful friends who wouldn't care who he slept with.

And hadn't Peni found that with Sloan and his friends?

Wasn't it *marvelous*?

The letter went on to say that Michael Mouse didn't know why he was gay, but he was thankful.

Thankful!

Michael was thankful from the very depths of his heart!

Peni had read those words and been shocked.

Michael was thankful for something that had cast him from everything he'd been taught to believe? Thankful he was something that, according to his church, was wrong? It reminded Peni—of course—of what he was going through. The only difference was that his religion—no, his *parents'* religion—said it was "okay" he was gay, but he couldn't act on it…. How insane was that?

It was like the words from that Barbra Streisand song—the one where she asked God why he would give a bird wings and then tell it that it wasn't allowed to fly! Wouldn't that be the same? Wasn't he born to love men but told by his religion that he wasn't *allowed* to express that love? Wasn't that just like telling a bird it wasn't allowed to fly?

And Peni knew he was gay.

Knew it from a kiss.

Two kisses.

The kiss of a woman that had meant nothing to him, breaking his heart, because oh, he had been praying that he would love the kiss of a woman and that all his fears about being gay would just go away.

And then the kiss of a man. A kiss that had healed his heart, showing him how wondrous a kiss could be, but then broken it as well. But it didn't matter that the man—Bobby—had wound up hurting him.

Peni was starting to see that now, with the passing of time and the company of gay friends.

(And oh, the way Asher looked at him!)

Peni was healing!

He had friends who loved him *just* the way he was. Friends with compassion and empathy for what he had been through.

Peni's heart was now more completely full and alive and loving than he ever dreamed possible. And if that was what it felt like "just" to have gay friends, what might it be like to be in love? To be in love with a *man*? A man who loved him back?

(Could that man possibly be Asher? A man who at first Peni had all but loathed?)

What irony!

But then Michael Tolliver's letter went even further—moving Peni more powerfully than ever. Michael said something that Peni could scarcely believe (although he wanted, *desperately* wanted, to).

At first it seemed impossible. Like Santa Claus or the Tooth Fairy (or an angel appearing before Joseph Smith and revealing the true lost Gospel of Jesus Christ?).

The letter said he was not only grateful he was gay, but that being gay had taught him about being truly alive! It taught him about acceptance and empathy and humility. Being gay had taught him about tolerance. About compassion. About being humble without being meek. That it had shown him just how much possibility there was outside the strict walls he'd been surrounded by for his entire life.

Or at least that was what Peni had interpreted through the author's words.

And finally, toward the close of that magical letter in that magical book about "The City," Peni had seen something he had to write down, to keep. He wrote it on a piece of paper, and he laminated it and put it in his wallet and pulled it out to read, over and over again.

This is what it said: "Being gay… has brought me into the family of man, Mama, and I like it here. I like it."

The family of *man*.

Yes!

The words had seemed like an impossible promise when Peni had first read them. But within one month, they had proven to be true. By not only coming out to himself and his family, and by embracing himself for what he was, and by gathering in gay men as his friends, Peni *had* joined a *family* of *man*.

Wasn't that just what Wyatt talked about when he spoke of his religion and his belief that there were some kind of spiritual beings called "Queer Ones?"

And weren't magical beings called Queer Ones far more comforting to him than his mother's God?

With every passing day, Peni couldn't help but think more and more of his heritage.

Of Tangaloa, the Samoan god who had created everything.

Of the story of how the earth was peopled and why Tangaloa chose the people that he did to have authority over the earth. Peni thought of how he loved the beautiful myth of *Le Pisaga: To Sua ma le To le Sua*. How Afona's—his grandfather's—gentle but powerful voice could make him *see* the story in his mind. See himself climbing the great plateau that looked out over the ocean, but also down into two cavernous holes. *To Sua*—water exists within—and *To le Sua*—for its lack of water. The poetry of the tale, with Afona's masterful storytelling, could make Peni feel an awe-inspiring presence that he'd never really felt at church. It made him *hear* the crashing of waves, *feel* the cool waters of *To Sua* and the rumbling of the ocean in the rock walls. To feel weightless in that water! And then, in the second part of the tale, being taken to *To le Sua*, feeling the weight of his body (it seemed so ponderous after the weightlessness of *To Sua*) when he was put out from the water and onto the rocks. And then—*then*—he would sense the Samoan spirits and gods and ancestors! Hear their laughter and song and *fiafia*—their celebrations—the celebrations of the *auti*, the ancient ghosts of Samoa.

Oh! And of course there had been the story of the long-toothed devil of Falelima! That story had thrilled him as a child!

It had been through all of this that Peni had always felt closest to anything "holy" and powerful.

And *oca*! How surprising it had been when Peni found himself telling Asher all these things over dinner. Over curried lentils and golden potatoes and pesto polenta and a puttanesca sauce served over sautéed spinach and spaghetti squash. Not that he'd ordered that much food himself, of course! No. He'd ordered the dish called Muladhara and Asher ordered Vishuddha and they shared.

Imagine!

Sharing food that way. With a man. Practically feeding each other off each other's plates!

I'm on a date, Peni realized over and over that afternoon. *I. Am. On. A.* Date! *With Asher Eisenberg!*

Peni told Asher so much, and Asher *listened*! He told Asher about the fact that his people had a place for gay men in their society. He told Asher about the *fa'afafine* and what he understood about them. And while the *fa'afafine* were not necessarily a group he would want to join, a group of men that lived *as* women—it was incredible that these men were still honored. His ancient heritage would have allowed him, if so many of his people had not converted to Mormonism, to have had a husband and to be held in high esteem amongst his friends and neighbors!

With every day that passed, he began to see that he wasn't sure that he could be Mormon anymore.

Peni spoke of all of this with Asher that evening at Café Namasté. It was the first time in his life he'd ever shared so much of himself with another person, even Wyatt, who would have completely understood.

And Asher was listening! He could see it in Asher's beautiful blue-green eyes. What it must be like to have eyes that color. Why, he would never stop looking at himself in the mirror!

Although he supposed maybe if it was all he had ever known….

"And that's why the pe'a is so important to you!" Asher had exclaimed.

Yes! Yes, it was.

"And you're thinking about it, aren't you?"

Oca! Did Asher know? Did Asher know what he was just beginning to know himself?

And then he found himself talking about Bobby. "He swept me off my feet, you know? I couldn't believe I held off sex with a man my whole life, and then he got me with some booze and"—he blushed—"a kiss."

Asher nodded. "A kiss can be a pretty powerful thing."

"I was so *stupid*! I thought he loved me. We barely even dated for a week, and I was hearing wedding bells. I was so happy, and then I was hurting *so* bad." He paused, wondering what to say, how much to say. "He invited me over for a candlelit dinner. It sounded so romantic. He told me he would show me what 'lovin'' was all about." Peni stopped. Felt a strange little lump in his heart. Still? It hurt still? Even with this man sitting across the table listening to his every word? He looked up, and what he saw in those eyes suddenly made it all okay. The lump? It seemed to just melt away. "I got there, and he had some other guy there. I mean, they were half undressed!" He laughed. Laughed? He was actually *laughing* about it? "He told me he 'accidentally' made two dates for the same night."

"Shit," Asher said.

"Then he wanted to know if I wanted to have a three-way. *Me!* A three-way! I threw this complete fit, screaming at him. Oca! I even started crying. And then he called me a big sissy and made me leave. He—made—me—*leave!*"

It had been horrible. *Horrible!* But now....

Now why did it seem so stupid?

"God," Asher said. "I am so sorry." He looked away.

What was it? Was something wrong? "Asher?"

"I was just thinking that might have been something I would have done once upon a time."

Asher?

He looked back. "I've used men a lot, Peni. I can't deny that. But you? I don't know what it is. You make me... different."

Peni's heart began to race.

Then what the silly man said next!

"Forgive me?"

"What?" Peni had asked. "Forgive you? For what?"

Asher had leaned in and whispered, "I keep getting lost in your eyes. Do you have any idea how beautiful your eyes are?"

The words had taken Peni completely off guard. Hadn't he just been thinking the same thing about Asher's eyes?

"I heard every single word. And the way you talk... I understand.... I understand why you want it. I—"

Peni sat up straight in his chair. And just as Asher was about to say it out loud, their waiter came and began to gather their empty plates. "Care for dessert? We have right now—for a limited time—a strawberry cashew cheesecake with almond date crust, topped with a chocolate-dipped strawberry. We also have a delicious mocha cheesecake. Or how about an after-dinner wine? We have an—"

Asher got a pained expression and the waiter, no dummy, snapped his mouth shut.

"I'm pretty full," Peni said.

"Me too," Asher said, finding his smile. "And Cedar's a pretty good cook. I'm sure he and Scott will have something for us to nom on later."

They paid their bill—Peni insisted they go dutch since it wasn't yet time for their date—(although it was a date!—it was! it was!)

—and Asher agreed reluctantly, with the promise that Peni would let him pay when they had that "first" date.

"You know, we're in luck. Because it's the last Saturday I'll have free for nearly a month. Hell, one of the last nights I'll have free for a month *period*."

Peni had looked at Asher with confusion. A month? There would only be one date? For a month? "Why?" he asked.

"Because the play starts the following Monday, and—"

"Monday," Peni exclaimed. "I want to go opening night."

"Ummm…," Asher said, looking uncomfortable. "I'm not sure you'd like it."

Peni laughed. He'd heard all about the vomiting. But there was no way he was going to miss seeing Asher's play, especially if Asher was even half the actor Sloan swore he was.

THEY DECIDED to go for a walk, and Asher felt nearly overwhelmed by a strange compulsion to take Peni's hand in his own. Had he ever wanted to hold someone's hand?

(Except in maybe helping a guy stroke his own dick? Teach him the speed and grip he liked best?)

Asher wasn't sure he ever had.

Then before he even knew what he was doing—and wasn't that happening a lot lately—he told Peni something he hadn't ever shared with anyone before.

"I loved my grandfather when I was a boy," he said as they walked along. The sun was quite low by then, and the street lights had come on, but they were walking through Terra's Gate's business district, and Asher could never remember hearing about any crime—not so much as a mugging—occurring in the little town. They stuck mostly to Green Street, past shops and stores and cafes, many thriving because of their appeal to the college kids who attended Wagner University. There was a sports clothing store, a comic book shop, several more restaurants—including the coffee shop The Radiant Cup 2—and a dress shop that looked like it catered to Stevie Nicks or Cyan Carrington. ("Has Cedar's mother ever seen this place?" Peni wondered aloud to Asher.) And of course, there was Treasures of Terra, the New Age shop Wyatt managed for the esteemed Katherine Grimsley.

But Peni's comment about the dress shop was about the only thing he did say during their walk. Because he was listening to Asher.

Really listening.

"My grandfather's name was Yeshiyahu," Asher shared. "And he was a rabbi. A very conservative *orthodox* rabbi. And Peni…. Oh, he was magic! He would cover his head with his *tallit*, his prayer shawl, and say his prayers, and it was…." Asher was at a loss for words and could only repeat what he'd said before. "Magic. And then there was Chanukah. Each evening, lighting another candle of the menorah, singing his prayer…."

Asher tried to remember the words.

Ba-ruch A-tah Ado-nai E-lo-he-nu Me-lech ha-olam a-sher ki-de-sha-nu be-mitz-vo-tav ve-tzi-va-nu le-had-lik ner shel Cha-nu-kah….

He spied a bench. "Mind if we sit down a minute?" he asked.

"Sure," Peni replied, and they did.

Asher paused and gathered his wits about him. Could he do this? Could he say it?

He looked over at Peni and suddenly saw just how wrong he'd been. This man wasn't judgmental. He wasn't sanctimonious. He wasn't condescending. He was *injured*. He was hurt.

Just like me.

Peni's trigger was alcohol.

Does he think how his father died every time he looks at me? Asher wondered. *What must it be like for him to even consider getting involved with someone like me?*

And that was just what was happening, wasn't it?

Getting involved?

This *was* a date, no matter what they were calling it. A date a week early.

"One day when I was in fourth grade, me and my best friend—well, I don't know that he was my best friend, but—hell. What difference does it make?"

Peni gave him a single nod. "It's okay, Asher. You can tell me."

Asher sighed.

"My friend Ronnie and I... well, I guess you could say we were playing doctor."

"Doctor?" Peni asked, confused.

"Doctor," Asher repeated and got a blank look in return. Peni clearly didn't understand the reference. "We were playing 'I'll show you mine if you show me yours.'"

"Your what?" Then, suddenly, "Oh!" Peni blushed and somehow that made telling this story a little easier. It actually lightened the mood, although for the life of him Asher wasn't sure why.

"I don't suppose you ever did anything like that," Asher said. In fact he couldn't imagine it. "Get naked with another boy when you were young."

"Actually," Peni said and blushed all the more (which was quite a sight, especially considering Peni's complexion and the fact that the sun had set and all they had was street lights to see by now). Peni grimaced. "Actually I used to do that with my cousin Tupe."

"You did?" Asher said, totally surprised. "I mean.... Whoa."

"Samoans are just like everybody else, Asher!"

"It's not the Samoan thing," Asher said. "It's the Mormon thing. I figured with all your rules and your magic underwear...."

Peni rolled his eyes. "I didn't wear 'magic underwear' when I was a kid. Do you know how much we hate people calling it 'magic underwear'?"

"So you've never worn them?" Asher said, surprised once again. "I just thought... I mean, I saw that movie *Latter Days*. And they sing about it in the Broadway musical *The Book of Mormon*, don't they?"

"I don't know," said Peni. "Disenchanted with my religion I might be, but there's a song in that musical that I can't help but feel is pretty offensive."

Asher realized instantly which one it must have been. "You mean the one where they...."

Peni nodded. "Yeah. A song called... well, 'Eff God.' That turned me off way too much to ever think about listening to the soundtrack."

Asher nodded. That made sense. Even *he* had sort of checked the sky for lightning bolts the first time he'd heard the equally sacrilegious and hilarious song. "So.... No.... Uh.... *Special* underwear?"

"They're called temple garments," Peni said. "And no. Not then. And not now."

"Commando, then?" Asher said. It was a nice image.

"*No!* Now stop. You're avoiding telling me your story. Have you changed your mind?"

"No...." Asher sighed again. No, he hadn't changed his mind. But he did know he'd better tell it before he *did*.

"Okay. I was playing with my friend Ronnie. I guess I was curious for my age. We were looking at these men's magazines, totally unimpressed with the naked women, but turned on to each other. And we got naked and got in the sixty-nine position, although we didn't know that was what it was called back then, and I suppose we were about to go down on each other. I mean that's what *I* wanted. I don't know *how* I knew, exactly, except I'd heard about blowjobs and they sounded pretty damned hot to me. And right then... my grandfather walked in on us."

"Shit," Peni said and slapped a hand over his mouth.

Asher nodded, and the pain of that long-ago day reared up and hit him again. After all this time! The horror of it. It was like some kind of fucking ALS ice-bucket challenge! Like being splashed into the cold and dark all at once. For a minute he wasn't sure if he could go on.

But then, knowing it was now or never (ever), he said, "He started screaming. Calling me an abomination. A sinner. Told me God hated me. Ronnie ran out of there and that was it for our friendship. He wouldn't talk to me at school after that. And Grandfather?" Asher flinched. "He slapped me!" It was like he could feel it even now, and to his horror, as if out of nowhere, tears once more threatened. What was happening to him?

No!

He. Did. Not. Cry!

"Oh my God," Peni said with a quiet gasp.

Asher looked away; then it was as if there were some kind of magnetic force, drawing him to look back. The expression on Peni's face. How had he ever thought this man sanctimonious? Condescending? How?

"I ran, Peni," he blurted. "I ran and ran and ran. I cried. I cried for what felt like a year. And when I finally stopped, I swore I would *never* cry again!"

And yet...

...here he was....

"And I decided that if Yeshiyahu's *fucking* God hated me, then I hated *Him* too."

Peni's eyes went wide. "Asher. Is that what you meant the day Wyatt got his tattoo?"

Asher stared at him a moment. He wasn't sure what Peni was referring to.

"You said… something like… sometimes the people that you think love you stop loving you."

Asher shook his head. Yes…. Yes! And Peni…. Peni really *was* listening to him…. Had been listening the other day. Really *listening*.

"Yes," he cried out. "And I decided that if I was an 'abomination,' then so be it. Because I *knew*, Peni. I knew even then I liked boys. I *wanted* to suck Ronnie's cock. I was mad, I mean *mad*, that I hadn't gotten to. So fuck God, I thought," and to his surprise he looked up for one instant. Lightning bolt?

Of course not.

But he saw the expression on Peni's face. It had bothered him too. Did he understand?

"I understand," Peni said. "Because that's how I've been feeling lately. Not so I can use that word. It's a rough one for me, Asher." He shrugged. "It just is. But it was like I was saying earlier: what kind of God makes me want to love men and then tells me I can't? Why should I have anything to do with him? When there's Tangaloa who would be just fine with me the way I am!"

Yes. Of course Peni understood! It was all Asher could do not to thrust himself into Peni's arms. Pull him tight.

Peni *did* understand.

He did!

They sat for a long time, just looking at each other.

Then Peni spoke. "What happened then?"

Asher closed his eyes. Took a deep breath, then let it out in a long sigh. "He died," Asher whispered. Why, he didn't know. Why whisper?

"Oh," said Peni, just as quietly. "Oh, I… I mean." He shook his head. "I was going to say I'm sorry, but…."

"Yeah," Asher said, and damn if the tears weren't ready to hit again.

Then, to his horror, he felt it. A tear. A tear! It was running slowly down his face. He could only hope Peni didn't see it. At least it would be on the shadowed side….

"My parents made me go the funeral, of course. It was a big deal. Even though neither of them were practicing Jews—and believe me, Yeshiyahu *hated* that. His daughter, his only child, walking away from her religion. And he never had a son to take up the mantle, or whatever it is, to be a rabbi. That's what a rabbi wants. What he frigging *needs*. A son to become a rabbi after him. And I think—no, I know—that *that* was what he was hoping for with me."

Peni shut his eyes. "And then he saw you with that boy...."

"Jews have a big problem with homosexuality," Asher said.

"And Mormons. Although they pretend they don't anymore."

"Wow," said Asher. "We're two boys who were fucked over pretty good by religion, huh?"

Peni nodded, and look. Was *he* about to cry as well? Those eyes were so big and dark anyway.... Oh.... He was. A tear to match Asher's rolled down Peni's cheek. "Fu—" Peni closed his mouth, opened it, closed it again. "It has put a pretty good hate on me."

There was another pause. Then Asher decided to finish and be done with it.

"The funeral was horrible, Peni. Do you know that I didn't even get to see my grandfather's body?"

"You didn't?" Peni said.

"It was an orthodox Jewish funeral. You don't see the body. And there is black cloth over everything. They cover mirrors. I don't understand it all, and I don't care, and my mom didn't explain." He shrugged. Lost another tear. This time on the side Peni was sure to see.

Fuck!

"And while we were there, all I could hear was him shouting 'abomination!' And that there could never be peace between us. For just one minute, I took it all back. All the 'fuck you, Gods' and everything. I told God that if he'd only bring my grandfather back, I would never do it again. I told him I'd marry a woman. That I'd become a rabbi. Anything!"

Asher looked away.

"But of course that didn't happen. And so I was done with tears. And I was done with *God*. And I was done with funerals...."

Peni let out a moan. "Until you came to my father's...."

An abrupt and unheralded sob hitched up through Asher's throat, horrifying him.

Peni only reached out and touched his hand.

The skin on his fingers was as soft as satin.

"Peni. I didn't even go to your father's funeral for the right reason. I went because I was going to hang out with the guys after."

Peni nodded. "Oh, Asher. Oca…." He squinted his eyes tight, then rubbed at them with both hands.

Asher wished Peni hadn't taken his touch away.

Then Peni looked up, and his eyes were all wet, and there were tears. They trickled down his face and—oh, no!—*please stop*, Asher begged without begging.

"Asher. I am so ashamed."

"You?" Asher asked, incredulous.

"For punishing you about that *muli elo* funeral!" Again Peni clapped a hand over his mouth, then just let it drop in his lap. "Oh God, Asher. I am so sorry…."

"*You're* sorry?" Asher was stunned. *You're sorry?* "Why?"

"I've been so selfish."

"No!" Asher cried out. "I don't think you know *how* to be selfish."

Peni shook his head. "Oh, I know. Oh, Asher, I was taking out my anger with the *kio* drunk that killed my father… but I took it out on you!"

But of course you did, thought Asher. *Of course you did. Why wouldn't you? Me. Thrusting my drinking in your face all the time. And then getting pissed off at you for getting upset.* "Oh, Peni. I *am* an asshole. I am one through and through. A total fucking goddamned abomination asshole!"

"No!" Peni shouted, echoing Asher's cry.

"Yes, I am! I am so sorry."

And then it happened.

Asher burst into tears.

It was hideous. It rolled up and out and would not stop. It felt like his heart was being torn apart. His lungs burned. A slamming like thunder, or hammers on anvils, filled his head.

It was the worst feeling he ever remembered.

After those days when he was a kid, of course….

But then something happened.

Peni's arms went around him. He cringed for a second.

And then melted into those arms.

Oh God….

It felt so good.
And so he just did it.
He cried. And Peni cried too.
They both cried.
Until they could cry no more.

WHEN THEY got themselves into some reasonable order, they went by Scott and Cedar's place. Scott showed off his new motorcycle—a Harley-Davidson FLHX Street Glide like Cedar's, except in black and red. He went on and on about their trip and how they found one of Cedar's patented deserted roads and rode naked together in the night. Asher didn't think of asking if Scott was crazy and had they thought about how badly it could have fucked them up if they crashed their bikes. He was too impressed with the fact that Scott had had the balls to ride a motorcycle in the first place. Let alone naked!

And he barely heard half of what the two of them were babbling about concerning… what was it? A house? Really?

He tried to be enthusiastic.

Thank goodness, Peni was making up for the both of them. It helped him.

And it wasn't that he didn't care.

It was a sudden and blinding awareness that was *so* huge there wasn't room for anything else.

He was struck with the shocking realization that he just might, for the first time in his life, be in love.

So when they found themselves on a love seat together, it was hard not to let his knee touch Peni's.

Besides, it was only a knee. Right?

CHAPTER TWENTY-ONE

IT WAS Monday night and that meant family night. Peni had been having a harder and harder time going to his mother's, especially over the last few months. But it was important to her. Even more so right now, dealing with the grief of losing her husband.

Family night meant they ate together. It was another way they actually didn't follow Samoan tradition. They always—as a family—all sat at the dinner table. In Afona's house only Peni's grandfather and grandmother would have sat at the table. They would have—Afona would have—been served dinner first. They didn't even sit at the table with their grandparents. It was even more important because Afona had been a chief. Then when he was done, the rest of the family could eat, children last. It was a sign of respect.

But Peni's parents had decided they would break with tradition. They wanted to raise their children in a more American way. To make Peni's and his brothers' and sisters' lives as much like their American friends' as possible, considering they were Mormon.

So on Monday nights, they had dinner. And after, they would sing and do their lesson and pray.

It was clearly his mother's favorite time. She glowed on Mondays. Family was so important to her.

Family was important to Peni too.

But with every passing day, the way of his ancestors called to him more and more. It made it hard for him to pay attention, especially to the lesson and the reading from the Book of Mormon.

But tonight?

Tonight *Peni* was glowing.

He couldn't help it.

As the evening broke up and his family headed their separate ways, Peni's mother asked him if he would stay and help her wash up, and even though it was over an hour's drive home, he said he would. It was his turn, and she didn't ask often.

So once more they practically washed the dishes by hand before putting them in the dishwasher. She gave him that "I don't want to hear another word about it" look when he tried to remind her that her new dishwasher could do the job, so he shut up and rinsed after she washed.

"So you seem very happy tonight, Peniamina."

Peniamina? Using his full name, was she?

Not that it was that unusual. But there was a tone there....

"I am, Mama."

She nodded, hummed to herself for a few moments.

"And is it because of the boy you are seeing?"

Peni froze. "*Boy?*" What would she know about—

"Well, I suppose I should say 'man,' yes?"

"Mama!" He could have fallen off his feet she had so startled him.

She looked up at him. She was a small woman, and older than most of his friends' mothers since he was the fourth child and there were several years between him and his sister Sala and their older brothers Poto and Mika. And oh, she had been looking very old since his father's passing. But now?

Why, now she looked... younger.

She smiled. "Are you in love with this man?"

"Mama!" he said with a gasp.

"Stop saying 'Mama!'" She laughed. "And tell me! Who is this man?"

"His name is Asher," Peni said, and he slapped a hand over his mouth and looked at her wide-eyed.

"Asher...." She looked back down at her hands, deep in the soapy sink. "He isn't Samoan?"

"I.... N-no, Mother." Admitting further that there *was* a man.

But *oca*! There wasn't a man, was there?

Crying on each other's shoulder didn't mean anything was really happening between him and Asher, did it?

"And this Asher.... He is special to you?"

"I—I...."

Peni's mother handed him a dish and then let the stopper out of the sink, allowing it to drain. She rinsed off her hands. "You want some cocoa, Peni? I made some this morning. I can heat it up."

Peni trembled. "Sure, Mama."

"Sit down," she said and got a half-gallon milk container filled with dark brown kokosamoa out of the refrigerator, poured some into a small pan, and began heating it up on the stove. No microwave for her. At least not with her kokosamoa.

"Now, tell me," she said.

"Oh, Mama. I don't know what to say. I don't know yet if there is even anything to tell."

"Do you love him?"

"Love him?" he asked, shocked. Had his mother just asked him if he loved a man?

"This is so hard to answer?" she asked. "Either you do or you do not. Which is it?"

Peni trembled again. Gulped.

This was it.

"I think I do."

She smiled, stirred the kokosamoa, and then turned off the flame. She got out a couple of mugs and poured. Handed Peni his. "Be careful! It is hot!"

She sat down next to him.

"Is he a good man, Peniamina?"

How did he answer that?

With the truth, perhaps?

"I didn't used to think so, Mama. I thought he was a...." He almost said *puki'o*, but that wouldn't have been a good idea, now, would it? Probably make her think something motherly, like "Is this what hanging out with this boy has done to you? Made you swear in front of your mother?"

"At first I thought he was a jerk. I didn't like him at all! I, I think I kind of hated him...."

His mother laughed and nodded knowingly. "It was the same with your father," she said.

It was? "It was?" he asked aloud.

She nodded. "He would wait for me to get out of school and then walk me home. I thought he was obnoxious. I kept telling him to leave me alone, but he didn't give up." She smiled. "I'm so happy he did not."

"Gosh, Mama."

"He turned out to be the most wonderful man in the world. Is this Asher turning out to be a wonderful man?" She blinked at him and reached out and took one of his hands in hers. It was warm from holding the hot kokosamoa-filled mug.

Peni smiled back. "I-I think so, Mama." He did. He did think so.

She let out a long sigh. "Have you two been… intimate?"

Peni's eyes went wide. "Mama!" He couldn't believe she'd asked him that.

But she kept looking, and it soon became obvious she wanted an answer.

"No, we haven't."

"Good. It is too soon. You need to get to know each other first. Make him walk you home from school."

He shook his head. He wasn't ready for this. His mother talking sex with him?

"I want to meet him, Peni."

Peni's eyes grew even wider. Meet him? "Mama, I think it is *way* too soon. We haven't really even gone on a date!"

"That is not what your friend Wyatt says."

What! "What?"

She pursed her lips and then relaxed them to take a drink of her kokosamoa. "Facebook," she said.

"*Facebook?*"

She held out her hands. "What can I say? If you won't tell me what's going on, a mother has to find out."

"And I thought you knew something was going on because I'm happy." He sighed.

Her mouth spread into a wide, huge smile. "That is how I *knew*, Peniamina." She patted his hand. "All your Wyatt said was that he thought it was cute that you were getting along with Asher. And that this Asher is acting differently lately. I think maybe you might be making him happy, no?"

Peni's heart raced. "Do you think?"

She gave a shrug. "I don't know. That is why you are bringing him to dinner. This Saturday."

"But—"

"Seven o'clock, for dinner." She crossed her arms. Her don't-argue-with-*me* look.

Dinner? Really? What would Asher say? Somehow Peni didn't think Asher would think it was a good idea. Not with all his talk of pushing people away before they could start hating you. "I'll ask, Mama."

She nodded. "Good. And if he is a good man, he will agree to come meet us."

Peni jerked up straight. "*Us?*"

"Your family, Peniamina. We all want to meet him. Didn't your brothers bring their lady friends home to meet the family? Didn't your sister Sala bring her man home?"

Oh, no. It could be an interrogation! "Mama. *All* of you? You'll terrify him!"

She shook her head. "If he is for you, it will be *just* like it was with Sala's Samuelu and Poto's Kelly and Mika's Teuila. We will not throw your Asher to the sharks."

This could be bad, thought Peni. "I'll ask," he said.

"Good," she said and stood and went to the stove. "I have a little left here...."

"I didn't even finish this," Peni told her.

But she took his mug anyway and topped it off and gave it back, and of course he drank it. Because it was rich and thick and wonderful, and because she had made it for him.

"Just remember this," she said, finishing her own and then washing the mug. "This man Asher? Any man should be happy to have you in his life. Lucky!"

Peni blushed—still amazed that his mother was saying such things. "Thank you, Mama."

It wasn't until he was halfway home that Peni realized his mother's command for dinner was the night he and Asher were supposed to have their first "real" date.

"OKAY," SAID Asher over the phone.

"And I know I can make an excuse. I'll tell her that you're in rehearsals—"

"Peni, I said I'll do it."

"Which wouldn't exactly be a lie because, you know, you are in rehearsals and—"

"*Peni!*"

Peni stopped talking.

Then it hit him.

"You'll do it?"

"I'll do it," Asher told him.

"I—I can't..."...*believe it*, he thought.

"You can't what?"

"N-nothing." Then: "You mean it? You don't mind being presented to my family like...."

"Like what?" Asher asked.

Peni shook his head. "I don't know...." *Like a potential husband.*

"Hey, I want to meet them, Peni."

"You do?"

"I do."

"And you don't mind that we were supposed to have our date?"

"We can always do that Sunday."

"You mean it?" Peni still couldn't believe what he was hearing.

"Count on it. That is, if I don't make a *puki'o* of myself and you don't want to see me after that."

Peni grinned so wide it hurt. "I don't think that's going to happen," Peni said. Didn't even bother to tell Asher to *stop* calling himself that word!

And somehow, he quite suddenly felt that everything was going to turn out right!

"OKAY," SAID Asher into the phone, shocking himself. Had he just agreed to meet Peni's family? Him? He, who had sworn he would never meet a guy's family?

"And I know I can make an excuse," he heard Peni saying. It was cute. Peni was trying to get him out of it.

"I'll tell her that you're in rehearsals—"

Which for some reason made him all the more determined. "Peni, I said I'll do it," he said.

"Which wouldn't exactly be a lie because," Peni continued on, oblivious, "you know, you are in rehearsals and—"

"Peni!" Asher cried.

Peni stopped talking. There was a pause. Then (in obvious surprise); "You'll do it?"

"I'll do it," Asher told him, before he could change his mind.

"I—I can't...."

"You can't what?" Asher asked him.

"N-nothing." There was another pause, long enough that Asher almost thought they'd been cut off. But then Peni spoke up, in a tone that almost shamed Asher. He really was a jerk, wasn't he?

"You mean it?" came Peni's voice. "You don't mind being presented to my family like…."

"Like what?" Like a bride-to-be?

"I don't know…."

It was then he quite suddenly realized something. "Hey, I want to meet them, Peni."

"You do?"

He did. He really did. "I do."

"And you don't mind that we were supposed to have our date?"

Well, of course he did. Meeting Peni's family wasn't exactly his idea of the date he'd been waiting for—

I've been waiting to date someone. Me!

—but then it wasn't like Saturday was the last day in the world. "We can always do that Sunday…."

"You mean it?"

Asher grinned. Peni sounded so sweet. Asher loved it. Who knew he needed sweet? "Count on it. That is if I don't make a *puki'o* of myself and you don't want to see me after that." And had he just pronounced *puki'o* correctly? Peni wasn't correcting him, so hopefully that meant he had….

"I don't think that's going to happen," Peni said.

I hope you're right, thought Asher.

Because quite suddenly he knew that it was a night he didn't want to fuck up. He wanted this to go right.

But there was something he had to do first….

CHAPTER TWENTY-TWO

ASHER DID not know how long he sat in his truck outside Temple Kol Emeth. He had lost the time. All he knew was that he hadn't made the service. Oh, he'd made it there on time. He just couldn't bring himself to go into the synagogue.

How many years had it been since his grandfather Yeshiyahu had taken him for Friday night services? Over twenty years, that much was clear. Twenty-five?

The images and memories were vague. Because of the walls that word "Abomination!" had slammed down around him. And also because what his parents had dismissed when he was small— Yeshiyahu taking him to services for a religion that they did not follow—they grew more unyielding about as he approached puberty.

"We don't want our son listening to that crap!" Asher's father would yell. "Filling his head with your antique nonsense. Next thing you'll be doing is trying to brainwash him into following in your footsteps and becoming a rabbi."

For all intents and purposes, Yeshiyahu snuck him to synagogue after that.

"Should we be going?" Asher would ask him during those rare Fridays in the last year or two before Yeshiyahu died.

"Oh yes," the seemingly ancient man had stated. "God's will supersedes the will of man. God *wants* you to go."

"But aren't we lying?" Asher had wanted to know.

"There have been many things done for the greater good," Yeshiyahu would explain. "Jacob stole his brother Esau's blessing and then went on to sire the twelve tribes of Israel! Didn't God allow that?"

At nine or ten, Asher wasn't sure how to answer. He wasn't entirely sure what "sire" even meant except it was what people called a king in movies like *The Sword in the Stone*. He also hadn't had the training he would have had if Yeshiyahu's wishes been met.

So Asher had not been all that sure of his grandfather's argument, but he adored the old man (and had he ever doubted that the old man adored him?), and there had been something sneaky fun in defying his parents' wishes. And after all, wasn't Yeshiyahu his mother's father? Didn't the Commandments say she had to obey him? Didn't Asher therefore have to obey Yeshiyahu as well?

"When a child begins to speak, his father should teach him verses from the Torah."

It upset the old man so much that Asher was being brought up in the ways of the world. It was why, whenever he could, he snuck his lessons in here and there, swearing Asher to secrecy.

Of course, those lessons had ended the day Yeshiyahu had caught him with Ronnie.

Oh, Asher had liked Ronnie.

Truth be told, he thought he might have loved him.

Which had scared him. You weren't supposed to love a boy. Not if *you* were a boy. Everyone said that. Even if the incredibly hot Ryan Phillippe played a gay character named Billy Douglas who was in love with a boy named Ricky on *One Life to Live.*

Asher would have to record the show each day on the sly on the VCR when his parents were at work, and then he would watch them when they went out on their Friday night dates and his sister was hanging out at the mall with her goofy friends.

He would fast forward through the episodes to get to the scenes with Ryan because he would have to catch up and had a few hours a week to do so. All Ryan, aka Billy, ever did with Ricky was hold hands a few times, but oh, it had been exciting!

To this day it was pretty men Asher particularly was drawn to rather than the burly or stocky or hairy.

Pretty men like Peni, who Asher just knew had a smooth, if not totally hairless, chest....

Asher had lost the love of two people that horrible day when his grandfather discovered him with Ronnie.

He'd made a vow during that funeral so long ago.

No God. Nothing Jewish.

But lately, the memories of that man screaming "Abomination" filled his mind more and more. Was that because of Peni?

When Asher rejected his grandfather's religion, had he somehow rejected everything along with it? Thrown the baby out with the bathwater? Had he made it so that fucking was "okay," but *feeling* something for a man… was wrong? He would sit and think about that verse over and over again. It was burned into his memory.

"A man shall not lay with a man as he would with a woman," Asher's grandfather had screamed that day. "It is an abomination."

Had he decided that "lay with a man as he would with a woman" was about emotions? Love? He read more than once that for hundreds of years, during ancient times (and Yeshiyahu's verses had certainly been written in ancient times), men being sexual with men wasn't something men *were*, but just something they *did*. It was rare for male couples to actually bond—to try and find some kind of life together. The prejudices in their cultures made such a thing hard to even conceive, let alone *do*. Had such thinking invaded Asher's thoughts?

Had he decided it was okay to "do" sex with another man, but the minute he could even think about *caring* for one—

"Abomination!"

—his grandfather's voice would come up from the dark, from the grave, and prevent him from being able to do anything *but* fuck?

Or was all of this just psychiatric, mumbo-jumbo bullshit?

Had he somehow decided that fucking a man made him less an abomination than loving one?

It seemed too crazy. Too surreal. Why did he even care about that fucking verse for? Hadn't he rejected it? Rejected the Torah? Rejected *all* of that Judeo-Christian shit?

Was it possible his grandfather was still very much a real and negative force inside his head and that it was keeping him from having a happy and normal life?

And would he have been able to think seriously about any of this—done any soul-searching—when he was almost constantly under the influence of booze?

It was only in the last few weeks that Asher had given any of this any thought at all.

It was all because of Peni.

He and Peni talking about their religious pasts….

Peni desiring to know more about his… and Asher *afraid* to know more about his own?

Talking with Peni about his Samoan heritage had reminded Asher of the heritage he had tried so hard to forget himself. Memories were filling the hours that were not befuddled by intoxication. Memories of the candles. Of the tallit draped over his grandfather's shoulders and head. The haunting and beautiful voice of Yeshiyahu as he sang his prayers.

Ba-ruch A-tah Ado-nai E-lo-he-nu Me-lech ha-olam a-sher ki-de-sha-nu be-mitz-vo-tav ve-tzi-va-nu le-had-lik ner shel Cha-nu-kah....

By why Peni? Why now? Asher had pushed this all out of his life!

It was Peni who longed to know more about the ancient Samoan ways. He'd ignored his Jewish traditions. Exorcised them, in fact!

But then Samoans had a place of honor for men who loved men, after all. What had Peni called them? Fah-fah-feen? Something like that? Yes, Peni wasn't crazy that it meant he would be considered female. But a gay man still had a place!

For Asher? Why, his only place was one where he was hated by God.

Of course the only way Asher had had to deal with that so-called truth was to reject it. But had he buried it deep and ignored it instead? Was the fear that he was hated still there?

It was too horrible.

But what could he do?

Now he *couldn't* forget it.

All for lack of booze! It made him want to dive headfirst into a bottle of gin!

But it was more than a new clarity of mind (even if he was confused at the same time!).

It was these new and growing feelings for Peni....

Love?

Was this love?

And was he actually going to go and have dinner with Peni's family?

Forget drinking. It was enough to make Asher consider running!

Forget booze. And forget Peni. Forget the coming play. Just jump in his truck and drive.

Of course how far would his beat-up truck get him? Why, he worried sometimes about the drive to Terra's Gate. It wasn't like the thing would get him to San Francisco or Chicago or New York!

When the tap came at the window, Asher was so deep in thought he actually let out a scream. He jerked his head to the left, and who should be standing there but an old, heavyset man in a suit, wearing a yarmulke and small round glasses.

The old man nodded. Made a motion with his hands that was clear—roll down your window. Asher stared until the man made the motion again, and then his only choice was to do what the old guy asked or hit the gas and peel out of here.

The second option would look pretty stupid, wouldn't it?

So Asher rolled down the window, cranking the handle like the old guy acted out—Asher's truck was that old.

"Excuse me," said the old man. "Do you need help?"

Asher shook his head quickly. "No!" Then more quietly. "N-no. I'm fine. Just resting…."

"Just resting," the old man echoed. "I saw you before services. I thought maybe you would come in. Then I saw after that you were still here, and I thought maybe…."

"Maybe what?" snapped Asher, then immediately regretted it.

The old man simply looked at him. For what felt like a hundred years. Finally he said, "Aren't you Asher Eisenberg?"

Asher started. "Y-yes," he said. "How did you know?"

"Because you're an actor. I've seen you perform."

Asher doubted it. He could hardly imagine, for instance, the old fart having seen him a year ago in *Tearoom Tango*.

The old man smiled. Nodded. "I saw you in *Tearoom Tango* last year at the Pegasus Theatre."

Asher gaped at the man. "You saw *that*?"

"You were wonderful. You got very good reviews in a play with very *mixed* reviews. I'm not sure Kansas City was quite ready for all the sex, even if the audience never really saw anything."

Asher gulped and was surprised to find himself blushing. "Ah, thank you, sir."

"Rabbi," said the old man. "Rabbi Dov Kushner. Look, won't you come in? You must be cold out here. There's coffee all made."

"I don't know," Asher said.

"Please. For a fan? I bet I can find the program. An autograph? You can be right on your way then…."

For a fan?

Really?

Asher couldn't help but smile.

You got me by my ego, Rabbi Dov Kushner, he thought. Asher nodded, rolled up the window in case it rained—the sky was so overcast that was entirely possible—and climbed out of his truck. It was dark, making Asher wonder how the rabbi had even seen him with only the streetlights haloing down through the skeleton-hand branches of the denuded trees that lined the city block. Leaves blew in great gusts and heaped into gutters. Asher pulled his collar up against the wind and followed the little man inside.

Lightning did not strike him dead.

At least there's that....

They went through a side door and down a staircase into the basement, then across a room with long tables and chairs. Probably used for temple functions—dinners or something? Asher wasn't sure. He'd lost touch, of course, knowing that God hated him. For choosing not to pretend he was anything other than he was. He knew other Jewish guys who prayed on Friday nights and fucked men—or got fucked—on Saturday nights.

That wasn't for Asher.

And how about all those married Jewish men? He'd actually had a guy beg Asher to fuck him while they both wore yarmulkes. Asher declined.

They went into a book-lined office piled high with papers and more books. In fact, Rabbi Kushner had to clear off a chair just so Asher could sit down. He did so, and the rabbi went off and came back with a steaming cup of coffee.

"It might be a little strong. I made it before services. The Sabbath, you know." He sighed. "I hope it's not too strong."

"Sure. I understand, Rabbi Kushner," Asher said, not really understanding at all. It seemed silly to him.

"Please! Call me Dov."

Dov? Really? Not even Rabbi Dov? His grandfather would be rolling in his grave. Asher nodded and drank, and yes, it was strong, but that was okay. He liked his coffee strong. While Asher sipped the very hot brew, Rabbi Dov—*Dov*—adjusted his glasses and began to go through piles of paper. Asher realized he liked this old man. Especially since he was told to call him Dov. He was sure the average congregant could never do such a thing. It made Asher more comfortable, though.

Who is this crazy man?

"I know I have it here somewhere...," Dov said. "Your program? I saved it...."

"I can't believe you saw that," Asher said.

"Why?" asked the old man. "Don't you think rabbis see plays?"

"S-sure." Asher laughed. "I just figured you were more of a *My Name is Asher Lev* kind of guy than the men-pretending-to-suck-each-other-off-on-stage type."

Dov gave a laugh of his own. It was really more of a hoot. Then he grinned and rubbed his hands together, adjusted his glasses once more, and then dove back into his hunt. "I like all kinds of plays. I have diverse tastes. My mind is open, Asher. By the way, do you think your parents named you after the character in Chaim Potok's novel? You could have been, no? The book—I believe it was first published in the early seventies?"

The rabbi stopped, stood up straight, and began to clean his glasses with the edge of his suit jacket. He looked thoughtful. "1972, I believe. Yes. It was the same year *Grease* opened on Broadway." He laughed.

Asher goggled at the rabbi. *Grease*?

"What can I say? I love the theater."

"I guess you do," Asher said. It explained why he went to plays, anyway. And as racy as the play *Grease* really was, with its songs about "pussy wagons" and "the chicks'll cream," let alone the lyric about getting "my rocks" off, maybe that was why the rabbi could see a show like *Tearoom Tango*.

"Here!" the rabbi cried. He held up a six-by-nine folded theater program. "I *knew* I would find it!" He held it out to Asher. "Sign. Please!"

Asher chuckled at Dov's enthusiasm and took the proffered program. "How do you want me to sign it?"

Dov smiled happily. "To my friend Dov... don't use 'rabbi'! Rebecca—my secretary—she will have a stroke!" He grinned even wider. "Write, 'to The Bear from the Actor!'"

So specific? Then suddenly Asher remembered what Dov meant. Bear. Even Wyatt knew that. Hadn't he used the word once or twice around Asher in jest?

Asher signed with a flourish, ending it with a, "Thanks for the coffee on a chilly autumn night. My name is not Asher Lev." He underlined "not." Then finished with, "Yours, Asher Eisenberg."

He handed it back and got another joyful hoot in return. "Oh, *wait* until I show this to Rebecca! She will shake her finger at me! I can see it *now*."

Asher grinned. He couldn't help it. Who was this old man?

Dov sat down. Drank some of his coffee. Grimaced. *"Oy vey!* Strong. *Too* strong. Do you think it would be okay for me to add water?"

Asher shrugged. He didn't have a clue.

Dov nodded. "Yes. God will not care. Wait! I will be back." He scampered out of the room and was back in a flash. "Don't tell Rebecca, all right? She will have problems enough with the autograph, but that is good clean fun. Fixing my coffee? The old lady might *really* have a stroke!"

"I promise," Asher said. "I won't tell."

"Besides, I really don't think God minds, do you? Didn't the Christian Jesus break off heads of wheat and eat them on the Sabbath?"

Asher gave him a funny look. "You don't believe in Jesus, do you?"

Dov touched his glasses again. "Well, I think it is pretty clear the man existed."

"Really?" Asher said. "I'm not convinced. You certainly don't believe that he was the Messiah?"

Dov shrugged, then leaned over his desk and peeked out the door. He sat back. "'There are more things in heaven and earth, Horatio, than are dreamt of in your philosophy.'"

Damn. This guy was a character, wasn't he?

"You are the grandson of Rabbi Yeshiyahu Avraham, are you not?"

Asher gasped in shock. The question came out of nowhere. It was like a punch to the stomach.

The rabbi sighed. "I thought as much." He nodded. "Brilliant man. *Brilliant!* But, and I hope you don't mind me saying so, very closed-minded. He thought he had *the* ear of God. No one knew scripture better than he. And I will give it to him; few did."

Asher's mouth fell open.

Dov leaned back and rested his hands on his round belly. After a long moment, Dov said, "What's wrong? Have you been struck dumb?"

Asher swallowed. "Y-you knew my grandfather?"

"Of course I did. It was hard *not* to know him in his day. He was the rabbi that nearly had a stroke when his daughter turned her back on God. He was *convinced* it was his fault. So he tried to make up for it. He did that with *you.* Sometime I would see you with him. He was so proud of you...."

Asher's eyes went so wide he was afraid they would pop out of his head. "You saw *me?*"

Dov nodded. "Such a boy! Such a *handsome* boy. And such a handsome man you've turned out to be."

Asher raised an eyebrow. Was this old guy…?

Rabbi Dov gave another hoot. "Oh no! Get your eyes back in where they belong. I am not, what do they say? Hitting on you? No, I am progressive, but I like the ladies. Well. I like my wife." He leaned forward, removed his glasses, and wiped his eyes. "But you, Asher Eisenberg. *You* like men, am I right?"

Asher froze again. This man was one of the most forward he'd ever met. No bullshit beat around the bush with him.

Dov put his glasses back on. He leaned forward on his desk, steepled his fingers before him, and waited.

He's going to make me say it. Well, fuck it. Why not? No bullshit with him, none with me. "Yes, Dov. I'm gay. Do you have a problem with that?"

Dov shrugged. "Not at all."

Asher had to fight to keep his mouth from falling open again. *What?*

"I don't have a problem with it at all," he repeated. Pause. "This surprises you?"

"It sure as fuck *does*!" Asher cried.

"Because I'm a rabbi?" Dov asked. "Because you think that *I* think you are some kind of—"

"Abomination," Asher blurted.

Dov sighed and leaned back once again. He studied Asher so long that Asher started to squirm.

"Do *you* think you're an abomination?"

Asher opened his mouth to answer. To say, *Fuck no!* But the words wouldn't come out. They wouldn't goddamned come out. God! *Why* couldn't he say it?

Dov nodded. "You do, somehow, don't you? Why? Your parents aren't religious. You have not attended temple in, what? Twenty years?"

Asher gulped. "M-more or less…."

"So what's the problem?" Dov asked.

And then he did it. It came like water pouring through the floodgates. Like with Peni, but more. Asher told Rabbi Dov Kushner everything. What had happened with Ronnie. What happened when his grandfather walked in on them. How Yeshiyahu had died and left such a hole, such a deep scar in his life….

And dammit.

He cried.

Like a fucking baby.

When he had begun to quiet, he felt a gentle hand on his shoulder and then a handkerchief pressed into his hands. He looked up with blurry eyes—up and across—to see that Rabbi Dov had pulled a chair next to him.

"Closed-minded," he said softly. "Rabbi Avraham had a *very* closed mind."

"W-what do you mean?" Asher asked, hating the way he sounded.

"He was stuck in the old ways. He didn't believe in the new and rising thoughts. Newer interpretations. And in *my* opinion, more than 'newer.' More *accurate*."

"What?" Asher asked. What was the man talking about?

"This verse you quote? 'A man shall not lay with a man as he would with a woman. It is an abomination.' It is not an accurate translation."

"What?" Asher asked again. *I'm beginning to sound like a parrot!*

"In the Hebrew, the word for man? Two words were used there in that verse, not one. The first was *ish*. *Ish* means man. Like you. Like me. A grown man. However…!" Dov held up a finger. "The second word that has been translated as 'man?'" He shook his head. "That word is *zakar*. Which means *young* man. Under thirteen."

"W-what?" Asher asked once more.

"'A man shall not lay with a *boy* as he would with an *isha*—a woman.' This scripture that has haunted you all of your life? It is not about a man lying down—having sexual relations—with another *man* as he would with a woman. It is about a man having sex with a *boy*. An *under*aged *boy*. It is about pedophilia. Of taking advantage of a boy. A boy who in many ways wouldn't even be allowed to say no. It is about taking advantage. And in Middle Eastern cultures, there is *nothing* worse than taking advantage of another person."

Asher fell back in his chair. He couldn't believe what he was hearing. "Is this true? You're not… not…."

"Bullshitting you?" Rabbi Dov shook his head. "No. I am not."

"B-but if that's true…. Why didn't my grandfather know? You said he was brilliant!"

Dov nodded. "He was. But some men are... *oy vey*.... They are set in their ways. Too old to change."

Asher's mind was reeling. He could scarcely believe it. It was... it was too good to be true. Dare he hope what the rabbi was saying was true? Could it be true?

"There's more, if you want to hear it," Rabbi Dov Kushner said.

Asher sat up. "Fuck yes, I want to hear more!"

Rabbi Dov Kushner laughed.

"Then maybe I should put on another pot of coffee?"

Asher jumped to his feet. "Nope. I'll do that. You sit and honor the Sabbath."

Asher did not leave Temple Kol Emeth until hours later.

And interestingly enough? The last thing Rabbi Dov told him was the meaning of his synagogue's name.

It meant "Voice of Truth."

CHAPTER TWENTY-THREE

ASHER ALMOST brought a bottle of wine to Peni's mother for dinner, and then he realized just how much he was set in his old ways. Wine? Really? But wine was what he had always brought to a dinner. Wine was *easy* to bring. Everyone appreciated a bottle of wine. Of course, in this case….

"My family doesn't drink, Asher."

"Of course not," Asher said. Paused. "Not even with dinner?"

Peni shook his head. "Not even with dinner."

"Not even wine?"

Peni laughed. "No. Not *even* wine."

Asher nodded and then lifted the lid off the pan he had simmering on the oven. "So I hope this will do instead," he replied.

Because he'd also learned that when you were invited to a Samoan household for dinner, you always brought something for the table.

It was his Bandgobhi Alu Sabji, a recipe he'd perfected over the years. It was fried cabbage and potatoes with tomatoes, cloves, cardamom, cinnamon, and just a touch of cayenne. He loved it and hoped Peni's mother would as well.

"Wow," Peni said.

"You think they'll like it?"

"Wow! I want to eat it up right now. I know they'll love it."

Asher hadn't been sure what to wear for the evening, but when Peni showed up, looking casual but gorgeous in khaki slacks and a white shirt with loafers, he was relieved to see he'd dressed appropriately. For him it was black dress slacks and a button-down long-sleeved blue shirt. He hoped it brought out his eyes.

The way Peni's eyes had gone wide, Asher secretly thought he was right.

He wanted Peni to like what he saw.

Oh, he wanted it.

He couldn't believe how much he wanted it.

And God, how much he wanted Peni.

He was dying to tell Peni about his evening with the Rabbi Dov Kushner. He found it hard to sit *or* stand with the excitement of it all. But wasn't tonight about Peni? He could save it until later.

Peni was talking a mile a minute in the car on the way to Independence, Missouri, which was only about a twenty-minute drive east from Kansas City. Asher found it terribly amusing. Peni was so obviously nervous it was the only thing keeping Asher himself from opening the car door and doing a tuck and tumble onto the shoulder of the road.

Him! Asher Eisenberg. Meeting a guy's parents? It was crazy. It was insane. Wyatt would have a field day. Damn. Did he already know? Asher was tempted to check Wyatt's Facebook page on his cell, but no. That would be rude. He hated when people were constantly checking their cell phones. Besides, he couldn't stop looking at Peni.

Asher got a little start when he saw the Mormon temple—a huge glowing building that looked like a nautilus seashell spiraling up into the sky. He wasn't sure why he was surprised. After all, the building dominated the Independence skyline. But he had never given it much thought. It was stunning, though. "Is that where your family goes?" he asked Peni.

Peni shook his head. "That's the Community of Christ Temple. It's RLDS."

"RLDS?"

"My family is the original branch founded by Joseph Smith. The Latter Day Saints. RLDS is *Reorganized* Church of Jesus Christ of Latter Day Saints."

"Huh? What's the difference?"

Peni just shrugged. "Don't worry about it, Asher."

"So do you believe that Jesus is coming again to Independence?"

"My mother does...."

His mother believed. But not Peni. Hmmmm.... Asher gave a single nod, and Peni told him to turn right at the next corner. A few minutes later they were there.

Peni's family's house didn't look any different than any of the other houses on the block. As they went up the walk to the front door— Asher carrying a big canvas grocery bag—he saw a lot of bushes and growing things out front. Or at least they would have been a month ago.

Most of it was now brown and yellow, leaves dying and ready for winter.

Peni smiled, gave Asher a nod, and then without knocking, entered the house. "*Talofa*," he called out, which meant "hello."

Right?

Asher had been asking Peni things he should say when they got there. It had pleased Peni too. It turned out that Samoans liked it when you tried to speak their language.

"It shows interest," Peni explained. "It shows respect."

"*Talofa*" came a cry from the back of the house, and then a small woman—slightly round, her mostly gray hair pulled back in a tight knot—appeared through a door at the back of the foyer. She was wearing an apron and wiping her hands on a dishtowel, and when she looked at Asher, her eyes grew wide and she smiled so brightly that he found himself blushing. "*Talofa!* Greetings!" She laid her towel over a shoulder and held her hands out. "You must be Asher. So good to meet you. So happy to have you here tonight."

"Yes, Mama," said Peni. "Asher, this is my mother, Tina." She hugged her son and turned to Asher.

"Tah-low-fah, Mrs. Fah-ah-maw-see-lee," Asher said carefully, putting down the grocery bag and trying not to stumble over the Samoan words (and God, had he ever pronounced Peni's last name correctly?) too badly. "Oh-ah my oy?"—pronouncing that last word just the way Rabbi Dov or his own grandfather would say the "oy" in "oy vey."

Her eyes went even wider, her smile even broader. "I am *good*! I am excellent! *O a mai oe*?"

"Man-we-ah, fa fah-tie," he said, hoping desperately that he'd gotten it at least close. *Manuia, fa'afetai*—fine, thank you.

Peni's mother took several quick steps forward and hugged Asher, her head coming in only at his chest. She gave him a big squeeze and then stepped back, joy radiating out of her. "Please. You call me Tina. None of that Mrs. Faamausili stuff, '*ioe*?"

"All… all right," Asher said, and looked at Peni, who was nodding.

Okay. Call her by her name. "I have something here for you," he said.

"You do?"

Asher bent and reached into the bag and pulled out a big bouquet of flowers. He hadn't been able to get any hibiscus (he hadn't gone out with Preston for drinks in payment for the first ones, and he could hardly do that now, could he?) but he had found a luscious collection of brightly colored lilies.

"Oh my! How beautiful. For me?"

Asher grinned. She was clearly pleased.

"*Fa'afetai,* Asher!"

"You're welcome," he replied, not being able to remember how to say it in Samoan. It was similar, he knew, but with his nerves, the words had flown right out of his head. "I have something else too."

"What is this?" she asked when he pulled the towel-wrapped casserole dish from the bag. He'd placed the Bandgobhi Alu Sabji into the dish before they left his apartment to make it easier to carry, and it made a better presentation as well. At least he thought so.

"It's nothing," Asher said. "Fried cabbage and potatoes. I hope that goes with what you made."

"Asher!" she said, reaching for the towel-wrapped dish. "You shouldn't have. Peni. Why did you let him bring food? He is the guest."

"She'll tell you that you shouldn't have," Peni had told him the day before. "But you should. It's the way. Just tell her it was no problem. Even if it was."

"It was no problem," Asher said, trying not to laugh.

"I will take it to the kitchen. Everyone is down in the basement. Why don't you join them? Dinner will be soon."

She disappeared through the doorway she had first appeared through, and Peni sighed and asked him if he was ready.

Was he?

He wasn't sure.

Then Peni did something Asher wasn't expecting. He began to take off his loafers. As he toed off the second one, he looked over at Asher. "You need to take your shoes off," he said.

"My shoes?"

Peni nodded. "You always take off your shoes in a Samoan home," he explained.

Take off his shoes? "But what would you do if your feet stink?"

Peni laughed. "Your feet don't stink," he said.

"How do you know?" Asher asked.

"Because I've been around when you kicked them off," Peni replied. "They *didn't* stink."

Peni had noticed? "No?"

Peni shook his head and winked. "In fact," he whispered, "they smelled kind of sexy...."

Asher blushed. He was doing a lot of that lately, wasn't he? Among other things. "You could *smell* them?" He was almost horrified.

"Just... a... *little*... bit." Peni winked with both eyes this time. "Nothing offensive. Just *aaaallllll* man."

Asher gulped.

Peni leaned in. "Turned me on," he whispered.

Asher felt his cock stir in his slacks and then thought, *when in Samoa, do as the Samoans do*, and squatted down to untie his dress shoes. He placed them on a long mat apparently there just for that purpose. There were at least a dozen pairs already, lined up in two rows. Asher put his next to Peni's and felt his cock twitch once more.

Really? he thought. *You're getting turned on by putting your shoes next to his? It isn't even footsie!*

Then Peni led the way down a short flight of steps with walls lined with dozens and dozens of photographs. It was an act of genius that had managed to get so many in such a limited space. Leis hung from several of them.

"Family pictures," Peni explained. "Brothers and sisters and aunties and uncles and cousins and... well...." His smile softened, almost turned to a frown. Sadness came into Peni's big, lovely eyes. "This is my father," he said, pointing at one of the pictures framed with a colorful lei.

Asher swallowed and turned to see the man in the picture. It was obviously nothing taken recently. The photography wasn't very good, and it had been blown up to a degree that it was ever so slightly fuzzy. The man was big, heavy, with a large belly. He was naked except for a short sarong that opened at one side, revealing a mass of black lines, arches, triangles, and jagged patterns. The Samoan tattoos.

"Wow," Asher whispered.

"Yes," Peni said, his voice almost reverent.

"He was dancing here. I was just a boy when this was taken. You can see his...."

"Pe'a," Asher finished. *He wants this*, Asher thought, remembering Peni's Halloween costume. When Asher had googled the pe'a, the pictures had been beautiful—even sexy. Just as sexy as Peni had looked with the Sharpie tatau. But the articles had been hard to read. It had to be an extremely painful process. How could anyone subject themselves to such an experience?

But what had Peni said? It was a symbol of manhood. Of honor. And if one wasn't able to finish the process, Peni had further explained, it not only brought shame and dishonor on the man receiving the pe'a, but on his entire family as well.

It was a lot to take in. Asher had hardly been able to read sections of the photograph-filled essays, let alone think of going through it himself.

"He was handsome, don't you think?" came Tina's voice.

They turned to see her standing a few steps above them, a facial expression that was a mix of happiness and sadness. It was quite easy in that moment to see she was Peni's mother. The features were all too clear.

"I see where Peni gets his beauty," Asher said aloud, unaware he was even doing so.

The smile on Tina's face once more became wider—happier. "You are a very sweet man, Asher."

If you only knew, thought Asher. What would Guy think if he heard Tina saying that? Nellie? Melanie?

Then they made their way down the rest of the stairs…

…and into the lion's den.

IT WAS a big area, probably the full length of the house, and the first thing Asher saw was a pool table and a foosball setup. What struck Asher second was the people.

There were a lot of them.

Asher actually stiffened. He knew Peni had some brothers and sisters, figured a few might be here tonight. Well, he had even been warned—he needed to be fair about that. But God! There must have been someone for every pair of shoes there.

Then to Asher's surprise, Peni took his hand—took his hand!— and led him into the circle of people.

He realized he was as scared as shit. But Peni's hand?

It felt nice.

Really nice.

Who'd a thought such a thing?

The hand was warm and soft and—wasn't this crazy?—it didn't embarrass him at all in front of all these strangers—strangers waiting to see the (*palagi*) gay boyfriend.

Wait. Boyfriend?

Was he thinking that he was a boyfriend?

Anyway, Peni's hand felt good.

To Asher's surprise, that hand in his—in front of a roomful of straight people—not only felt good, not only didn't embarrass him, but made him feel strong.

It was completely amazing.

So when the introductions started, he smiled and he shook hands and exchanged a few hugs and made "*talofa*s" and "*o a mai oe*s" where he thought appropriate. They were just as impressed with him using Samoan as Peni's mother had been.

First, there was Poto, Peni's oldest brother—oldest by quite a few years, Asher guessed. He was a big man, really big, heavy in girth and thick-necked and round-cheeked besides. His hair was short and spiked up, and he had an elaborate wrist tattoo that reminded Asher of the pictures of the pe'a he'd googled. Poto liked to play the "see how hard we can squeeze when we're shaking hands" game. Which Asher supposed was okay. Poto probably didn't want his brother getting involved with some sissy, right?

Or did he? Was Poto caught up in traditional Samoan thinking? Was he worried that his little brother might be the *fa'afafine*—the woman of the relationship?

Relationship?

Are we in a relationship?

Asher didn't know what to do, so he squeezed back, and after a moment saw a sparkle in the man's dark eyes—

(so much like Peni's, but smaller in his plump face)

—and then a nod of approval.

Poto's wife was next, and what do you know? She was white with thick red hair.

I'm not the only palagi *here*. Asher felt his stress drop down at least two levels. Her name was Kelly, and she was pretty and a bit plump, but it worked for her. She eyed him suspiciously as well. Asher wasn't sure if it was the Mormon thing or love for Peni, but after he told her how beautiful her hair was, she was smiling and blushing, and Asher cast aside any worries he may have had there.

Next was Mika. He was solidly built as well, although not as overweight as Poto. There was a lot of muscle on this guy, and if he'd had a hairy chest, Asher supposed Wyatt would be about melting by now. His hair was cut short and combed tight to his head, and he had a goatee cut very short as well. He looked a lot more like Peni, but more handsome versus Peni's beauty. Mika was willing to smile, didn't try to break the bones in Asher's hand, and liked the "*talofa*" quite a bit. His wife—Teuila—was obviously Samoan, with her deep tan skin and black hair and black-black eyes. She was a big woman and not in height, with at least two chins to her husband's one. Her eyes flashed, and she eyed Asher up and down, her gaze lingering *just* a bit too long at Asher's crotch. Mika actually had to nudge her, a move that Asher caught. He pretended not to, though, and, blushing, moved down the line.

Sala was cut from very different cloth than her older brothers. She was shapely and bore an incredible resemblance to Peni. Her hair, like Teuila's, was thick and black but hung down in a luxurious waterfall, piling up around her shoulders. She was wearing makeup, unlike her brothers' wives, and it made her dark eyes luminous. She hugged him tight and told Asher how handsome he was and then introduced him to her husband, Samuelu, a dashingly handsome man himself. He gave a firm handshake and an up-and-down perusal as well, although Asher strongly doubted it was in the same vein as Teuila's lingering gaze. He was sizing Asher up, that was clear.

God, I hope there isn't going to be wrestling later on.

Finally there was "little" Lagi, who was not really little at all. Like her sister, she was stunningly beautiful, although Asher supposed she must look more like her father, because he would never have guessed she was related to Peni. She looked like she was in her early twenties, and she giggled and threw her arms around Asher and pulled him close.

"You better be good to my brother," she said. "Or you will hear about it from me!"

The words startled Asher, and he made himself cover an expression that showed it. And when Lagi let go and leaned back, he saw her eyes were flashing mischievously. Was she joking or was the threat real?

Somehow, Asher figured both were true. She was small, like her mother, but somehow he didn't think that made her any less dangerous.

"Don't worry," he told her. "I don't have any plans like that at all."

Why would I? he thought and turned and looked at Peni. His heart swelled. He couldn't believe he was here, in this house, meeting these people, with this beautiful man. He was scared. He was nervous. He was anxious. But to his surprise, he didn't want to be anywhere else. That desire he'd felt sitting in his truck outside Temple Kol Emeth—to run away, to hit the gas and get as far from Kansas City as possible—was gone.

He was exactly where he supposed to be.

THEY ALL sat down around a huge dining table and feasted. Asher could hardly believe how much food was on the table. Sala and Lagi served everyone, and when Asher was handed his plate, he was stunned by how much food was piled there. "You're too skinny," Teuila told him from across the table. "Peni needs to fatten you up." For some reason, this brought much laughter.

There were three kinds of meat. Corned beef, something that looked a lot like a hot dog—

"That's exactly what it is," Peni said, chuckling.

A hot dog? Asher wondered. *With this kind of banquet?* It seemed so incongruous.

—and a chunk of something he couldn't identify.

"It's turkey tail," Peni said when Asher poked it with a fork.

"Turkey tail?"

Peni nodded. "It's my favorite," he said. "But eat too many of those, and you'll lose your washboard abs."

Asher blushed and there was more laughter.

There was also something that looked kind of like ramen noodles, only they were thinner, darker, and softer. Limper.

"That is Samoan chop suey," Peni explained.

It was the last thing he would have guessed, Asher realized. He tried it but thought it really didn't have a lot of flavor. Peni grinned and wolfed his down. Well, obviously Peni thought it did.

The most unusual item, though, was the bananas. They were skinned and darker than the familiar pale yellow. Like maybe they had been dipped in a brown sugar solution. "Dessert?" he asked.

"No! No!" cried Teuila. "Eat. You will like. *I* brought them."

So Asher went to cut a piece and was surprised by its density. More like a mostly cooked carrot. He took a bite and found it was nothing like he imagined. He was expecting sweet. But it wasn't sweet in the least. It was more like a baked potato, denser, without any butter or even salt. In fact, it had less flavor than the "chop suey." He wasn't sure he liked it at all.

He smiled, though, when he looked up and saw Teuila's expectant expression. "Wow," he said. Then, so he wasn't lying, told her his inner thought—that it was nothing like he thought it would be. "It doesn't taste like a banana."

She nodded vigorously. "It is boiled. We use very green bananas."

"It kind of reminds me of a potato," he said.

"Yes," said Peni's mother. "We eat them a lot like that."

Lagi grimaced at him and stuck out her tongue. It lasted only a second. Then she was grinning, and he couldn't help but laugh. It was his thought exactly.

But if they had a potato-like dish, had he brought the wrong thing?

"Asher," cried Peni's mother. "This is wonderful! What is it?"

He sighed inwardly in relief. "It's Bandgobhi Alu Sabji, Mrs.... I mean, Tina."

That earned him a smile.

"It's a Middle Eastern dish. It's a well-worn recipe for me."

"Well, it is very good!"

That made everyone try it, and he was pleased when everyone seemed to like it.

"I can't believe there's so much food!" he said. "Thanks for doing all this."

Lagi shrugged. "This is the way we always eat," she said.

"*Really?*" He was astonished.

"Why do you think we Samoan men are so big?" Poto asked, and once more there was much laughter.

Asher joined in. It felt good. It felt wonderful. He couldn't remember being so happy.

He felt a gentle squeeze on his thigh and looked to see Peni's hand resting there. Then he looked up into his eyes, and once more felt a surge he never really felt until the last few days.

I think I'm falling in love, he thought and felt tears welling up in his eyes. Peni's widened in surprise and seemed to get wet as well.

But then he cleared his throat and forced himself to look away. Tried the turkey tail and found it was delicious. It was almost entirely fat. But God, it was good!

"This is wonderful," he said. "But you're right, eat too many of these and...."

"You'll look like *me*!" declared Poto.

"Oca!" cried Tina. "That would take a *lot* of turkey tails."

Howls of laughter.

Poto stood up and clutched his big belly. "I'm dedicated!"

Asher tried not to laugh, but he couldn't help it and joined in.

He looked around the table at the big family, all of whom obviously loved each other so much. So different than what he remembered at his own family's table. He supposed his parents loved him. His mother had told him so as a kid. She said it as they hung up the phone—*when* they talked on the phone. But jokes? No. Loud boisterous laughter? *Never*. His parents were serious. They were masters of serious.

Asher looked. He watched. They were talking, poking each other, passing food, teasing....

It was all so *not* what he was expecting. These people were Mormons. He'd expected serious and....

God. Had he expected a table of Yeshiyahus?

He had.

He'd watched those "What Mormons Believe" videos on YouTube, and somehow he'd expected a room of people just as smiley and pretentious and affected as the woman *in* those videos. These were people who were supposed to be thinking that what was happening with him and Peni—

(and was there something happening?)

—was wrong. But from what he could see—

(he turned and looked at Peni, and his breath caught)

—that's not what they were thinking at all. Or they were the most polite people he'd ever known in his life. Or they loved their brother and son—

(*Oh my God! I'm in love!*)

—and wanted what was best for him.

(Could he be the best for Peni?)

"What?" Peni asked. "Do I have something stuck in my teeth?"

"You're perfect," Asher said. And meant it with all of his heart.

CHAPTER TWENTY-FOUR

AFTER DINNER they went out back. It was chilly, and Asher was allowed to get his shoes, much to his relief. A big metal fire pit had been set up and lit, and they sat and talked.

Tina put on some Samoan music and had soon talked her boys into dancing. And even as chilly as it was, they all went in and took off their pants and put on sarongs—they called them lava-lavas—and how they danced!

After two numbers they pulled Asher into their midst and decreed it was time for him to learn. He didn't want to, but one look from Peni and that was all she wrote. Again, there was laughter, but hell, so what? And it was fun, and he even threw in a few of his own moves, which earned him many hoots and hollers.

Then Tina served them all the kokosamoa Asher had heard so much about and—*whoa!*—it was thick and sweet and strong. It was actually gritty from all the tiny chocolate nibs that had not quite melted. He was almost buzzing from all the sugar and caffeine, and he found himself imagining having more, here in this place, with these people.

At one point, as a discussion he was having with Sala and Lagi ended and they left to do whatever it was that Tina had asked them to do, he found himself joining Peni and his brothers—and almost immediately wondering if he was intruding.

"Are you sure, little brother?"

"I've never been so sure of anything in my life."

They were all nodding and froze when they saw Asher.

"Ah, do you need me to go away?" he asked.

"No, Asher," Peni said and reached up and touched his arm. "Stay."

"Peni," said Mika. "Have you told him? Have you told Asher?"

"Told me what?"

Peni sighed. "About the pe'a," he said.

Asher nodded. "That you want to do it?"

Peni's eyes widened slightly, then relaxed. "Yes."

Asher looked at Peni's brothers. "It's dangerous?"

"It can be," said Poto. "Not like it used to be. But yes. It can be dangerous."

Asher reached out and touched Peni's face. "I don't want anything to happen to you now... now...." He swallowed.

"Now what?" Peni said.

Could he say it? But looking into those beautiful eyes, he knew he could.

"Now that I've found you."

Peni's eyes went wide again, and they welled up with tears. "Oh, Asher."

Asher realized he had never wanted to kiss someone so much in his life. He wasn't going to do it in front of Peni's brothers, though.

But he could hold him. Couldn't he?

The question was moot an instant later when Peni stepped forward and wrapped his arms around Asher, buried his face in his chest.

To Asher's surprise, when he looked over Peni's shoulder's, his brothers were smiling.

CHAPTER TWENTY-FIVE

PENI HAD talked nonstop on the way *to* his mother's house. He'd been so nervous! But as it turned out, there really was no reason. He shouldn't have been worried. Everything had gone wonderfully. From beginning to end. His mother had been wonderful. Asher had been wonderful.

Asher *was* wonderful.

He could hardly believe Asher was the same man that he met all those months ago at a huge Fourth of July party for gay men thrown by one of the richest men in the world.

Every time he looked across a room and saw Asher standing there, being charming with his mother and sisters, doing his best to find something he could talk about with Peni's brothers, he heart just raced. They were accepting Asher.

And it wasn't until tonight that he realized how much he wanted that.

What was going on?

Peni had not had any intention of letting this go anywhere. But oh, it had, hadn't it?

It was one of those times when he met eyes with Asher over dinner that something... happened. He wasn't sure what. They were talking, just talking, and they looked at each other... and suddenly it was like... like they were looking into each other's souls.

He was so startled, he made some kind of stupid comment—like, "What? Have I got something caught in my teeth?"

Then on the very tail of that, something quite clearly occurred to him.

I think I'm falling in love with this man....

It seemed an impossible thought to have immediately after making such a stupid comment. But there it was.

And now? Listening to Asher talk faster and faster, he realized there was no "think I'm falling in love" about it.

He was. He was in love.

Alofa ia te oi… I love you.

"Peni," Asher was saying. "It's like… like mountains have been lifted off my shoulders. It was like there was a cage around my heart, and then suddenly it was open. I wish I could explain… but Peni. I feel free!"

It turned out that Asher had had a very powerful and wonderful experience. He had done what he didn't think he could do. He had gone to a rabbi and talked.

And apparently let go of demons that had been buried deep inside him for a long time.

"Oh, Asher," Peni said, heart swelling, the love growing. "Why didn't you tell me about this before?"

Asher leaned back in his seat. "Because *tonight* was about *you.* Not me. *Last* night was my night."

"But Asher! It was just a dinner. What you're saying now—"

"Was something that could wait. Hell, Peni. I waited over twenty years to talk to that rabbi—or someone like him. I could wait a few more hours to tell you about it."

How amazing was that? Everything Peni had ever heard about Asher, and everything he had seen until just these past weeks, was that the man was totally self-absorbed. Needed to be in the limelight all the time. After all, hadn't he chosen to be an actor? And yet despite all that, what Peni had been seeing more and more of was a very different man. A man like he saw tonight. Who was putting others first.

Who was putting *Peni* first.

"You should have told me on the way to my mother's house," Peni said. "I wasn't talking *about* anything!"

"I just love listening to you talk," Asher said.

Peni's heart skipped. Asher meant that. Asher meant it!

"Peni—I owe you so much."

"Me?"

"*You,* Peni. Y-you were right. I *do* have a drinking problem. I don't know if I'm an alcoholic, but I *have* a problem. Fuck. I have a bunch of problems. And when you challenged me not to drink?" He sighed. "At first I was kind of pissed. I thought, how dare he tell me I'm an alcoholic? I thought you were… forgive me, but… well, kind of sanctimonious."

Peni shrugged. *Maybe I am?*

"But I was going to prove I could do it. I was going to *show* you!" Asher shook his head. "I'm so sorry."

"You don't have to be, Asher."

"Don't you see? I did it for the wrong reasons."

"Did you, Asher? These last weeks, you and me. I think it's been pretty—"

"Special," said Asher. "Wonderful."

"I think so too," Peni said, his heart speeding up.

Asher was smiling now. "You know what? I may have started that thirty days to spite you. But then something happened. I began to… to think… *differently*. More clearly."

They had pulled off the highway and were now moving down a quiet city street. They would be back at Asher's any moment. But the thing was, Peni didn't want to go home. He wanted to stay with Asher.

As they drove the last blocks, Asher told him about what had been happening with his play. How the lines of dialog ripped and tore at him. "At first I thought the script was funny" Asher was saying as Peni parked the car. He was able to get a space almost directly in front of Asher's building. It was a Saturday night, after all, and everyone must have been out on dates.

Like us, Peni thought. *We've been on a date. Our first. And it was at my mother's!*

"But as each night passed and I began to *hear* the words, I began to wonder if I could even *do* the show. I started seeing myself in the characters. All of them. And you know what? That is what an actor *tries* to do. Find something in the character he can relate do so he can bring them to life. But *this* character?" He shuddered. "These *characters*? Drinking and drinking and *drinking*…. I saw that is what *I've* been doing. Drinking until I didn't even know what I was doing. I hate it! I hate that I was that way. And now I have to stand up on that stage, night after night—for a *month*!—and be a drunk. I don't know if I can do it."

"You can't quit the show," Peni said. "Aren't they depending on you?"

Asher nodded. "It's going to be hard," he said. "But hell! I'm an actor. I'm not the characters I play—even if sometimes I pull on my own life to create them onstage. Maybe this is karma? Maybe it's the final thing I have to do to start putting this all behind me?"

Peni turned sideways in his seat and reached out and placed a hand on Asher's thigh. He did it to assure him. But oh, oh the muscles in that thigh!

Get your mind where it needs to be, Peni!

"I'm so proud of you, Asher."

Asher looked at him in astonishment. "You are? For what?"

"For everything. For your talent. For what you've done this month. For *not* drinking. You've changed so much. I'm the one who should apologize."

"For what?"

"For ever thinking you were a—" No. Say it in English. "An asshole."

Asher sighed. "Aren't I? An asshole?"

"No, Asher. You're not. And I suspect it was the alcohol all along. *It* was the asshole."

"But doesn't booze bring out the real person?" Asher asked him.

"I don't think so."

Asher shook his head. Looked back at a lifetime. Looked back at the way he'd treated three men that were supposed to be his best friends. He'd been doing that a lot lately. "God, Peni. I've been ugly to so many people. Even people I care about!"

"But that's not necessarily you anymore, Asher."

"You know what I hate? The predicament I've put my life into! I *like* drinking, Peni. What I said to you before? It wasn't a lie. I get so much pleasure from finding some new and delicious cocktail and sharing it with friends. But now I'm afraid I *can't* drink anymore. Not at all. What if that's the case? What if I can't?"

Peni sighed. "Then that's the way it will be, Asher. What if you found out you were diabetic? Or allergic to something? What if you had a heart attack, and you couldn't eat certain foods anymore? You could do it, couldn't you?"

"Yes," Asher said with a sigh.

"And Asher?"

"Yes?" Asher asked, his beautiful eyes big and heavy lidded.

"I'll be here. Right here. Every step of the way. I will be here for you not drinking. And if you decide you want to test if you can drink like a normal person, you know, by having just one or two? I'll be here too. I'll help."

"You'll be here for me?"

The look on Asher's face broke Peni's heart. Asher looked so vulnerable. Being vulnerable, especially where others could see, was not something Asher did.

"Yes, Asher. Right by your side."

"Peni?" Asher was looking at him, his eyes wide. Was… was he crying?

"Yes?"

"May I kiss you?"

Peni nodded. There was nothing he wanted more.

Peni closed his eyes and leaned in, and then those lips—*Asher's lips*!—touched his at last. And even was so soft and gentle, his heart begin to pound like Samoan drums.

Then they were kissing harder, mouths parting, tongues touching, caressing—Asher's hand now touching Peni's cheek, stroking his face. Peni reached for Asher's cheek, touched him the same way. So gentle but so… powerful.

His heart was racing now, his heart pounding in his ears.

And then he was pulling back.

"Asher," he said. "Take me upstairs."

Asher looked up at him in surprise. "Upstairs? But…. Do you…?"

"I want you to make love to me, Asher."

"B-but I thought you said that wasn't going to happen on our first date."

Peni laughed. It was pure joy pouring out of him. "Let's be real, Asher. We've been dating for a month."

Asher grinned. "We have, haven't we?" he said. "That's just what I've been thinking."

That sat for another minute, neither saying a word.

And then they got out of the truck and went upstairs.

CHAPTER TWENTY-SIX

THEY KICKED their shoes off by the front door first—it made them laugh.

Then Asher took Peni to his room.

Peni's heart was racing. It had been months since he'd been touched. Touched and made love to... and then it had ended so badly. That man, that big sexy man, Bobby Brubaker, had broken his heart. Oh, but then Peni had been foolish. Bobby had never professed to want anything but sex. Peni had chosen to be blind. To think there was something there that wasn't.

And tonight?

He was scared. He wanted to be with Asher so badly. But what if....

Asher lit candles, and that surprised him. Candles. He turned on some soft music. Somehow that didn't seem like the kind of thing Asher would do. Peni imagined he was more of a Marvin Gaye kind of man. *Sexual Healing* or some such thing.

The candles and music were... romantic.

"Peni?" Asher whispered—as if anyone could hear....

"Yes, Asher?"

"I have to tell you something." *Did Asher's voice just crack?*

"What?" Peni asked.

"Peni... I... I've never done this before...."

Peni looked at Asher, puzzled. Never done this before. Done what before...? "What, Asher?"

"I've...." Asher leaned in and kissed him, very lightly.

Kissed? Surely he'd kissed.

"Peni... I've never made love to anyone before."

Peni trembled. What? What was Asher saying? Never.... "Never made love to anyone. But...?" What was he saying? Because he *knew* Asher wasn't a virgin.

"*Peni*... I've only... well... *fucked*. I've never taken a man to bed before that... that I cared about."

Cared about? Peni's heart began to pound once more. That drumming had come back. So like Samoan drums. "Cared about?" he asked aloud.

"And... I'm kind of scared."

Peni's eyes widened. He couldn't help it. Scared? Asher scared? It was hard to believe. "Scared?"

Asher nodded. "Yes. I feel like... like a virgin." He laughed. "Is that crazy? *Me?* A virgin? But dammit—and if you ever tell Wyatt I said this, I will deny it—but it's like that damned Madonna song, Peni. My heart. It's *pounding*! It feels like it could explode in my chest. I've never felt like this before. *Oh, Peni...!*"

Peni kissed him. Kissed him hard. He threw his arms around Asher's shoulders and pulled himself up against that chest, that muscular, hard body, and *kissed* him. He moaned, almost sobbed, only to hear Asher returning the same sounds. He tore at Asher's shirt, not caring if he ripped off the buttons, and then Asher's big strong hands were stopping him.

"No!" he commanded. "No... I want this to last. I want this to last forever."

And so, with a strangled whine, Peni let Asher lead the way.

They took all night.

CHAPTER TWENTY-SEVEN

BIT BY bit they cast off their clothes.

They marveled, the both of them. Marveled at each other's bodies, the solid muscles, the smooth, flawless skin. They kissed, they touched, ran lips over fingers and the inside of elbows. Suckled gently (at first) on hard nipples. Explored.

For Peni, it was still all new. Bobby had been the boss in bed and, surprisingly, done most of the work. So he was trying things he'd never gotten to try before. Kissing in places that he'd never dreamed of when he first realized he wanted to be with men. Asher's armpit, his waist, the groove that traveled from his hip to his... his cock.

And it *was* huge. It was everything Wyatt and Sloan had said. It was beautiful and terrifying. How would he ever take that into his body? He didn't see how he could take it in his mouth!

FOR ASHER it was new because he was taking his time. He wasn't showing off. He wasn't forcing and cajoling and proving that even the most dedicated top would melt in Asher's hands and let himself be taken. That didn't mean he wasn't showing off, wasn't showing Peni the most magical time he could.

But now?

Now, somehow, it was all new. He wasn't playing with places—like toes and the tips of fingers and behind Peni's ears—just to shock and surprise and show how good it felt to have those places explored. Instead he wanted this to be magical for Peni. Wondrous. He wanted to play the man's body like an instrument. He was running sweet little kisses down Peni's chest and tight flat tummy to his beautiful hard cock. It was glorious. Perfect. Exactly the right size. Smaller than his own—

(and yes, Asher's ego needed that)

—but not small by any means. It was thick. Maybe thicker than Asher's. And yes, perfect! Not darker than the rest of Peni. It was Asher's (rather plentiful) experience that most men of color had a much darker cock than the rest of their body. But not Peni's. It was the same lovely shade as the rest of him. He loved how the crown flared wide and triumphant, the trunk throbbed in need, the tip extruding a glistening pearl of Peni's nectar. Asher licked it away, and it was salty sweet, and he knew he could hardly wait to drink this down.

But not tonight.

Tonight he had something else in mind.

He was doing all of this not to show off, but because he wanted to make love to every single inch of Peni. He was doing it for his own pleasure as much as for this man he loved.

Loved.

"Peni?" he whispered, on top of him, chest to chest.

"Yes, Asher?"

"I—"

God. Could he say it?

Yes.

He *had* to.

"I think I love you."

"Oh, Asher!" Peni cried. "Asher, I love *you*."

Too much! thought Asher. It was too much. Too much to believe. It was perfect!

"Peni?"

"Y-yes?" Peni could hardly seem to talk. It was more a sob than anything else.

"I want you inside me. I want you to *cum* inside me."

"What?" Peni asked, beautiful dark eyes going wide. "But...."

"I know I'm clean. I get tested all the time. And I *never* fuck a man without a condom. Almost never. There was one man...."

Sloan. It had been Sloan.

Crazy.

But he'd been feeling a little of what he was feeling tonight.

Imagine if he'd waited to take Sloan to his bed instead of hauling him off that night they'd met. They might still be together.

But no. He could never have waited in those days. He hadn't been ready.

Tonight he was ready. He was also ready for something he'd never let any man do before.

Because it would have made him an abomination.

If he had let a man take him, then *he*—Asher—would have been taking the part of a woman. Something that men weren't supposed to do. At least that was what his grandfather's culture would have said…. What any culture from that part of the world would say.

But he knew it was a lie now.

Because he was a man in love with a man. Not a woman. Being fucked or fucking didn't change that. Tonight he would prove it.

"There was one man," Asher said. "A long time ago. But I know I am safe. And I topped him. You?"

PENI FELT he might faint. He was dizzy.

"I've been tested, Asher. Over and over these past months. I was so scared. But they're sure. The doctors. They think I'm okay. But Asher. Are you sure? You want…." *Me? You want me to… be inside you?*

"I more than want. I *need*."

AND BROOKING no further argument, Asher got the lube. He coated Peni's length—and it was so hard, so rigid, he could hardly pull it up and away from Peni's body—and then straddled him. He reached back. Touched himself, touched his hole, coated it with lube—

This is going to hurt….

—and he began the arduous process of taking that length inside him.

A little bit… and back…. A little bit more… and back…. A little bit…. Back.

Then to Asher's surprise, the head popped right in!

"*OH!*" SHOUTED Peni as the heat and wetness enveloped him. Tight! So tight. So wet and smooth and like velvet and God! Hot. So hot.

He almost came in that instant.

Asher froze, and Peni looked up and saw the muscles standing out in his strong neck, saw eyes widen and feared he was in pain—

God no! I don't want you to hurt!

—but then he saw it. Asher wasn't in pain. He was…
…surprised.

PENI WAS so hard and God, Peni was inside him. And full!

God! I'm so fucking full!

But it wasn't pain.

Not exactly….

And as he slid down Peni's length—slowly, slowly—he quite suddenly *knew* what he was feeling.

He was feeling *alive*. More alive than he'd ever felt in his life.

Then, as his asscheeks met the soft curls of Peni's pubic hair, the head nudged firmly against Asher's prostate, and he almost came in that very instant.

But no! Not yet. I can't yet.

So he just sat there for a moment. Breathing deep. Accepting Peni into far more than just his body. He looked down into that impassioned face and knew it was over. Peni was in his *heart*.

"I love you," he said.

To his joy, Peni echoed him. "I love you, Asher."

ASHER LEANED in close and kissed him, and then somehow, Peni wasn't sure just how, did some kind of roll, and Peni was on top.

"Peni," he gasped.

"Yes, Asher."

"How do you say fuck me in Samoan."

Peni laughed. "I told you. We don't have words for so many sexual things. We just do it. But…. But I know there is this phrase—*ua fia mea*. It means something like that. Like, 'do you want to go….' That's not it. That's not right, but…."

"*Ua fia mea*," Asher said. "Please, Peni. *Ua fia mea*."

So Peni did. He had to find the rhythm. He wasn't sure at first. Had to find the angle.

But then a million years of instinct took over, and he was doing it. Fucking Asher. And nothing had prepared him for the exquisiteness of it. The exquisite pleasure.

"Oh God," cried Asher.

I DIDN'T know! Asher marveled. *I didn't know it could feel like this! My God! My God my God my God*!

How could he have known?

How could he *not* have known?

All those men who had so loved it when he fucked them? Why, it wasn't just his big cock taking control—possessing. It wasn't just those men who wanted to give up control—who wanted to be possessed. No—

(although that was surely part of it)

—this was pleasure! This was exquisite pleasure.

They fucked and *fucked* and then cried out and came, both at almost exactly the same time.

Peni, seeing the utter, unbelievable joy and thrusting deep into this man he loved and planting his seed, pumping it, deep deep deep, into Asher.

Asher, seeing and feeling the pumping, the jets, the pulsing of the blood in Peni's cock, the wetness of the seed planted deep within him.

He shot his semen in great arcs, high and thick, jetting over his shoulder, hitting the damned headboard, and it was like he was shooting his very soul out of his body.

Then Peni collapsed on top of him, and they became even more one than when they were locked together, their bodies conforming to each other.

They held each other, and they breathed into each other's mouths, breathed each other's breaths, and enfolded each other in limbs and hearts.

CHAPTER TWENTY-EIGHT

RESTING HIS head on Peni's chest, Asher lay marveling at what had just happened.

Neither said anything for a long time.

Then, finally, Asher sat up. He sat Indian-style and looked down at the beauty that was Peni. He reached out and caressed his chest—his hips—his thighs. Thighs that still had the shadow of his Sharpie tattoos. Sharpie markers didn't wash off that easily. He chuckled.

Then he did something else. He splayed his fingers out, raked them gently, once more, over Peni's hips and thighs... imagined the shadows of black pathways and arches and jagged lines...

...and knew.

"You'll be beautiful...."

"I'll be... what?"

"When you get your pe'a. You are beautiful now. But then? You will be beyond beautiful. Not just because of the lines. But because... because.... It is your people."

Peni's voice caught. "B-because it *is* spiritual, Asher. It *is* my people. It is my heritage...."

"Yes, Peni," Asher said and bent to kiss all the places those lines would one day cover.

"Asher?"

He looked up, locked eyes with those bottomless black orbs. "Yes?"

"Samoan men... when they get the pe'a. The take their best friends. Their brothers. Those most special to them. I know it might be horrible... but would you...?"

"Yes," said Asher. "You honor me."

And Asher knew it would be horrible. To watch this man he loved be put through so much pain, so much blood—

And danger! People died!

—but he would also be witness to Peni's transformation.

If he loved this man—

I do! Oh, I do!

—could he do anything less than be there for Peni?

No. He couldn't.

The look of wonder on Peni's face. Look!

"I love you, Asher Eisenberg."

"I love *you*, Peniamina Faamausili."

From the smile, Asher knew he got it right.

"May I ask one thing?" Asher asked.

Peni sat up, his smile wondrous. "Anything."

"Anything?" Asher said and gave Peni his most mischievous look.

Peni giggled. "Anything."

"Can you wait until my show is over?"

Peni laughed and threw himself into Asher's arms.

"Oh yes! Yes yes yes yes yes!"

And then they made love again.

CHAPTER TWENTY-NINE

OPENING NIGHT. A full house. Asher was in character as Matt, along with Melanie as Cindy, Louis as Don, and Linda as Kensie. It all came down to this. But Asher had no time to think about all that. He *was* Matt.

"Where's my gun?" Cindy asked.

"I tucked it in the pocket of his bag," *Matt* said, pointing to Don. "I didn't want the maid to see it and freak out." He left the room and came back with it a moment later. "See, here it is." He looked at it. "Oh, *fuck* me. No wonder it didn't work. The *safety's* on!"

Matt released the safety, and when the gun immediately fired, he jumped and let out a startled shout.

He wasn't the only one in the room to do so!

Kensie's eyes flew open wide, and she jerked back and grabbed her shoulder and fell over backward. Don and Cindy stared, stonily silent, then looked back and forth between Matt and the fallen Kensie.

"Fuck," said Cindy.

Matt trembled—staggered. "Oh, God. I killed Kensie. I didn't *want* to kill her. I *liked* her. What did I do?" He put the gun to his temple, and as his fellow actors froze, there was a gasp from the audience.

"I'm okay," said Kensie, the producer. "Put down the gun, sweetie." She tried to sit up. "Actually, not okay." She winced in pretend pain. "Been shot. This hurts like a bitch."

"Call 911," Cindy cried.

"No 911!" Kensie shouted and grimaced again. "*No* cops."

"You're okay?" said Don.

"No, I'm *not* fucking okay! I've been *shot* in the shoulder!"

The audience chuckled in uncomfortable laughter. Kensie's shoulder was bleeding. Stage magic at its best.

"Does it hurt?" Matt asked.

"Yes, you moron. It hurts like a *bitch*."

After that the end came quickly. Kensie swore them all to silence. The characters had finally done what they were supposed to do in the first place: sign off on a movie script so that it could go into immediate production. Action was also determined on the gunshot wound. "Okay," said Kensie. "We're going to go to this guy the studio has on retainer. Someone who will take care of this without having to call the police."

"Like a mob doctor?" asked Cindy.

"I think he *was* a mob doctor."

(And yes, there was the hoped for laughter. There had been much laughter tonight, much to Asher's relief. The gun shooting Kensie was far from the darkest moment in the play. The audience could have gone either way with this show—loving it or hating it.)

"He's pretty good with gunshots," she continued. "I think he can notarize these too." She held up the now signed contracts (and yes! More laughter).

Then they started to carry Kensie out the door (offstage) to a "car" to take her to get help.

Meanwhile, Matt had had his phone returned to him. He looked down at it with dread. He had done something very stupid when he was drunk.

(Asher could identify. Hadn't he done enough stupid things?)

"Hey," he said. "My ex left me a message."

Louis was looking at his phone as well. He sighed. "My wife has left me many, *many* messages."

Cindy walked over to Don and kissed him lightly on the cheek. "We'll make it better. See you on the set."

"Let's go before I fucking die, please," moaned Kensie.

"Gotta go," said Cindy (getting the last line of the show). "Miss bossy over here...."

They all walked offstage except for Louis (who Asher knew was now looking around the room, at the disarray, the damage, and the empty bottles of booze). He was shaking his head by now, booting up his laptop, and sitting back down to write. There was only the sound of typing. Then silence as he stopped and walked over to one of the coolers—grabbed another beer. The house lights faded as he took a final drink.

There was silence then. A silence that seemed to go on for hours.

This was it.

This was the moment.

Asher held his breath.

Then it came.

The applause. It went on and on, and they hadn't even taken the stage.

He looked at his fellow actors, who were all beaming. Melanie actually gave him a quick hug, and then they were walking out onto the lit stage and the clapping continued, the audience now on their feet. Asher could only see the first row clearly because of the bright lights, but yes. Everyone was standing.

Including Peni, who was in that first row and—*God!*—he was crying! Why was he crying? Was the play too much? Did it remind his lover *too* much of how Asher was in real life?

But no! How he *had* been. He wasn't that anymore. And with Peni at his side—

My side. I have someone at my side!

—he was going to keep it that way.

Then he saw the rest. All in the front row. Sloan and Wyatt and Scott, his best friends—

I have best friends! I can't be that bad with friends like them.

—and of course Max and Cedar.

The actors bowed and bowed again, and then it was time to leave the stage, and they all hugged each other fiercely backstage. Melanie hugged him again, tight.

"I had my doubts, Asher. But…. You've… changed."

Asher's heart swelled. For one instant, he almost fell back into a dark place—thinking of how bad he must have been—but then there was Peni, running to him, and any darkness was gone. Peni leapt into his arms, and they were kissing—kissing hard and deep—and Linda told them to get a room.

So they did.

Right at the Meridian Hotel.

Care of Rodger, Asher's boss.

Miracles never ceased.

CHAPTER THIRTY

ASHER AND Peni had just finished making love—

(and Peni had topped again—he found he liked topping, and lo and behold, Asher found he liked bottoming)

—and were spooned tightly together. It was the second time that night. They were full of nervous energy, couldn't sleep, too excited about what was coming.

The tickets were bought—had been for a month—the contacts made, the *tufuga ta tatau*—the pe'a artist found, the appointment made.

In four days they were flying to Samoa.

There had been challenges to overcome. Sure, tourists arrived and tracked down men who would give them the pe'a rather easily these days. A time when only high chiefs could get the exotic full-body tattoos were past. Money was money, and the people in Samoa were often poor.

But that was not what Peni was after. He needed his work done by the tufuga ta tatau. Otherwise, as far as he was concerned, he might as well get tattoos done by a gun from an artist in Kansas City.

The words tufuga ta tatau were hard to translate, Peni said. Like so *many* Samoan words. One word could mean many, many things, depending on the context. One word or phrase in English could also be said several different ways in Samoan. But the best that he could express tufuga ta tatau was "those whose special talent is to put pictures in the skin."

In Samoan society, the tufuga ta tatau have a very high rank and honorable place—a lot of trust was placed in them, for obtaining the pe'a is a great ordeal and (as Asher constantly worried) sometimes dangerous.

At first Peni found reluctance greeting his wishes. He began to suspect it might have something to do with his sexuality—although he had no proof. If the Samoans considered him *fa'afafine*, then that meant they considered him a woman. Women were *not* allowed to receive the pe'a for *any* reason. To find a tufuga ta tatau that would give the pe'a to a woman was an impossibility, no matter what the payment.

Just as Peni was about to despair, Poto, his oldest brother, stepped in and saved the day. He was going to go to Samoa and get his pe'a as well. He explained that as the eldest son of a chief, it was his responsibility. "And if you, little brother," Poto said, rubbing his knuckles briskly against Peni's close-cropped hair, "can rise to such a challenge, then who am *I* to sit at home and watch the Chiefs game?"

His wife, Kelly, showed a lot of concern. She was not Samoan—did not understand the importance of the pe'a. But in the end she relented. "But I am going!" On that she put down her foot.

So when Poto stepped in, doors magically opened. It was happening.

Asher couldn't help but worry—couldn't help but be astonished at Peni's calm and seeming lack of fear. Yes, his lover—

Lover! Me! I *have a lover.*

—had a remarkably high threshold of pain, but this was no scrape, no sprained ankle (Asher and Peni had been running lately with Max and Sloan's Front Runner's Group and Peni had fallen and hurt himself one Saturday morning and wound up very black and blue without more than a few winces of pain), no teddy bear tattoo. This was going to be day after day of what Asher saw as torture.

But Asher knew he had to support Peni. As Peni explained, his whole life had led up to this moment. "That," he said, "and meeting you."

That night had been like the other nights recently. They would fight off the anxiety with lots of loving (and sometimes crazy-wild) sex. And also because sex would be off the table for several months after Peni's ordeal, while he healed. How would he keep his hands off of his lover?

And it was while lying there satiated (but still with sniggles of worry) that Asher was jolted just as he had finally *almost* dozed off by his cell phone ringing again—for the third time. "What the *fuck*?" he cried.

What hadn't he just turned the damned thing off?

It was then that it hit him. It was ringing the Beethoven's Fifth ring!

He reached for the phone, looked at the flashing screen. God.... It was the Pegasus Theatre. Why would they be calling at this time?

"Hello?" he said into the phone.

"Asher!" came the almost shout from the other end. "We've been trying to get a hold of you all day." It was Jennifer Leavitt.

They had? "You have?" he asked. He would have to check messages.

"Asher, are you sitting down?"

"Yes," he said, even more curious now.

"All right—hold on to your hat."

Asher sat up straight, now completely intrigued. Peni gave him a curious look. "Is everything okay?" Peni asked.

Asher shrugged and gulped hard. "What's wrong, Jennifer?"

"Nothing's wrong, Asher. Nothing could be further *from* wrong. Asher, the last week of the run of *Drunks*? There were three different nights we had people there from HBO."

Asher's back went rigid. *HBO?*

"Asher, they want to do the show. And they want you."

"What?" What had she said? Surely she hadn't meant what it sounded like she'd said—and if he even dared respond to what he *thought* she'd said, she would laugh at him and tell him he was—

an asshole

—wrong and, "Boy, you sure do have an ego don't you, Asher?" and—

"Asher, what's wrong?" Peni asked, reaching out and giving him a little shake.

"Asher," Jennifer said again. "Did you hear me?"

"N-no," Asher replied quietly. "The cell crackled out on you. I didn't catch it...."

Jennifer laughed, and quite clearly Asher could see it was happy laughter. Almost a giggle. "Oh, Asher! I said that HBO has contacted us. And the playwright, Pete Bakely." She laughed again, and yes, that was *joy* in her voice. "HBO is interested in optioning the show. Possibly for a series. And they want *you*. Asher, my boy. You have to pack your bags. They want you in LA on Monday."

A thrill of near unparalleled power raced and jolted through Asher, electrifying him, making him want to leap from the bed and—

Wait.

Monday?

"Jennifer, I *can't*...."

"You can't what?" cried Peni (and Asher spared him a wild look).

"*What?*" cried Jennifer. "Why *can't* you?"

"I'm leaving for Samoa on that day."

"Then I suggest you change your plans, Mr. Eisenberg. This is the moment you've been waiting for. This is *it*, my friend! This could—this almost certainly *will*—make you a star."

Asher looked at Peni again, saw the wide-eyed alarm on his lover's face—

Lover! Me! I have a lover.

—and his heart did a crazy somersault along with the trip-hammering it was already doing, and—

I can't go. I'm going to Samoa. I cannot go to LA.

—for one tiny instant there was a flash of *Fuck you! This is it! I'm finally going to do it, I'm going to be a star*—and then it was gone and—

I love you so much, Peniamina Faamausili.

—that was it.

"I'm sorry, Jennifer. I can't go."

And instead of falling into a river of sorrow and despair, he could only smile and his heart could only dance. Because he was going to Samoa with his lover—

Lover! My lover!

—and *nothing* else mattered.

THEY TRIED to talk him out of it.

Peni: "You have to go, Asher! Thank you for what you're willing to do for me. But you might never get an opportunity like this again."

Asher: "And when will I ever get an opportunity to be with you for the most important thing that's ever happened to you?"

And Jennifer: "Asher! Have you lost your mind? This is HBO! *Spencer Morrison* wants you. Spencer-*fucking*-Morrison—"

(who was once a down on his luck Kansas City actor and now an Academy Award nominated star)

"—wants you—"

and wasn't it funny to hear Jennifer swearing?

"—and you *can't* turn down *Spencer Morrison*! Asher, Spencer Morrison is going to be playing Don, and he wants *you* as his costar. This isn't some little indie film company with a budget of two thousand dollars making a movie on video tape. This is *it*! And they don't give a shit that you have a boyfriend who wants to get a tattoo!"

Asher: "It's not 'tattoo,' Jennifer. It's 'tatau.' It's the pe'a. I *have* to be there. I cannot *not* be there for him. I don't care what that means for my career. This—*he*—is more important than anything else in my life."

And there was Sloan, his best friend: "You're crazy, you know that? Can't Peni change his appointment for whatever it is? You go to LA, and then you and Peni go to Samoa another time?"

Asher: "It's not like that, Sloan. This is huge. He almost didn't get to go at all. And I've learned something, Sloan. Sometimes there are more important things than me. The world doesn't center around me. The world doesn't give a shit if I'm the next big star. There are a million stars and a million people waiting right around the corner to be stars and a million more stars who are being forgotten about today because their latest movie or show or what-the-fuck-ever flopped. If I don't go with Peni? *That* is what I will regret. That I *won't* forget."

And in the end…

CHAPTER THIRTY-ONE

THE FLIGHT into Samoa was stunningly beautiful. Peni sat by the window, and Asher put his chin right on his lover's shoulder so he could see. The ocean had gone quite suddenly from a deep blue-black—almost like dark polished steel—to the most gorgeous blue he'd ever seen. Then the view from the window was filled with the beaches and forests and green, green, green.

After the plane landed—and Asher was so glad they had finally landed; it had been a long flight—they were picked up by two men, relatives of Peni's. Both studied Asher suspiciously. But Asher didn't mind. Of course they would. Wasn't he the *palagi* who was in a relationship with their nephew?

Asher's stomach was tied up in knots. He'd tried not to think about what his lover was about to endure. Tried not to think about it at all. But once they'd made the drive along the coast and climbed out of the beat-up car to meet the men who would be performing the long process of painting Peni's body?

There was nothing else to think about.

Now it was real.

For one moment, simply thinking about it made Asher feel faint. But no. He had to be strong. Nothing had even happened yet! And he was here to hold Peni, hold his hand, be the strength he needed. Asher *would* do this. He had to.

Somehow.

The sudden *need* for a drink hit Asher strongly then. Hit him powerfully strong. Like a truck! The need to deaden his senses so he could get through this.

But no.

No, no, no, *no*!

What he, Asher, would be going through was nothing. He wasn't going to be in pain. He wasn't going to have those mallets pounding and tapping ink-filled spikes all over his body for hour after endless hour. Peni was the one.

Somehow, he would find the strength to be there for the man he loved so much.

Love. He was in *love*!

It hardly seemed possible. When he thought about it, Asher grew giddy. When he thought back to a time without Peni, it seemed impossibly long ago. A different era.

A different Asher.

It was then that Asher saw the men were arguing. Peni was upset. Poto was yelling. A tiny old man was shaking his head. They were speaking in Samoan, and of course they weren't saying "hello" or "how are you?" or "I love you" or "*ua fia mea*—do you want to go," for that matter, so Asher had no idea what they were saying. Until he heard one word.

Fa'afafine.

The old man looked angry, and when he said "*fa'afafine*" he was pointing at Peni and shaking his head vehemently.

That fast Asher knew what he had to do. He turned to Kelly, Poto's wife, and said, "Kelly, I need your blouse." He pulled his T-shirt off over his head. "Hurry!"

She looked at him and blinked. "What?"

"Please! *Now.* There's a sarong for you to cover yourself in the car. Give me your blouse!" It was a command and not a request.

She blinked at him in confusion—

"Hurry, Kelly! Please!"

—gave a nod, and turned, went to the car. Then, what seemed about a year later she returned, handing him her pink-hibiscus-covered blouse. Asher put it on in a flash, tying it at the bottom, and went to the arguing men, making sure to put a slight sashay in his walk. After all, wasn't he an actor?

"Hey!" he said, and the men froze and turned to him, eyes flashing. "Peniamina is not *fa'afafine*! *I* am *fa'afafine*."

They stared for a long moment, Peni perhaps the most surprised of all.

And an hour later, the ceremony began.

CHAPTER THIRTY-TWO

THERE WAS nothing to prepare Peni for what happened next.

He had a high threshold of pain. He always had.

But this?

This was pain.

IT LASTED for hour upon hour upon hour.

The tufuga ta tatau used tools call *au* to make the pe'a. These tools were basically a wooden handle with a small flat piece made from fish bones or boar's tusk attached at an angle. There were little teeth carved into those pieces, making them resemble miniature combs. Except those teeth were needle- and razor-sharp. They came in different sizes, depending on which designs they would be used for. There were broad ones with twenty to thirty teeth used for long lines and large areas, and smaller ones with as few as four for the tiny detailed patterns. The tool's teeth were then dipped into the ink and placed upon the skin. Then the other men would use their hands to stretch the skin taut (and also to secure the man who was receiving the pe'a firmly in place) so that the *tufuga* could hit the handle of the tool with a long, heavy mallet, which would drive the ink-filled teeth together and into the skin. This created tiny black dots.

Unlike the tattoos done in most of the world, where only the upper layers of skin received the ink, in Samoa, the teeth of the instrument were driven deep into whatever lay beneath the skin.

This was repeated hour after painful hour until the designs were complete.

It was the job of Peni's family and his lover, Asher, to help him through his weakest moments—talking to him, praying with him, singing to him, or just by *being* there for him.

There were only a few things that got Peni through the almost feverish hours. The decision that he would *not* let the artist think of him as a woman, or even *fa'afafine*, for even one minute—and the fact that

Asher was there. He would pour his concentration into being strong for Asher, trying to pretend that all was well, that he could do this.

In the end he failed at the latter.

Because in the end it was Asher who got him through. Lying there, head in Asher's lap, looking up with blurred vision into his lover's beautiful blue-green eyes—finding himself even then marveling at their color.

In the end, through a haze of suffering and pain unimagined—pain that at times seemed passionate—he fell more deeply in love than ever.

IN THE evening Asher helped Peni into a tub of salt water. He wanted to cry. Wanted to cry while his beautiful lover—laying out on the floor of a tiny house—was being pounded and pounded and pounded and the blood flowed and flowed and was wiped away again and again and again. At first Asher didn't think he was going to be able to do it. But then Peni had looked up into his face, eyes wide and wild—and something... happened inside Asher.

Man up! cried some inner spirit...

...and he *did*.

He gave Peni a firm nod, made his eyes like steel, his only acquiescence to emotion a mouthed *I love you*, and gave his lover's hand a firm squeeze. Then Peni's eyes filled with gratitude—Asher could *see* that was what it was—and Peni bore on.

I must be his strength.

PENI CRIED out as he lowered himself into the tub. The salt water— *Oca! It hurts!*—more pain on top of the endless hours of pain, but it was so important. In the old days, the man receiving the pe'a would bathe himself in the ocean, but today—with the pollutants in the water—it wasn't possible.

He worried about Asher even during the pain, worried that what *he* was undergoing was too much for his lover. But then he just didn't have the strength to worry for him. He had to trust that Asher really did love him as much as he claimed.

And now? When he climbed into the tub? Asher had to massage his freshly tattooed skin—only *more* pain! But it was critical. The massage was needed to work out pus and impurities that collected under the endless scabs while the salt water disinfected and cooled his wounds. The tattoo had to be kept cool—it made it more difficult for infection to set in.

Asher brought him food, *forced* him to eat it even though eating was the *last* thing he wanted to do. He wanted to shout at Asher, tell him to *fuck off*! But then he saw the love and pain in his lover's eyes and knew that the food was pressed on him to help him heal and replace all the blood he had lost.

Peni thought he wouldn't be able to sleep—that the pain would keep him awake. But he fell off into a troubled darkness almost the instant he lay down.

Only to be woken every couple hours to be rolled over—

No! Leave me alone. Please!

—because otherwise his wounds would stick, *did* stick, to the sheets.

Through it *all*, Asher was there,

Was there and was there and was there....

SOMEHOW, THEY both made it.

ON THE last day, after the designs were at last in place, Peni was surrounded by family and friends and "baptized" by having an egg broken over his head and coconut oil poured on his scalp.

It meant he was done!

The tattooing process was complete!

There was a huge feast—and even though Peni didn't feel like eating, Asher was there, feeding him by hand.

That night, after another careful washing, Peni and Asher stood side by side in front of a mirror, and Peni saw his new body and wept.

They both did.

For even with all the swelling, it was clear to see.

He was beautiful.

He was Samoan.

CHAPTER THIRTY-THREE

IT WAS actually Peni who took the long-distance phone call, and for that he was eternally grateful. Asher had gone for a long walk—Peni had insisted—and so Kelly brought the phone to him.

"Peni?"

It was Sloan.

"Yes," he said.

There followed hurried words of concern, of encouragement, of goodwill—but it was clear to Peni that his pe'a was *not* why Sloan had called.

Then, *finally*: "When will Asher be back?"

"I'm not sure, Sloan. Is everything okay?"

Sloan laughed. "Oh, it's more than okay. A miracle has happened."

Peni sat up. "What?"

"The people from HBO? They heard what happened. I guess they were impressed. They said that if Asher can be in LA next week—he might still get the part. He's who they want, Peni! *He's* who they want!"

It was all Peni could do not to weep with joy.

"Of course," Sloan added, "it certainly helped that Peter Wagner—who it fricking turns out is one of the *producers* of the show—insisted that he wanted Asher as well."

"Oca!" cried Peni. "How did he even find out?"

Sloan giggled. "Well... I *do* work for the man...."

"YOU'RE GOING," Peni told him. "And that's final. I am putting my foot down about this, my love."

Asher's mouth was open to argue until those final two words.

My love....

His heart rushed, his breath caught, but then of course he saw the stunning, gorgeous swirls and lines over his lover's lower torso and legs and.... "Peni. You *need* me."

Peni smiled at him. "Of course I do, Asher. I need you with all my heart. I need you for the rest of my life!"

The rest of his life. A wonderful *zing*! raced through Asher's chest.

"But please—you were here for me. I know now that I couldn't have done it without you. Whenever it got to be too much—just when I knew I would *have* to tell them to stop—I would look up and see you looking down at me, and I was able to go on. Now let me do this for you. I can't *be* there, but.... But, Asher.... You said you knew I had to get the pe'a. Now *I* know that you *have* to go to Los Angeles. Do it for *me*."

That was what it took.

Two days later, Asher flew back from Samoa...

...and into the rest of his life.

CHAPTER THIRTY-FOUR

IT WAS not the first Saturday of the month, so it was *not* Porch Night, but it was a sweet and nostalgic night, with only the tiniest note of sadness. That note was the fact that Peni was not there. He was still recovering in Samoa, not quite ready to fly. But of course he was the first with whom Asher shared the news.

And these men? The men surrounding him? They were second to know, of course. The most important friends Asher had ever had in his life. Friends who had loved him despite it all. Despite his arrogance. Despite his drinking. Despite love withheld. Despite the fact that he'd been an asshole.

The Fabulous Four.

And how wonderful it was to be here. *Drunks* wasn't even a full week into production and he'd been able to fly into Kansas City to be here with his friends tonight. He would be flying back tomorrow.

Asher looked around his small screened-in porch. It was quite chilly, but the space heater helped, and they so wanted to recreate the feeling of Porch Night.

Tonight it was just the four of them.

There was Sloan, unarguably his best and closest friend. A man who knew him better than anyone. A man who had carried a torch for him for a long time—but one whose love had frightened Asher too much to accept—to even acknowledge. Through some miracle, Sloan had stayed his friend, despite all the drunken nights that had come close to destroying everything they had. And through another miracle, Sloan had transitioned into a wonderful relationship with another man—and that relationship had not ended their friendship. So many times, it seemed, when a gay man found love, he abandoned his friends.

Not so in Sloan's case.

Tonight, he was smiling, he was laughing, he was happy. Yes, part of that was surely that he had found love in a man named Max—a man Asher heartily approved of. Asher had not been ready for Sloan's love. Thank God—*yes, God*!—that Sloan had found Max.

But Asher also knew that a huge reason Sloan could smile today was the friendship here, now, tonight, on this chilly porch in November.

And then there was Scott. Oh, Scott! King of Pessimists, the killjoy of all killjoys, but fiercely loyal and willing to step in front of a gun—literally—for a friend. Despite all that, the FF loved him. They knew that deep under that curmudgeonly exterior was a beautiful man. Who knew that he was also a spiritual one as well? It had taken the magic of fairies and of a sexy man named Cedar to help Scott finally see that. Cedar had cracked the shell that the Fabulous Four could not. But was there ever a group of friends that he could come out of that shell better with than the FF? A group that loved and supported him— even if he was a little over the top these days? Who knew a man could get nearly too optimistic? Asher laughed inwardly. Scott was almost a caricature of a New Ager.

But who gave a ratfuck?

Did it matter if some of his positive-attitude talk got a little out there?

Conceive—Believe—Receive?

Really?

Did Scott *really* believe he could create his own reality?

Yet who was Asher to doubt? Wasn't he seeing a miracle right before him? Scott. Laughing! Joking!

Asher *knew* that a huge reason Scott could smile today was the friendship here, now, tonight, on this chilly porch in November.

Finally, their sweet little bear, Wyatt. Brokenhearted. Now— ironically—the only one of the Fabulous Four who was single. After ten years living with Howard, Wyatt was now without both his boyfriend and the home he had loved.

Yet Asher knew this, even if Wyatt didn't: he was so much better off without that motherfucking son of a whore! Howard was despicable.

In the last nine months, Asher had seen people redeem themselves. Why he, Asher, had himself!

But this he knew: Howard? Howard was beyond redemption.

Wyatt saw himself as lost, but Asher knew better.

Wyatt was lost long before Howard left him.

Now Wyatt could be found.

Would it be with a man like the rest of the Fabulous Four had found?

Did Wyatt *need* a man?

Why, no. *Hell* no!

But somehow Asher thought that Wyatt had a very good chance at finding love. What was it that Scott was always spouting these days? Nature abhors a vacuum? And only when you get rid of what you don't need can something wonderful come to take its place?

Why, look what had happened to Asher when he had finally let go of the image of a hateful Father-God, floating up on a cloud somewhere, thinking that Asher was an abomination?

A lot had happened! A lot indeed.

Asher didn't think Wyatt would be alone for long.

This time the Fabulous Four would be there, and they would not stand by idly! Any man who wanted Wyatt in his life would have to measure up to the approval of his best friends.

And despite all the grief and changes and losses Wyatt had experienced, why, look at him tonight. Laughing! Joking!

Asher knew this much: a huge reason Wyatt could smile today was the friendship here, now, tonight, on this chilly porch in November.

"All right, everyone," cried Sloan. "The time has come!"

He pulled a bottle of sparkling grape juice from its ice bucket.

"Hear! Hear!" they all shouted.

Sloan popped the cork with a gratifying sound and poured.

"Hold up your glasses!" said Wyatt.

They held them high.

"To Asher!" exclaimed his friends.

"The new star of the HBO show, *Drunks*!"

"HURRAY!"

A star! He was going to be a star.

Of course, Asher knew something else even more important. The men sitting around this chilly little porch?

They were the stars.

He looked out the screen into the night. It was a city, and there were city lights, so he couldn't really see the sky, and he had no idea if he was even looking in the right direction—but out there somewhere, was the *real* star of his life.

Peni would soon be home.

And then?

It would only be one more step in the beginning of the rest of the most wonderful life a man could have.

RECIPES:

Okay…. The e-mails have spoken. Readers want recipes. So here they are!

<u>Corpse Reviver #2</u>

3/4 ounce gin
3/4 ounce Lillet Blanc
3/4 ounce lemon juice
3/4 ounce Cointreau
3 dashes orange bitters
approximately 1 teaspoon absinthe to rinse glass (optional)

Rinse a martini glass with a small amount of absinthe; discard. Combine remaining ingredients, shake with ice, and strain into the prepared glass.

<u>Bandgobhi Alu Sabji</u>

1 pound cabbage
2 whole cloves
2 cardamom pods
1 cinnamon stick, 3 inches long
4 tablespoons ghee or vegetable oil
4 medium-sized potatoes, peeled and cubed
2/3 cup water
1 tablespoon grated fresh ginger
1/2 teaspoon cayenne pepper
1 teaspoon turmeric
4 medium-sized ripe tomatoes, each cut into 8 wedges
1 1/2 teaspoons salt
1/2 teaspoon sugar

Wash the cabbage, shred it, and let it drain. Grind the cloves, cardamom, and cinnamon stick into a fine powder and set aside.

Heat 3 tablespoons of the ghee or vegetable oil in a saucepan over moderate heat. Put the cubed potatoes in the pan and stir-fry them, scraping the bottom of the pan frequently, until they are lightly browned. Remove them from the pan and set them aside.

Put the remaining tablespoon of ghee or oil in the same saucepan and stir-fry the grated ginger, cayenne pepper, and turmeric. Fry for a few seconds more. Add the shredded cabbage and fry for three or four more minutes, stirring regularly to mix it with the spices and prevent scorching. Add the tomatoes, fried potatoes, salt, sugar, and water. Cover the pan and simmer over low heat until all the vegetables are tender. Before serving, sprinkle the previously prepared ground sweet spices over the top and mix gently.

Blue Boy Dip

8 ounces cream cheese
3 ounces blue cheese, crumbled
whipping cream to thin
Worcestershire sauce to taste

Mix the cheeses together. Thin the cheese with cream to a dipping consistency. Add Worcestershire sauce to taste.

Asher stuffed individual endive spears with this mixture, but it's good as a plain old dip as well!

Don't miss how the story began!

Spring Affair

Seasons of Love: Book One

By B.G. Thomas

Sloan McKenna is going through a tough time. His beloved mother has recently passed away, leaving him her house and beautiful garden. But should he keep the house? Sell it? To make matters worse, he's in love with one of his best friends, Asher, a man who can't (or won't) love him back.

Sloan's neighbor, Max Turner, is married to an ambitious woman with far-reaching dreams, including moving the family to France. But Max is happy teaching at the local college and living in their nice, quiet town. Then he discovers his fourteen-year-old son is not only gay, but out and proud as well. That throws him into complete disarray, for more than one reason....

When Max's wife leaves on a two-month business trip to Paris, circumstances throw the two men together. As they become friends, Sloan finds himself falling in love with Max, who is completely unavailable... just like Asher. As for Max, he is discovering that both his son's coming out and his new friendship with Sloan are stirring up feelings he thought buried long ago. Spring is a time for rebirth—Is there any way the two men can find happiness and a new beginning?

http://www.dreamspinnerpress.com

Summer Lover

Seasons of Love: Book Two

By B.G. Thomas

Scott Aberdeen doesn't believe in Santa Claus, the Easter Bunny, or God. Or love—at least, he knows no one will ever love him. After all, he has carried a torch for his best friend Sloan for a decade, hoping his feelings will be returned one day. But when Sloan finds springtime love with another man, Scott's fantasies are crushed and his skepticism confirmed.

Cedar Carrington, raised by rock star parents, leads a free-spirited, nomadic life, never staying in one place for long. Due to a dark past he refuses to share or even think about, he is willing to let men into his bed for sex, but never for the night.

When Scott finds himself camping in the middle of nowhere with over a hundred men who all believe in love—and faeries and a magickal gay brotherhood—he's pretty sure he's in the wrong place. And when Cedar connects with cynical, critical Scott, he wonders how he could be falling in for this man of all men. But hearts and lives have been transformed at the Heartland Men's Festival before, and it might be just the place where two very different men can release their pain and find true love at last.

http://www.dreamspinnerpress.com

B.G. THOMAS lives in Kansas City with his husband of more than a decade and their fabulous little dog. He is lucky enough to have a lovely daughter as well as many extraordinary friends. He has a great passion for life.

B.G. loves romance, comedies, fantasy, science fiction and even horror—as far as he is concerned, as long as the stories are character driven and entertaining, it doesn't matter the genre. He has gone to literature conventions his entire adult life where he's been lucky enough to meet many of his favorite writers. He has made up stories since he was a child; it is where he finds his joy.

In the nineties, he wrote for gay magazines but stopped because the editors wanted all sex without plot. "The sex is never as important as the characters," he says. "Who cares what they are doing if we don't care about them?" Excited about the growing male/male romance market, he began writing again. Gay men are what he knows best, after all—since he grew out of being a "practicing" homosexual long ago. He submitted a story and was thrilled when it was accepted in four days.

"Leap, and the net will appear" is his personal philosophy and his message to all. "It is never too late," he states. "Pursue your dreams. They will come true!"

Website/blog: http://bthomaswriter.wordpress.com/
E-mail: bgthomaswriter@aol.com

http://www.dreamspinnerpress.com

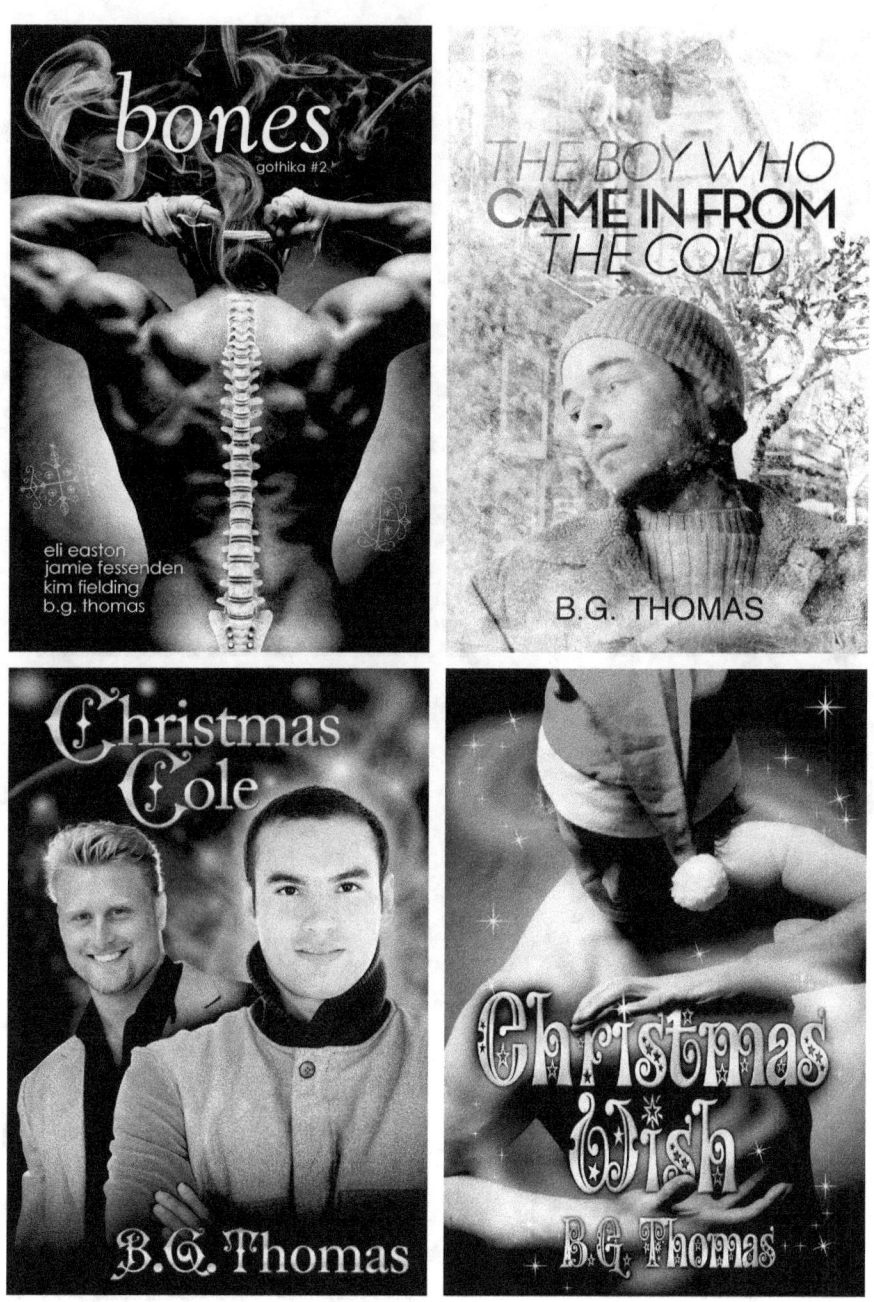

http://www.dreamspinnerpress.com

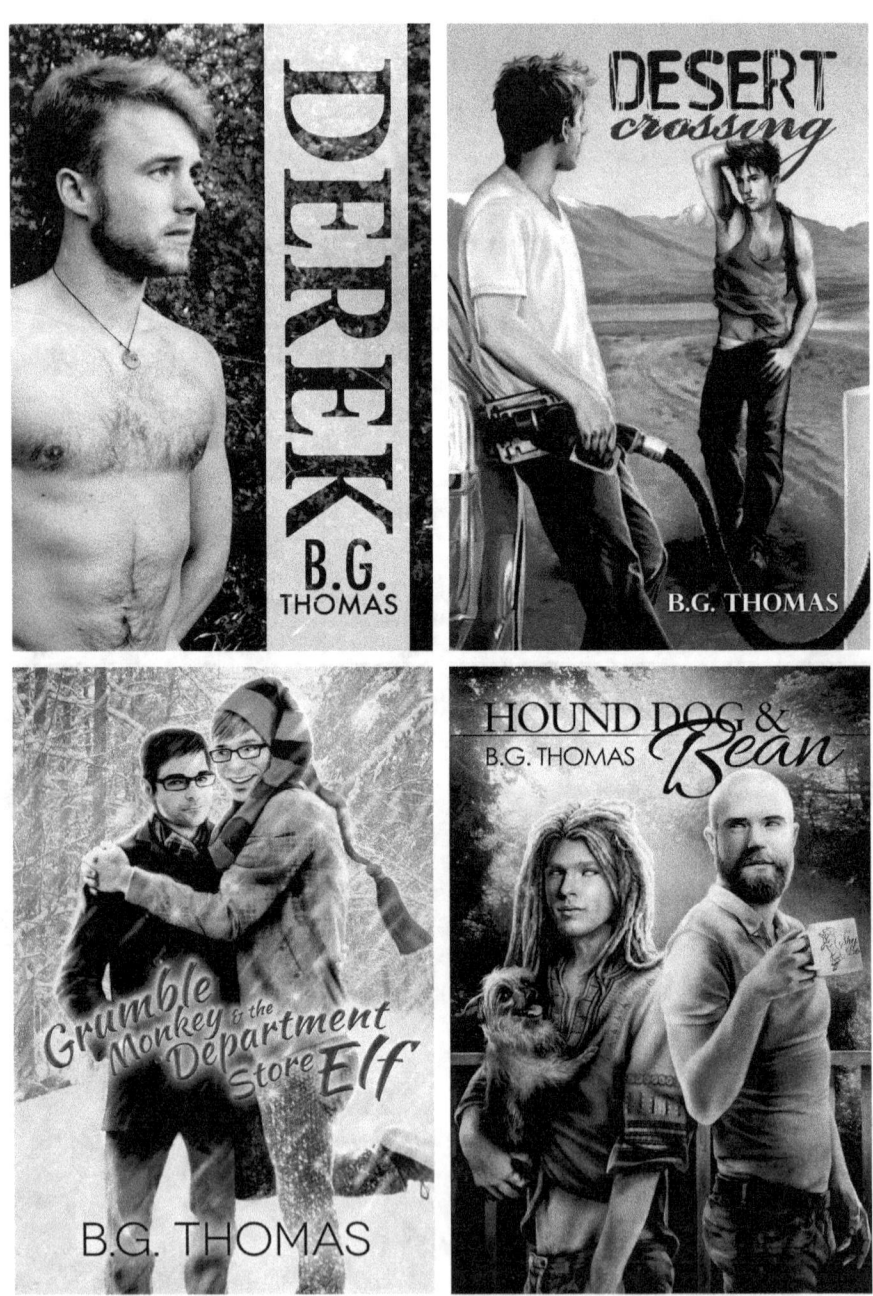

http://www.dreamspinnerpress.com

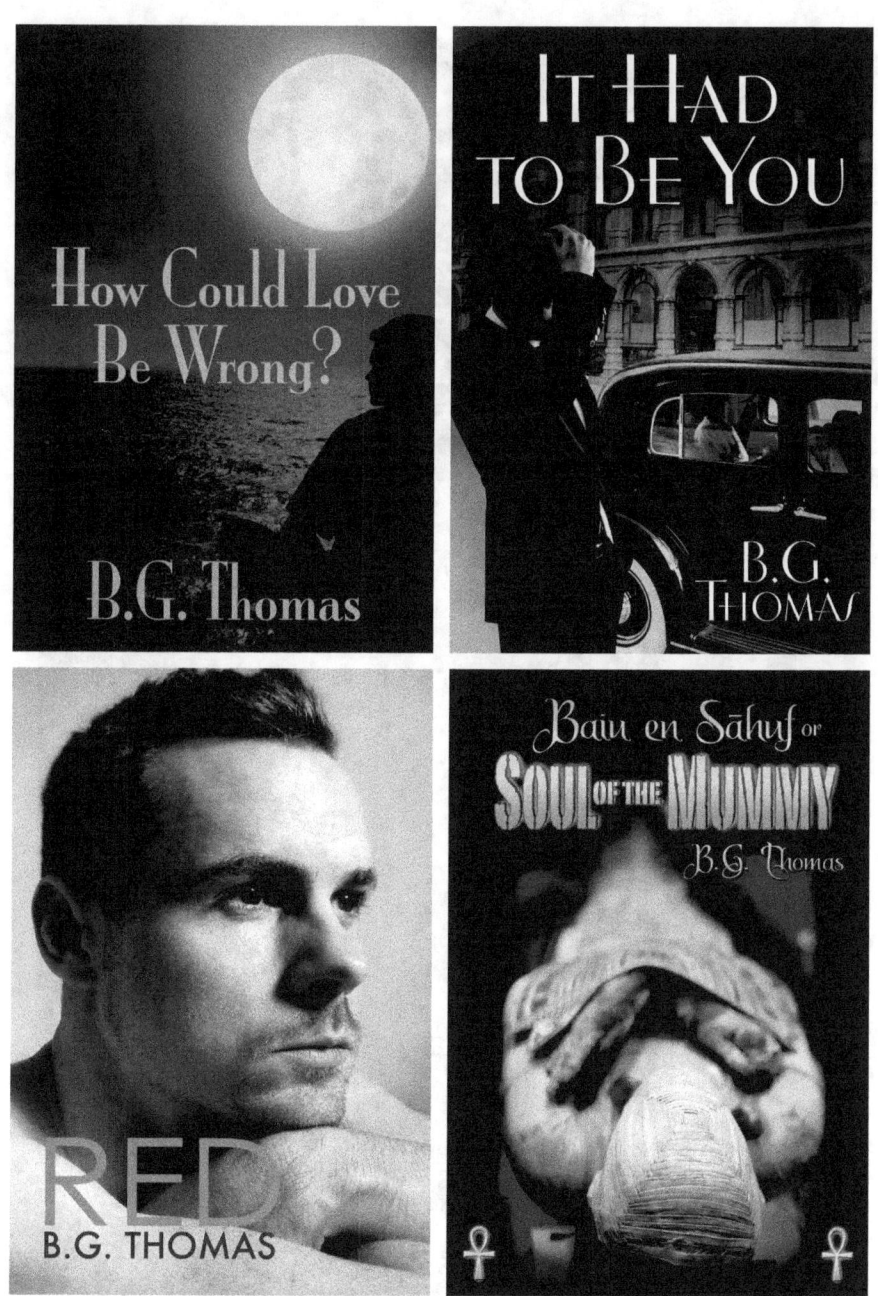

http://www.dreamspinnerpress.com

www.ingramcontent.com/pod-product-compliance
Lightning Source LLC
Chambersburg PA
CBHW051629260626
47170CB00004B/1094